Harp of Joy
Book Two

Yvonne Harlech is the author of Female Parts: the Art and Politics of Women Playwrights, under the name Yvonne Hodkinson. Mistress of the Temple is her first novel, followed by Book 2, Harp of Joy. The author was born in Edinburgh and grew up in Montreal, Canada. She studied English at Concordia University and now lives in Cheshire with her husband. Her novels reflect her deep love for Egypt and the ancient temples, which are a portal to the past and the deities, once venerated within the sacred chambers.

Also by Yvonne Harlech:

Mistress of the Temple
Book One

For more information on books, ancient Egypt, gods and goddesses, visit our website:

www.hathorpress.co.uk

Visit Yvonne Harlech on Facebook:

www.facebook.com/pages/ Yvonne-Harlech

Harp of Joy

Yvonne Harlech

Hathor Press
2012

Published in the UK by Hathor Press in 2012.

A CIP catalogue record for this book is available from the British Library.
ISBN 978-1-908451-02-6

Hathor Press,
A division of SF Products UK Ltd
PO Box 3436, Chester, CH1 9DG

www.hathorpress.co.uk

Foreword

Summary of Book One, *Mistress of the Temple.*

1290 BC in the Egyptian city of Abydos, the young priestess Bentreshy is renowned for her spiritual powers — a medium between Isis and the temple. But when she falls in love with King Sety I, her spiritual life is thrown into question. By defying the temple laws the couple pit themselves against the omnipotent priesthood, but King Sety believes their love is sanctioned by the gods and they are destined to change history.

3200 years later, Dorothy Eady is born into an Edwardian family in London. She begins to remember a past life in Abydos, when she lived in a beautiful temple as a follower of Isis. Only Dr Budge, a Keeper at the British Museum, believes her story and helps her unravel the past. Dorothy realises she must return to Abydos, where the truth lies hidden in the arcane temple, but how is she going to get to there? When she meets Imam Meguid, an Egyptian student, she finally sees her chance. Much to her parents' horror, Dorothy agrees to marry him. In 1933 Dorothy sets sail for Egypt to join her fiancé, a man she knows little about . . .

I am the pure one in his eye, not shall I die a second time.
(*Egyptian Book of the Dead*)

1. Initiation
Abydos, 1290 BC

King Sety stood under the persea tree, his body appeared to be emerging from the trunk, his limbs extending from the branches. The leaves were pink in the setting sun, his flesh dyed crimson, waiting for the cool night air. Seshet wrote our destinies on the persea leaves, he remembered, words written on green veins, spelling our fate.

"Bentreshy, my love," he whispered from the tree, words leaping from the leaves. Bentreshy thought of the bennu bird rising from the burning tree, moulding himself out of the sacred flames. She felt herself leap forward, as if jumping into a dark pool, not knowing how deep she would plunge, but craving the cool water below her feet. Their lips merged, then opened into a secret cavern; she was a hungry wolf exploring the dark crevices, seeking out this new pleasure. Inside this kiss a shroud was lifted and she had a moment of recognition; love fell upon her like soft rain, soaking the dry earth and awakening the seeds below; the potential for new life.

Sety's desire was like the sunrise; his face glowing with strange emotions, his bewildered eyes—brown, purple, almost amber and then brown again. He parted his lips and whispered, as if uttering his last words, "I love you, Bentreshy."

Noses rubbing together, his breath exhaling into her nostrils. "We have found each other. Our *Kas* are one." She inhaled his sweet breath, his *sekhem* travelling through her body, their union sending shockwaves through the universe, and they felt the world tremble, sensing the power of this relentless love. They faltered, not knowing where to stand, fearing they may slip into a deep chasm. No, they couldn't fall—the garden was their earthly paradise, their names carved on the trees, their bodies bound to this green sanctuary.

Time had disappeared behind the mountains, sliding into darkness then rising into light again. It all seemed to happen in an instant, like a black cloud moving across the sun.

"I must get back for morning prayers," she remembered, seeing the sky turn violet.

"Meet me here tomorrow night," he implored, covering her face in soft kisses; Bentreshy laughing, drowning in kisses, stumbling

11

along the slanted path. "I don't know if I can—I have to meet Inhapi, learn about the Mysteries." More kisses, cuddles, tongues meeting in tender words.

Back in her room Bentreshy washed her face with rosewater and applied ochre powder round her eyes to conceal the dark circles of fatigue. The attendant, Kiya, wrapped her in a voluminous white robe and secured it with a wide blue sash. Bentreshy made her way to the Chamber of Isis, carrying a tray of offerings for the Holy Couple, containing wine, bread and apricots. After prayers Inhapi would teach her about the Mysteries and the sacred fertility rite she would be performing. Finally Bentreshy would learn the ancient secrets and become one of the chosen few, possessing insights that must follow her to the grave. She placed the offerings by the false door of Isis and then repeated the ritual before Osiris, filling the chamber with billows of frankincense. Bentreshy stood before the painted figures of Isis and Osiris, inhaling their beauty through the blue smoke.

"I thank you for the honour bestowed upon me. I don't understand its nature or why it has happened to me—why the Divine Lady has chosen me—but if it is your will then it cannot be wrong. Please help me understand." Bentreshy stared up at Osiris on his throne, Isis standing by his side, her hand affectionately resting on his shoulder.

"Do not question what is happening to you, my daughter. Perform the rituals with all your heart and open yourself to receive the wonders of creation," Osiris told her, his words sounding like music. The channels were unusually receptive that morning; she felt the energy rising from the victuals, their *sekhem* spring to life.

She uttered the magic rites, "Let this food and drink restore the Holy Mother and Father to life, so they may enter the mortal realm and indulge their earthly pleasures. May these offerings give them sustenance and nurture all living creatures." Bentreshy wafted the incense over the plate of offerings and watched the food begin to change colour: the bread turning light brown, the apricots revealing their orange down, and the wine becoming a deeper red, a blue tinge glistening on the surface. Bentreshy noticed the smells intensifying, the sweet-sour scent of the grapes tickling her nose, the mouldy smell of yeast rising from the core, colliding with the fresh smell of warm bread. The essence of the offerings had been evoked, called forth into the chamber, and Bentreshy stepped back a few paces, as if blown about by a sudden wind; she was ready to receive. She performed the Opening of the Mouth ceremony, waving the ankh over the provisions to awaken the *Ka* in each article. Then she waved the ankh round Isis and Osiris, feeling their *Kas* struggle against the stone; no longer frozen images on the wall, they were breathing, living creatures, exuding light and colour through their painted flesh.

Bentreshy closed her eyes and slipped into a trance, waiting for the *Kas* to reveal themselves. In the darkness she saw a tiny light shining by the false door, which grew into a sheet of white, taking the shape of a translucent robe. A figure transmogrified out of the fabric, her gold flesh forming into arms and legs, twisting into a beautiful face with luminous brown eyes outlined in purple kohl, eyelids painted shiny blue. Out of the wall came a splash of green, like liquid malachite dribbling down the stones, then settling into a solid mould. Bentreshy watched transfixed as the face of Osiris appeared out of the green mass, arms folded across his chest, carrying a hook and flail. The Divine Couple floated round the chamber, eating morsels of food and drinking wine, enticing the images to come alive, urging the figures to pump with blood, their limestone limbs to become flesh.

Bentreshy watched the figures peel off the wall, and soon the chamber was full of lively people, chatting, singing, playing music and dancing round the pillars. The guests drank large amounts of wine and lost themselves in joyful revelry, dancing wildly and falling over each other with good-humoured abandon.

Bentreshy participated in this great festival of life, a celebration of earthly delights so appealing that even the gods came down to indulge in them. Singers, musicians, and dancers shaking their cowry belts; cavorting, feasting, everyone uproarious; fire-eaters gorging on peaches in between vomits of flame, red-faced dwarves intoxicated with wine and laughter, dancing round with elated abandon, saluting Bes with every swig.

Bentreshy felt utter joy in the goddess' chamber, surrounded by the love of Isis and her magic symbols. She felt most at home in this little vaulted chamber, completely loved and accepted by Isis, and she sat on the floor gazing up at the lady with the ochre skin, her streaks of blue hair braided into pleats and interlaced with strips of ribbon. Then she saw her mother's kind face smiling through the mural, and remembered her painting flowers on the mud brick wall, the cow-eared face of Hathor emerging from the reeds.

The next few days were absorbed with preparations for the three day Osirion Mystery Plays. As the servants beautified her for the event, Bentreshy thought about her meeting with Inhapi the other night. How the priestess had spoken in a low voice, dismissing the attendants from the room and carefully shutting the door behind them.

"I need to talk to you about the Mystery Plays . . . you remember our initial discussion about the fertility ritual—the resurrection of Osiris and how it's the most important ceremony in all of Egypt? ..." Inhapi stared at Bentreshy intently, "You know it's a complex ritual involving a great sacrifice, the death of Our Lord Osiris."

"I will do my best to honour the Lord's sacrifice, considering the goddess has chosen me," Bentreshy replied, beginning to feel uneasy, wondering what was about to unfold. They'd gone over the procedure two years ago, when she'd agreed to be the Receptacle of Isis, but it still seemed a mystery to her. Bentreshy fidgeted with her beads, anxiously spinning them round on the string. "I'll perform the rites with passion—if it will help restore Osiris to life and ensure a good harvest." If only she knew what was expected of her...

Inhapi noticed the uncertainty in the girl's face; *the poor child is apprehensive, she doesn't understand. It's time she knows the truth.*

Inhapi grabbed Bentreshy's arm with a sense of urgency. "The Resurrection Rite is the most revered part of the Passion Play. Isis unites with Osiris in this sacred act of love, one that permeates the land with fecundity, compassion and healing energy. Through this divine union barren women will become pregnant, impotent men will regain their manhood and the arid earth will become productive."

Bentreshy began to understand what Inhapi was trying to tell her. She'd seen the reliefs in the Temple: Osiris lying horizontal on a stone bed, his erect penis throbbing with life, thanks to Isis who initiates the sacred renewal, with Horus hovering above, witnessing his own conception. . . A ritual so arcane that only the Adepts knew the details of this cherished act.

Bentreshy wondered who would play Osiris, knowing the Pharaoh usually performed the role, or in his absence, the High Priest.

"Last year Master Kahotep performed this rite with Woserit—they call her a priestess but she's really an administrator, not an ounce of magic in her. She was ordained by the Wives of Amun in Thebes, not in Abydos," Inhapi grumbled, her disapproval evident in her voice. "The inundation was low and the harvest was meagre. We are hoping King Sety will take part this year as he did several years ago—we had the best flood that year and the crops grew with divine abundance," Inhapi recalled wistfully, remembering the delicious fruit and vegetables, rich in minerals and tasting of goodness.

Bentreshy's heart leaped at the thought of Sety playing Osiris...but the Pharaoh hadn't played the part in years and although his devotion to Osiris was profound, he avoided the emotional intensity of performing the resurrection rite, fearing the great surge of excitement may release untold passions which he'd concealed in his soul, and the outcome, like a flash flood, could be devastating.

"I doubt the Pharaoh will take part in the rite—they say his presence is urgently required back in Thebes." Inhapi noticed a woeful flicker in Bentreshy's eyes, but couldn't imagine the extent of the girl's ardour. Bentreshy fiddled with her beads and lowered her gaze, "Surely the Queen would play the part of Isis—I mean, if the Pharaoh chooses to play Osiris."

Inhapi rumpled her brow, "The King and Queen once took part as a couple. It was not a successful union—there was a certain amount of discord in their marriage at the time, and Queen Tuyu seemed anxious to get back to Thebes. As a result, the ritual was impaired and the resurrection was a rather limp affair. Osiris struggled to return to life—and it was only due to the Pharaoh's devotion, and his sophisticated irrigation methods, that the harvest was so abundant."

"Perhaps the Queen would enjoy it better this time—it may even rekindle their marriage," Bentreshy suggested, hoping to gain insight into the royal marriage. To her relief Inhapi laughed at the idea, "The Queen shows little interest in the festival—the couple have become estranged of late—such a shame for the Pharaoh."

Inhapi leaned towards Bentreshy and said earnestly, "I hope you aren't having any doubts about performing the part. You have been selected by the Oracle and the rite requires your total commitment. You will need to participate with every fibre of your being—only then will Isis awaken into carnal ecstasy and the sacred libido of Osiris can spring to life. The pleasure will be of unearthly proportions and will cause the whole universe to radiate with magic; pure energy pouring through the earth, wave after wave of fertile furrows ready to nurture the new seeds."

"I am ready for this sacred union," Bentreshy declared, with more enthusiasm than was necessary and her cheeks turned crimson, lest her ardour be revealed through the faint veil. She was eager to offer herself to Isis, to be the receptacle of her *Ka*, so that the goddess may love her husband once more in earthly form, with the passion of human flesh, as in the days when they were royal lovers, when they ruled the land with their benevolence; before the tragedy of death and destruction, and the subsequent chaos of Seth's reign.

Inhapi kissed the girl on the head with approval. She was reassured by the girl's devotion, her eyes shining like blue stars and her lovely face, hiding her mysteries behind a shroud of mist, hinting at uncharted lands.

She is a true Daughter of Isis, Inhapi told herself, glowing with pride. Inhapi had spotted the child's potential and had helped her develop, rearing her like an abandoned fledgling. And now the child was ready to fly with Isis and test the power in her wings.

2. Mother Country
Egypt, 1933

Dorothy stood on the deck, watching a faint mound in the distance. After ten days at sea the sight of land seemed like a mirage.

"That's Port Said, Miss," the sailor shouted, gallantly tipping his cap as she turned round. Dorothy smiled and nodded to the sailor, "I know—isn't it wonderful?" He gave her a comical salute and disappeared into the swarm of sailors. She saw the flurry of lights shining from the port like a cluster of stars; the violet shadows skulking over the desert hills. As daylight emerged, Egypt revealed herself, metamorphosing out of the night sky, a giant Earth Mother discarding her black cape and exposing her soft folds of flesh. Dorothy would never forget her first sunrise over Egypt: the world opening into a fusion of life and colour, starting with purple, crimson and pink, and igniting into pure gold, then turning pale yellow as the sun bleached the horizon. The sun wasn't remote like the London sun, but soft and ethereal—almost liquid. It had a purity about it, like spring rain, and she felt cleansed by its golden rays. The sky looked translucent, if only she could pierce the film and gaze into eternity, beyond the boundaries of human sight. She felt herself awaken into this new land, the light rising from the Underworld, each ray gushing like a stream, flowing over the earth. For a moment Dorothy felt a little ashamed, as though staring into the private quarters of the gods who'd carelessly left their curtains open, and she a voyeur, catching an illicit glimpse of the heavens, before she'd been invited to do so.

The urban lights were fading into oblivion, overpowered by the explosion of sunshine. With this invasion of natural light, she could see Port Said was an industrial force of some magnitude, the urban sprawl carving its way into the desert, with the odd patchwork of houses, palm trees and crops. Beyond the swell of human activity the landscape melted into endless sand, like a sea of milky coffee; it was hard to tell if they were clouds or dunes, hovering in pink puffs—then Dorothy could make out several layers of hills, unfolding in a swirl of red, bronze and gold, exposing layer upon layer of wavy sand, concealing then revealing a new desert, as if dancing behind a veil.

17

After ten days at sea the impact of this fluid world was overpowering, where nothing was distinguishable, where there were no fixed lines. Now the permanent objects on land seemed a revelation to her, gifts from the green god; this land a refuge from the perpetual flood. She found herself counting objects: houses, trees, animals—absorbing their existence, letting them colonise her being. She wanted to ground herself in this ancient world, where they were soon to anchor.

Dorothy imagined how many conquerors had landed on this coast before her, from the Hyksos in the 2nd millennium BC to the British in the 20th century. Everyone wanted to conquer Egypt, but each invader was seduced by the charms of the country and ended up adopting the local customs. Dorothy imagined how miserable the Egyptians must have felt when the Persians invaded them, as they hadn't been conquered by a foreign power since the Hyksos, over a thousand years earlier.

She thought of Alexander the Great sailing ashore with dreams of conquering this land, only to find himself dressing like a Pharaoh and bowing to the sun god. How they rejoiced when Alexander came ashore and chased away the Persians! They welcomed him as a liberator of the people, crowned him the first Macedonian Pharaoh. . . . but little did they realise this was the beginning of 2500 years of foreign rule: from this momentous beginning a terrible trend was set, which would later see the demise of ancient Egypt; her language and religion trampled into the dust.

The Greeks, the Romans, the Christians, the Arabs, the Turks, the French and now the insufferable English, thought Dorothy. 150 years ago Nelson and his crew had sailed to these shores in a wave of blood lust, pouncing on the French sailors who'd grown soft on Egyptian luxury (they too had fallen for her charms). The French were no match for the brawny English sailors raised on Spartan discipline and forced to achieve Herculean tasks, sweetened with the promise of material rewards beyond their dreams: all they had to do was beat the French and claim Egypt for themselves.

She felt a sadness for this land that had once known glory but was now at the mercy of foreign cultures much inferior to her own. *When would Egypt be free again?* she asked the wind, blowing warm air from the desert; *free to rule herself, as in the time of the great Pharaohs.*

The sun was firmly in the sky now, the bright rays flooding the land in white light. She would always remember this first sight of Egypt rising before her, the desert floating like peach meringue, the mythical sun burning into her brain, and she vowed to stay here forever.

As this solemn declaration was taken by the wind, a throng of Arabs rushed on board like a gang of pirates invading the ship. She was enchanted by the strange tongues, drowning out the English voices with their compelling language, undulating from gentle melodies to deep guttural inflections, evoking alien emotions in the baffled listener. The contrast couldn't have been greater: one minute Dorothy had been basking in ethereal serenity, the next, deafened by a swarm of frantic locals, rushing around the ship in a burst of colour and movement, laughing, shouting, gesticulating like circus performers, their limbs flying left and right, like whirling dervishes lost in a mystical rhapsody. They paraded across the deck, voices and robes flowing behind them, and the ship succumbed to their world; she was captivated by these charming invaders.

Dorothy stifled her laughter, seeing Mr Scammell's stunned expression, his rotund body squeezed up against the railing to let four locals pass: tickling, punching and embracing one another in a strange ritual of friendship. Then all hell broke loose as the men climbed over the railings, shimmied across the outside of the ship and jumped onto the gangplank. Some dangled from cables and swung themselves ashore like death-defying acrobats. She was in Egypt now: different rules applied here, and everything she'd learned in England seemed suddenly irrelevant.

Dorothy ran down the gangplank and leaped onto the dock, falling to her knees and kissing the ground. "Dear Mother, I've come home, and I promise you I'll never leave!" Great tears rolled down her cheeks, followed by a wave of laughter, realising how funny she must appear to the locals: this English lady with her head bowed to the ground, her face covered in sand. "I am in Egypt at last!" Her joy was uncontrollable, like the flooding of the Nile. She caught sight of Mr and Mrs Scammell out of the corner of her eye, and they pretended not to see her crouched on the ground, her skirt smudged in dirt. The couple busied themselves with a swarm of locals, whom they ordered about with veiled contempt. Dorothy didn't care what the Scammells thought of her; she wouldn't be mixing with such awful colonials, and she expected they were glad to see the back of her, what with her radical ideas. Good riddance to them.

The sun burned her face like a branding iron. "Amun-Ra," she whispered, and stared with closed eyes into the heart of the sun, seeing a flash of fire ignite her vision.

Dorothy stood in this state of rapture for a few moments, enjoying this rare episode when the world was suspended in motion, like the huge candyfloss clouds hovering over the hills, as if glued onto a collage. Suddenly a firm hand grabbed her arm and pulled her forward, jerking her out of her golden reverie.

"Dorothy, are you all right. Did you have a fall? You are covered in dirt."

She turned towards the concerned male voice and saw a dark figure towering over her, obscuring the sun. When she adjusted her eyes she realised the man was Imam, his face a portrait of anxiety. Dorothy laughed when she saw his troubled expression, remembering how earnest he could be. "Don't worry, Imam, I haven't injured myself. Quite the contrary. I'm simply overjoyed to be here!"

Dorothy spun round in a circle and spread her arms to the sky, her polka dot skirt flaring, like a ladybird in flight. Then she grabbed Imam's hands and twirled round in an impromptu dance. She felt his body stiffen—like dancing with a wooden plank, she thought. Imam let out a nervous laugh and tried to straighten his suit. "Come on, Dorothy, the carriage is waiting and if we don't hurry the driver will pick up another customer." Imam motioned to a young man in a gallabiya to take her suitcases.

They sat holding hands as the caleche drove to the train station, the clip-clop of the horse's hooves filling in the silence. At the docks they had kissed each other on both cheeks and then Imam had taken her arm, but that was the extent of their affection up to now. Dorothy suddenly realised how little she knew about this man and how foreign his physical presence was to her, despite the flood of intimate letters. But she was too enthralled by the novelty of the experience, casting her doubts into the dark crevices of her mind. She watched in awe as the caleche driver weaved his way between the bicycles and donkeys laden with piles of vegetation, the carts overflowing with fruit.

"I'll find our first class carriage and come back for you in a minute, my dear—you don't want to wade through the hordes of people," said

Imam, his affection tinged with decorum. How formal he seemed, after the passionate letters he wrote, thought Dorothy, standing in the railway station, barefoot children clamouring round her hips, veiled women with baskets on their heads, and men in gallabiyas flashing their white teeth, their robes flapping like sails.

Imam went off to find their carriage, speaking to the porter in a rush of Arabic. Dorothy stood alone on the platform, feeling the essence of Egypt sink into her being. She breathed in the smell of spices, salt, mint and an exhilarating sensation: the warm wind of the desert, the dry scent of crushed rocks and withered bones.

She spotted Imam waving to her from the front of the crowd, his dark suit and hat looked out of place, she thought, he looked like a man strolling in Leicester Square. Despite his Egyptian features he looked so English, compared to the locals in their gallabiyas, their leather sandals flapping up and down the platform, their woven baskets overflowing with market goods.

Once on the train, the couple settled into their first class carriage and sat in silence, both finding conversation rather difficult. "I trust you had a safe journey, my dear," Imam inquired, trying to be more intimate with his bride-to-be.

"Oh yes, wonderful. Quite wonderful," Dorothy replied in a dreamy voice, staring out the window, transfixed by the scenery. This English lady was going to be his wife, he mused; how he longed to discard the air of formality and enter into unreserved intimacy, as only a husband and wife can experience. He was anxious to recapture the passion from their correspondences and hoped it was possible to be that intimate on a physical plane. Not that he'd had many intimate encounters with women, except an embarrassing visit to a brothel with his cousin Ahmed. In fact, he knew very little about women, he confessed, due to the unfortunate segregation of the sexes in Egypt. He'd grown up with a rather puzzling perception of women, adoring them from afar and fearing them when confronted with their presence.

"It's wonderful to be here—you don't know how happy I am to finally be here, after all this time," she smiled at him and squeezed his hand, then continued to stare out the window, engrossed by the lively streets teeming with merchants and beasts of burden. She was surprised by the energy of the place, by how industrial Port Said was and how busy everyone seemed to be, caught up in a flurry of motion, darting like bees from flower to flower.

21

"Cairo is more cosmopolitan than Port Said—there are some delightful areas in Cairo, like Maadi and Manya el Ronda—perfect for an English lady, and there are lovely shops just like in London and Paris." Imam tried to draw her attention away from the window, but she offered him a faint smile and kept gazing into the horizon.

Dorothy felt her heart contract with the reference to London and Paris. What did he mean? She certainly wasn't interested in the latest fashions; she hadn't come to Egypt to live as a colonial, or as an English lady for that matter. But she decided to reserve judgement until they arrived in Cairo. She trusted his family would live according to Egyptian customs and banished all fears of colonialism from her mind. She was too caught up in the excitement of it all to worry about the future. She was back in her ancient home, "I'll never leave you," she repeated, her promise escaping out the window, disappearing into the heat haze.

Dorothy sat in a state of rapture watching the fields drift by, the villagers tending their crops with handmade tools, the cattle drawing the water from the well as they had in ancient times. Imam buried his head in the newspaper, as he could see his wife-to-be was lost in some sort of stupor, probably caused by the exhaustion of her journey. She'd ignored his attempts at conversation and had kept her eyes glued to the window. *The poor dear must be shattered, not to mention bewildered by it all. To an English lady Egypt must be a shock to the senses.* Imam glanced out the window and saw a group of dirty children carrying huge bundles of greenery on their backs, their spines bent over like hooks. He felt ashamed when he saw the mud huts and people squatting like animals, without shoes or proper clothes. He wondered what Dorothy thought of it all, seeing the children in their dirty rags, toiling the land in primitive conditions, unable to read and write because they'd never been to school. With Dorothy by his side he would help to change all that. He'd seen the modern world, he believed in social progress, and it was about time Egypt dusted herself off and faced the future. There was no time for medieval sentimentality in this new world: a mud hut may seem romantic to the tourist, but what is romantic about a life of squalor? To Imam the old ways embodied a life without options; the villagers were like beasts of burden, locked in a cycle they were powerless to change.

Dorothy was unaware of Imam's malcontent and took delight in every living creature she saw, as if they were long lost relatives. She absorbed the sweep of fertile fields, the strip of green to which the villagers clung, sheltering them from the imperious desert. The enormity of the desert was like the sea, she thought, or the frozen north pole, and she was amazed that life could take hold here, forged out of barren sand. Human existence seemed so precious here, surrounded by this desert of death. This determination to exist in a sea of sand struck her as a miracle, and every tree, bush and vegetable took on special significance; this emanation of life, a green strike against death. The greenery invaded the wasteland with its will to regenerate itself, transforming the Delta region into an abundant oasis, an earthly paradise bursting with tropical fruits and palm trees. Dorothy finally understood why the ancient Egyptians had chosen this place, for life by the Nile was a transcendence of death. Eternity was promised along the river's edge, the boundary between life and death. Dorothy embraced the scenery through every pore, her senses sucking in the landscape, her mind mapping out the new space. She was being brought back to life, like a flower in the desert, sensing the rain. The surrounding images awakened ancient memories buried within her, and each snapshot of Egypt was like a fragment of memory being made visible. It was like looking through a tarnished bronze mirror, and once polished it revealed a golden world forgotten by time.

Imam scanned his newspaper for the fourth time, having read all the pages that interested him; he glanced out the window, following Dorothy's incessant gaze. How could she tell him she'd seen this all before, and that she knew the place like the back of her hand: the fields, the reeds and the river imprinted on her psyche; the tracks in the sand written on her skin, the fig trees moulded into her backbone.

The train came to a grinding halt and Dorothy was jolted from her reverie, her body catapulted towards the floor. Imam grabbed her arm and pulled her safely back to her seat. "Are you all right, my love?"

Dorothy smiled awkwardly and struggled to compose herself, just as the train lunged forward again. She felt terribly woozy, as if she'd been asleep, or drugged, the sunlight beginning to sting her eyes.

"I forgot to warn you about Egyptian trains. They are known to stop and start at unexpected moments. Are you sure you're all right, my dear?"

Dorothy nodded, "I'm fine. I'm not made of glass. In fact I'm very well padded," she laughed, slapping her hips, then spreading her wide skirt over the seat. He would certainly be an attentive husband, she realised, taking his hand with affection.

They finally arrived in Cairo, and as they got up to leave their seats Dorothy heard a British man shout, "These trains are a downright danger—I'm amazed they can even stop at all, what with these dreadful brakes—and these tatty seats are a disgrace—this certainly isn't first class."

Dorothy recognised the arrogant voice of Richard Scammell, and she watched the couple gesticulating to the porters on the platform, posing in their haughty manner. She did her best to avoid them, and soon the snooty couple were engulfed by the crowd as if they'd never existed.

Dorothy and Imam took a caleche to his parents' flat, and she nervously stepped into the hallway, hoping his parents would approve of having an English daughter-in-law and not find her too peculiar. To Dorothy's relief, Imam's parents welcomed her into their home and made her feel one of the family.

The next day Dorothy wrote to her mother, *"Imam's parents are gracious, affectionate people and they've planned a traditional wedding for us—they don't waste any time! Sayyida Meguid is a stylish woman in her late forties—she's made me very welcome, and Sayyid Meguid has already adopted me—he calls me Bulbul because he says I sing like a nightingale! For the moment we're living in their Ottoman style flat near the citadel, the flat is full of character, with wooden architrave and lofty oriental furniture. I'd love to live in a flat like this, but Imam has his heart set on the suburbs, he says we'd be better off there—but we'll have to see. Tomorrow I'm going to meet the entire family and that could take days as they are scattered all over Egypt, much like Osiris's remains."*

The impromptu wedding happened like a dream, she later wrote, as a dozen female relatives descended upon her, shaving her body, styling her hair and painting her hands in intricate floral patterns. The women loved Dorothy's blue eyes and fair skin, and ran their fingers through her blonde curls, swooning in Arabic as if singing a love song, or so it sounded to Dorothy, who longed to master this melodious language. Sayyida Meguid was delighted with her daughter-in-law-to-be and kept kissing her on the cheek, uttering affectionate words in Arabic, "anti jamilah!"—you look beautiful!

When Dorothy was sufficiently adorned with makeup and gold jewels, the women helped her into her white and yellow dress, which was rather on the tight side. She squeezed her flesh into the tight fabric and her hefty bosom cascaded into the open neckline, like a waterfall plunging into a pool. The women fondled her ample mounds approvingly and caressed her round hips, uttering squeals of delight, "You have great childbearing hips, and big breasts for feeding babies—you never run out of milk," said Shama, full of admiration for her new sister-in-law.

"Yes, I'm built like an ox and feel rather ridiculous in this dress," Dorothy laughed uneasily, finding it hard to breathe. She was amazed by the women's intimacy, and the way they openly touched her breasts and buttocks. You'd never get this in England, she laughed, imagining her mother surrounded by these sensuous women, devouring British reserve with their slaps and kisses, their Arabic love songs.

Considering the wedding was an off the cuff affair, Dorothy was surprised how well organised the ceremony appeared to be. *"The whole event came off spectacularly well, even though I looked like a lemon cream cake in this outlandish dress and had to sit on a stage for all the guests to gawp at, as if they planned to devour me at the first opportunity."* Dorothy later wrote to her parents, describing her unusual wedding.

The wedding started at noon. The family were escorted in a horse drawn carriage to the local mosque, where the Mullah placed the couple's hands under the prayer cloth and chanted to Allah for an eternity. Dorothy wondered how many prayers you could say about marriage (obviously a whole book's worth), and she worried what they were signing up for, as the Arabic sermons went on and on, uttered in a foreboding manner (not that she understood a word of it). The Mullah expected the bride's father to join hands with the groom, but as he wasn't present, Imam's father stepped in and the cloth was placed over their hands. The whole process was repeated with another length of prayers, and Dorothy doubted they would ever get to the wedding feast (and she was getting rather hungry).

The final blessing was made by the Mullah, and the female relatives began to laugh and cry, appealing to Dorothy to throw the prayer cloth. She turned her back on the women and tossed the cloth in the air, the women raising their arms, desperately trying to catch it and be the next woman to marry. "Allah, throw it to me, Dorothy! Throw it to me, your cousin—Allah Akhbar!" The women shouted in ear-splitting Arabic, raucous enough to sound like a burst of expletives. To Shama's delight the cloth landed in her right hand. "You're a good sister—you bring me luck," she cried, collapsing on the floor in a fit of joy.

The wedding party was an exciting event for Dorothy, with the vibrant procession, the *Zaffa,* ambling down the street, shaking tambourines, playing flutes, bagpipes and drums, compelling the women to ululate in shrill voices. They made their way across town in an explosion of colour and sound, people dancing and clapping, the men twirling their shouba sticks round in the air. Such a contrast to her simple life in London, walking to work each day under a blanket of grey sky. And here she was marrying an Egyptian man, wearing a fantastic gaudy dress, surrounded by friendly women drenched in jewels and makeup, resembling a dozen Cleopatras. Shama had done her best to make Dorothy look like a queen, with Egyptian almond eyes. "But I look more like a lewd panda," Dorothy giggled, quite taken with her garish transformation.

They arrived at a hotel run by one of Imam's uncles, the dining room decorated with flowers and streamers, with fruits and vegetables carved into floral patterns. The couple walked up the stairs and were urged to come down again, pausing by the chandelier for a photo, the belly dancers surrounding them in a tangle of torsos, shaking their hip scarves in a jingle of bells. For a moment Dorothy closed her eyes and imagined the dancers in ancient times, producing the same hypnotic sound, shaking their sistra and pounding their feet, calling upon the goddess. When she opened her eyes the belly dancers were leaving the stairs in a slow procession; Dorothy and Imam followed them to the stage decorated in white flowers, where they sat on their koshas—their ornate wedding thrones, painted in gold and green.

"You are the King and Queen," said Shama, handing Dorothy a bouquet of flowers. All newlyweds were given this royal treatment, Dorothy later realised, but for this brief moment she felt like the Queen of Egypt. A group of attendants were at their beck and call, and the couple were encouraged to stay in their koshas, unless they needed to go to the bathroom. At one point Dorothy wished to stretch her legs as all this sitting around was giving her cramp. "Do you need anything?" the waiter inquired, as she tried to get up. "I would like to walk about for a bit, I'm tired of too much sitting," Dorothy explained. "I bring you rose sherbet drink—no need to get up from your kosha," the waiter insisted, running off to the bar. Dorothy realised that leaving the stage was a sign that the couple were dissatisfied with the service and that their every need hadn't been catered for. In the end she pretended to go to the loo so she could sneak outside to stretch her legs—and smoke a cigarette.

When Dorothy returned to her throne the professional musicians and singers began their performance. The *Capella* band wore cream coloured gallabiyas with white turbans, and they performed several traditional wedding songs. Then the *Toura* dancer spun round and round like a top, performing tricks with his long tunic, folding the lengths into intricate patterns. At the end of his performance he started to turn with tremendous speed, unwrapping his turban as he twisted round. He rolled the turban into a ball as he spun, and then suddenly came to a halt, holding the bundle in his arms like a newborn baby. He walked towards the couple and presented the 'baby' to Dorothy, who accepted the heap with an awkward smile, as everyone started to clap and cheer. Then the attendants surrounded the couple with incense braziers, the spicy mix of musk and jasmine filling Dorothy's senses with dreamy pleasure. One of the attendants handed the couple a glass of rose water and they all waited while the couple drained the contents. "Now you kiss!"

The couple performed their clumsy kiss, their lips smacking together as they leaned over their koshas. Then there was more clapping, music and cheering, and the whole room stood up to make a toast, everyone drinking glasses of rose water, which tasted like strawberry sherbet to Dorothy. After the couple exchanged rings it was time to cut the cake. It seemed an odd way of doing things, as they hadn't eaten the main course yet. The cake was several layers high, covered in icing sugar, nuts and gold coloured ornaments.

"Throw your bouquet," Shama shouted, hoping to seal her future marriage with a second blessing. Dorothy tossed the bouquet in the air, thinking what a strange medley of rituals this was, what with incense and thrones, and wedding cakes before the meal. A girl called Aisha caught the bouquet—a cousin or sister-in-law, Dorothy wasn't sure which, but Shama gave her a tongue-lashing for spoiling her luck.

Then the couple were asked to come forward for the first dance.

"Thank God we can get up," Dorothy sighed with relief. The pair performed an impromptu foxtrot to an Arabic love song and they managed to keep in step with one another, which surprised them both as they'd never danced together before. "I'll have to take you dancing more often—you have an Egyptian rhythm and you can shimmy like a belly dancer," Imam laughed.

"And I will certainly accept, as you haven't stepped on my shoes once!"

By the time the buffet was brought out Dorothy was beginning to feel rather faint with hunger and a little sick from the atrociously sweet cake. But she managed to eat a plate of salad and a little bowl of lentil stew. The great feast was arranged on a long table and looked very sumptuous, with Shish Tawouk—spicy grilled chicken and vegetables served on skewers, and endless trays of grilled lamb and beef. There were huge bowls of Kushari, a tasty vegetarian mix of lentils, rice, spicy tomatoes, pasta and onions, silver plates piled high with crisp bread, rice, salad, fruit, and tantalising sweetmeats.

With the music, the dancing and the wonderful feast, Dorothy felt the ancient memories begin to stir. The old ways were never far from the surface, she knew, even in this modern hotel with the fancy chandeliers. The people couldn't help themselves: a little music, dancing and good food, and the ancient customs sprang into being. The people hadn't changed in thousands of years, she realised; the rituals flowed through the blood, like the canals through the desert. They were stored in the memory like shafts of wheat. And like the granite cliffs, they could never be erased.

∧∧∧∧∧   ∧∧∧∧∧   ∧∧∧∧∧

Dorothy wrote a letter to her parents describing her first month in Cairo.

Dear Both,

I am amazed by the diversity of Cairo, a wonderful medley of Arabic, Egyptian and European cultures. In one day it is possible to see schoolchildren in English uniforms, old men shuffling to the mosque in red fezes, women in long robes with baskets on their heads as in Pharaonic times, and European women wearing the latest fashions! The English men go around in bowler hats and double breasted suits, as if they were in Trafalgar Square. There are many French people here and some of the boutiques are straight out of Paris, including the bistros and patisseries selling fresh croissants. But my favourite places of all are the Egyptian souqs where they sell carpets, antiques, and all sorts of marvellous trinkets from the Orient, and there are spice stalls and exotic fruits of every colour, and Turkish cafés right out of the Arabian Nights. It is possible to eat a French pastry, drink a Turkish coffee and pomegranate juice all at once! How I would love to live in this fascinating area, but Imam has got us a house in the diplomatic area, as he says I deserve to live in style! Manya El Roda is a posh neighbourhood, with gardens and stately homes. But there are so many British people I keep thinking I'm in Kensington! I can't complain, Imam tries his best to make me feel at home, and he really loves everything English—more than I do I fear! Tomorrow we are going to an Egyptology lecture at the British Civic Society—I'm hoping to meet some kindred spirits...

In fact Dorothy found Manya El Roda an insufferable place full of pretentious expatriates, and she told her husband, "I would much rather live near the citadel, like your parents." Dorothy had come to Egypt to live with the local people, the old houses, the dovecotes and the braying donkeys. But Imam hated the Old Quarter, "It smells awful and people live in primitive ways—they're still in the Middle Ages. All the modern young people live in Manya El Roda—it's perfect for a liberal couple like us." Imam reminded his wife that he was now a teacher and government official—he couldn't live in such a backward place as the Old Quarter, with its crumbling ruins and dubious hygiene. "No respectable person would ever visit us if we lived there—the houses are outdated: they still have outdoor toilets. Manya El Roda is where all the educated Egyptians and Europeans live. It's just the place for an English lady, with all the pretty gardens and tree lined avenues."

Dorothy had been swayed by Imam's glowing description of Manya El Roda in his letters, but she disliked the area right from the start. "The place is full of snobs, Imam. The worst kind of English people who do not appreciate Egyptian history or culture—they only wish to throw their weight around. They are attracted to a lifestyle they couldn't afford back in England, with their servants and their pretentious airs."

29

"Everything is very strange to you right now, just give it some time. You will grow to like it, I'm sure." Imam was an eternal optimist, but sometimes it blinded him to the truth, Dorothy realised. *I will never grow to love this place.*

She met a few of the neighbours, like Mr and Mrs Denham who'd managed a clothing shop in Leeds. They'd come to Egypt to export cotton back home and they'd suddenly made a huge amount of money. "They live like Lord and Lady Muck, with their chauffeur and Bentley," Dorothy scoffed at their pretensions. Then two days later Dorothy discovered to her horror that Mr and Mrs Scammell lived on the same street. One evening she passed them along the Corniche el Nile, arm in arm with her Egyptian husband, and their jaws dropped, but they pretended not to notice her. She knew what they were thinking by their condescending expression: how could she marry a native—it just isn't done! There was a clear division between the English and the locals, as in any colonial country the English ruled, and as she had crossed that divide—made a mockery of the conventions—the price to pay was ostracism. How she despised these insular people! Why did Imam want to live with these people? He didn't seem to notice their disapproval—perhaps he was accustomed to their arrogant ways.

The following evening the couple went to a lecture, and to her dismay, Dorothy found the hall was full of tiresome colonials. When Dorothy and Imam walked into the British Civic Society everyone suddenly went quiet and gave the couple a dark stare. She'd seen several of them before, and they knew all about her rebellious sentiments on Egyptian independence and her penchant for living like a native. In their company Dorothy felt even more of an outsider than she'd felt in London.

The lecture was given by a young American called Dr Wilkes, who told the audience about the recent discoveries at Giza. Dorothy was fascinated by his talk as she knew there were countless wonders still hidden in the sand—if only she could help unearth them and protect them from greedy collectors. She saw the lecture was wasted on this audience, who were only interested in discovering hordes of gold that would make them filthy rich.

After the lecture Dorothy chatted to some Egyptologists and an interesting English lady called Teresa, a painter who wore Eastern clothes. Dorothy admired her Turkish pantaloons and red waistcoat, her hips draped in multicoloured scarves.

"Look at these buffoons in their mess jackets and blue patrols—there's even a chap in an Expeditionary Force uniform and a pith helmet—don't they see what's happening? The resentful faces..." she confided in Teresa by the punch bowl. "An uprising is festering right under their noses and all they do is order another martini."

"They are quite wretched, darling, the worst sort of bourgeoisie you'll ever come across. Marx would have had a field day with them." Teresa mimicked their pompous mannerisms: bossing the locals and smoking cigars they couldn't afford back home. The two women collapsed into fits of laughter, a welcome relief from the oppressive atmosphere of the evening, but people thought they were drunk, the way they tittered by the punch bowl.

Imam found a group of local officials and chatted away in Arabic. How she envied him speaking the language: he could always escape from these silly colonials, and he could rest assured none of them spoke Arabic. Speaking Arabic gave them a secret power over the English, the language of the majority they didn't understand.

I must learn this language, vowed Dorothy, then I can find a way into their culture, their hearts—instead of sticking with these unilingual expats.

"You should go to the Khan el Khalili bazaar," Teresa suggested, "I go there to paint—it's full of colour and extraordinary light filtering through the Arabic arches." She said there were many bohemians wandering around, attracted by the mysterious souqs leading to Eastern wonders, the real setting for the *Thousand and One Nights*.

"That seems more my cup of tea—black and sweet, Egyptian tea." Dorothy would go to the bazaar and lose herself in the oriental alleys, make some sketches of arabesques, domes and market traders; the brocade of light streaming through the porticos.

I will have to go there on my own, she decided; it was no good asking Imam to take her, as he disliked the bazaar, with the oppressive awnings leading to endless shops; the crowds, the loud noises and suspicious smells made him feel ill, almost claustrophobic. In fact his parents' place was near el Khalili, and to think all those weeks they'd stayed there and he'd never taken her to the bazaar.

Dorothy wanted to go home—the Egyptologists, Teresa and her bohemian friends had gone to a party near the citadel, fed up with

31

these boring old codgers. Dorothy and Imam were on their way out when she overheard a man say, "Of course the Egyptians couldn't run the place without us—they've got no experience of running a civilised society. It's best to quell the rebels before they get out of hand."

Dorothy turned to face the man and interrupted, "ancient Egypt was the most civilised society the world has ever known, when your ancestors were living like animals they were building magnificent temples. The revolution will come sooner than you think and when it does, you better hop on the first ship back to England, because they'll slit your throat sooner than you can say the Feast of Ibrahim!"

As Dorothy turned to leave a man in a uniform approached her, "We'll not tolerate such incendiary remarks in the British Civic Society. So don't bother coming here again as our doors will be closed to you."

"I would rather visit a pack of jackals—and I would trust them a good deal more!"

Everyone stared at this English lady with the flaming eyes, who insisted on making a grand exit, with her discomfited husband shrinking behind her.

Word soon got round about Dorothy—Mrs Bulbul Meguid, and she found herself excluded from colonial circles: mainly for her anti-Imperial views, but also for marrying a native. But Dorothy felt sorry for these snooty people in their elite clubs and societies, with no idea what was happening around them.

"Don't they hear the students in the streets, shouting slogans—their angry eyes? These ridiculous colonials strolling along the Corniche in their fineries, who don't notice the poverty, the discontent in the air."

"Don't be so controversial, my dear," said Imam, wishing his wife wouldn't rock the boat so violently; as a government official his job required a certain degree of compliance. The British were still in charge: they ran the police, the army and the financial structure. They certainly had the power and the wealth, which meant that even King Fuad's loyalty could be bought. In London Imam had been free to express his views about Independence, but back in Cairo he could easily be branded a radical and lose his position.

Later that evening Dorothy realised she must curb her tongue. "People are thrown in prison for making such insurgent remarks about the British, about Independence—don't be so foolhardy," she admonished herself. One of Imam's colleagues had written a play criticising the military, and he'd been arrested and charged with 'civil unrest.'

She did her best to avoid the colonial types—but if she heard one more comment about the lazy natives she'd smack the sod over the head with her wicker basket, "and no doubt he'd charge me with assault!"

Dorothy found solace in the Khalili Bazaar with the labyrinth of souqs dating back to Persian times, the hidden archways and tiled alcoves reminiscent of Constantinople; the spice mounds, the brass tea sets, the Eastern rugs and star-shaped lanterns. There was little chance of meeting the Scammells in this Oriental spider's web. Occasionally she spotted the odd Westerner in search of real adventure, but most of the time she was the only English person in sight. She entered a numinous world of Arabic voices and painted mazes, the coloured lanterns casting geometric patterns on the ceilings. Islamic design was a reflection of the beauty and infinite nature of the universe, the intricate motifs revealing the complexity of life on earth and the human capacity to reinvent itself. Dorothy sat in the café reading the book on Sufi poetry she'd found in the antique shop. She lingered on a poem by Jalaluddin Rumi:

"We come spinning out of nothingness, scattering stars like dust..."
"Let the beauty we love be what we do."
She sipped her tea and let the cosmic wonders permeate her soul.
"The song of the spheres in their revolutions
Is what men sing with lute and voice."

There were a few Sufi proverbs in the last chapter and one caught her eye:
"A donkey with a load of holy books is still a donkey."
She choked on her tea, trying not to laugh, as a group of old mullahs shuffled by on their way to the mosque, their Turkish slippers flapping on the cobbles.

3. Passion Play
Abydos, 1290 BC

The Mystery Plays began with the life and death of Osiris; the drama exploding on the scene, the villagers' weeping as they heard the dreadful news: "Our beloved King Osiris is dead, murdered by his evil brother Seth!" Inhapi ran along the shore as Isis, searching for her husband in despair, her primal screams resounding through the land, raising the hairs of every creature and sending them into a spiral of grief. The gong was struck and with every clang the sound of doom multiplied, announcing the Lord's death and the inevitable destruction to follow. Isis gave a dramatic performance; her healing powers awakened, her soliloquy echoing through the bulrushes, all the way to Canaan and then onto Lebanon; they heard her sonnets of distress in the royal palace, and even the great King of Byblos was reduced to tears. Nephthys joined in the tragedy, the two sisters running along the muddy shore, screaming and covering themselves in dirt; the people across the bank followed in a cathartic outpouring, acting out their collective grief, searching the reservoir of emotion hidden within. They were wailing, shaking and writhing in the mud, as they watched the sisters across the canal; the watery divide ensured the people observed the drama from a slight distance, allowing the drama of their own emotions to unfold. This Passion Play, this inchoation of theatrical tragedy—the seeds that would later take root in the Ancient Greek imagination—first awakened on these Eastern shores.

Bentreshy and Kebi ran down to the shore and squeezed their way through the throng of mourners; they positioned themselves on a mound of clay, their feet sinking below the surface, soaked with tears and the swirl of the river, whipped up by the frantic bodies sliding down the banks. They ripped through the earth in despair, turning the river into a deep wound, the mud forming brown pools of blood beneath their feet, the remnants of a great sacrifice.

Bentreshy watched Inhapi across the canal, her reflection a mirror of doom, sending deep ripples of grief across the shore. Bentreshy and Kebi waded into the water, their robes clinging to their legs as if in fear, and they ran along the bank following the priestess' movements, wailing in anguish like dying birds shot out of the sky. The girls covered themselves in mud, scraping at the ground on all fours, as if digging a way out of their misery, searching for a glimmer of light in the darkness. *"All is lost. Our King is dead! The most righteous Lord that ever lived, who brought peace and harmony to his people. Alas, Our Saviour is no more!"*

Then the goddess-sisters lay silent on the shore, their grief spent, their anguish washed away by the river. The girls lay down in the mud, eyes bulging like scarabs and they let their sorrow sink into the mire where it writhed and gurgled underground, reminiscent of an ancient species that once crawled upon this shore, a limbless creature with a strange impulse to live on land.

Bentreshy dived into the river and cleansed the dirt from her body, emerging with a new sense of purity, her eyes shining with clarity. Kebi turned backward somersaults and then burst to the surface, arms splashing and causing waves on the shore, the girls plunging into spirals of laughter. The villagers wallowed in the river like lazy hippos and the fish were so surprised by the mass of visitors that they jumped out of the water and lay flapping on the shore. Some of the villagers caught the flying fish with their bare hands, and the children ran up the bank with squeals of laughter, the scaly fish tickling their palms.

The evening ceremony began after sundown, with the villagers expending the last of their grief in a final cathartic wailing, followed by a great feast to fill their barren bellies. Their sorrow was diminished with the promise of dawn, knowing that tomorrow would bring the resurrection. But they were careful to conceal their joy behind a cloud of woe, part sing-along, part lament, the people dancing and chanting with devotion, the wine blurring their senses, so it was hard to distinguish whether they were laughing or crying, so dramatic were their outpourings, everyone trying to outdo the other, as in a country opera, shrill voices piercing the night sky. Then they cooked endless fish on open fires and roasted the pintail ducks the fowlers had boomeranged out of the sky, and all the food was shared so that no one went hungry on the Feast of Sorrow.

On the second day of the Passion Plays, Isis and Nephthys stood by the shore in their golden robes, the people cheering as the sisters spread their powerful wings towards the sky, their grief and ragged appearance replaced with a serene composure.

35

"Oh great people of Osiris. We will find the remains of your King and bring him home to you. We will scour the land until we find his murdered body and we will restore him to life. Our Lord will transcend death and the light of truth will return to this great land."

The villagers roared with approval, "Find the King and bring him back to life!"

The sisters searched for the remains of Osiris, crawling through the reeds and papyri, retrieving arms and legs, fingers and toes, and when they'd collected all his body parts they stitched him back together, as if they were making a quilt, placing his handsome head on the crest of their creation.

The part of Seth was played by Amenkef. Many priests refused to perform the role but Amenkef seemed to relish the idea, and he staunchly defended the wicked slayer, "Without Seth the Lord would not rise again—and there would be no resurrection. Thanks to Seth the King was reborn as a god, his resurrection a testament of life after death."

The audience knew the priest was telling the truth, but they were troubled by his enthusiasm for the role and the pleasure he took in the King's demise. Their only consolation was that Seth would be overthrown by Horus, then torn to pieces by a pack of wolves.

The priests gathered by the shore for the Final Act of the day. They scoured the undergrowth in search of the monstrous Seth and when they discovered his hiding place they shouted, "Oh Great Horus, son of Osiris, eliminate the evil power from this land. Avenge thy father's death!"

In a flash Rameses leaped from the undergrowth, as though materialising out of reeds, and raised his sword of vengeance. He drove his sword into Seth's villainous heart, and his uncle exhaled his last vicious breath with great drama, his body collapsing to the ground, his malice sinking into the mud. The villagers cheered, "Seth the evil usurper is no more! Egypt is free from chaos! Oh hail the great Horus, our new King, merciful son of Osiris!"

Rameses' performance was a special surprise as no one had expected the prince to play Horus, or even knew he was in Abydos, for that matter. He'd come through the desert with the nomads, dressed as a Babylonian trader. (He was co-ruler of Egypt and yet he'd walked unnoticed through the crowds, his face hidden behind a red scarf.) Once Seth had been slain and the chaos had been eliminated, Rameses made a dramatic bow and returned to the palace to practice his archery, and everyone praised him as the Liberator of Egypt.

On the third day Bentreshy prepared herself for the fertility ritual in the chapel of Isis. The light streamed through the window, a bright ray of sunshine stretched towards her like a golden arm and seized her in its radiance, tossing her out of bed. She remembered last night's party with misty pleasure, her head spinning with too much wine and lack of sleep. But there was no time for indolence, she realised, splashing cold water on her face, forcing her heavy eyes to open wide and clear the vapour from her mind. Then the attendants arrived to shave her body hair—except for her blonde locks, deemed too beautiful to cut off (Inhapi said her hair was a gift from Isis and not to be tampered with). After the ablutions, Kiya anointed Bentreshy's body in neroli oil and applied her makeup, creating sultry eyes with a charcoal stick and dramatic waves with malachite eye shadow. Kiya rubbed ochre powder into Bentreshy's cheeks and darkened her lips with wine residue and bees wax. She clapped her hands, "Osiris won't be able to resist you—even though he's a corpse, he'll be bursting with carnal desires!"

Bentreshy blushed under her rouge cheeks. "The passion is only symbolic—I am not really Isis—it's only a ritual," she reminded Kiya, who was busy sorting through the glass beads, not really listening; she'd been swept along by the fantasy of it all, and she wasn't about to come down to earth.

As the attendants adorned her in the guise of Isis, Bentreshy felt herself transforming, the way a bud turns into a lotus flower. She was slipping away, as if melting into the ground; about to be possessed by another being. A seed was germinating within her belly and she felt a rush of hot sun radiate throughout her body. She was suddenly powerful, imbued with an invincible strength. How wonderful it would be to always feel this way, she wished, for Bentreshy was bursting with exuberance, as if still tipsy on wine, yet with the mental clarity of Seshet, who could store a million verses in her head and never forget a single word.

When the transformation was complete Bentreshy stood before the attendants in her gold and blue gown, embroidered with lapis lazuli, garnets, citrine and turquoise stones, shimmering with the gaze of the

Immortal One, and she wore the Royal Headdress with the dancing uraeus, poised to strike the demons of the netherworld. Her arms were draped in gold snakes, which slithered up her shoulders and around her neck, and she wore a splendid collar of jade, carnelian and moonstones. The attendants held their breath for a moment, and then cried, "Oh Lady Isis! We welcome you, our Great Mother." They fell to their knees in astonishment, their eyes sparkling with tears, like diamond splinters.

Isis was alive within her now. Bentreshy could feel herself lying dormant, as if given opium to drink; the goddess possessed her body, her power rising like the Dog Star. Isis flung open the doors and a gust of wind travelled through the chamber. The initiates drew in a collective breath of air, pausing for a moment in reverence before uttering, "Hail to the Great Mother Isis!" This outburst released them from bewilderment and they absorbed the warmth of the goddess, never one to be worshipped from afar. Isis drifted into the Great Hall, suspended by an intake of breath, the Adepts inhaling the image of beauty, the air heavy with divine radiance and joy. Isis mounted the steps to the golden canopy and called out:

"Osiris, my beloved husband, oh come to me my sweet husband. I long to feel your breath on my face, your soft lips on mine." The goddess exhaled with emotion and drifted towards the figure on the bed, a lifeless corpse in the shape of a mummy, his hands folded across his chest. Isis discarded her robe and headdress, revealing a radiant body, both primeval and divine, the Eternal Mother who heals the wounded and nurtures the abandoned; her skin the colour of pale gold, her rounded breasts offering sacred milk, hips shaped like half moons. The goddess lay down beside her dead husband and gazed at him with such tenderness, seeing his broken body, his face twisted with pain and she cradled him the way she would a child, drawing the withered figure to the warmth of her breast. Isis ran her healing hands over her husband's bruised body and uttered the magic incantations, *"Oh my beloved Osiris, rise from the dead and walk with me through the land of Geb, and our love will last forever. Open your ears so you may hear my words of devotion, open your mouth so you may speak the language of eternal love!"*

The drums began to beat through the Underworld, and then the beat grew louder, pounding through the ears of the Adepts until the chamber became one giant heartbeat. The rhythm was hypnotic and no one knew its origin—whether it came from within their own hearts or from a manmade instrument, or from a primeval source at the centre of the universe.

"Rise, my Lord Osiris! Awaken to your loving wife and let us be as one!"

Isis kissed Osiris, her red lips lingering on his faint lips. *"Rise, my love,"* she whispered in his ear. And rise he did—his lips trembling with new life, parted to receive his wife's warm mouth. He rose again, overcome by sheer love and female force of will, and the Lord opened his eyes and stared into the radiant face of his wife who had saved him from death, and he opened his mouth in wonder, his nose breathing in her intoxicating perfume, his eyes leaking tears of joy, and he knew he was alive.

Osiris reached out and touched the goddess' perfect breasts, her body like a golden tree bursting with fruit. He trembled with rapture, the memory of human passion awakening in his veins, and he turned his bruised being towards Isis and let her lead him to ecstasy. He didn't have long to wait—his passionate spouse leaped upon him, covering his body in loving kisses, taking his royal member into her warm mouth until it grew like a shaft of wheat in the sun, radiating with golden seeds. Then Isis rolled onto her back and opened her body to receive, a sacred boat offering herself to the sea. Pulsating with desire, Osiris made love to Isis, the Eternal Couple uniting in a state of rapture, their passion melting into memory, clutching at each other with a human sense of urgency. They recalled their physical love on earth, when they once lived as King and Queen of Egypt, when their generous spirits radiated through the land, and the people lived in paradise. Thanks to this yearly ritual, the Eternal Couple made love in human form, reliving their precious time on earth, a fleeting yet precious gift from nature. Due to its ephemeral quality their physical love seemed all the more desirable, a thin shroud taken by the wind, its beauty hovering over the trees. The transient element imbued their love with intensity—on earth they were evanescent beings, they could die at any moment and suffer the agonies of death, or worse, the anguish of a broken heart. When they made love in Amenti they reached a state of bliss unknown to mortals, and yet the couple missed this frantic earthly passion, charged with longing and the desire for eternity. Here on earth they had to seize every moment, like a sunset before it fades; they didn't have time to languor in divine luxury, they made love in a feverish manner, their instincts roused like animals in the dark. Isis felt overwhelmed by this love; a riverbank succumbing to the force of water. She was a woman again, with fleshy folds, dark mounds and hidden devices, and when her husband entered her body, all of creation burst within her, wave after wave of mortal pleasure.

Outside the Temple the villagers united for the Resurrection Feast, roasting the Phagrus fish on open fires, the very creature that nibbled Osiris' penis and carried the seed of his fertility in its scaly flesh. The locals ate platefuls of fish, the men shouting, "Osiris, Lord of Fertility, may the fish make my member productive, and turn me into a potent love god!" And the women cried out, "Oh, Desirable One, Beloved of Isis, impregnate me with your fertile seed, swim inside my womb and leave a child behind!" They consumed the fish with chants and prayers, and then they started dancing and singing, stripping off their clothes in the heat of the fire and slinging their garments into the flames.

"Hail to Isis and Osiris, bonded in Eternal Love! Isis who rises the limp penis from the dead and makes it pump with life—Lady Isis, White Goddess, who resurrects the Green Lord, so we may live!"

Men and women came together in a desperate frenzy, copulating on the ground which would later bear their harvest, human passion seeping into the earth, enriching the soil with potent energy. They called upon the earth to be productive, and the women called upon their wombs to swell like the belly of Isis, who offered conception on this very night. The couples rose from the ground reeling with animal pleasure and rushed back to their homes to continue their lovemaking, running naked with wild nobility, the majestic children of the black land; tonight they would be fruitful and multiply, under the tender gaze of their Divine Parents.

Bentreshy awoke in the dark chamber, her head reeling with hallucinations, her dress torn and covered in dirt. Sety staggered to his feet and rubbed his face with his hands, the lotus potion still clouding his vision. The oppressive air burned their lungs, the eerie silence unsettled their nerves. "Take my hand—I know a secret way out of here," he whispered; he would take her back to the light.

She followed Sety through the maze of passageways, the sound of her feet emulating her throbbing head, down into the bowels of the Temple, passed the embalming chamber where she'd once hidden. But she hadn't realised the Temple had such an intricate underground network, leading to tiny chambers and antechambers, their stone doorways intimating covert domains. Then they scrambled up a dirt tunnel, the sand wedging under her fingernails as she crawled her way up, the sand slipping inside her sandals. The moonlight revealed a dark sky on the west side of the Temple, where the desert plain slowly lifted itself towards the hills. The couple ran towards the hills, Bentreshy not knowing where they were going, but she felt safe, knowing they were alone in the wilderness. They fell over the dark mounds of sand as they ran, falling into the soft moulds, laughing, gasping and spitting sand. Their laughter was uncontrollable and they inhaled great gulps of air, their minds intoxicated with the ripples of cold wind, they were seized by a sort of joyful madness. They made their way down the other side of the mountain, half sliding half falling, the sound of her robe ripping, like a branch torn from a tree.

"We are in the land of the desert people now—where the Berbers follow their wandering spirits. Their homes are in constant motion, like the stars in the universe." Sety whistled into the empty sky, the sound disappearing into infinity. There was nothing around but an endless terrain of dips and arches leading to oblivion. Bentreshy felt like a tiny speck of dust, engulfed by this silent void. To her surprise she heard a horn in the distance and the sound of voices coming over the mounds. What a marvel to come across human life in this barren place; a whole tribe of people came towards them, some on foot, some on horses, and she saw their white teeth in the moonlight, flashing in collective joy: oh, to be walking in the desert at midnight, with the stars shining like specks of sand in the sunlight.

An old man stepped forward, his leathery face illuminated by the moonlight; the lines on his face were like bits of old string, thought Bentreshy, woven into a mysterious pattern.

"Good-evening, Men-Maat-Ra, I have your horse ready for your journey." The man was called Senwhet and he motioned to Bentreshy to mount the grey and white horse.

"I've never been on such a big horse—I don't think I can handle him," she faltered, staring up at the beast's great haunches, broad muscular torso and towering shoulders, and the thought of mounting this haughty creature seemed an impossible task.

"His name is Raia—named after a famous charioteer. He's very gentle—I'll get on first and help you up," suggested Sety, grabbing hold of the horse's neck and swinging himself into the air, landing effortlessly on the horse's back. Then two Berbers lifted Bentreshy off her feet and she managed to cling on to Sety's back and settle into an ungainly position. She held onto Sety's torso and in an instant they were flying through the desert—the horse galloping in a ball of thunder—she felt connected to this powerful beast, his energy vibrating through her legs and up her spine; his hooves sinking into the soft sand, whipping up a cloud of dust. She felt herself letting go, relinquishing her hold on reality, as if falling through space and surrendering to the reckless unknown. What a thrill—to gallop through the desert on horseback, the rush of danger mingling with her desires, her pores open to the cold air, and a wave of excitement ascended inside her thighs, sending arrows of pleasure through her nerve endings. She wrapped herself round Sety's frame, her hands caressing his chest, his nipples, and her fingers came to rest on his heart, pounding with the horse's hooves.

They came to a settlement of black tents where a group of people were gathered round a fire, clapping and singing as a man played the flute and told stories between tunes. The couple joined the tribe by the fire, eating figs and sharing a jug of beer, passing it round the circle after taking a generous swig. The nomads wore dark woollen robes, their turbans pulled over their brows, making it hard to see their faces, but their eyes shone like turquoise stones.

"How strange they have such blue eyes," Bentreshy whispered to Sety, glancing at the women through the flames.

"Yes, the Berbers are a mysterious people, their origins are lost in the memories of time. Some say they came from Canaan, Achea or Crete. Others believe they are the descendants of an advanced culture that vanished in the Great Flood. Their stories talk about Atlantis, the Island of Fire that existed somewhere in the Western Sea, long before Egypt began. Some sages believe they were a highly developed society, well versed in astronomy, science, mathematics and literature. And they had dazzling blue eyes and fair hair—sometimes bright red." Sety looked round the circle of faces, the odd wisp of red hair escaping from a scarf, revealing their noble origins. Bentreshy's hair looked golden in the moonlight, he noticed, the blaze from the fire infusing it with russet tones.

She looked like a descendant from the Island of Fire, the land of volcanoes and rugged mountains raging with hidden flames.

"I heard these stories when I was a child," Bentreshy recalled, "our teacher said they were folktales, and it was doubtful that such a land ever existed—especially one more advanced than Egypt! Nevertheless, one story told how Thoth was born in a faraway land, across the Western Sea. He was King of this land and taught his people writing and esoteric wisdom—and all the tools necessary to build a sophisticated society. But one day their harmonious world turned to chaos. The mountains erupted with fire and the sun was eclipsed in darkness. The people were terrified as their island was consumed by flames and smoke, and they feared their home would explode into the sea. They gathered by the shore and listened to the wise words of King Thoth. He told them not to fear: he would lead them to a new world where they would be safe. As the Controller of the Sea, Thoth calmed the waves so even the weakest citizens could cross in safety; that way he led his people across the rising waters to the Eastern Land. There they started a new civilisation on the banks of the Nile, and thanks to the wisdom of Thoth the people created an advanced society in this foreign land, much like the one they'd lost on the Island of Fire."

Sety threw a log on the fire and watched the sparks wriggle through the sky, like insects transforming into stars. "Don't forget about his wife Seshet. She taught women how to read hieroglyphs and how to understand the universe. Their feminine energy created a balance in the world—they became a civilising influence over the brutal aspects of men. Without the nurturing elements of Seshet, men would be obsessed with war and domination."

Sety was a wise King, thought Bentreshy, to understand that women created a balance in the universe. Inhapi also reminded her girls that Egypt was an advanced society, because women were equal to men and were encouraged to foster their talents. A country where women were suppressed and kept in ignorance could never develop. "The entire land would be thrown into turmoil, like an instrument out of tune, producing a cacophony."

The women began to sing again, clapping their hands in rhythm; one woman loosened the scarf round her chin as she stretched her vocals to hit the high notes. In the warmth of the fire they all began unravelling their scarves, leaving the fabric in piles, like sleeping snakes. It was safe to take off their scarves by the fire, as the flames sucked the dust into its core and away from their hair.

Their red hair shone like carnelian filaments, disappearing into the dark folds of their robes. *Perhaps I am descended from these nomadic people*. Bentreshy thought about her mother's auburn streaks and how she loved to tell tales about floods and mythical beasts rising from the sea. Bentreshy examined one of her own strands; her golden hair didn't seem so unusual out here in the desert, nor did her blue eyes. The women gathered round Bentreshy, running their fingers through her soft curls, singing about a girl who came from a distant land and turned the head of a handsome prince. Bentreshy blushed as she listened to the words, her face burning with embarrassment and the heat from the fire. Sety laughed when he saw her complexion, shining like a ripe pomegranate. "They have an old legend about a young girl who swam across the sea and was taken in by a nomadic tribe. She grew into a great beauty and amazed the prince with her intelligence, her knowledge of mathematics, astronomy and the arts. They fell in love, got married and spent their lives educating the people, travelling from one end of the desert to the other, and watching the sunset over countless horizons, claiming that each one was better than the last, as they believed the world improved with each day."

The couple withdrew to their tent, resembling a giant bull standing on the horizon. They lay naked in the candlelight, their bodies entwined in silent bliss. The smell of horse, fire and beer rose in the warmth, their adventure exuding from their pores. Bentreshy nuzzled under Sety's arm, her fingers exploring the fissures of flesh leading to her own paradise. He turned to her with such a loving gaze, and she saw the adoration in his eyes, beseeching, like a man lost, and with a kiss she inhaled a rush of emotion, as if emanating from an eternal spring, known to replenish those dying in the desert.

That night she experienced all the delights of carnal pleasure, crescendos of bliss rising like the milky dunes and subsiding into gentle plains. Their bodies rolling on sheepskin; unfurling like a scroll of papyrus, carving their secrets into each other's body. She sensed his thoughts, his desires written inside her, a language only she could decipher.

And then all was calm, their bodies sedated with drunken pleasure, fading into a mute serenity, the sound of slow breathing replaced the frantic gasps of breath, and their racing hearts subsided into a sleepy rhythm.

"I love the desert—the endless sand, the wind, the eerie silence. The desert has its own laws that no king can influence. No wonder they say Seth controls this land, with its boundless shape and irrepressible spirit. But even Seth cannot rule here—he too is subject to its natural whims, its blinding sandstorms and bewildering dunes that offer no bearing." Sety could see the mythical connection between Seth and the desert: both were wily and unpredictable, capable of changing shape; born tricksters.

The desert was a shape-shifter, the wind whipping the dunes into huge mounds only to flatten them the next morning. Bentreshy knew the desert played tricks on the mind, offering shimmering pools to the thirsty traveller, a tantalising illusion planted on the dusty horizon, what a callous joke to play on the weary. "One of the market traders told me how he once saw a pink castle in the desert. He walked all day to reach the castle and when twilight came he approached the mighty walls illuminated by the golden sunset, then he watched in horror as the entire castle crumbled to the ground, disappearing with the dying rays of the sun. Beyond the dust he came across a group of nomads who laughed at him for being so gullible. They told him not to get downhearted, that everyone gets taken in by the desert until they understand its powers. And once you walk through a mirage you find untold wonders on the other side. The market trader realised the nomads were right, as he met a kind group of people who gave him food and water and a tent for the night, and they showed him how to reach the caravanserai where he could sell his trinkets for a fair price. But he never found the castle again...The desert tells us truths we don't want to hear, that's why people fear it." Bentreshy rolled over on her side to face Sety, his eyes fixed on the dark ceiling. "You hear things in the desert—Senwhet says there are rumours of unrest—talk of rebellion."

"What kind of rebellion—surely not against the court?" Bentreshy couldn't believe such a popular Pharaoh could have enemies.

"The Pharaohs have always had enemies—usually they are small insurgent groups, radical extremists who wish to seize power. Most of the time their efforts are diminished, confined to the margins of the desert. Our family has known its fair share of dissent. You see my ancestors once worshipped Seth as well as Osiris, believing we need to acknowledge the forces of chaos and order if we wish to achieve a balance in the world. By honouring Seth we were able to understand his destructive nature and learn to master his realm of chaos. But this reverence for Seth fell out of favour with the priests, and soon anyone who worshipped him was deemed guilty of heresy. My father didn't agree — he believed Seth was part of the cycle of life and death, the demise and resurrection of Osiris, and should not be cast aside. He pointed out that an angry Seth existing in the shadows would be far more dangerous, and this has proved to be correct. Now Seth is against us all and we know nothing of his whereabouts, or when his wrath may strike. I used to quell his anger with an offering or two — by pouring bull's blood on the desert, and it seemed to work — his wrath was less furious back then."

Bentreshy rested her head on one elbow, a sense of unease spiralled through her belly. "Does anyone know about this — I mean, the priests at the Temple?" She imagined what Amenkef and Kahotep would make of this news, those who interpreted religious law in such a rigid way. And what of Inhapi, for that matter?

"The priesthood is enlightened enough to understand the complexities of religious ritual and the delicate balance between chaos and harmony. Our survival has depended upon it. But there are a few ignorant and fanatical priests, and we must root them out and render them powerless. My soldiers have done a fine job so far and the Laws of Ma'at have been kept in balance — and I haven't been poisoned yet!" He gave a reckless laugh and rolled across the bed, wrapping his arms around Bentreshy, kissing her nose and cheeks.

"Let's have no more talk about chaos and rebellion. I have the protection of the gods — and now we've surrendered to the desert, no one can harm us." Sety lifted the ceiling flap and the night sky poured into the tent, the stars perforating the darkness with pinpricks of light. This was Seth's land and yet Bentreshy felt at peace here. Her thoughts drifted into space, tracing the contour of Orion's Belt, following the whims of Nut who fashioned the Milky Way. The moon was controlled by Thoth, but the millions of stars were Nut's domain. Like Seshet, her halo had a seven-pointed symbol that resembled a starfish floating to the sky. Long ago when the desert was a primeval sea, marine life swam near the sandy bottom and burrowed into the crevices for safety. Now the sea had become dry land, the shellfish were embedded in the rocks and left to fossilise in the sand.

Bentreshy watched the Milky Way expand, as Nut stretched her torso over the horizon. The sky resembled a vast sea swelling into infinity with no land in sight, the constellations shining like starfish. She lay on his torso watching the pools of moonlight gather in his fleshy hollows, illuminating his being in fractions, as if he lay in broken pieces. With our four limbs and one head we were five-pointed stars, struggling to shine through the unseen. One day their *Bas* and *Kas* would ascend to the Afterlife and live together as new stars in the Great Cosmos. Until that day they would bathe in the phosphorous moonlight, their limbs entwined in silver stardust, resisting the forces that would pull them asunder.

4. Egyptian Wife
Cairo, 1933

After Imam left for work, Dorothy took the bus to the Cairo Museum to see the new collection of artefacts. She often visited King Sety's mummy and chatted to him about her day, providing the tourists and guards were out of earshot. "I saw a heron flying over the Nile — at first I thought it was an ibis — perhaps it was, just like in the old days. Well, I must be getting on with my chores — I have to get to the market before it shuts. I'll come and see you on Thursday, my love," and as the guard wasn't looking, she leaned over and kissed the glass case.

She'd been in Cairo for three months now, and King Sety's presence was growing stronger, like a radio gaining reception. He followed her like her own shadow; his breath flowing with the heat of the sun, his eyes radiating from the silver moonlight. She heard him whispering through the narrow souq, *"How I love you, my Lotus Flower, how wonderful to have you back home, now we can be together in our sacred land."*

Dorothy walked through the old citadel, finding a sense of intimacy in the claustrophobic streets; the sound of papyrus sandals tapping on the cobbles, footsteps softened by a layer of dust. "King Sety...is that you? When will you visit me again?" Her question echoed down the tiny alleys; an old man turned his head and then carried on walking, realising the emotional plea was not for him.

A reply came through a gust of wind, "I will visit you on the crescent moon," the voice mingled with a cloud of dust and settled into the stones. When would that be — which crescent moon? Dorothy traced the ancient walls with her fingers but found no clues. She would have to keep checking the sky . . .

The walls were so high they obscured the sun, creating a dark labyrinth of streets, like rivers through a deep canyon. The walls were built by the Arabs in the 7th century, the traders who originally founded the city on the spice trade, turning Cairo into a wealthy empire. Frankincense and gold had made the city's fortune, a relentless supply shipped across the sea to the Christian world; these

African treasures were a symbol of wealth and power, coveted by bishops and aristocrats alike.

Dorothy lingered in the spice market inhaling the mysterious potions, her senses overlapping with cumin, ginger, paprika, turmeric and saffron, rising in red, orange and yellow mountains. With a bag full of spices and her mind reeling with Oriental odours, she took refuge in the nearest café and moulded herself into the Turkish cushions, where she sat reading her book and listening to a group of locals arguing over their card game. She drank her black tea and ate her basboussa cake as old men in red fezes shuffled by to the mosque, and black-robed women negotiated the price of pigeons, their thrifty shrills rising from their veils.

Dorothy puffed on her shisha pipe, ignoring the lewd stares from the man standing at the bar—she'd seen him there last week, with his tight black trousers and greased-back hair, his eyes flashing with lust as she ate her basboussa. The other men didn't take any notice of her, and they tolerated her presence because she was a foreign woman and not bound by the same conventions as their women, although some of the old men disapproved of her pipe smoking and her intrusion into their café society. They could see by her ring that she was a married woman and could have an important husband, for all they knew, possibly a government official, or a businessman who could make their life a misery if they gave her any trouble. It never occurred to them her husband may be Egyptian, as they assumed English women married their own kind, and being the ruling class, they didn't normally mix with locals. Dorothy was supposed to be shopping for the evening meal, traipsing round the market in search of fresh meat and vegetables, bargaining for the best price of lamb. By now she should be heading home with a basket full of groceries.

Dorothy spotted a young boy in the street and called him over, "You look like you could do with a meal—would you like to earn a few piastres? My name is Dorothy, what's yours?"

"Ashraf," the boy managed to say, staring bashfully at the floor and shuffling his grubby feet from side to side. He was wearing a grease-stained gallabiya, which was practically in rags, and his hands and face were covered in dirt.

"All right, Ashraf, all you have to do is help this tired lady buy some food for her supper. I'm sure you know where to get some fresh lamb—and I'll bet you could get a decent price for it too—better than I could, for that matter."

Ashraf smiled at this unusual confession from a foreign lady and finally let his eyes drift up from the floor to meet her gaze. He stared into her playful blue eyes and saw that she was full of kindness and good humour.

He responded with a nervous laugh and grabbed the note from Dorothy's hand. "I know every inch of the market—sometimes I sleep under big stalls, when everyone go home—all except the donkeys who sleep standing up and the cats who look in garbage for food."

"Don't you go home to your parents at night? Your mother must want you home for supper," enquired Dorothy, who didn't like to think of this poor boy sleeping in the streets on his own.

"I am orphan—I eat what I can find once the market is closed—there always something lying around. Last night I find a bunch of bananas inside the bin, and I find a ta'amiya too, wrapped in a paper napkin, not even one bite from it."

"Well, if you get my shopping you can have a whole plate of ta'amiyas —and bananas too, if that's what you fancy."

Ashraf's eyes went wide, "*Maashi*—OK lady, I get you food," and off he ran towards the meat market, where he disappeared in a sea of stalls and Arabic voices. The boy was soon lost in a maze of gallabiyas.

"That's the last you'll see of that filthy ragamuffin—and your money," a Frenchman laughed, finishing his coffee and getting up to leave.

"What little faith you have—he'll be back," Dorothy replied, disgusted by the man's cynicism. The man responded with a scornful snort, adjusted his cravat and went on his way. How she detested some of these arrogant people, strutting around as if they owned the place. The Frenchman had left the money on the counter—twice what she paid for a coffee. She was glad to see the café owner made him pay for his insolence.

Dorothy noticed a young man sitting in the corner of the café drinking Turkish coffee and writing in his notebook, seemingly lost in a world of ideas. He had luminous eyes and a grave expression, intensified by his thin face and ruffled brow.

"This café is a great place to write—all of life collides right in front of your eyes—it's like watching a wrestling match between chaos and harmony—just like in ancient times. And I think chaos is winning today." Dorothy pointed to the donkey being dragged through a small doorway, deafening the customers with its incessant braying and flying kicks, while two cats rolled around in the dirt, intent on ripping each other's ears off for the sake of territory.

The writer was called Nabil Sayeed, and he peered over his spectacles at this intrusive woman in a conventional floral dress, draped in peasant beads and amulets. He'd never seen anyone dressed so strangely; he'd seen the bohemians in their Eastern gowns and embroidered Turkish slippers, but never dressed in such an ill-assorted fashion.

"What are you writing about?—you seem very involved in it all, quite taken to another world." Dorothy drew her chair closer to the man who looked up to meet her inquisitive eyes and playful smile. Nabil was immediately disarmed by the woman, unsettled by her frankness. Despite his interior nature and his need for contemplation, the man felt himself drawn to this woman, and against his usual reserve, he found himself engaging in conversation.

"I write what I see, and all I see is injustice. My country is a land of oppressed people, thanks to the Ottomans and now the Europeans, the people have been turned into miserable dogs."

To Nabil's surprise Dorothy responded with a hearty roar, as if life was a big cosmic joke and she knew the answers to its many riddles.

"Well, I can't speak for the Ottomans, although I've heard they were a bad lot, but I can tell you the sooner the British and French get out of here the better! It's time Egypt ran her own affairs and it's high time they had that revolution they've been talking about for the last twenty years."

The writer looked round the café with unease, "Be careful what you say, Madame," he whispered, "we can end up in prison for making such claims. It is not safe to talk about revolution. The government fears anarchy more than they fear the British. They do not want real change, and so they keep the people silent and ignorant."

Dorothy lowered her voice, "I'm sorry for speaking so rashly. I can't help myself sometimes. I saw you writing and I recognised a kindred spirit. Everything you say is true—I've seen the students together, bursting with a new kind of vision—incendiary ideas, according to the government. But one day change will come, I feel

51

it in my bones," Dorothy slapped her thigh, conveying a sense of physical urgency.

Nabil's attention was drawn to her shapely hips hidden beneath her cotton dress and her bare legs protruding from under the table. It amazed him how some European women dressed, seemingly unaware of the local customs, blatantly disregarding the tradition of dressing modestly. But Nabil felt compassion for this English woman—she hadn't been here long and everything must seem strange to her. All the same, he was surprised to learn she had an Egyptian husband and that he let her go out in such a flimsy dress.

He realised what little contact he had with British people: he worked as a journalist for an Arabic newspaper and he lived in the Old Quarter, where Europeans rarely ventured.

"Most Europeans don't see the need for change here. They are used to being the bosses, having people work for them. They don't seem to notice the children in rags, the hungry eyes—but the rich Egyptians are no better—they take it for granted that the majority of people are illiterate and at their mercy," said Nabil, rubbing his weary eyes.

"I expected better from the Egyptians—but I suppose rich people are the same everywhere, loathe to give up their privileges." Dorothy hadn't been in Egypt long enough to grasp all the cultural nuances, but she could tell Nabil was an educated man and that he was in a state of conflict. He hated the elite echelon who ignored the plight of the poor and yet he was part of that elite world, due to his privileged education and middle-class family. She could sense Nabil didn't belong anywhere and that he was searching for some kind of truth. That search had led him to writing. He wrote about people trying to find dignity in positions of squalor, socialists and nationalists struggling against oppression, and writers trying to express themselves in a world of censorship.

"You could write a story about young Ashraf, living out of the bins and yet so full of childish optimism," Dorothy suggest. She was beginning to wonder where Ashraf had got to, but she refused to believe he'd run off with her money. Just as she was thinking about going home empty handed, Ashraf appeared with her shopping basket filled with vegetables and lamb cutlets. His face and hands were clean as he'd stopped to wash them in the fountain on the way back; he'd been looking forward to his meal with the English lady and this pleasant rendezvous had kept him going through the searing heat and the crowded market.

"I get all you shopping," the boy beamed, slamming the basket on the table.

"What a wonderful splash of colour—with those purple aubergines, red and yellow peppers, you've nearly got every colour of the rainbow! Go and order yourself a plate of ta'amiyas, and anything else you fancy." Dorothy stroked the boy's head and he ran off to the counter. She watched in anger as a well-dressed Egyptian tried to chase the boy away, "We'll have no street urchins in here, go tend to your donkeys!"

Dorothy shouted back, "His money is as good as yours—it's even better, because at least he earned it through honest work!"

The rich man forced a laugh and lit his fat cigar. He puffed out a tail of smoke and made loud snorting sounds, much like a pug nose, thought Dorothy, and he sat watching in disgust as the 'little urchin' joined Dorothy at the table. "The boy probably has lice—and a number of diseases, no doubt," he said to a local at the counter.

Dorothy walked over to the man with the cigar and smiled, "Then I suggest you get out of here immediately, as I have leprosy—although it doesn't seem to do me any harm!"

The man laughed nervously, he was surprised she'd overheard him as he'd muttered in a low voice. Dorothy patted him on the arm and she felt him recoil. "You don't really have leprosy do you—you're just pulling my leg."

Dorothy shrugged, "I've had it for several years now, but I feel fine. My feet have started to rot, but other than that I am in perfect health. I think people exaggerate about the dangers of leprosy, don't you?" she grabbed the man's hand.

The man backed away from the bar, "You should be in quarantine," he muttered, then fled the café like a streak of lightening, leaving his cigar smouldering in the ashtray.

Dorothy returned to the table as Ashraf was devouring his second ta'amiya, chatting away in Arabic to Nabil, who was astonished by this verbose street boy. Although he often wrote stories about the needy, he rarely came into close contact with them, maintaining a detached interest. He realised his academic nature had made him aloof, removed him from life, and that he knew very little about the poor people of Cairo.

"A present from the rich," Dorothy handed Nabil a box of cigars which the man had left on the counter. Nabil couldn't help but laugh, "They look Cuban—from one oppressed country to another."

When he'd finished eating, Ashraf rubbed his belly, enjoying the unusual sensation of a full stomach, the warm food settling inside him like a full moon. "You very kind lady, Dorothy. I take you to my home—you meet my mother and family."

"I thought you were an orphan," Dorothy grabbed him playfully by the ear.

"I have to say this to get money. Now you my friend, I tell you truth."

Ashraf jumped up, beckoning her to follow him up the street towards the old citadel, "is not far, only 10 minute walk—we live in the baqi."

"You mean to say your family lives in the cemetery?" Dorothy was suddenly intrigued, as she'd heard about these people who lived in the old tombs, preferring the houses of the dead to modern flats. "If you want me to come you'll have to slow down—and don't think I can squeeze through those gaps in the walls—I'm not as skinny as you are."

Ashraf carried Dorothy's basket in one arm and held onto her elbow with the other, gallantly leading her through the tight stalls.

Nabil walked with them to the Alhazar Mosque and then suddenly rushed off ahead, "I have to get back to the newspaper. I have an article to finish by six o'clock. I was supposed to be writing it in the café." He looked sheepishly at his notebook in his left hand, full of character sketches and snippets of dialogue he'd overheard. The article was about the construction of the new Bank of Alexandria and how much money they needed to complete the ultramodern interior—when most Egyptians lived a hand to mouth existence, he noted, but he wasn't allowed to write that.

"I hope to see you again. The café is my favourite place to write, surrounded by the chaos of the souq. The place feeds my soul after the sterile office I work in every day." Nabil winced at the thought of returning there, walking up the concrete steps to his soulless desk.

"I'll tell you about the cemetery. Next time you'll have to come with us—just think of the story you could write."

Nabil watched Dorothy walk up the street with the young boy in the gallabiya. She walked with a natural ease, as if she belonged to these streets, talking to the boy as she would to her own son. It didn't seem to concern her that there were no Europeans around and that she was walking into the poor part of town.

They entered the gates of the old cemetery and walked along the dusty path to Ashraf's home, passing mausoleums the size of garden sheds, but more like miniature palaces, she thought, their marble exteriors glistening in the sun. The women squatted round the fires cooking the evening meals, eyeing Dorothy through a veil of steam, stirring their bean stews with a look of amazement. What was this Ingiliziyya doing here? Perhaps she was lost, they considered, and the boy was showing her the way home. But she didn't appear to be lost: she walked with a confident manner, as if she'd been here many times and seemed to be enjoying every minute, the way she waved at the children and stopped to appreciate the Arabic carvings on the tombs.

"This my home," Ashraf smiled with relief and laid the basket down with a thud, "And this lady my mother—her name Nawes." Ashraf kissed a tiny woman in a black robe and headscarf, her face and hands covered in henna tattoos. The woman kissed Dorothy on both cheeks, *"Tasharrafna." Pleased to meet you.* The woman was fascinated by Dorothy's hair and reached out to touch her blonde curls, like the fluffy feathers on a baby chick, she thought.

"My mother never meet English lady before," Ashraf explained, trying to divert his mother's attention away from Dorothy's hair and pointing to the basket of food, speaking in a flood of Arabic. How Dorothy wished she could understand, listening to the rush of words, her ears enjoying the operatic sounds and the rich throaty intonations that seemed to resonate from a subterranean cavern.

"Tell your mother she has a lovely home," Dorothy gazed at the limestone tomb covered in Arabic patterns and the reed canopy which sheltered the outdoor kitchen. What a great way to cook—with a sandy floor, and no need to wash it with a mop—just like in ancient times. My kind of kitchen, thought Dorothy, wishing she could trade her fancy kitchen for this rustic model. She imagined Imam sitting on the woven mats, the smoke billowing from the open fire and she had to suppress a giggle, knowing what he'd say: "Have you lost your mind? This place is only fit for animals!"

Nawes was pleased to show Dorothy around her house as this Ingiliziyya genuinely appreciated the place, admiring the alcove carved into the wall, displaying the items she'd found in the cemetery: rosaries, braziers, lace handkerchiefs and vases of flowers.

"Tell your mother I would love to live in a house like this, but my husband wouldn't hear of it. It's much better than our stuffy apartment. Here you have birds, fresh air and the stars at night." Considering it was a cemetery, it was livelier than that snooty neighbourhood where Imam insisted on living. Their neighbourhood was full of pampered corpses, privileged people who were severed from real life and real passions.

Dorothy peeked into the small antechamber at the back of the tomb, decorated with reed mats and a mound of blankets to sleep on; an alabaster sarcophagus served as their dressing table and a couple of rough benches were piled high with wicker baskets, containing their worldly possessions. Nawes had decorated the house with colourful rugs and wall-hangings she'd woven herself, with floral patterns, flocks of birds and branches teeming with fruit, earthly wonders from the tree of life.

"My mother say you stay eat with us," Ashraf squatted by the fire, stirring the embers so his mother could fry the omelettes.

Dorothy motioned to the basket of food, "This food is a gift for you—let's make a real feast. I'm in the mood to celebrate." There was something about these people that made her want to celebrate, surrounded by this atmospheric cemetery with the old spirits and the children playing in the dust, their young limbs running alongside the old bones of their ancestors. I have found Egypt, she thought, this is the real place. Perhaps that's what she was celebrating: feeling at home with these people, gathering round for a communal supper; the women in their long robes, kohl eyes and jangly jewellery, sitting under the reed canopy gossiping and minding the children, waiting for the flatbread to bake, stirring the cauldron on the fire as they had for thousands of years.

Dorothy listened to Nawes talking to her children and slowly she began to recognise certain words: *aywah* meant yes and *la* no, and she gathered *ayyil* meant child. How she longed to understand their meaning, to read the language of their emotions; to hear their stories, their thoughts and dreams...

Dorothy sat on the mat slicing vegetables with Nawes and her two cousins. "I know nothing about cooking," Dorothy confessed, "Maybe you can show me a thing or two."

The women laughed when they realised this English lady couldn't cook.

"How you eat? How you feed babies?"

"Well, we eat mainly in restaurants—and regarding babies, well I haven't got any."

Dorothy laughed when she saw their sad faces. "No babies," the women repeated forlornly; Nawes rubbed her belly and then placed her hand on Dorothy's belly, "I have three babies—I give you next child."

Dorothy realised Nawes was transferring her own fertile powers to her. "Your belly awake now—you have baby soon."

Dorothy looked alarmed. "I've only been married three months. I'm not ready for motherhood just yet—I have so much to learn—so much to do." She thought about her connection with Sety, her desire to explore the ancient sites and gain the truth about her past.

The women found this very funny and wriggled on their mats in a wave of laughter and strange words.

Nawes noticed Dorothy's grave face and hoped she hadn't offended her. "You ready for baby. You have strong body. You have hips made like oud—a lute," Ashraf translated for his mother.

A lute wasn't such a bad shape, she conceded, at least I'm not like an oboe . . . Dorothy helped the women skew the lamb on the fire and coat it with herbs and spicy oil. They made a babaghanoush with the roasted aubergines and tahina paste with lots of garlic. When the food was ready the children gathered round and filled their clay bowls with generous helpings.

"We have lamb—just like at Eed il Adha, Feast of Ibrahim," the children cried, tucking into the glistening lamb morsels, their mouths round with pleasure.

"It's the Feast of Lady Bulbul Meguid," Ashraf told them, having returned with a bundle of stalks strapped to his donkey. The children stared at this venerable lady with gratitude, "The Feast of Lady Bulbul!" they shouted, dancing round Dorothy.

When they'd finished eating, Dorothy helped the women collect water from the fountain and they washed the dishes in a giant trough, the soapy water scented with jasmine flowers. *They have so little and yet their dish water smells like perfume*, Dorothy marvelled, for once enjoying the experience of washing up. The women worked in a cooperative manner, singing songs, washing and drying in harmony, until all signs of their lavish feast had been cleared away, leaving behind an invisible sense of pleasure.

Dorothy closed her eyes and saw a group of women sitting round the fire, laughing, singing and playing games with the children. They wore long white robes, their thick hair woven with beads and ribbons. "Such a long time you've been away—so happy you came to visit us." The women engulfed her in kisses, hugs and morsels of food. She knew these women like her own spirit, her deepest self she revealed to no one else. They walked towards the lake and she saw the temple in the distance, frozen in the moonlight, the great walls bathed in sallow silence; the world with the sound switched off, waiting for the dawn prayers to infuse it with life. The moon was like a hidden window revealing the world through a thin curtain. The lake was black as kohl, with shards of silver dancing on the surface. She was diving into a black hole, both terrified and exuberant; the warm water, the girlish shrieks breaking through the darkness. The unknown suddenly made intimate.

Ashraf gave Dorothy a nudge, "You fall asleep. I make cup of tea for you."

Dorothy sat in a daze sipping her mint tea, the black water like her dream, a miniature misty lake. She watched Nawes grind some seeds on a stone palette, adding multihued powders until she produced a deep green paste.

"What are you making—is that some kind of ointment?" Dorothy was intrigued by this green concoction, as it resembled crushed malachite, which the ancient Egyptians painted on their eyelids.

Nawes explained in Arabic and Dorothy listened attentively, picking out remarkable words: *ba'doonis*, *kurumb*, *rihan*—parsley, cabbage and basil.

"I make cure for baby cough—green colour, same as baby cough."

Dorothy suddenly understood her meaning. "Oh, the baby has phlegm, the colour and texture of the paste—you use green paste to heal the cough."

"*Maashi.* That's right. Green also colour of life, green make baby grow, make him strong," Ashraf explained, watching his mother pound the plants with increased vigour, forming green spirals in the mortar.

Dorothy sat by the fire staring at the crescent moon and the emerging stars, her toes sifting through the warm sand. Reluctantly she had to leave, "I must be getting home to my husband, he'll be wondering where I am." She'd lost track of time again and he'd be disappointed with her (again). Before she left, Dorothy peeked into the tomb and saw the children curled up under their blankets, their faces shining like little brass bowls in the lamplight. Her attention was drawn to the child wheezing in the corner, his neck plastered in green paste. "Just like Osiris—the Green One," Dorothy bowed her head to the vegetation god. "Please heal this poor child, restore him to health—let him be a happy, healthy child. He is such a sweet boy and his mother loves him so—as Isis loved Horus."

Nawes heard the lady mutter something to the child, waving her hands over his chest in circular motions.

She stroked Dorothy's arm, "You more than English lady—you like Egyptian. You heal sick, I see what you do," she said, nodding as Ashraf translated the words.

Dorothy laughed, suddenly feeling uncomfortable. "I don't know very much. In fact sometimes I feel I know absolutely nothing. I don't know why I did that, but it just felt right, what the child needed me to do," Dorothy floundered in mid sentence, "I'm eager to learn how to heal people, make people better, every day I gain new knowledge— one day I'll have the answers."

She kissed her new friends goodbye and promised to come again soon. Ashraf walked with her in silence to the main road and as she boarded the carriage to go home, he slipped something into her hand. Dorothy realised it was a small piece of bone. "From the ancestors, so you come back, so you don't forget. This way, Afreet remember you."

Dorothy listened to the clip-clop of the horse's hooves and rolled the bone over in her palm. Then she remembered she'd forgotten her basket. "Oh well, it didn't have any food in it—the Feast of Bulbul made sure of that." The evening had filled her with good-humour and she decided to buy some kushari for her husband, to make up for her shopping fiasco.

"I've been sick with worry," Imam pounced on her as she walked through the door, noticing her dress covered in dust. "Are you hurt— if anyone has hurt you I will go straight to the police—they'll pay for this."

"I am perfectly fine. I've brought you some supper," Dorothy handed her husband the kushari and he eyed the cardboard box suspiciously. "If you are fine then where is the shopping basket and why weren't you home to cook the dinner?" That's what normal wives did, instead of returning home covered in dust and claiming to be all right.

"If you must know, a young lad helped me do my shopping, and then I visited his family in the cemetery. When I heard they only had vegetable soup to eat, I offered them the food I'd bought in the market. They made a great feast and it was such fun. We laughed and told stories and had a grand time, without a drop of alcohol."

"You mean to say you went with a strange boy to the cemetery and you ate in a tomb?" Imam was furious with her, "What you did was very dangerous, not to mention quite foolhardy. You could catch a terrible illness there—and you could have been attacked. Those people live like animals in caves, with no hygiene or clean water."

Dorothy felt compelled to defend her friends, "That's not true. The people there are very clean. They live with very little and yet there is no sign of filth. They live simply, but I wouldn't say they live in squalor. I was very impressed by their clean tombs and the creative way they decorated their homes." She didn't say anything about the hole in the ground that served as the toilet, as that would only give him ammunition. It would have been easier for him if she had been attacked, she imagined, then at least he could lay the blame somewhere.

"I was just worried about you," Imam tried to diffuse the situation. "Promise me you won't go there again. We can get Zenna to do the shopping from now on."

Dorothy ignored his plea as she could never promise such a thing, and began scooping the kushari onto the plate. "I'm sorry about your supper, but this smells delicious." She inhaled the rich aroma of noodles and lentils blended in a spicy sauce.

"I'm not hungry. The lady from downstairs gave me some stew— the one who cooks for the bachelors." Imam was getting used to calling on the woman from downstairs, feeling like a bachelor himself, with his tin bowl. He was beginning to realise his wife was a walking domestic disaster and he was embarrassed to invite anyone for dinner. Either she burned the dish or covered it in a revolting brown sauce. He cringed when he remembered his boss coming to dinner, and Dorothy had made a chicken that resembled an old boot. She even tied the vine leaves together with a pair of laces! How could any woman make such a mess of Waraq Einab, one of Egypt's favourite dishes (it was downright unpatriotic, the domestic equivalent of burning the Egyptian flag).

Imam retired to his office to finish some work, and Dorothy sat on the balcony eating the kushari and enjoying the cool night air. She knew she was putting on weight, but she couldn't bear to see good food go to waste. The tasty food took away her empty feeling, the stodgy noodles coating her belly in a blanket of warmth. "I can't believe I'm still hungry after that huge feast," she laughed at herself, "maybe I have a tape worm."

She stretched a mat on the floor and lay down under the stars, staring into the indigo sky. She thought of the solar priestess on the lookout for the Star of Isis. She drifted into a dream world, where shooting stars streaked through the sky and the cool wind blew the sand into soft ripples.

∧∧∧∧∧   ∧∧∧∧∧   ∧∧∧∧∧

Imam was annoyed to be sleeping alone again, stretching his arm across the empty bed. "Why does she insist on sleeping on the balcony like a peasant girl?" he wondered, you would think she'd never slept in a bed. Sometimes she didn't seem in the least bit English—the way she went around barefoot and chatted to the servants in broken Arabic.

That night under the stars, Dorothy dreamed about the cemetery. She awoke remembering fragments of the dream: the fire, the women laughing and cooking in a circle of intimacy, their long robes protecting them like wings, flapping like happy birds. She rose from the floor feeling transposed, full of new possibilities, as if standing by a portal. She thought of Nawes in her tombhouse: how different my life is with Imam, living in this grand yet sterile flat, in this privileged part of town.

Dorothy felt drawn back to the cemetery. "Those people can teach me about the ancient ways." They slept with the spirits and ate their meals in the courtyard of the Underworld, their timeless faces ascending to the stars. She could see it in their eyes, their movements;

61

the way Nawes mashed the aubergine on a stone slab and used a piece of flat bread as her spoon—just like the old times.

I will go and sketch them tomorrow, make a plan of their tomb, she decided, reminding herself how she used to draw with acute precision—but that was a long time ago, maybe she'd forgotten how. Since her arrival Dorothy hadn't done any drawing—what with meeting the family and getting married. Yes, she would go and sketch Nawes and her children, capture their colourful lives in shades of ochre, burnt sienna and a touch of ultramarine.

Dorothy realised it must be after nine o'clock as Imam had left for work and she could hear Zenna clattering in the kitchen, trying to wake the dead. She went to the bathroom and leaned over the sink to wash her face, suddenly feeling queasy, her belly churning like a cauldron. "I hope I'm not coming down with anything."

She knew Imam would say, "I was afraid this would happen—you shouldn't have eaten in that filthy place." She couldn't stand him being right, when those people had been so kind, given her so much. Dorothy struggled to the toilet, a wave of nausea rising like a sea storm, and she held onto the bowl, clinging to a solid force, longing for the sick feeling to subside. "Oh help me, dear Isis, and I promise I'll never miss another supper again." But she realised Isis wouldn't care about such trivialities. "And I will help to heal people in your name." That was better, she muttered, unaware of the figure standing behind her. "You all right, Sayyida Meguid?"

Her nausea made everything seem blurry as smoke, but she could make out Zenna's face staring in a concerned manner. "No. I'm not all right, Zenna," she struggled to speak, her eyes wouldn't focus— something strange was happening to her, something she didn't understand, as if her body wasn't her own.

Dorothy tried to talk to the maid, but another surge of nausea walloped her senses and she flopped onto the floor, her head resting on the toilet seat. She always dreaded being sick. It was never a straightforward affair: she writhed and retched, moaned and gasped like a dying animal. She couldn't simply be sick, bring it up like other people. She had to enact the last throes of death.

She heard Zenna shouting, as if from across the street. "I fetch Sayyid Meguid! You are very sick. He fetch doctor to come."

Dorothy managed to crawl back into bed, slinking into her warm cave, seeking the comfort of darkness.

Half an hour later her husband arrived with the doctor. Dorothy wished everyone would leave her alone, but they insisted on fussing. First the doctor, who examined her for signs of food poisoning, then her husband, who urged her to take a sip of mint tea, which made her nauseous again.

"You shouldn't have eaten with those primitive people. And to think you drank the tea—with water straight from the Nile—you may as well have drunk from the toilet! It's no wonder you're ill, with the appalling hygiene. I feared this would happen! Who knows what ghastly disease you've picked up," Imam scolded her, his concern turning to anger. Dorothy groaned and turned over to face the wall.

Those people are very clean and they have a fountain with spring water, she wanted to say, but she didn't have the strength to argue. She thought of Nawes, washing her hands and face in the metal bowl, sprinkling fresh sand on the floor before a visitor sat down to eat, as they'd done in ancient times.

The doctor finished his examination and said, "You don't have food poisoning, Sayyida Meguid. Your condition is more complicated than that, more long term shall we say —I'd say you are pregnant, Madame. You are going to have a child."

Dorothy was astonished by the doctor's news. "How can I be pregnant—Yes, I missed a period last month, but I thought it was the heat, all the upheaval. I can't be—I've only been here three months."

"Just enough time, Madame. My guess is about eight weeks pregnant. I see this baby couldn't wait." The doctor packed up his bag and got ready to leave.

Imam stood in the doorway beaming with joy. "This is wonderful news, my habibi, much better than food poisoning!" His angry eyes softened with tenderness, great orbs radiating affection.

"She will need plenty of rest and a good diet," the doctor told Imam, "and nature will see to everything else."

Dorothy felt her belly squirm at the mention of food. All she wanted was pomegranate juice, with lots of sugar.

Imam laughed at this request. "I'll ask Zenna to get you some. And now I'll leave you to rest awhile. Later on Zenna will fix you a healthy lunch—the baby needs to grow strong, like a shaft of wheat. He cannot live on pomegranate juice."

"What makes you think it's a boy?"

But Imam was already out the door, on his way to tell his family the good news.

Dorothy lay in bed, overwhelmed by her impending motherhood. She felt a confusing mixture of dread and joy. Can I cope with this unknown creature growing inside me? Will I endure the pain of childbirth? She wondered if she'd be a good mother, with her whimsical tendencies, and felt a sudden panic, more acute than her nausea. "Pull yourself together, Dorothy. Women have been giving birth since the beginning of time." She thought of the ancient women with their birthing bricks, amulets and herbs, praying to Taweret.

Imam proved to be an attentive husband throughout her pregnancy, "too attentive," she thought, as he insisted Zenna accompany her into town, so she couldn't sneak off to the Old Quarter or visit Ashraf and Nawes in the cemetery. But Dorothy soon grew tired of the pleasant streets and longed to wander through the bazaar. "I've had enough of being wrapped in cotton wool. I'd like to visit some people in the cemetery, pay my respects," she told Zenna."

Zenna reluctantly agreed, as she knew it was important to honour the dead and feared their wrath if they didn't appease them with prayers. "If you must visit a dead friend, I not stand in your way. We buy some flowers."

They walked in silence to the cemetery, Dorothy resting the flowers on her large belly and Zenna reluctantly carrying a basket of fruit. When Ashraf spotted her walking towards the tomb, he shouted, "Mama, Dorothy is here, I say she come back!"

Nawes smiled when she saw Dorothy's pregnant belly. "You have baby—just as I say," she beamed, rubbing her own belly in sympathy.

"I thought we come visit a tomb, place some flowers," Zenna snapped, realising Dorothy had tricked her. "I am here to visit a tomb and offer flowers. But it's a living tomb full of lovely people, very much alive." Dorothy hugged Nawes and Ashraf, and introduced them to Zenna, embarrassed to admit she was her maid. "She is more like a friend to me, and she teaches me how to cook and how to sing in Arabic."

Zenna looked around anxiously, "Just don't let Sayyid Meguid hear you say this. I promise look after you. I promise keep you safe."

"Keep me locked up more like it," Dorothy laughed. "What I need is fresh air, good company, and lots of old bones to remind me of the past."

"I promise not to take you to the cemetery, Sayyid Meguid be angry with me," Zenna started to fret.

Dorothy stroked Zenna's hand. "You didn't take me—I took you, remember? He doesn't have to know. Women should have some secrets, life would be insufferable without them. It gives us a bit of mystery," she winked at Zenna.

The women sat down on the mats, and Dorothy was given a stool as she couldn't get down on the ground with her swollen belly. It is like a birthing stool, she noticed, I could give birth in one of those empty tombs, then we could have a proper feast with the ancestors.

Dorothy thought about birth in ancient Egypt, when they believed the placenta was imbued with magical powers. They made a drink out of mother's milk and the blood of the afterbirth. If the baby drank the concoction, it would live, if not, then the baby would probably die...

Dorothy was glad to see Zenna enjoying the women's company, sitting cross-legged on the mat, talking in a rush of Arabic. Then she told Dorothy, "In my village when a woman want a child, she make a little doll out of old cloth and leave it in the house of pregnant woman. She sleep with doll for forty nights, then she give it back to her friend—and soon she pregnant. I see it with my own eyes." Zenna was no longer a servant, she had transformed into an assured woman with shining eyes, talking about the ancient ways in her village. She knew a lot about magic and healing: how to cure a child's earache with ochre and honey, and quell tummy pains by burning a wisp of hair in the fire. Dorothy listened transfixed; she'd never seen this side of her before—Zenna usually made the breakfast and cleaned up the mess. But suddenly she was a knowledgeable woman who knew about folkloric remedies. "Every village woman know these things. They come from the past. Some things they don't need to learn, they just know."

Nawes said something in Arabic, her voice ringing with enthusiasm as Ashraf translated her words. "My mother she pleased you have healing woman to look after you—she know about old medicine, like my mother."

As they walked home, Dorothy wanted to hear more about Zenna's life in her village. "I would love to learn more about your village cures, how to heal people in the Egyptian way."

Zenna's face darkened, "I not talk about it anymore. Sayyid Meguid not like this talk. He say we have modern medicine now—better than old ways."

Dorothy felt her blood rise, "You are allowed to talk to me about the old ways. In some respects, they are far superior to modern ways. I promise I won't tell Sayyid Meguid, you have my word."

Zenna studied Dorothy's face and saw her sincerity, deep as the sand in the desert. "Tamam, all right. I tell you stories about my village—if you show me how to write in English. I don't understand writing words, all sticks and circles."

Dorothy agreed. She would teach Zenna the English alphabet and in return Zenna would show her how to get rid of an enemy. "First you draw person on piece of paper—then you curse him, spit at him, make loud hissing noises like a snake. Then you take a needle and stab him, tear through paper skin. Then you must make fire, fill brazier with hot coals and sandalwood—best is frankincense and myrrh. The people go behind mosque where they leave garbage—sometimes they find incense there—burn drawing in brazier and wave smoke in every room. Then evil die in the fire, the enemy cannot hurt you anymore."

The magic could also be used for good purposes, Zenna pointed out, and there were many ways to get pregnant, like jumping over a tortoise seven times—tortoises were in great demand, she said, "they like film star, women go crazy for them," and the tortoise was passed from house to house before the midwife took it to the next village.

When Dorothy entered her final trimester, Zenna gave her some leftover frankincense from the local mosque and placed it in the brazier. She waited until Imam had gone to work and then she cleansed the house with the magic smoke, in case an evil afreet was jealous of her baby. Then she tied a cowrie belt round Dorothy's belly. "Women do this in my village. It keep evil spirits away, make baby a *shugo shakhs*, a brave soul, like the shell, tough outside, soft inside."

Zenna started to sing a song about chasing demons from a mother's womb and Dorothy shook her hips in time to the melody, her belly wobbling up and down. She imagined this was the ancient origins of belly dancing, the pregnant women gyrating and rattling abdomens—

the shells in the shape of vulvas, calling to the goddess to bless their foetus.

Zenna rubbed Dorothy's belly, "Baby grow into strong man, like pyramid."

Dorothy stopped dancing for a moment, "How do you know it's a boy?"

"By shape of your belly—you can tell is a boy—boys always lower down." She glanced up at Dorothy, surprised at her lack of knowledge in these matters. What did women talk about in England? For they didn't seem to know anything about childbirth, or their own bodies, for that matter.

Dorothy tried to explain, "Where I come from bodily functions and pregnancies aren't talked about much. Women are taught to draw a veil of silence over such matters. They're not seen as polite topics of conversation."

Zenna looked perplexed, "I can understand they keep these things from men—from their husbands, but why not talk about them with women? They share same bodies. They all have monthly blood, babies, same joys and pains. It make it easier to share—it make the joy bigger and the pain smaller."

Dorothy thought about her mother's embarrassment concerning menstruation. She called it the French Relatives. She never talked to Dorothy about her monthly cycle except to remind her it must be kept away from Father. "Men are not to know about these matters, they would be terribly repulsed if they found out."

"That's a terrible burden to bear," Dorothy thought. She hated the fear, the secrecy, the respectable facade. Her mother offered her no comfort, no explanation. There was no female celebration, as Zenna described. She had to laugh as she pictured her mother and friends casting aside their tight corsets, rubbing each other's bellies and shaking their hips as they called to the fertility goddess.

Zenna sang along to the radio as she made the breakfast, something about dying of love. Zenna translated, "I make a coffin out of rubies and sapphires, love coursing through my veins like blood flowing down a mountain. I will drown in this dark love." Dorothy couldn't help laughing at the lyrics—so melodramatic for this time of day. "Couldn't they just start with a cup of tea?"

Zenna said not. "This is Arabic love song, feelings are like battle of the heart."

Dorothy opened her morning post and suddenly cried out in surprise, "My parents say they are coming to stay with us." Dorothy ate her omelette and flat bread as if she were eating pebbles.

"You don't look happy about your parents coming," said Zenna, noticing her glum expression.

"Don't I? I can't hide anything from you. You are more perceptive than my husband, he never notices." *How is it she can detect my emotions and yet Imam is totally oblivious to them?*

"We women, we feel things," Zenna smiled knowingly. "You don't have to be professor or politician to do that."

Dorothy folded the letter on the table and pushed it aside. "I love my parents—it's just that they never understood me, they made me feel like a misfit. I don't blame them—I was a difficult child." She faltered, remembering her mother's abrasive words, "You really exasperate me, Dorothy. What will become of you?"

And her father interjecting, "You must face reality, child. You can't live in this fantasy world forever."

Why couldn't she? And years later she was finally living in Egypt. She was still searching—she wasn't there yet. But one day she would find her place...

Part of her didn't want her parents to come. They would trample on her dreams as they'd always done; uproot the flowers in her sacred garden. She suddenly dreaded them coming to Egypt, her own Promise Land; she dreaded their disapproval, the disappointment in their eyes.

Zenna gave her a friendly nudge on the arm, "They will be happy you have baby. They think you are good daughter—you give them grandchild."

Dorothy laughed, "Oh I hope so," wishing she could gain some of Zenna's optimism. *They should be happy—they were going to be grandparents.* Any Egyptian parent would be overjoyed. How she envied their family bonds, their intimate connection with one another. But Dorothy knew it was more complicated than that: they wished she'd been married in England, to an Englishman, and they would prefer an English grandchild...

∧∧∧∧∧   ∧∧∧∧∧   ∧∧∧∧∧

Mr and Mrs Eady sat in the parlour drinking tea, feeling bewildered by the heat and the strong smells coming from the kitchen.

Imam leaned over to Mrs Eady and squeezed her hand. "I'm so glad you've come to stay, you don't know what it means to us, especially to Dorothy at this delicate time, with the birth date approaching." He squeezed her hand a little tighter, reassuring her that everything was going to be all right. "You are very kind, Imam. You take such good care of Dorothy."

Dorothy rolled her eyes, "Mother just wanted to know if my husband really existed, she thought I made you up."

Imam laughed nervously, "Of course we are married, it is the honourable way to live."

Mother just wanted to see what kind of mess I'd got myself into, Dorothy felt like saying, *and then she'd try and persuade me to come home.*

"You've got a lovely home, Dorothy. I didn't expect it to be so palatial. You live just like the queen of Egypt."

Too good for little old Dorothy, she imagined her mother was thinking.

Her mother's eyes swept from floor to ceiling, admiring the grand rooms and ornate furniture, the mahogany cabinet glistening like an otter's pelt. "They certainly love their high polish over here," Mr Eady whispered to his wife.

Mrs Eady vigorously fanned herself, a layer of sweat forming above her lip. "I don't know how you cope with this heat, Dorothy, especially in your condition."

Dorothy simply shrugged, "I've grown accustomed to it. I feel I've always lived in this heat, I've taken to it so well."

Mrs Eady shifted awkwardly in her seat, and asked Zenna for some more tea.

Mrs Eady hoped Dorothy wasn't going to spoil it all with her reincarnation fantasy, her obsession with ghosts and her ridiculous notion of a past life in ancient Egypt.

That evening she had a quiet word with her daughter. "Father and I think Imam is a fine fellow. He obviously loves you very much, the way he dotes on you, the way he cares about your wellbeing."

"Yes, he is a good man, I cannot fault him," Dorothy confirmed. She knew her mother was leading up to something.

"You are lucky to have married at all, Dorothy, at your stage of life, just remember how lucky you are. And I thought you'd remain a spinster the rest of your life—and here you are with a well-to-do husband and a baby on the way—with a charming house and even a maid! I never imagined you'd do so well for yourself—you've really fallen on your feet, Dorothy, mark my word."

"Yes mother, Imam is a saint to put up with me, I know," Dorothy humoured her mother, hoping she would end this gushing barrage and go to bed.

"Just try and be a good wife, Dorothy. Think about your husband's needs—not just about your own." Mrs Eady's voice sounded more urgent, "Don't slip into that strange place you used to go to. Try to live in the real world. If you can remember to do that then everything will be fine. And you will have a happy marriage."

How could she tell her mother it was too late? That she slipped into that strange place on a regular basis and that the spirit of King Sety had started visiting her again?

"But I do live in the real world, Mother, so stop worrying about me." The real world was full of spirits and magic, and it was more powerful than any physical world. She could feel herself slipping into this deeper world at this very moment, as sleep invaded her body, creeping into her bones. "I'm sorry, Mother, I'm very tired. You must be exhausted yourself, after your long journey," noticing her mother's heavy eyelids. She kissed her goodnight and felt a wave of relief as her mother traipsed off to bed. Dorothy longed to lie down on the balcony, where she could breathe the fresh midnight air and gaze up at the stars, her mind drifting into the dark realm.

Mrs Eady lay in her bed unable to sleep, swathed in a cocoon of heat. "It's surprising anyone gets any sleep in this country—it must be over 100 degrees," she reckoned, and decided to sit on the balcony for a while, where the air was slightly fresher. She could see her daughter sleeping at the other end of the balcony, her pregnant belly rising with each laboured breath.

"Poor dear—her pregnancy hasn't helped her weight problem." But not to worry—over here they liked their women on the plump side, and Imam seemed to love Dorothy's chubby shape.

Mrs Eady could see Imam standing by the mattress, watching Dorothy as she slept, with such a sense of devotion. "I can see he loves her very deeply," thought Mrs Eady, the way he bent down to stroke her face and then tenderly kiss her on the forehead. She watched him take off his blue robe and sit down beside Dorothy; he tried to embrace her but each time he suddenly pulled back, as if separated by a sheet of glass. Mrs Eady found his behaviour terribly strange and she struggled to make sense of this baffling scene being played out before her eyes. She imagined he was overcome with physical passion—after all, they'd only been married a short while. He obviously didn't wish to wake Dorothy, which was very considerate of him and a great strain on him, judging by the enormity of his ardour. Mrs Eady remembered her husband's amorous feats in the early stages of their marriage; she felt a tingle of passion, stirring in a forgotten part of her memory.

Mrs Eady watched transfixed as Imam stood up once again and fumbled with his blue robe. Why didn't he return to bed? He paced anxiously around the balcony, as if he might throw himself over the railing. Then he placed a large hat on his head. "What on earth?" She suddenly realised the man was wearing a large crown; he stepped out of the shadows and the moonlight shone on his noble face, illuminating his dark-rimmed eyes. Mrs Eady nearly fainted with surprise, as she stared into the face of the Pharaoh, his gold headdress glittering like the stars. He didn't appear to see her, gazing only at Dorothy, as if no one else in the world existed.

Mrs Eady ran into the house, her heart pumping with fear. As a child, she'd seen the ghost of her great-aunt Emily float across the window, an ethereal figure who'd disappeared into the morning mist. But the ghost of the Pharaoh was something different: real passions pumped through his veins and he exuded incredible energy and power. The ghosts in Egypt were of a different nature—they seemed to materialise into real beings and could even possess the living. She must rescue her daughter from this ungodly place, where the dead never seemed to die, where some phantom Pharaoh had taken possession of her daughter's soul.

Dorothy knew nothing of her mother's nocturnal distress. She dreamed about a desert realm with fleecy folds of sand and yawning caverns, the pink horizon dissolving into ruffles of sky. She left her physical body asleep on the balcony, her astral being leaping into the moonlight. Sety was waiting for her, his blue robe swelling like the firmament. Her astral body was much more powerful in Egypt; at night her *Ka* could leap out of the present realm with ease and wander

71

through the ageless desert. She simply walked out of the current millennium and into a more ancient one, where jackals howled at the moon, where the temple opened its gateway to the east, waiting for the sun to rise.

Mrs Eady awoke from her troubled sleep and tried to convince herself the encounter with the Pharaoh had all been an awful dream. She poked her head through the balcony door and saw her daughter lying peacefully. Dorothy opened her eyes and stared at her mother with an expression of dreamy euphoria. Then she closed her eyes for a moment, as if to veil the secret pleasure she felt. *Keep it hidden from disapproving eyes; the disbelieving eyes of the uninitiated.*

"I've made some scrambled eggs for you and Imam," said Mrs Eady, her voice cheerful and full of promise. She wore a yellow apron she'd bought in the souq, embroidered with floral patterns, skilfully sewn in gold thread. Too good for scrambled eggs, she thought, an apron fit for royalty.

Dorothy stretched like a pregnant cat, baring her belly to the sky. "I'm afraid Imam won't be joining us—he left at four o'clock this morning—he has an important meeting in Alexandria."

She noticed her mother suddenly looked frightened, her light suntan turning to alabaster. "But I saw him this morning—just after the call to prayer." Mrs Eady remembered hearing the chants from the local mosque, *Allahu Akhbar*...waking her up with their haunting cries of devotion; she'd got up for a glass of water, and then she'd seen a male figure walking on the balcony.

"It must have been Imam—who else could it have been? He was wearing a blue robe..." Mrs Eady gave a gasp, "Don't tell me the dream was real—but that's impossible!"

"You've seen him, haven't you, mother. You've seen King Sety in his blue robe," Dorothy whispered, closing the balcony door.

"Just don't tell Imam or your father—they'd think we were both mad. I can't see any husband playing second fiddle to an old Pharaoh." This was just the sort of thing she'd been worried about: her daughter making a mess of it all, thanks to her penchant for the paranormal.

"You have to get away from this place, Dorothy—why don't you all come back to England? Imam could get a job in London—for the sake of your marriage and your child, you've got to get away from this evil poltergeist!"

But Dorothy would hear nothing of the kind, "Sety is a very kind man and he means me no harm. He respects my marriage to Imam. I have no reason to fear him," she defended the Pharaoh, perplexed by her mother's state of alarm.

"I don't have the strength to discuss this right now, Mother," Dorothy began to breathe heavily and sat down on the chair, feeling a stabbing pain in her lower abdomen. "I need help. I think I'm going into labour!"

Mrs Eady ran into the bedroom to wake her husband, "Fetch the doctor, Reuben! Dorothy's about to have the baby!"

The doctor gave her chloroform to inhale and soon she drifted into a drugged induced state, seeing the doctor and nurse from a far-flung place, staring down a long tunnel at the white coats.

Several hours later, within a pool of sweat and pain, Dorothy gave birth to a baby boy. The household exploded into squeals of jubilation.

"It's a boy! We have a grandson!" shouted Mr Eady, embracing his wife with enthusiasm.

Dorothy decided to call the child Sety, much against her parents' wishes, who wanted to call him George.

"Let's see what Imam says about that," Mrs Eady said in a critical tone. The doctor had phoned the school in Alexandria and Imam had taken the first train home.

Imam burst into the bedroom, hugging and kissing his parents-in-law, forgetting the English rule of restraint. "I have a son! Thank you Allah! We have a son—may Allah bless him. Culla suna winta tyab! Happy Birthday little boy! We will call him Tariq," he kissed Dorothy several times on the cheek. She drew the child to her breast and said in a firm voice, "His name is Sety. I have made up my mind." Then Dorothy fell into a deep sleep, with the baby gurgling by her side. Imam had wanted to name him Tariq, after his great-grandfather. But somehow the name Sety stuck, despite Imam's attempts to call him Tariq Abdul Meguid.

Dorothy lay in a cocoon of contented exhaustion, her body trembling with pain and the thrill of new life. This little baby had set her free—she was no longer a waddling whale; she felt suddenly unburdened. She stared down at the tiny life form; he would need feeding, cuddling and educating. I will take him to the Cairo Museum, she vowed. Together they would have many adventures.

73

His birth made her feel strangely replenished, reconnected to life, as if she'd been reborn. New life stirred within her as she imagined the dormant potential in this child, like the desert at dawn, about to reveal its hidden treasures. She felt a new sense of urgency, her unexplored self stumbling in the darkness, an amoeba struggling to take form. The room suddenly seemed oppressive, like a sealed tomb. She longed for the desert air and the endless landscape of whipped sand and sky, the transmutation of light and dark; the changing moods that swing from gold to pink and then to sullen purple, finally sinking into melancholic aubergine, only to emerge with the pale yolk of dawn, an embryo revealing a new creation.

5. The Lovers
Abydos, 1290 BC

Bentreshy sat in the art class staring out the window and thinking about Sety—he'd left for Thebes early that morning, and she imagined him sailing up the Nile, his sad eyes swollen with tears, his face contorted with remorse; his crew wondering why a mighty Pharaoh would be so troubled. They'd been led to believe the image of god on earth was invincible, and yet here he was crying like a forsaken soul. But Bentreshy knew the Pharaoh was plagued with fears and uncertainties, despite his divine connection, and that he was capable of untamed passions. The way he'd looked at her, that first time in the garden—as if calling out to her; a glance of recognition and yet there was something else—the look of surprise, the wonder of discovery, the excitement of finding oneself in a foreign place, and the anxiety of not knowing where the journey would lead. It was like being alone in the darkness and seeing a light, his path illuminated for a moment, only to go dark again. Bentreshy saw the Pharaoh through a shaft of light, the sun creating a triangle of rays, the heat rising through white mist; she discerned his strong features, his straight nose and prominent jaw emerging from the vapour. But beside him there was a less defined shape, almost invisible against the bright background. The thing had an ethereal quality, like a diaphanous robe, blowing this way and that, about to vanish in the atmosphere. But as she stared at the object it began to take shape, breaking out of the ether and forming the face of a man. It was the face of Sety, and yet he was more gentle and delicate looking, like an ageless child. She was seeing his *Ka*, his astral self that had suddenly leaped free from his body; his higher self that was free to roam the universe, liberated from the shackles of his physical being. She stared at the Pharaoh and noticed his eyes were closed, his body lulled into a trance. While his mind was in a daydream his *Ka* had sprung to life—his *Ka* had spotted Bentreshy and wanted to dance and sing in a spontaneous expression of joy. His *Ka* cared little for protocol or public obligations. He could see Bentreshy through the swarm of people, a yellow pool in which he wanted to bathe. Yes, she was a lagoon of light, her fair hair drifting out to sea like a floating island. He was carried away by the stream, so full of joy; he would stay here forever and never come back to land, to obligations, to responsibility, to marital duty. His *Ka* had been set free: he would never enter the cage again; the bars had melted and he'd seen the invisible, with a clarity of vision that made his former life seem like death.

Bentreshy thought about their last meeting in the garden, Sety's arms wrapped around her, and for a moment she stopped singing, overwhelmed by his physical presence. Her *Ka* recognised the ethereal figure as a manifestation of her own being, as if witnessing her own rebirth, as if giving birth to herself. She continued singing, her voice calling out from the hidden realm, where bodies melt into amorphous shapes and drift into distant clouds. Her voice was deep and resonant, and for the first time (for it felt like a beginning) she felt she occupied the world, her body spreading into the atmosphere and laying claim to it, her pores like a swarm of bees settling into a hive. (Bees, she recalled, were a sign of rebirth, a glob of honey the teardrop of Ra.)

Her voice was awakening to the music of the lyre, the lute and the drums, taking on its own identity. The birds singing, the reeds blowing and brushing up against the boats and the voices bouncing over the water, creating a beautiful sound—they were all influencing one another and producing a universal music; the music of the spheres...

Bentreshy heard a tapping on the reed blind: a beetle had hit the window, its black body climbing up the ridges. She could see its shiny form through the reed slats. At that moment it mattered more to her than the teacher and the statue, the drawing slates and the sticks of chalk. She noticed the small things, the things concealed that people failed to notice. It was the tiny things lurking in the shadows which brought her into the invisible and hinted at a more magical world unseen. No one noticed the beetle on the blind, the pupils bent over their slates as they tried to reproduce the statue in chalk. Since meeting Sety she had begun to see life differently—oh it all sounded ridiculous, trying to explain it now: they'd bonded on a deep level, their *Kas* uniting as one; some schoolgirl fantasy her friends would say, and they would laugh at her for being so foolish. Perhaps Kebi would understand. Could she trust her with such an intimate secret?

"Bentreshy," she heard someone calling, hearing her name from the back of her head, as if from the bottom of a mountain.

"Bentreshy, you've been sitting there idle as a statue. I gather from your indolence that you have finished your drawing." The art teacher marched over to her desk and peered down at the slate. Bentreshy could feel the teacher's eyes looking down at the empty slate, her anger filling the blank space. The beetle clicked its brittle wings and flew away—how she wished she could fly away, follow the beetle into the desert and take refuge under a bush.

"I'm sorry Priestess Sebah, I must have fallen asleep." Bentreshy stared at the vacant slate; if only she could draw what she felt: about the beetle, the music, meeting Sety, his *Ka*...about the world unseen. But no—she would stay after class and be forced to draw something tedious; she would produce an inferior likeness because her heart wasn't in it, and the teacher would give her that disappointed look and say, "You have talent Bentreshy, you've produced some exceptional drawings. But lately you've become lazy, and all you do is stare out the window—such a pity with your aptitude."

This time she would try and produce something of worth, an echo of her great promise. She closed her eyes and conjured up the face of Sety, his gentle face urging her to create. Bentreshy took up her chalk and began to draw, following the contours of Sety's eyes, using dark lines to shape his nose and soft smudges to create the fullness of his mouth and then she applied bold strokes to form his strong jaw. And when the drawing was finished she was closer to understanding its meaning: that art existed to reveal the unseen. She thought of the artists in the temples, bringing the images to life, helping us to see the invisible; creating a visual picture of what we feel in our hearts but cannot fathom.

Priestess Sebah came over to assess her drawing and for a moment she stood in silence, poring over the portrait, baffled by the unusual composition. "You've drawn it like a statue, full front. That's most unorthodox."

Bentreshy knew the great masters didn't draw this way. In all the murals the bodies were side on, always walking to the right or to the left, but never facing the viewer. "I wanted to draw the whole face—I wanted to capture the entirety." Bentreshy wanted to see what was on the other side, the one concealed from view. It was a shift in perception, with the model keeping his head straight, staring right at you. And yet this simple position led to a whole new dimension of seeing.

"You haven't drawn Osiris the way I asked, it's all wrong—it's not the god at all." Priestess Sebah stared into the oval eyes—who did she see? She finally recognised the Pharaoh, his soulful eyes smudged in dark shadows, the layers of shading suggesting deep emotions. It was a fair likeness, she had to admit, and yet it was unsettling. The girl had dashed it off in a few minutes—just a few flicks of the wrist, the lines falling in perfect symmetry.

"It's not what I asked you to do," the teacher muttered, feeling defeated, disconcerted by this solitary flash of genius. She knew the drawing was exceptional but her apprehension prevented her from accepting it; she must set limits, teach her pupils to honour the boundaries, if only to maintain order in her class.

Bentreshy erased the drawing with her sponge, the striking features dissolving into mud, the bold lines washed away, as if by a flash flood.

"That's all for today, class. You are free to go. Next week we'll be working in clay." Sebah turned away and went to collect her basket, then she covered the statue with a linen cloth and tucked the corners round the stone slab.

Bentreshy picked up her slate and left the classroom in a cloud of gloom. She felt angry with herself: why did she erase the drawing—just to spite her teacher? She'd let her anger mar her judgement, destroy a moment of insight. The tears welled in her eyes, great bubbles of pain straining at her eyelids. She would go and see Kebi—tell her how horrible the teacher had been, "what a stickler for the rules!"

∧∧∧∧∧ ∧∧∧∧∧ ∧∧∧∧∧

Since meeting Bentreshy, the Pharaoh realised human love was the closest we come to the divine, to comprehending the essence of the gods. It had taken him thirty-four years to understand this and he wasn't about to ignore such a revelation. How could he turn away from truth, tenderness—the experience of pure joy? These vital elements manifested from the gods...

When Sety returned to his palace in Thebes he felt his *Ka* being pulled back to Bentreshy, as if caught in the river's current, feeling the force of nature's tempestuous whims. It was painful to be separated from her *Ka* and he felt a sudden emptiness. His isolation was apparent in his private chambers, the walls echoing like a deep cave; he was stranded in a labyrinth, not knowing which way to turn. He missed the sense of impletion he felt with Harp of Joy: this total understanding and acceptance of himself, his *sekhem* responding to her radiant being.

The Pharaoh was beginning to understand the nature of love: the energy generating the universe, the light illuminating the world, transforming the barren wilderness into a creative oasis. He thought of Isis and her deep love for Osiris: her adoration so infinite that she defied death and restored her husband to life. The resurrection of Osiris was an inimitable expression of love—and the acceptance of love, because you have to want to be reborn.

Love was the essence of Sety's own rebirth, and he was sure this transformation emanated from the goddess herself, as who else had the power to awaken a dying man and fill his being with unknown wonders?

For Bentreshy, this expression of love was heightened by the intensity of adolescence, the surge of raw emotion and unbridled passion leaping from her young heart. Unlike Sety, Harp of Joy did not analyse her emotions, she simply responded with every fibre of her being, her nerve-endings bursting into flames. She accepted this love as a gift from Isis, and in gratitude she burned incense before her effigy, leaving mimosa flowers beneath her feet. Bentreshy had no reason to suspect divine disapproval—when praying to Isis she felt her gentle gaze upon her, filling her heart with warmth.

Perhaps it was Bentreshy's naivety that made her think their relationship would be embraced by the Temple priesthood. She assumed if the gods approved, then so too would the mortals of Abydos, whose lives were ruled by divine authority. But when Bentreshy revealed her lover's identity to Kebi, her friend nearly fell off her stool, sending her snake hissing and slithering under the table. Kebi was suddenly worried for her friend, as she knew the court's history for intrigue and treachery. Sety also had opponents in the Temple, and the priestesses had to apply their considerable powers to impede the malevolence. "Promise me you won't tell anyone about your affair with the Pharaoh," warned Kebi, troubled by her friend's dreamy eyes.

"You make it sound so sordid—all this secrecy and fear of reprisals. The Pharaoh loves me—his *Ka* has united with mine for eternity," Bentreshy spoke with a new sense of assurance, "This sacred bond between *Kas* should never be broken and to come between them violates the Laws of Ma'at, tipping the cosmos out of balance."

Kebi felt such tenderness for her friend. Bentreshy was an ingénue when it came to love—oh, what a burden to fall in love for the first time, and discover this love is the eternal kind, your soul infinitely bound to another. And yet Kebi envied her friend's sense of rapture; it was the kind of love poets write about, the stuff of myths and legends that inspires the imagination. It was evident her love was immeasurable, like the boundless river, emanating from a mysterious place. And Bentreshy was like a gazelle standing by the water's edge, mesmerised by the crystals of light dancing on the surface, drawn into the swirling currents.

Kebi could only imagine this intoxicating love from the shore, her feet embedded in the sand. She loved Teshen deeply, but their union wasn't inspired by the gods, she admitted; yet there was real affection between them, and they shared a passion for snakes, at times elevating them to a place of magic. Kebi could honestly say she was happy with her lot, bound by serpentine enchantments and physical joys.

Kebi's earthly bearing gave her a practical sense, rooted in the affairs of everyday life, and she could smell danger with the sharpness of a jackal's nose.

"Think about it, Bentreshy, you should keep quiet about your love affair for the moment—Sety has enemies, people who would use this information against him and see to his demise."

"You mean like Amenkef?" Bentreshy knew the priest was a troublemaker, and that he was looking for any violation of protocol; his beady eyes were watching, disapproving, waiting to clamp down on you like the jaws of a hippopotamus.

"He is a bureaucrat who doesn't understand the true ways of the divine, the subtle Laws of Ma'at. These great laws are flexible and include a degree of tolerance, as they are inspired by the goddess of cosmic order, and there is always room for interpretation and exception to the rule." Bentreshy hated blind obedience and narrow ways of thinking; the gods were far from conventional and it required a radical leap into the unknown in order to experience the divine. In order to understand the gods you had to unleash your deeper self, stoke the flames of creation.

Kebi smiled at her friend, detecting the magnitude of her spirit's longing, "What you say is true, Bentreshy: the gods want us to liberate our beings from ignorance, awaken our imaginations. They reward us for being original and innovative, for striving to live as gods. But as you pointed out, Amenkef is a bureaucrat and his understanding of the law is black and white, with no room for interpretation. And he is not the only one—Kahotep is even more dangerous and he has a small number of followers who have been swayed by his fanatic zeal. Since the demise of the gods under Akhenaten, the priests have been wary of radical notions and they are suspicious of change—anything that might upset the balance of Ma'at and tip the scales into chaos." Kebi reminded her friend that Akhenaten was a revolutionary who started out with good intentions, but in the end he brought all of Egypt to the brink of destruction.

She knew Kebi was only trying to help and that she was right about the need for balance in all things. "Our love isn't immoral or wrong—our love is sanctioned by Isis herself. How can anyone associate this sacred bond with something depraved?" Bentreshy thought of Amenkef with his shrivelled face and mean eyes, unable to see the munificence of the gods, and for a moment she felt pity for him. But there was something heartless about him; something ruthless.

Kebi grabbed her friend's arm, "Think rationally for a moment—not with your heart, I implore you. The Temple laws claim that once a girl becomes a fertility priestess she belongs to the Temple. She must remain a Receptacle of Isis, so the goddess may possess her body and restore Osiris to life. But maybe it is the will of the gods that you and King Sety unite in a sacred bond, like Isis and Osiris…I'm sure Inhapi will understand the prophetic nature of such a bond—but Amenkef is another story—he would use it against you—he will quote Temple laws, he will try to blacken your name." Amenkef would claim the laws had been violated: the renewal of the earth and its people jeopardised.

Bentreshy knew her Temple duties better than anyone. She had made a pledge to perform the secret rites. It was a great honour to be selected for this role, she realised, as the goddess rewarded her Vessel Priestess with bountiful gifts, including untold privileges in the Afterlife. Bentreshy looked at her friend and burst into tears, burdened by the weight of her holy obligations. "I know the laws inside out, and how I regret the vow I have taken! When I made my oath I never expected to fall in love with a Pharaoh," she wailed, burying her head in her hands and pulling at her hair, as if in mourning.

Kebi put her arms round her friend, suddenly aware of her small frame, "how young she is," thought Kebi, too young for this immense responsibility.

Bentreshy pulled herself away from Kebi and dried her tears. Sety would not abandon her. Their *Kas* had welded into one and he would never forsake her—that would be like rejecting his own soul, and abandoning his chance of eternal bliss. Kebi noticed a sudden change in her friend's demeanour and felt her grow in stature; her shoulders straight, her eyes glowing with a new confidence. Kebi had to step back, as her friend's rapid surge of energy was overpowering, like a flash of lightening, leaving a tremor of fear in its wake.

Bentreshy kissed her friend goodbye and made a hasty retreat; she would discuss the matter with Inhapi, she decided, declining Kebi's invitation of vegetable stew and duck egg fritters. Kebi watched her run down the dusty track towards the Temple, hoping Inhapi would offer her support.

She looked back and saw Kebi sitting by the huge cauldron, slicing a pile of carrots and leeks, her figure overshadowed by the reed canopy. Such a cosy house, she thought, I am happy for Kebi; she'd found a safe refuge and a man who was her equal, a man who shared her passion for snakes and spells.

Walking back to the Temple, the warm sand was losing its heat, drawn out by the cool air of early evening. She crossed the old acropolis with the piles of pottery offerings, the dusty shards poking out from the heaps of sand. There were clay pieces with blue, red and yellow patterns, once moulded into a fine jar, containing incense, dried jasmine flowers perhaps, or even frankincense if the deceased were very rich. This whole landscape was a giant offering, she realised, with the Mountain of Offerings embracing the village, the Temple complex, the ancient tombs—the living and the dead existing side by side.

Bentreshy hurried through the garden towards the House of Isis, mulling over what her friend had said: *promise me you will keep your affair with the Pharaoh secret.* Bentreshy knew their love was too immense, too intense for most people to comprehend.

Darting through the archway to the House of Isis, her sandals made a clapping sound on the limestone floor as she hurried towards the shrine. She expected to see Inhapi commencing the ritual, filling the jugs with holy water, but the priestess was nowhere in sight. She had

82

decided to unburden her soul to the priestess, who had always offered her solace and sound advice whenever she'd been in need. Finding herself alone in the Temple, Bentreshy began her nightly ablutions, the silent pose of the goddess engulfing her in stillness. She disrobed and dived into the clear pool, the bronze sunset creating a gold shield on the surface. The healing waters began to seep through her skin, turning her senses into delicate receivers, ready to hear the voice of Isis. She performed her synchronised movements with ease, twisting her body into a series of symbols: the knot of Isis, the ankh, the sun, moon and stars, the lotus and chalice; drawing the energy of Isis down from the sky, calling on the goddess to awaken within her and hear her prayers.

Bentreshy emerged from the sacred pool, her feet radiating on the marble steps, the water dripping from her skin in gold ripples. She completed her cleansing rites with a deep sense of devotion, pouring the jug of holy water over the statue of Isis, her arms extended, palms open to receive. She offered her naked body to the goddess, her pores rising, feeling both vulnerable and powerful, as she sensed the goddess getting closer to her. Bentreshy sprinkled the water over the statue and saw the goddess smiling through the stone effigy. Placing the incense jar on the ground she heard a rattling sound inside. She peered into the jar and noticed a piece of pottery lying on the bottom. It was a small ostraca with a message carved onto the surface. *"Meet me by the canal under the willow tree, when the crescent moon sits on the mountain like a fat scribe."*

She stifled her laughter and pressed the ostraca to her breast. Then she traced the letters with her fingers and placed them to her lips, savouring their meaning. Bentreshy stared up at the goddess and felt her all-embracing smile, her all-knowing eyes burning through the ostraca. *Scratch out the message and throw the ostraca into the pool.* She followed the instructions, scratching out the message with a pebble and when it was illegible she threw it into the centre of the pool, watching it ripple through the surface, through the effigy, the gold light, and then her damp skin. She absorbed it all: the ostraca, the goddess, the sky bleeding into pink, the thought of seeing King Sety in the moonlight. Bentreshy had the approval of Isis, she sensed it in her bones, as if carved in stone.

Staring into the serene face of the goddess she felt the nurturing energy embrace her, the turquoise eyes emitting waves of heat.

Bentreshy rubbed oil into the effigy's marble skin, taking extra care over the ritual, making each motion an act of love.

"I know the Temple decrees that a fertility priestess belongs to Isis—and yet I have broken that promise through my love affair with Sety." There was a tremor in her voice, a sudden frisson. She felt vulnerable, as though standing by a cliff, her words disappearing into a hollow space. *I cannot fool Isis. Isis knows my intimate secrets; she detects my every weakness and knows the nature of my imperfections. She shines her light of truth through the centre of my heart and exposes my shortcomings. And yet Isis loves me, she is a generous mother who sees the goodness in me. She is the reflection of my deeper self; my potential made divine.*

"I know I have failed in my duties and I am sorry. But the Laws of Ma'at also decree that I must follow my *Ka*, which knows no human boundaries. I am in a state of terrible conflict, Great Mother! How can I follow the desires of my *Ka* and the restraints of the ritual? How can I obey the laws of the priesthood and the Laws of Ma'at? Please help me understand!" She waited for an answer on bended knees, palm turned open to receive a divine message from Isis. She concentrated on opening her mind and heart, emptying herself of all mortal thoughts, until she could see only white nothingness. A flash of light appeared somewhere in the blank space, a speck of yellow dust, swelling into a grain of wheat; then an embryo bursting open, filling the space with swirls of colour and forming into beautiful patterns. A figure of a woman began to take shape, her body moulded out of liquid fire. The form of Isis appeared with long black braids, wearing a diaphanous gold robe, her head crowned with the horned sun disk and the uraeus coiling from her forehead, her wise eyes radiating waves of light. Despite her stunning appearance, Isis was a good-natured, playful goddess, who didn't like to stand on ceremony. Bentreshy knew the goddess wanted her followers to feel comfortable in her presence and to think of her as a close friend, rather than a deity to be feared and venerated from afar. Bentreshy felt herself surrounded by compassion and kindness, the goddess filling her with love and acceptance, offering her complete understanding.

Isis parted her soft lips and a flood of messages spilled out, filtering through Bentreshy's senses, as if they were her own thoughts and feelings. Later she claimed the words didn't reach her in an oral sense—how to explain...imagine the water could speak, or the wind talking through the trees, the words sounding green, due to their abundance.

The Laws of Ma'at are difficult for mortals to understand, as they are the great labyrinths of Truth that make up the universe. You must let go of the physical boundaries, the limitations of reason to fully understand. Try to think and feel like a child, with a sense of openness and innocence, before social imprints made its mark on the mind. Open yourself as a child and you will understand as a goddess.

Bentreshy meditated on this message: *Receive as a child, understand as a goddess.*

The words uttered by Isis were forming into tangible symbols; the sight of the invisible, turning into pictures, resounding into waves. She would never forget the message and she felt suspended in its very essence, transported to the core of memory. Bentreshy concentrated on being as vulnerable as a child, and yet as wise as Horus, who gazed into the heart of things with his unflinching eyes.

Opening her eyes she saw the chamber bathed in gold, a slight mist hovering near the ceiling. She stared at the stone wall and became aware of its inner essence, it's journey from the limestone cliffs of the quarry, and then further back—to the bowels of the desert where the stone once lay, where the quarrymen had hauled it out using pulleys and ropes, bound together in a collective struggle—and back even further, when the slab belonged to a great rock face, long before man began chiselling lumps into squares and building temples—back to the time when the stone lived at the bottom of the ocean, when all was a primeval sea...

Bentreshy could feel the memory of water oozing from the stone; her *Ka* rising to greet the sea, when she too sprang from its source. Seeing zigzags marked in the stone, the aqueous symbols recalling our primal being. The sea was her first home, the beginning of human time; the watery womb was another ocean, the beginning of her life on earth.

She lay on the floor and watched her own *Ka* floating out of the water, heading towards a liquid mass shaped like a foetus. Then she saw the Pharaoh inside the ovum, spinning in the yellow yolk; she leaped towards him like a shooting star, their bodies merging into an explosion of colour; a numinous transformation began to happen, right there in the pit of the universe, where the cellular life forms spiral through the abyss, absorbing all sorts of strange matter and evolving into peculiar shapes and textures, emotions and desires; the green, red and blue flames of creation. The alchemy, once completed, faded into a pink glow, illuminating the land, the river and mountains in the final throes of creation.

The earthlings responded to the cosmos by dancing, chanting and sprinkling the ground with holy water, lighting torches and fires in honour of the burning sun and stars. Two beings floated through the pink firmament, protected by a layer of light brown skin, and they hovered in the nucleus, amazed by what they saw on earth.

Isis gazed at the woven *Kas*, her face almost blue in the descending light, and she smiled through a veil of empathy which resembled a cloud to the naked eye below. Isis embraced the two *Kas* in her vast wings, concealing them in a mass of feathers.

"The love between two Kas emanates from the seeds of creation and this love inflames the universe. It shall never be impeded or destroyed by mortal or god."

Isis flapped her wings and the earth felt a tremor, sending shock waves through the ground and the people dashing for shelter. The few who stayed in the fields saw that the earth had been disturbed, the atmosphere suddenly altered. The whitewashed huts darkened by violet shadows, the sun sinking from pink to purple and then to granite grey, like a bruise changing colour. For a frightening moment the sun disappeared behind a black mask, plunging the earth into darkness. "Anubis!" the villagers cried, running out of their houses to greet the god, who grinned at them as he devoured the sun with his canine jaws. Within this black orb a pink light began to seep through, the people rising with anticipation, eyes wide, inhaling sharp breaths of air, lips formed into circles of awe.

The crimson light bled through the horizon, the people fell to their knees, and the sun continued its journey to the West, sinking behind the hills—then the people stopped being afraid, as the darkness came every night. They knew Ra was safely in the Underworld.

Bentreshy sat in meditation, the goddess expanding through her being, like the sinuous vines stretching over the trellises, overflowing with plump grapes; Isis whispering in her ears:

"People will have difficulties understanding your union. Your love will be fraught with conflict. In times of darkness always remember your love has been sanctioned by the gods. Men are often ignorant of

the gods' wishes—no wonder the universe slips into chaos—and we must work night and day to restore the balance."

When Bentreshy opened her eyes again, the chamber had gone quiet and night had fallen. The effigy stared in stony silence, without breathing or moving, like any object carved in stone. Her knees began to ache on the flimsy mat and she was desperately thirsty. All her physical needs cried out at once, demanding to be satisfied. She was no longer in the realm of the divine—her hunger was an obvious sign. But there was no time to eat, *"I must follow my Ka,"* she reminded herself, slipping on her blue robe and running to the window. The moon was nearly sitting on the Mountain of Offerings; it was nearly time to meet the Pharaoh.

Her whole body leaped towards the moonlight, emotions rushing in like a flash flood, her heart thrashing in excitement. She picked up her basket of healing herbs and knew no one would question her, for they'd think she'd gone to attend a woman in labour, her basket full of chamomile flowers and hippo-shaped amulets.

Bentreshy quickened her pace to the canal and walked along the water's edge, the frogs rumbling like distant thunder. She paused to study her reflection in the runny moonlight: her hair was plaited in tiny braids and gathered in a bronze clip decorated with turquoise gems. Her light blue robe was fastened with a beaded belt and drawn at the centre by a large brooch, depicting the Knot of Isis in tiny carnelian stones. Her eyes were finely contoured with black eyeliner, so that her blue eyes appeared to spring from the darkness.

Standing by the willow tree, she watched the moon's reflection tremble on the river's surface; the moon was hovering on the tip of the mountain, like a portly old scribe about to fall over. Then she heard a bird call, unusual for this time of night, filling the emptiness with its sweet song. Which bird sang so beautifully in the dead of night, with no one to appreciate its melody but me? *"Tweet, tweet, tweet, Bentree, Tweet, tweet Bentresheeee!"* she detected her name in the middle of the song and her spirit leaped towards the sound, her ears straining over the frogs' croaking. She saw the Pharaoh sailing towards her in a rustic boat, holding a net above his head and casting it out in the river, as she'd seen the fishermen do. Bentreshy couldn't help laughing at this irreverent image of the Pharaoh: he'd got the fishnet caught in his hair and nearly toppled the boat. Running down the bank she waded out to the boat, her love mounting in the inky water, flooding her senses with immeasurable passions.

She leaped into the boat with wild enthusiasm, nearly capsizing it for the second time. Sety laughed at her clumsy exuberance and pulled her towards him, "You have the dainty feet of a gazelle, yet the strength of a crocodile, an unusual combination in a woman."

The couple fell to the ground in a spiral of kisses, hair tangled in the fishing net, "We're trapped in the labyrinth, we'll never get out," Sety laughed; they tussled like two leopard kittens, trying to free themselves from the net. He realised he hadn't laughed for years—not that jovial kind of laughter that made his ribs ache and his head giddy. With Harp of Joy he felt like a child again, full of innocence and impetuous pleasure. Bentreshy gazed up at her lover, drawn to his sudden vulnerability, his naked torso lustrous in the moonlight, his arms slumped over his head in acquiescence. It was surprising to see this great Pharaoh in such a tender pose, submitting himself to her, his body trembling with desire, receptive to her every touch. Bentreshy lay down beside him, his beautiful skin coming alive under her fingers, her gentle kisses. She felt his body relax, his head sinking back in bliss and he stared up at the sky where Nut arched over the world in a shower of stars; he surrendered to the unconscious, the intuitive wonders fermenting behind the veil of reason, the impulsive life-force that fuels the universe. Then his calm demeanour suddenly changed, his muscles tightening round his chest, his torso contracting with alarm. "I need to get away from here—let's sail into the next canal—a great surprise awaits you there." Sety stood up and grabbed the long oar, steering the boat into the central current. Bentreshy felt the elusive forces tugging from below, the watery abyss that was a law unto itself. The little boat bounced to and fro, sucked into the maelstrom where it spun like a mad dog trying to catch its tail. Bentreshy held her breath and clung to the sides, seized by fear and excitement. She watched him battle with the whirlpool, shifting the oar from side to side, his arms bulging as he struggled against the force of nature. "It's that damn irrigation channel—I told the engineer it was too steep." Sety's vulnerable stance had disappeared, his tenderness transformed into brute strength and Bentreshy saw the warrior within him, a man capable of subduing his enemies and the unruly elements that threatened the balance of things. Sety skilfully guided the vessel out of danger and then he erected the sail, nudging it to catch the wind.

The lovers sailed away in a gush of wind, zigzagging across the water as they followed the airstream and the unseen whims of the river. Bentreshy's legs were wet from wading in the shore, her robe wrapped around her knees like a bandage, the swift air creating ripples in the fabric. He could see her pores through the blue gauze, seeking out the warm air. Her wet robe formed a puddle in the bottom of the boat, and she spread the water with her toes, her foot touching his heel. Their feet intertwined and she felt the power of their physical beings, fusing like minerals in the earth; his strong bare foot, the sole that ruled the two lands of Egypt. They sailed in silence, overwhelmed by the darkness and the magnitude of the river, which was growing wider by the minute. Finally they emerged into a rectangular pool where the canal diverged into several waterways, spreading out like black fingers, pointing to the unknown. Bentreshy spotted a hippopotamus wading by the shore, its craggy flesh squatted in obese tranquillity, masking the terror that could erupt in a primeval instant. Sety recognised her fear and gently held her hand, "Don't worry, Lotus Flower. The beast has eaten his fill of waterfowl and he's dozing in the mud—look at him—he doesn't have the energy to stand, let alone devour a priestess."

Narrowing her eyes she focused on the stubby silhouette, lying comatose in the shallows, like a giant tree stump lodged in the mud. Her eyesight sharpened by fear, she perceived several crocodiles protruding from the surface: nodular snouts waiting for a helpless victim. Bentreshy turned her mind to Sobek, the crocodile god, knowing the energy of the river monsters could be harnessed for the power of good. The crocodile tenderly cradled her babies in her deadly jaws, and even the fearsome hippopotamus was devoted to her young. Without thinking, Bentreshy began to chant: *Oh Fearsome Sobek, protect me from the demons in the unseen depths, and I will honour you with an offering in the Temple. Oh Mighty Sobek, turn the river beasts into gentle lambs!*

Sensing the awesome power of these creatures, their instincts the epitome of raw nature, she knelt down to honour the water beasts. Sety watched in amazement as the crocodiles swam back to shore in a slow procession and crept into the undergrowth. Then Bentreshy leaped off the boat, inspired by the crocodile's impulsive spirit. "It's

89

a wonderful night for a swim, and the water's really warm—like a Temple bath at the Great Feast."

"Come out, my love, it's very dangerous to swim at night, the crocodiles are looking for a meal. Swim back to the boat, I beg you." Sety sounded terrified.

She responded with a reckless laugh. The river beasts were under a spell; she had harnessed their *sekhem* and there was no way she could come to any harm. "Why don't you join me?" she enticed him, amused by his trepidation: the man who had subdued the Hittites was afraid of going for a midnight swim. She dived under the boat, Sety watched her dart like a fish and then disappear into the depths. A sense of panic pricked his heart, he would have to go after her, he realised, suppressing his fear and taking a blind leap into the river. He feared the worst as he hit the water, imagining himself torn to pieces by a crocodile, the hungry jowls staining the water with royal blood. But to his surprise, when he poked his head out of the surface, there were no river beasts in sight, the night submerged in a strange silence. The moonlight dressed the water in a silver cloak, and he saw the sky sink into the earth until there was no more divide, no sense of here or there, of this world or the next; the endless stars raining down on him—did they consist of fire or water? he couldn't say; their compound was a mystery to him, like the alchemy inciting his soul. He caught a glimpse of Bentreshy emerging like an amphibious creature, the moon igniting her face in a white dome, pearls of fire and water dripping from her chin, and she, too, was a mystery to him, and he wondered whether she was made from earthly compounds or fashioned from the heavens; her eyes cast from stars, her hair spun from wheat. The river seemed to have given birth to this floating creature. All the natural elements were part of her composition: the black mud, the fathomless water, the monsters retracting in her wake; the land of Geb and the sky of Nut. There was no beginning and no end, just the amorphous swamp where life leached out, twisting its way through the cosmos.

Sety swam towards the aphotic shape, following the sound of laughter under the water, reminding him of the distant yelp of a jackal, muffled by the mountains. Sety caught her in his arms, her body slippery as an eel, writhing with a supernatural force, as if she belonged to this place. Their lips came together, their mouths filling with murky sediments and the musty taste of silt. They swam along

90

the river, moving through endless streaks of water, parting the surface with their arms. Sety realised he'd lost all sense of fear, as the river was most accommodating, his body darting like a Nile perch, he believed he could swim all the way to Heliopolis. They swam towards a little inlet where an arch of stars sparkled above their heads, making diamond splashes in the sky, the same way their arms made splashes in the water, leaving a trail of glitter in the darkness.

The couple floated into a lagoon with a sandy beach that led to a lush garden of flowers and palm trees, with fruit hanging from every branch. "This is my secret place. I come here when I need to get away. You are the only person I want to share it with." Sety kissed her on the lips and she inhaled his sweet breath.

"I have a surprise for you, as promised." Sety scrambled up the bank, where two men were hiding in the shadows, rigid as statues.

"Who are those men?" Bentreshy jumped towards Sety in fear, seeing the size of their pointed spears, the blades gleaming in the moonlight. Sety laughed, "Just a couple of my guards, no need to be afraid." He motioned to the men and they retreated into the bushes.

Bentreshy noticed their boat moored in the shallows and realised the guards had discreetly rescued the abandoned boat and brought it to the shore. In the world of the Pharaoh, even a wild adventure was not without a plan, impulses guarded by an attentive eye. The sentries were there to ensure divine will was maintained, every need and desire catered for—in a seamless flow of protection that almost went unnoticed. Sety appeared oblivious to these shadowy men, spears at their sides, ready to take orders and lay down their lives for King Sety if the need arose. They believed Pharaoh was the persona of Horus on earth, and all of Egypt depended on His Majesty's wellbeing.

Bentreshy could see the shape of a round hut made from reeds and decorated with streams of flowers.

"Come and see your surprise," Sety whispered, leading her through the dark entrance. She stumbled as though blind, her feet probing each step and then in a flash of an eye the torches were lit, illuminating a circular space draped in multicoloured flowers and foliage like the jungles of Africa; life-size sculptures of strange animals she'd never seen before, with long necks and spotted bodies, white horses covered in black stripes and portly beasts with long ivory tusks.

The couple sat on a bed of plump cushions and a servant appeared with fresh linen robes and a tray of makeup and oils. Bentreshy stared in the bronze mirror, the room reflected in bowl-shaped fragments, like a dream unfolding in patches of fabric, alluding to the whole story. She dressed and anointed herself, catching glimpses of light and motion, aware that something wonderful was evolving behind her, but frightened to turn round and break the spell, or discover that it was all an illusion. Gradually she heard a vibration coming through the floor, rising in a thunder of drums and dancing feet, followed by the most wonderful music that lifted her soul into a state of bliss, making her want to laugh, cry, dance, sing and roll about the floor all at once. There were harps, flutes, tambourines and sistra, shaking to a primal beat, overlapping into waves of dreamy melodies. Sety lifted her onto the bed of cushions where they wriggled like serpents, kissing, laughing and biting one another, the tribal music awakening their animal natures. Next to the bed there was a table of food, with plates of spiced quail, duck glazed in pomegranates, vegetables carved into star shapes, bread moulded into little fish, cakes dripping with honey, and fruit covered in spirals of cream.

The couple indulged in every earthly pleasure, revelling in their romantic retreat; as if the world only existed for them, as if the whole event had happened by magic. Yet Bentreshy knew the evening had been carefully orchestrated, and that there were several attendants waiting in the shadows, the invisible conductors that made it all appear spontaneous, flawlessly improvised. They had the illusion of being alone, enjoying a secluded night of romantic intimacy: there was no one else around, except the echoes of singing and music, the only sign of human life.

They writhed in naked rapture, their bodies rolling round the cushions in waves of pleasure, their *Kas* seeking out the other, desperate to unite as one being. They drifted into a state of ecstasy, the fusion of their mortal and spirit beings ascending in bliss, bringing them closer to the source of the gods. They reached a dizzying climax and clung to each other in disbelief, as their beings hovered in paradise. Their eyes locked together and they saw within the other a flame of recognition, a flash of enlightenment, suspended in a vapour of colour and sound, all the wonders of the universe exploded within them: pearls of beauty, the gods smiling in approval, watching these mortals suddenly poke through the divine realm and look around in amazement, as if to say: *so this is what the poets and the visionaries have been talking about—the paradise that is only a shift in perception away, a place reached through earthly joy. Oh mortals of the world: we must indulge in earthly pleasures, for how can we experience divine bliss, or perceive enlightenment when we chastise our physical beings and deny them the very provisions that feed our souls? The gods are insulted when we deny sensual pleasures, the sacred gifts they've bestowed upon us.*

They lay back on the cushions, a slither of dawn creeping into their pleasure grove, the leaves drooping over their heads with a sense of melancholy. Bentreshy felt a sadness slink into her belly—soon it would be time to leave and return to the world of duty. She crawled out of bed, feeling the dull weight of responsibility surround her heart.

"Don't despair, my love," Sety whispered in her ear. "You must return to the Temple and prepare for the evening ritual, the renewal of the land depends upon it. Keep the memory of this experience fixed in your mind and we will be united soon, I promise."

Bentreshy would remember every detail of their river date; the night of mortal passion and divine pleasure, the night her body had taken flight and soared into ecstasy, riding on the wings of Isis and ascending through the stars. She glanced at Sety and felt his hidden sadness; only hours ago they had flown through the cosmos and now they sat here harnessed to the earth, weary and overcome, as if they had died a beautiful death.

Bentreshy bathed her face in the bowl, clearing the despondency from her eyes, the water refreshing her memory of the invisible and reviving her spirits.

As they sailed back to the Temple they mapped out a plan for their next encounter: they would meet again after the Mystery Plays, when all of Egypt radiated with new life, seized by the euphoria of rebirth, and the two lovers would take flight on the wings of this exuberance and steal away to their own private heaven.

The lovers docked by the quay, their boat knocking into the immovable dykes. They embraced in a final burst of passion and then Bentreshy (against her better nature) struggled to free herself, feeling that flicker of death again, followed by a rush of life as she charged up the bank to the Temple. The sky was neither light nor dark, waiting for the sunrise to infuse the world with gold. For a moment the earth hovered in a state of apathy, devoid of life or motion. She cherished these moments of stillness before sunrise, as though she were the only being on earth, slipping through the world like ether. The Temple seemed enormous after the green bower by the river, the stone columns making her feel like a tiny insect. Humans needed these great monuments to confirm their faith—if only they knew the divine could be drawn from a wild flower, or the flap of a butterfly's wing, or a stone worn smooth by the river.

6. Finding Bentreshy
Cairo, 1934

Dorothy made herself a cup of tea and sat down to listen to the radio, the baby fed and sleeping in his basket, the rest of the house blissfully silent. She heard the broadcaster report in a sombre voice, "Sir Earnest Wallis Budge, retired Keeper of Antiquities at the British Museum has died at the age of seventy-seven after a long illness..."

"He can't be dead—he had the constitution of a bull—he was never ill!" Dorothy cried, listening to the professor's achievements through a stream of tears: his books, his lecture tours, his knighthood in 1920, and his vast contribution to the British Museum. She was amazed to learn he'd written 150 books—she'd read about thirty of them, but had no idea he was so prolific. The British Museum had been his life's passion and thanks to his obsession with hoarding Egyptian artefacts, the Museum had the largest collection outside Cairo (of course she believed the artefacts should be sent back to Egypt—how they'd argued about this!).

The professor had done a great deal to preserve antiquities, but not many people knew about his nurturing side—how he had fostered a young girl's development and directed her studies. Before meeting Dr Budge, Dorothy had been wandering through the rooms without purpose, cast adrift amongst the artefacts; he'd given her the power to read the symbols, the tools to inscribe her own destiny...

Dorothy thought back to those early days in the Museum, how Dr Budge had taught her to decipher the papyri, and let her handle the ancient objects—even though she was just a child, he trusted her with these priceless artefacts. *His faith in me was like the Nile rising after a drought, permeating my being with medicinal waters. Now I can read the hieroglyphs, date the relics and place them in the proper Dynasty...Egyptology is my Field of Reeds...*

On the eve of their voyage back to Southampton, Mr and Mrs Eady tried to persuade their daughter to return home with them.

"Come away from this ungodly place. Strange things happen here— frightening things. Come home to England, Dorothy, we beg you!"

Dorothy laughed nervously, "Don't be silly, Mum, I have a family here. I am Egyptian now." They were watching the sunset from the balcony; blood-red, like a dying bull.

She wanted to tell them—ever since she'd stepped off the ship King Sety's presence had intensified, and now he was appearing in her dreams—she could never return to England. She sensed his deep love, his silent passion and remembered why she'd come to Egypt. In her astral dreams he appeared not as a mummy but as a handsome man in his early thirties, still fit and full of vitality, despite his broken heart. The Pharaoh had something to tell her, she could read it in his sad eyes, but at the moment he was unable to utter a single word.

∧∧∧∧∧ ∧∧∧∧∧ ∧∧∧∧∧

One day, after Imam went to work, King Sety appeared in the bedroom wearing a simple tunic and a beige cape which fell to the floor in great folds. He sat quietly on a stool at the foot of the bed, gazing at Dorothy through the elusive light, her face a golden orb illuminating the space above, her lips trembling like two flames. Dorothy half opened her eyes and saw the Pharaoh in particles of sleep, his face appearing in fragments: his furrowed brow, his flushed face, his feet fidgeting in the chair. *This is no vision*, she mused; *he is made of flesh and bone, with shadows under his eyes, a slight bruise below his elbow.*

"Why have you taken so long to come back to me?" Dorothy asked him; he'd been visiting her dreams for the past five months, but this was the first time he'd sat at the end of her bed, watching her lips tremble with sleep, her eyes flickering like butterflies. He watched her eyes open and then close, straining against the morning light. He sat like a statue, unyielding, a staunch figure fixed in place. She had waited sixteen years for this moment—when he'd first appeared to her as a mummy, when he'd torn her nightdress.

King Sety stood up, his cape blocking the light in a swirl of fabric. He reached his arms out towards her and then suspended them in midair, as if he'd turned to stone, and she had the sense that all motion had ceased, all words abandoned. After a length of silence she was surprised to hear him speak: "I'm sorry for my absence over the years. It has been torture for me, to refrain from visiting you. I was warned by the Council that I had frightened you, and that your *Ka* was not ready for such a responsibility."

"Who is this Council?" Dorothy demanded to know, feeling hostile towards this elusive force; she imagined a council of old men deciding her fate, preventing Sety from visiting her. Could such a Council really exist—it was too absurd!

The Pharaoh tried to explain, "I'm afraid such a Council does exist—but not a council of men, rather a Council of the Gods." He said they were a group of enlightened souls who were selected by the gods for their wisdom and sound judgement. Their job was to see that the Laws of Ma'at were upheld and to act on behalf of the gods. "It was the Council's decision that I keep my distance from you all these years—that I shouldn't come to you until you returned to Abydos."

"But I haven't returned to Abydos—and yet you are able to visit me. The gods must have changed their minds!" Dorothy reasoned; this intangible figure had come back to her, his being materialised out of the ether.

King Sety looked around anxiously: he had the feeling that any moment a great wall would divide them, and he sensed a mountain of doom descend upon him, his eyes darkening with dread. He whispered, as if the walls had ears, "I wanted to see you every day, tell you I love you, to unburden the depths of my soul to you," Sety reached out for her hand, and to his horror it felt cold, like a block of ice in the winter desert, and then he saw a sheet of glass separating them, just as he'd feared. He remembered a cold morning in the Libyan Desert when he stared down at the ice, the sand frozen beneath the surface, the insects trapped as if in amber. Dorothy tried to touch him, but she, too, felt this glacial barrier, and the impact knocked her backwards onto the bed.

Sety paced the room in a stream of anguish, "How they torture me! It's because you are a married woman—that is why we cannot pass the barrier into physical contact. They are trying to tell me I must honour this union."

"Well, if that's the case we must sit together and talk," said Dorothy, slipping into the armchair by the window. She gazed at his profile across the room, an image of perfect clarity, like the bright sky on a cloudless day, his body glowing with a million particles, and for a moment she doubted the existence of this invisible obstacle between them.

97

Although Dorothy longed to unite with Sety on a physical plane, she would have to be content with their ephemeral meetings, relying on their imaginations to fill in the gaps, overcome the obstacles. Despite the restrictions they were overjoyed to see one another, talking about the priests, the Temple girls, the antics of the gods, the great feasts and fabled floods, and they chatted so intensely about the past that they quite forgot about the burdens of the present. She felt a terrible sadness when it was time for him to leave, her body trembling with cold, a fog descending over her vision. She never believed it possible to feel such a connection with another being: this sense of complete understanding and trust; a serene state of bliss. Dorothy realised this was the most profound expression of love—she had dreamed about it but never thought it could exist, like the horse with wings; something to be imagined but never attained. It was now apparent that dreams could leap from the darkness and find their place amongst tangible objects.

This sense of bliss was the deepest state of existence, which the sages and mystics spent their lives pursuing, their devout footprints visible on the horizon. She hoped Sety would show her the right path to follow; she needed a guide through the desert, with a key to open the Temple door... *The potential lies within us: it is the journey of the Ka towards the light. I am opening like a lotus drawn to the sun, the pink mist rising into dawn.* Then she heard Sety's voice, "I will be your guide. In your dreams your *Ka* will be liberated from this realm and will travel to the Beyond. Only then will you know of the wonders that await you after death, and how one day we will be united for Eternity. But first you must make your own journey, discover the truth."

"How will I know which path to take—how will I find the truth?" Dorothy asked, fearing she would make a wrong turn and lose his love, lose the chance to live in Amenti.

"You have a great task ahead of you: seek out the old festivals, search the truth in the tombs and temples. Unearth the old stones, the amulets and papyri, and they will give you clues. Your journey is written in the symbols scattered in the desert. There you will find which direction to take, buried in the sand." And then King Sety disappeared, leaving Dorothy feeling quite bewildered. She heard the baby crying and rushed onto the balcony where he lay in his basket, his fretful face conveying his hunger. She picked him up and drew him to her bosom, "My poor Little Sety, what a scatty mother you have!" She danced around the balcony, his baby eyes laughing with joy, mouth firmly attached to his mother's breast.

∧∧∧∧∧ ∧∧∧∧∧ ∧∧∧∧∧

Reluctantly and with a heavy heart, King Sety returned to the Netherworld. Usually he loved descending to the eternal realm, but today he was feeling melancholy: he had left earth without fulfilling his objective, and he felt that terrible sense of failure, of leaving things unresolved, like an incomplete mural. He remembered how frustrating life on earth could be: we had such great potential and big plans, yet life was filled with obstacles to thwart our goals. It is amazing how mortals achieve anything at all, he pondered, when they are constantly distracted by chaotic forces, social obligations, visitors and other calamities. He marvelled at the temples he'd managed to build in his lifetime, the expeditions into foreign lands, the political shenanigans he'd laid to rest, the battles he'd fought... Of course life in the Netherworld had its drawbacks. He had to admit he loved being amongst the immortals, in a world that was very much like earth, yet in an idealised form: imagine nature in its most sublime state, an existence without disease, pollution, poverty or strife. Amenti was the highest expression of the imagination, transformed into reality; the most potent images of beauty, the rousing rhymes of poetry, and then there were the deepest emotions, endless visions — in Amenti all these delights could manifest themselves into being. I could wax lyrical all day about the wonders of the Afterlife, but no mortal would really believe me, he sighed. If only they knew: higher, wider dimensions could unfurl, like orange blossom in the sun; first springing from the imagination and then mutating into life. If only human beings could envision this existence: that the divine realm lies within them, buried beneath the rubble, and that they were only a blink away from this infinite dimension.

King Sety had done his best to open Dorothy's eyes, lift her gaze from ground level to the heart of things. It required a slight shift in focus, like adjusting your eyes to the light of the moon and seeing with a new intensity, the clarity of things revealed through the darkness. It was extraordinary, Sety thought, what is perceived in the nebulous region when the light is concealed. There were fleeting

99

moments when Dorothy would see through this fog and King Sety's image would come to light before her eyes, transmuting out of the ether, the way a star suddenly becomes visible in a pale sky. Alas, her acuity was short-lived; some days she couldn't see him at all, despite his obvious presence and desperate pleas, the blinkers descending over her eyes.

Things were getting frightfully muddled, Sety realised, and he decided to take his concerns to Isis, known for her wisdom and tolerant nature.

He prostrated himself before the golden goddess, who motioned him to stand, embarrassed by the Pharaoh's excessive reverence. She was a kind and loving goddess and she wanted people to feel comfortable in her presence, like children playing in a beautiful garden where they could let themselves run free.

Sety sat down on a plump cushion with his legs crossed, sipping pomegranate wine and opening his heart to Isis. "It is time she learned her true identity. I'm afraid she'll never reach Amenti if she doesn't understand her past. The journey to the Afterlife starts with self-knowledge." It was written in the temple walls: *Know thyself.* The priests had taught people this simple message for thousands of years; they had recorded their philosophy of self-knowledge in the Wisdom Texts and artisans had carved these aphorisms on the shrines and tombs.

"Sometimes the truth is best untold." Isis studied the Pharaoh's face and saw how he suffered over this woman, his ancient soul-mate trapped in a mortal body, her vision tempered by human boundaries and her mind prone to mundane thinking.

"I see how it pains you, Nisou, and you are right—it is time this woman known as Dorothy discovered her past identity—that her name was once Bentreshy, and she was loved by a great Pharaoh... but what about the huge scandal that ensued—shaking the Temple to its foundations...how can you tell her this dreadful tale? Where to begin...do not burden her with too much, as the shock may unravel her and you could lose her forever," the goddess warned him. The spirits in the Afterworld had a precarious relationship with the human realm. People on earth existed in a material maze, driven by their senses and desires, their actions determined by corporal stimuli and emotional responses to others (alas, their relationships were often unsuitable). People today had little connection with the spirit world and most had forgotten it even existed.

"We must keep the channels open," Isis insisted. Long ago there had been an open border between Amenti and Earth, but times had changed. Less tolerant religions had sprung up in the last two millennia and things had become difficult. The experience of the Divine had been replaced with fear and ignorance, and people were prevented from reaching the old gods. It was a struggle for Sety to visit planet Earth in these times; it was like visiting a foreign country ruled by a dictator, with inaccessible border crossings. Only there was no single ruler to blame—people were ruled by something less tangible: mundane thinking, bureaucracy and dogma. Their world no longer encouraged astral travel or communing with animal-headed gods.

Do not burden her with too much. King Sety spun the warning round his tongue, his head whizzing like an angry bee. How he resented the Council, with their watchful eyes, spying on him like tyrannical policemen. How supercilious they were—how misguided! They said they couldn't risk losing Harp of Joy to the Red Land, as the Pharaoh would no doubt follow her, straight into the entrails of hell. They had to keep her hidden, protect her from the desert demons. But King Sety wouldn't let it rest, he had to keep searching, waiting around for three thousand years...he was no ordinary lover, his obsession was of epic proportions, like his colossal temples and finely crafted statues of the gods.

The great sages had taught him the truth must be told, to uphold the Justice of Ma'at. *Truth is sent by God...*

"Those who sail with a lie will find no berth, and their boat will not tie up in port," he recalled this proverb from his childhood—from the *Tales of the Oases* his mother used to read to him, the fables created by the desert nomads who followed the stars in search of enlightenment. Sety would keep searching like the ancient nomads, knowing that eternity was a million grains of sand, a billion stars piercing a boundless sky. *Righteousness appears in the heart of the Divine Light.*

If only the Council would leave him in peace. Why couldn't they understand? He would never stop visiting his true love, he'd never abide by their rules. He'd rather be banished to the bowels of the

Underworld—try his luck against Ammit, Devourer of Souls, Beast of Destiny.

But Isis wouldn't hear of it—King Sety one of the damned, a member of the Red Land—she'd never let it happen. Yes, he may wade through the Lake of Fire, but she expected him to brush off the sparks and find his way to the Field of Reeds, to live with Osiris like all great Pharaohs.

"Think of the consequences, Sety." Isis had a duty to caution him, "If you stay in the Lake of Fire you will become a shapeless being, a nonentity drifting in the waters of chaos, with no chance of rebirth or eternal life. You would be turning your back on Ma'at's cosmic order and your entire world could turn to chaos."

Sety buried his face in the cushion to stifle his anguish, within the silk folds he released a strangled scream.

Isis saw the enormity of the Pharaoh's rebellion. But it would be far worse if Sety were taken by the demons, where his anguish would fester and he would have time to devise ingenious ways of destroying the Divine Council. The goddess knew what his namesake was capable of, and the Pharaoh would no doubt call on the evil powers of Seth, who would seize the chance to wreak his revenge. Isis knew better than anyone Seth's penchant for destruction and it had taken all her powers to lay his malevolence to rest.

Isis laid this ominous future before the Council and applied every ounce of her eloquence in favour of Sety: to let the secret history be told and allow the ancient *Kas* to unite. In the end the Council was moved by her wisdom and decided to be tolerant in this matter. But they feared Sety was too emotionally involved to handle the situation, as he was governed by three thousand years of pent up feelings, and he was bound to get carried away. First, the woman must know about the past—and the revelations must be conveyed by someone suitable; someone of a detached, rational disposition.

Isis knew just the person and approached King Sety with her proposal. "The story must be told by a scribe—someone who will proceed with care. We mustn't upset the woman's equilibrium and tip her into despair. There was an unfortunate episode in her life when she was committed to an asylum—we cannot risk that happening again. I've seen how terrified some people can be of spirits; such encounters can lead to mental breakdowns, the poor souls fearful of their own shadows." Isis affirmed there must be balance in all things—Sety knew this was her gift to the universe, as a disciple of Ma'at. Whenever there was fear, suffering, a grain of ill doing in the world, then the cosmos was pushed further out of balance. She looked at the world with sadness—the planet was out of shape, like a shrunken head; she feared a vile war was looming and many millions would die. The Laws of Ma'at were being ignored and planet earth was tipped towards despair. But it wasn't too late or irreversible, Isis knew. People could be made to see again, guided by the symbols on the temple walls, the wisdom found in *The Pyramid Texts*, *The Book of the Dead*, and *The Story of Sinuhe*... For the ancient ways lay dormant within people, waiting to be restored to life. The gods had no real influence without the power of belief; they needed people to believe in them in order to give them form, animate their existence. She remembered the days of the priestesses, Bentreshy singing and dancing in the Temple. Isis missed her melodic voice, her songs drifting round the pillars, as if emanating from inside the stone. It was a shame she'd gone into hiding—but Isis didn't blame the poor child. She'd been treated abominably; the whole affair had been completely mishandled. It was time to make amends, Isis felt, and it was up to her to set things right.

"I have found a suitable scribe," she told King Sety, "he may be a little slow, some would say dim-witted, but he can tell a story with a pure heart, as he is utterly devoid of malice. No demon would ever devour his heart, for its rare purity would choke the creature to death."

The Pharaoh was pleased to hear it. "Tell me, Lady Isis, who is this good scribe?"

Isis hesitated a moment before revealing his identity. "His name is Hor-ra."

King Sety burst into laughter, "You don't mean that old scribe who falls asleep in his dinner and never remembers what day it is! You're right about his absent-mindedness," Sety guffawed, imagining the farcical scene, the scribe creating a monumental muddle. But when he realised the goddess was serious about her choice of messenger, he tried to conceal his ridicule, "I'm sure the scribe will overcome his shortcomings for such an important task—and his purity of heart will give him strength." *As long as he can stay awake*, Sety muttered under his breath.

"Well then, it's settled. The scribe Hor-ra will tell Dorothy about her past—and we will have to deal with the consequences—let's hope the damage will be minimal." Isis kissed the Pharaoh on the cheek, sealing her divine approval and floated off to the turquoise pond for a swim, while the lute players made beautiful music under the sycamore tree.

King Sety met Hor-ra under a leafy canopy, where he liked to sit and pass the time. He remembered the scribe from his father's court—he was an old man then and died when Sety was still a child. He looked much the same today, with his wrinkled old face, bulbous nose and weepy eyes that struggled to stay open. Why he chose to live as an old man when he could exist in any form, Sety wondered. Perhaps he liked the freedom from responsibility, the reverence granted to the aged, although Sety saw no signs of greatness in the scribe's demeanour: he seemed rather confused, lost in a muddled sense of rapture. He spent the day sitting in a rickety old chair listening to the children singing, and remembering the great tales he'd once written. The occasional lonely child would sit by his feet and listen to his literary ramblings about the festivals, the lives of the pharaohs, who wished to emulate the Immortal Ones, like Sety and his precocious son Rameses.

The scribe seemed rather insulted by his new assignment and King Sety began to feel like an unwelcome guest. "I wish to enjoy my old age in peace. I haven't the strength to interfere in the affairs of men—they are an arrogant lot and they think they know better than the scribes," Hor-ra closed his eyes and grumbled to himself. But Sety detected a tremor in one eye like a clam straining to open, and he realised the man was bluffing. The scribe was desperate to prove that a doddery old man could save the day; his vanity would get the better of him.

"Isis is counting on you—we need your help. You are the only one who can be trusted in this matter," Sety cringed with indignation, having to plead with this insufferable old fool. "But if you think you are past it—lack the strength, I'm sure the goddess will understand."

The old man peered through a slit of light, his left eyelid quivering like a feather; the scribe may feign indifference, but Sety noticed a glint of triumph in his veiled eyes. "I suppose it is my moral duty to offer my services. And if it will please Our Lady Isis, then how can I refuse?"

^^^^^   ^^^^^   ^^^^^

When Imam returned from work he found the house in a frightful mess and the baby asleep on the floor, his face buried in the cat's belly. Imam glanced at the cluttered countertop: she hadn't cooked supper again; there were no tantalising smells wafting from the stove, in fact the oven was quite cold.

How could Dorothy tell him she had spent a fascinating afternoon with the Pharaoh, discussing eternity—and how she must search for her destiny on slabs of stone in the desert? "He already thinks I'm a little mad, but with this revelation he'd think I'd gone completely batty!"

Imam was a kind husband and she couldn't fault him on his decency: he was what you would call a good provider and he always came home in time for dinner. The problem was the dinner was never on time. Dorothy would rush around at the last minute, and when Imam walked through the door she'd say, "Hello darling—is it that time already?—and I haven't even started peeling the potatoes—now where did I put that recipe Zenna gave me?"

For a moment Dorothy would step out of herself and could see their marriage as a comic farce. Seeing this disorganised woman dashing round the kitchen, throwing ingredients into a huge pot, indiscriminately stirring it all together, the culinary outcome left to chance. Occasionally she would produce an unintentional gastronomic wonder, or an inedible disaster, depending on the forces at work. And the man: how miserable he looked! Drawing his fork to his lips with a wince, as if each mouthful gave him a nasty sting on the tongue. He was not surprised to find a toothpick or a long piece of string in his dinner; some unexpected object used to bind the concoction together, although he knew not why, as the meals were usually shapeless. How discordant this couple were: painfully incongruous, as if existing in different timeframes, out of step with one another's very existence. If only Imam could step back, she wished, and see how absurd their lives were—what with Dorothy trying to cook Egyptian meals—so awful they'd kill the Pharaoh's food taster—and Imam, sweating in his smart suit from Oxford Street, as half a cup of chillies had been added to his dinner in a burning fit of creativity, a sudden deviation from Zenna's trusted recipe.

But alas, Imam couldn't step aside and see the comedy, nor the slapstick moments that made her howl with laughter. He didn't see her comic flare. He was too busy choking on hot string, desperately trying to loosen his tie. His face breaking into a chilli-red rash, eyes bulging like a dying ram. Dorothy could see the red string dangling from her husband's mouth, his tongue distended over his bottom lip.

"Hold still," Dorothy ordered her husband, leaning over his swollen face. She got hold of the string and inserted her fingers in his mouth and he yielded himself to this suddenly capable woman. He let his mouth go limp and let his fear dissolve into her eyes. She has beautiful eyes, he thought, the way they caught the light they looked like polished turquoise, and their intense gaze exuded a white heat, burning through the fabric of things. He had to admit she sometimes frightened him, with her peculiar expressions and faraway eyes, as if she had vacated her body. She had the ability to shift in and out of reality, change direction without appearing to move.

"Silly me for leaving that string in the pot—I thought I'd fished it all out." Dorothy pulled a long piece of string out of Imam's throat, and he felt his lungs burn with heat.

Dorothy handed him a glass of water. "I'm not trying to kill you darling, honest," she laughed, kissing him on the forehead, "although my cooking may tell you otherwise!"

"Just promise me you won't put any more string in the dinner, or bits of wood or metal wires—they are simply indigestible and I cannot stomach them."

Dorothy heard the desperation in his voice. "Of course I won't, Imam. I don't know how the wire got in there—the butcher must have bound the chicken with it. I'm awfully sorry—you must think I'm a dreadful wife." She suddenly felt sorry for him. He was a practical, conventional man and he just wanted a simple life. He had no time for spirits or flights of fancy, or Pharaohs in search of lost love. He just wanted a wife who could at least cook a decent dinner. The fact that his wife could discuss politics and the importance of education didn't seem so appealing on an empty stomach. And the baby was crying on the floor, writhing like a startled jellyfish. He was obviously hungry and needed his nappy changing, judging by the smell. Imam gave a sigh, "I will ask Zenna if she can stay and cook the evening meal from now on." He had to do something: they would fall seriously ill living on Dorothy's cooking, and the baby would grow up deformed.

Despite feeling like a domestic disaster, Dorothy realised there were some advantages to having someone else cook the supper, like being able to spend more time at the Cairo Museum.

After lunch she dressed Sety in his yellow smock and set off for the Museum, enjoying the carriage ride through town, gazing at the French ladies in their outlandish Parisian fashions, being upstaged by a succession of braying mules and wailing women dressed in black robes, drowning the city with their haunting lamentations. As the bus crossed the Khedive Ismail Bridge, the Nile spread out towards the sea, it looked passive in its blue robe, as if fast asleep. Today the river had an eerie calmness, other days the currents rushed with a sense of urgency, as if running from an enemy. Some days the river looked bright purple, then jet black; she'd seen it in the midday sun appear white as snow, the surface glistening with a sheet of ice. Dorothy disembarked on the Corniche el Nile and walked the rest of the way to the Museum, breathing in the warm air, which filled her senses with the taste of molasses, thick syrupy air that stuck to your lungs and made it difficult to breathe. The sky was intensely blue, like a holiday poster that had been touched up to seduce the tourists. She would never grow tired of these skies, and they were always a revelation to her, even now, after a year and a half of unfettered blue horizons. The blue skies reminded her of unexplored territory, her own fallow potential, the galaxies she had yet to explore, if only she could get out of the house more; if only she had the chance to visit the ancient sites, not as a tourist, but as a woman of scholarship, an archaeologist perhaps, or a priestess as in days gone by. She was dreaming again. She would have to be content with the bountiful treasures of the Museum, and at night she would dream of these ancient artefacts and see them in their original context, amongst the pillars and secret chambers of the temples, where they shone through the eyes of the initiated.

She stepped inside the great hall of the Cairo Museum and held her breath for a moment, her eyes drawn to the statues in the corner, their stony personas towering over her and reviving old memories, like people she'd met at a party but couldn't remember where. She could feel Baby Sety's warm breath on her neck, his body moulded round her belly. He was a contented baby, she thought, an amenable soul who happily followed his mother round the Museum or the market, tied to her front in the African style. When he fell asleep Dorothy

107

would unravel the long scarf and lay him on the floor, snoozing at the foot of an illustrious scribe, while she went in search of enigmatic hieroglyphs to decipher, filling her sketchbook with statues and stelae from the Old Kingdom. She drew the delicate features of Ptah, careful with the oval lines that formed his eyes, letting her wrist relax in order to capture the softness in his gaze. Her pencil barely touched the paper, the delicate image emerging with a life-like quality, the skin malleable and the lips about the break into a smile.

Ahmed, one of the guards, offered to keep an eye on Sety, "You go see the Pharaohs, Sayyida Meguid, Baby Sety he be fine with me, I give him sugar cane to suck if he wake up — but he sleep like the dead."

"Thank you, Ahmed. Sety has taken a shine to you — and he certainly loves your sugar cane — he chews it like a real fellah. I'll be in the mummy room if you need me."

Ahmed watched over the child like a guardian of the Underworld, thought Dorothy. She bolted up the steps to the top floor to see His Majesty, who lay sleeping in the dimmed room, his 3000 year old face staring into infinity. His image shocked her, even after her countless visits — she felt he might rise from his sleep at any moment and shed his aged disguise.

His skin was like an old book of verse, the rough hide protecting the immortal substance within. The surface skin was dried up and warped with time, its very existence defying the laws of nature. Dorothy squatted next to the brown body, drawing her face close to the mummy, her breath inhaling the musty smell of the dead. Fixing her gaze on King Sety's face, she began to see beyond the parched exterior, and there she saw something all together different, as though staring into the distance and seeing a clearing in the mist, the shapes appearing out of the mountains. She felt herself being drawn under the surface, past the organic plane to the amorphous core. Would he speak to her here — surrounded by exhumed mummies, guards and brash lights? This wasn't what King Sety had in mind, all those years ago when he wanted to live for eternity — to end up in some dusty collection, a freak show in the annals of time. What did it all mean, this preserving the physical body? Dorothy wondered. Once the *Ka* was set free it could wander at will, materialising into any form. Perhaps mummification was more for the living: to remind us that the dead once roamed the earth and should never be forgotten.

Staring into the mummy's familiar face, she remembered the first time he'd appeared to her eighteen years ago; his shrunken face should have terrified her, but she'd felt no fear. She had stared into his deep eyes and had seen the young man within, an invincible being, beyond the boundaries of death.

The Pharaoh's voice came through her head like an echo in a tunnel. *"I will visit you tonight. Go home and make your husband a nice supper—I have no grievance with him. Go to sleep on the balcony, and when the half crescent moon sits on the tree like a fat scribe, I will pay you a visit."*

Dorothy was baffled by this request, "Your Majesty must know I am an awful cook—but I'll do my best."

Dorothy waited for another message from King Sety, but when none came she decided to head home and prepare herself for this evening and her royal visitor. Dorothy drifted down the steps, passing the granite statues of pharaohs, royal wives, children, scribes and viziers; the gods and goddesses they most revered. Dorothy stood outside the Museum squinting in the brightness, the late sun burning her eyes. She pulled her hat over her forehead and looked around the courtyard with the huge statues. She loved this Museum, home to thousands of ancient artefacts and treasures from the tombs and temples. It was like a giant burial chamber housing the sacred relics within their dense walls, protecting them from tomb robbers and guarding them for eternity. Of course she'd much prefer the treasures to remain in their original locations, buried in the ground with their immortal owners. But there was an unfortunate side to human nature that was driven by greed and power. There were people who didn't care about honouring the dead, or the Laws of Ma'at, and were even willing to risk their own salvation for a few gold trinkets. Were archaeologists any different? she wondered. They plundered the resting places of the pharaohs and nobles, laying them bare for all to see, the tourists flashing their cameras, the whistle stop tours and the hordes of curio seekers, poking their sunburned noses into the sacred realms of the Underworld, and leaving their pistachio shells as tasteless offerings. It was either the tomb robbers or the archaeologists—and the archaeologists were the lesser of the two evils, Dorothy believed, despite the unsavoury element of mummy-seeking that had tainted the field. A man was shouting by the entrance, there's one of them now, she thought, making a spectacle of himself. "Come this way, folks, you've got to see the fiendish mummies—they still have their toenails intact!"

Dorothy heard anther man shouting and turned to give him a piece of her mind. Then she realised it was Ahmed and he was waving a cotton bundle in his arms, crying, "Madame Meguid! You forget Baby Sety! He eat all my sugar cane, he cry for more food! Oh Madame Meguid, you not leave poor Baby Sety in the Museum!"

Her face flushed with shame, "Oh, Ahmed, you must think I'm a terrible mother. I was so absorbed in the past that I ...I am so absent-minded sometimes, a right rattle-brain." Dorothy took her baby from Ahmed's arms and made soft cooing noises, reassuring him with maternal love. Sety was howling like a jackal and Dorothy fumbled through her bag, desperately searching for his bottle. She stuck the bottle in the baby's mouth and sighed with relief as he suckled in contented silence.

"He was just hungry—I missed his two o'clock feeding. I was in the middle of a sketch."

Ahmed sensed her embarrassment, stroking the child's head, "You never go home without him—you always come back." That's true, she comforted herself, she'd never actually left him at the Museum and gone home without him. However, once she'd gone as far as the main gates before returning in a panic.

"Don't worry, Madame Meguid. You do many important things. Your head full of information. I see you in the Museum, making drawings and they look so real. I look after Baby Sety—you don't worry about him," Ahmed reassured her. "I watch Baby Sety. My head not full of information like you. I'm good at watching things—is my job." Whether they were ancient artefacts or babies, it was all the same to him—he would keep a watchful eye out and make sure they came to no harm.

"*Mut shukran, anta lateef*—thank you, Ahmed, you're a very kind man. *Ashufak ba'dayn*—see you again soon." Dorothy wrapped Sety in the scarf and tied it round her shoulder. Then she strapped the child to her chest, his sweet saliva dripping down his chin, sugarcane icing his lips. Sety lapsed into a deep sleep as his mother walked along the road to the Nile, a faint trace of sugar and milk drying in the corner of his mouth. He was such a cooperative baby, the perfect sort to be an Egyptologist's progeny, with his easygoing temperament and amenable nature. All she had to do was remember to feed and change

110

him, and he was good as gold. How she longed to work again—if only she could get a job on an archaeological dig as a draughtswoman, or even a gopher digging in the desert. But Imam wouldn't hear of her working on digs. "Why don't you get a job in the tourist department? They could do with someone like you to encourage British visitors. It would certainly help the economy." The tourists had been scared off by the recent demonstrations and fear of revolution. Imam thought she should get a job in Cairo where it was safer for her health. But Dorothy disagreed, "I think it's a lot safer out in the desert, where people live close to nature and the air is clean. There's little talk of revolution out there—people live the way their ancestors have done for thousands of years." But Dorothy knew she couldn't change her husband's mind. He was a city man and he thought a proper job consisted of working indoors, either in a government office or a school.

Later that evening Dorothy tried her best to make a decent meal, and carefully prepared *tagen firakh*: an Egyptian chicken casserole. She popped the vegetables, rice and chicken into the oven and went to read on the balcony. Sety lay contentedly on a cushion, making happy gurgling noises and sucking on his blanket. If only Imam were quite so accommodating.

What with the visitations, her obsession with ancient Egypt and her poor domestic skills, Imam was beginning to realise he'd married the wrong woman. His wife took little interest in his career and most of the time she had her nose in a book on Egyptology, or was copying out endless pages of hieroglyphics. Just the other night he'd found some strange writing in a language he didn't recognise. "What does this mean, Dorothy?" He needed a rational explanation, he was anxious for something to make sense. But Dorothy could offer him no such reassurance, "I don't really know what it means. It's just something I wrote while I was asleep—I don't remember doing it." She examined the pages with a puzzled look, wrinkling her brow in amazement, turning the pages upside down and sideways, desperately trying to understand the writing which was supposedly done in her own hand.

"I can't make head or tail of it, Imam. I must have been dreaming—they're just meaningless scribbles. They're nothing to worry about. The supper will be ready soon—I've made tagen." Dorothy leaped up and made her way to the kitchen, anxious to end this awkward conversation and return to the domestic realm where Imam felt more comfortable.

Nothing to worry about, Imam reminded himself. But the strange writing did disturb him, and the characters played on his mind. He gazed at the pages and felt anger well in his heart. He didn't understand the inscriptions, no matter how long he stared at them, he couldn't unlock their meaning. How they mocked his limited understanding of things; he felt they revealed a hidden world, an inaccessible world that was forbidden to him. They reminded him of how far removed he was from his wife; she behaved in a way he didn't understand, and like the illegible scrawls, he could not make sense of her.

"Oh blast and damnation! I've burned the tagen. I've left it on the high setting." Dorothy threw the lid on the countertop, the casserole billowing steam and smoke. "I think it's only the top bit that's burned—I'll try and scrape it off, I can pick out the black bits."

Imam shook his head in dismay. Couldn't this woman ever cook a meal without burning it? Everything she made tasted of charcoal. The foul stench followed him round for days and he feared his taste buds would never recover.

That night Dorothy lay in bed unable to sleep, listening to the sound of Imam's laboured breathing, his sporadic inhalations that included an occasional snore. As she lay awake, she wondered if the Pharaoh would visit her tonight as planned, and she played the message over in her head. *"When the half crescent moon sits in the tree like a fat scribe."* He had something important to tell her, she was sure if it, and spotting a sliver of moonlight through the curtains she flung herself out of bed, a quiver of excitement rising in her belly, shaking her brain out of sleep.

King Sety was sitting on the balcony, his long blue cape draped over his feet, his crown casually thrown on the floor. He squatted on the rustic stool like a shoeshine boy, and the comical image made her smile, as he looked rather ungainly for one so noble. Dorothy sat on a chair beside him and for a moment they savoured the intensity of their feelings, the ancient memories forged in the desert sand, their love emerging from the wilderness, unfolding in the rock and rubble. Sety held his breath and began to tremble, seeing her eyes in the moonlight, blazing like two shooting stars and piercing a hole in his armour. He'd known these eyes for thousands of years and the memories came flooding back to him in a great surge of emotion: the countless inundations, the water drowning the fields, the dog stars rising in the desert sky, the equinoxes, feasts and famines, the parched land and the waterlogged pastures, the people sailing by in makeshift rafts, the cattle staring in dumbfounded silence, sinking to their knees in Nile sludge. Her eyes, forged out of the gems hidden in the rock, pulled from the rock by the rush of water. His Harp of Joy reflected all that was dear to him: she was the mortal world he remembered with such delight, and the invisible realm of his deepest dreams, the kingdom of his imagination, where his *Ka* existed in boundless bliss.

Dorothy began to awaken, her pores tingling, flesh crawling, as though changing into a new form. She felt lighter, as though discarding a heavy coat and feeling the fresh air on her skin. She was an adolescent girl again; she started to laugh, her exuberance and high spirits plunging like a waterfall over a cliff. She wasn't afraid of falling; she would float over the rapids and end up in a gentle pool below, full of lotus flowers and wading birds. King Sety emerged from the dark water; he ignited her heart with fire, breathed new life into her lungs, a primeval creature leading her to a deeper world.

King Sety had come to reveal the past, she could read the stories in his face, like ink on papyrus, his features lined with words she struggled to decipher. He was bursting with stories, bursting to tell their secrets, as though he'd read an arcane book, outlawed by the authorities.

"I wish I could tell you myself, Lotus Flower, but the task has been given to someone better equipped: an illustrious scribe, a noted historian and raconteur from my father's Kingdom. He is a little senile, but he comes highly recommended. He will reveal your true identity and tell you about your life in Abydos." Sety kissed her on the forehead and retreated into the shadows. Dorothy could see tears in his eyes, "What's the matter, my love?" She wanted to reach out and comfort him, but he backed away from her until he was hidden in darkness.

"Go back to sleep, my flower," the voice rung from the shadows, "and when you have discovered the truth about yourself, then I will visit you again."

She rushed over to the dark space concealing the Pharaoh, but he had vanished, leaving only a faint odour of sandalwood oil. Dorothy stood in the vacant space for a moment, absorbing the Pharaoh's apparition through her pores, shivering on the empty balcony. She felt alone, slightly dejected, staring into the night sky; the stars seemed infinite and out of reach to her. Her emotions twisted like sinews, buckling under the strain; he had abandoned her again.

I'm being too hard on him—I shouldn't blame him, she told herself, he isn't mortal anymore—he no longer inhabits the earthly plane and cannot easily enter its unbending dimension. How precarious it was, this divide between the invisible world and our own, and how difficult it was to navigate from one realm to another, and virtually impossible to predict travel times and arrivals. Quite shaken by his visit, Dorothy began straightening the sitting room, smoothing out the creases in the cushions, trying to settle her nerves with orderly strokes. She felt suddenly altered, taken to a place of great beauty—enriched by the experience, and yet she sensed herself unravel, like a jumper caught in the briars. How could she feel both enhanced and undone? Perhaps it had to do with the way King Sety perceived her, seeing the world through a different lens—a wider, deeper dimension. He saw her as an ageless being he'd loved for millennia, and through his imaginative rendering of her she began to transform into this enchanting creature, who had the power to captivate a Pharaoh's heart and mind. He saw through to her core, her *Akh;* her potential for greatness, and in his presence Dorothy saw herself through his immortal mirror, filtered through the eyes of the divine, where she appeared as a celestial being. And then she saw herself as Dorothy in a dressing gown and slippers, and the vision began to unravel.

She crawled into bed and tried to fall asleep, listening to Imam's snoring followed by the occasional smothered silence, when he appeared to have stopped breathing. Despite the erratic patterns, Dorothy drifted into a deep sleep, unaware of the strange noises she was making, or that she was kicking her legs as if swimming in a pool, rubbing her arms in an attempt to wash herself. Nor was she aware that Imam was watching her in amazement, having been awakened by several sharp kicks and the odd flailing arm. He awoke to find his wife sitting bolt upright, seemingly in a trance, mumbling strange words which sounded like a prayer, although not like any he'd read in the Koran. Then Dorothy slipped out of bed and floated over to the desk, with a lightness of touch he'd never seen before, as his wife was not known for her dainty footsteps. She was generally sure-footed and walked with the confidence of a man, yet she was quite feminine. She had always puzzled him, Imam admitted, the way she single-mindedly clung to her own ideas and believed in the power of ancient Egypt.

A man dressed as a scribe appeared in Dorothy's dreams and motioned to her to get out of bed. He wore a simple tunic and his torso was bare, save for a large collar decorated with reed-shaped amulets, forged in lapis lazuli to draw the attention of Thoth, patron of writing. He seemed anxious to get on with the job, as if he had better things to do. The scribe poked her with his reed pen and tickled her nose with the fibrous quills. "My name is Hor-ra and I have been appointed to tell you about the past," he stated officiously, expecting Dorothy to follow him to the dressing table. As he pulled out the chair he stifled a series of yawns and covered his shrivelled mouth with his hand. He seemed rather put out by the whole affair, as if it were an imposition—a strange attitude for an immortal scribe, she considered. Perhaps he'd fallen from grace—it was a long fall from Amenti…

When Dorothy was sitting comfortably, the scribe placed his hand on her head and concentrated with all his might, towering over her in silence. "Write this down," he told her, and Dorothy picked up the pen and began copying the dictations: *I was born in a little village by the river, a couple of miles from the temple, and yet I didn't know it existed until I was three years old, when my mother died and I was sent to live there…*

Imam watched his wife writing with a sense of urgency, words flowing like spilt water. He crept alongside her and caught a glimpse of her face, only to discover she was fast asleep, her eyes rolling like white marbles and her lips quivering with fragmented words. Dorothy wrote with great speed, her pen moving from right to left across the page in random streaks. The writing looked like hieroglyphics, Imam noticed, but it could be anything—hieratic, Aramaic of some sort— or maybe she was just making it up. But it was astonishing to him the way she formed the symbols in sporadic spurts, as if waiting for dictation.

Imam stared in bewilderment as she remained asleep throughout, her breathing laboured and white eyes unblinking, like those crazy people in his grandmother's village, who were thought to be possessed by demons. He stumbled back into bed, although he couldn't get back to sleep. He found his wife's behaviour very unnerving and he tossed and turned thinking about her curious dictations; he wondered who this strange demon was, using his wife as a nocturnal secretary, filling the pages with unreadable words.

The next day at breakfast Imam asked his wife, "What were you writing last night? You were up half the night — I'm surprised you are so lively this morning." By comparison, Imam had dark bags under his eyes and hadn't slept all night.

Dorothy fidgeted nervously in her wicker chair. She examined the pages she'd supposedly written and didn't recognise her own hand writing, unable to make head or tail of the scribbles. "I don't remember writing this," she stared incredulously, "It comes to me in a dream — but I haven't the faintest idea what it means. I'm sorry to keep you up, habibi, maybe some camomile tea would help me sleep better." Dorothy tried to make light of the incident — Imam would be upset if he knew about the ghostly male scribe, as most husbands would be, she imagined.

Dorothy tried to prevent her nocturnal writing by hiding her notepads in the spare room, but every morning she found a new batch of symbols and squiggles on the desk — she must have gone from room to room, searching for paper and pen. If only she could remember more about it: Dorothy vaguely recalled a dream about an irritable scribe who nudged her in the ribs, but that was all she could remember. As the nights continued, she hoped her husband would grow accustomed to her writing exercises, but he always noticed her get out of bed and wander into the next room.

"I wish you would stop this outlandish behaviour, Dorothy," he pleaded with her, "it isn't normal to write through the night — and to write such gobbledygook, it makes no sense."

"I wish I could stop these strange dreams and this mad writing, but it just keeps happening to me. Perhaps if I start taking sleeping pills the problem will go away." Dorothy was willing to try anything, as she wasn't getting any sleep and her husband was growing increasingly frustrated by the whole affair. Imam mentioned the problem to his mother, who told him, "Women often behave oddly after they give birth, your wife is coming to terms with motherhood." After all, Dorothy wasn't responsible for her nocturnal behaviour — how could she control her actions whilst asleep? He should be more patient with her, give her time to adjust to her new life.

After several weeks of writing Dorothy had amassed a large pile of notes, and decided to take them to the Cairo Museum, hoping to decipher their meaning. She left the baby with Ahmed, slipped him a few piastres to pay for the sugarcane, and headed for the papyri department. Due to her work with Dr Budge, Dorothy was given access to the archives' office, where she could sift through the papyri undisturbed. She began comparing her writing with the ancient texts, scanning the lines for any similarities. "It obviously isn't hieroglyphics," she surmised, "It's too erratic and slapdash for that." Then Dorothy examined several scrolls of hieratic text and wondered if her squiggles could have been written in this informal style, used for everyday writing, like letters, shopping lists and quick memos. Most of her notes didn't resemble any of the handwriting—but she'd written the pages in great haste, mostly in the dark. She spent many days in the archives' office mulling over the ancient scrolls and copying down any repetitions in her writing, but she failed to interpret their meaning.

One day Dorothy was sifting through a pile of papyri when she found a page copied in what looked like a child's hand, probably from the Wisdom Texts, she gathered, as children often copied out these moral instructions, the earliest form of proverbs once taught in temple schools. A flicker of understanding awakened her foggy mind, lifting her out of obscurity and sharpening her senses. She dusted off the ancient script and narrowed her eyes as she followed the undulating lines. On second glance it seemed too neat for a child's hand, but lacked the confidence of an adult's pen. An adolescent's perhaps? Dorothy's brain leaped from word to word, stringing connections like a spider making a web. Placing the writing side by side she realised to her amazement they were written in the same style. "I think I've finally found something!" she cried out in delight, dancing round the room in a wave of relief.

The archivist popped his head above the filing cabinet, looking anxiously around. "Is everything all right, Madame?"

Dorothy tried to steady herself and cleared her throat, "Everything is fine, Aziz. I've found a rather intriguing papyrus, perhaps you could shed some light on it."

The old man shuffled over to the desk, a twinkle of interest returning to his pale eyes. His hands shook as he held the papyrus and he mumbled a few words to himself. "Hmm. You're right about the adolescent hand—probably a young woman. The text is a unique script, often used by pupils. They had to copy down pages of moral instructions and religious poems, much like young Islamic scholars today. This writing, possibly from a temple school, is a formal kind of hieratic, or a formless kind of hieroglyphics, you could say—that's why you had such trouble deciphering it. It's a rare find, Madame. I've only seen one other example, and that went to a private collection, I'm afraid. And to think it was here all the time. Where did you find it?"

"It was in this mound of papyri, stuffed in the bottom drawer." Dorothy wondered how many other literary gems lay waiting in the drawers of obscurity.

"Follow the path of the scribe; there is no greater vocation in life. Your pen will record the deeds of history and the wisdom of the gods. Be a scribe and you will open hearts and minds; you will live forever in the written word."

Aziz read out the sentence in ancient Egyptian, then Arabic, and finally translated it into English. Dorothy gasped in disbelief, "You mean you understand the text?"

The old man smiled triumphantly, enjoying this sudden moment of glory. "Of course. A German scholar was very interested in a similar piece of temple writing. He spent months deciphering the text and I helped him interpret many of the words. He was heartbroken when it was sold to the private collector. It was supposed to stay here in the Museum, but then the First World War broke out and it ended up in America. Who knows where it is now."

Dorothy wouldn't let that happen to this important scroll, even if she had to smuggle it out of the Museum for safekeeping.

"Would you translate the writing for me?" she asked the old man, "I'm doing some research about life in ancient temples."

"I'd be glad to help, Madame," Aziz adjusted his spectacles, the sheet trembling in his right hand. His voice rang out in a dramatic tone,

"If you gain command of your pen you will live a life of ease. Be a scribe! Your body will be fat with lack of exercise and too much praise. Everyone will admire your lavish words: the peasant, the

washerwoman, the carpenter and cobbler, even though they cannot read and have no time to do so. Oh be a scribe and they will build you a mansion in the marshes, where you will lose your mind in so many words!"

Dorothy had read some of the *Instructions*, but she'd never come across a text like this. "The part you read, it reminds me of a *Schoolbook Text* that Dr Budge translated in the British Museum, but the style is very different." She recalled Dr Budge saying such verses were copied down by young scribes, in order to teach them the importance of language, education and social refinement. They dated back to the Old Kingdom and students continued to learn them up to the Roman era—but under Christianity they were outlawed.

"Yes, this version is very different. More like satire—the writer is making fun of the tradition, the way she plays with the meaning, ridiculing the veneration for the scribe."

Aziz recited the text again and Dorothy jotted down his translations, enchanted by his sudden transformation from old man to animated scholar; she remembered the scribe in her dreams who baffled her with cryptic words, and she was grateful to this modern day scribe who leaped from ancient symbols to Arabic, and then to English. She wrote from left to right, conscious that she was going in the opposite direction, as most early scripts flowed from right to left, or up and down, and she thought how dull the Western alphabet appeared, compared with the aesthetic forms of the ancient world.

Thanks to this forgotten scribe gathering dust in the crannies of the Museum, Dorothy learned to decipher the temple writing, and when she could understand the texts without the old man's assistance, she began the task of deciphering her own writing.

Dorothy spent the next few months deciphering her notebooks, searching for her past identity, and slowly she put the pieces back together, like Isis gathering the remains of Osiris. She waited until Imam had left for work and then she sat the child down to play with his building blocks. She watched Sety build a shaky pyramid, carefully placing the blocks with his little hands. We are both reconstructing the past, she noted, Sety with his pyramid, and me with my temple writing...restoring ancient memories, retrieving the pieces from the rubble. Dorothy had a sense she was gathering her own remains, picking through the parched desert, where her past had withered into dust.

119

My parents and I lived in a simple village, a couple of miles from the Temple. My mother's name was Nafrini, which meant earth, a fitting name as she lived closed to nature, and my father's name was Gahiji, which meant hunter. He was a soldier in the army of King Sety I in Abydos.

The local midwife warned my mother not to get pregnant because a kitten had died on her lap, a sure sign that she would die in childbirth, the midwife had told her. But my mother prayed to Taweret and asked her to reverse the bad omen. She asked the goddess to protect her from harm and left her daily offerings to win her favours. When she found herself pregnant she believed the evil had been averted, and she soon forgot about the midwife's ominous words.

My mother gave birth to me without any complications, and she named me Bentreshy, Harp of Joy, because I was a gift from Isis, who loved harp music. As soon as I was given the slap of life and inhaled my first breath, my mother said I started to sing, and I have been singing ever since.

Three years later my mother died of a fever. She was pregnant at the time, and had she lived I would have had a baby sister, but instead I lost both my mother and my sibling. My father couldn't cope with a young child and so he sent me to live in the Temple of Abydos...

Dorothy had to admit it was also a tremendous feeling, to finally know her past identity, to acknowledge the other self that had walked alongside her, whom she'd known very little about. And now this presence was written in black and white: Bentreshy, Harp of Joy.

The memories were like forgotten scrolls hidden in the desert; scraps of paper that had the power to uproot history, turn lies into truth.

The year was 1290 BC in the reign of Sety I, and the Passion Plays had just begun: the Temple was in a flurry of activity, the priests darting like cats in a sandstorm; the sculptors polishing their new statues, the painters adding the final colours to their bas reliefs in preparation for the Royal visit. In honour of Isis and the resurrection of Osiris, the royal palace was swarming with foreign dignitaries, emissaries and pilgrims come to celebrate the most important festival of the year. The King sat crownless in a scented garden, a simple tunic draped across his abdomen. His presence was concealed by a sycamore tree, which absorbed his royal aura in its dark sweeping leaves. A girl sat next to him, dressed in a light blue robe, her golden hair falling round her breasts. Her name was Bentreshy, Harp of Joy, a priestess of Isis who delighted the Temple with her glorious singing and votive dances.

The couple strolled under the floral archway, their heads brushing against the cascade of bougainvillea and jasmine. It was obvious the couple were in love, the way they looked at each other with misty eyes, their vision distorted with intense emotion. They saw a world more beautiful, with brighter colours and deeper textures; the glorious scent of flowers and trees, the rush of water, the chorus of birds, a vast channel of sensory splendour, opening a new dimension in their brains. How could you not fall in love in this bountiful garden? A fusion of natural beauty and human creativity; the essence of nature bursting from every angle, the temple murals, monuments and columns adorned with the finest carvings the world had ever seen. Isis and Osiris once loved each other in this landscape, their smiles, their laughter, their flesh and bones infused the earth with life; their deaths brought desolation and chaos, their resurrections brought hope and eternal life.

Wait—what happened next? Dorothy knew there was so much more to this tale ... she would have to wait for the scribe's next visit.

7. Death in Abydos
1290 BC

It was three months since the Passion Plays, and three months since her last menstrual cycle, Bentreshy noted. She went to see Kebi about her health concerns, as she often helped the village women with their moon cycles and pregnancies. Kebi was busy sieving liquids into glass phials; a cauldron of herbs bubbled on the hearth, filling the air with intoxicating aromas.

"So this is what you've been up to all this time—mixing magic potions and charming snakes, no wonder you've had no time to come to the Temple!" Bentreshy embraced her friend affectionately, feeling her slim frame beneath her robe: Kebi wasn't pregnant, she could tell (unlike most of the women in the village), her ochre sash snug around her waist. Kebi sensed her friend's thoughts concerning her fecundity, "Just because I know the fertility charms doesn't mean I have to use them—I can't afford to get pregnant this time of year, it's my busiest season, with all the women wanting herbs and medical advice—so I made sure I was protected: a little sponge dipped in vinegar works wonders. I administered quite a few at the festival," she laughed mischievously, "their husbands didn't even notice! When will they realise women don't want to have a child every year. I don't understand it—some women are desperate to have children and others say they have too many," Kebi shook her head, "The fertility festival is so much more than reproduction—it's also about the renewal of the mind and spirit."

Kebi suddenly stopped talking and looked at her friend intently: a beam of light illuminated her silhouette and Kebi noticed a slight swelling through her gossamer robe. "Oh, Bentreshy, don't tell me you're pregnant!...But you can't be—you've taken the vows."

Bentreshy's eyes flickered, exposing her secret joy, and then she burst into a flood of revelations. "We are deeply in love, our nights ruled by untamed passions, but Sety and I have been sensible—we always used protection. I wore the vinegar sponge, like the ones you make for the villagers. I must have conceived a child during the Ritual—it's all a blur to me now, as it occurred in a dream state, but at one point I awoke and drifted to the ceiling. I looked down on

122

a naked couple making love, their eyes full of tenderness and their bodies entwined in a spiral of passion. For a moment I recognised them as Isis and Osiris, but then the light changed and the curtain parted and I saw myself lying on the bed next to a man." Bentreshy paused to catch her breath and looked around to make sure no one else was listening, and then continued in a tremulous voice, "The man beside me was His Majesty! Osiris had become Sety! "

At that climactic moment the pot boiled over and the contents sizzled on the flames. Kebi leaped up in surprise, nearly dropping her phial on the floor.

"Do you understand the enormity of this conception? If what you say is true, you could be carrying the divine child of Isis and Osiris." Kebi sat down on the stool, her mind struggling with the complexity of the situation. "And if you think about things logically, the Pharaoh is the embodiment of Osiris on earth and you are a receptacle of Isis. You could be housing a miracle in your womb—the reincarnation of Horus!" Then Kebi suddenly went calm. "We must act responsibly— this is such a portentous event and we need support and guidance from the Adepts."

Bentreshy looked at her friend in disbelief. "I can't be nurturing the child of the Divine Couple—I am a simple girl from peasant ancestry." She rested her hand on her belly, as if protecting the child from what she was about to say. "They would hardly choose someone like me—I've been having an illicit affair with the Pharaoh, and I'm not of noble birth. Oh, I'm so confused by it all. I'll go and see Inhapi tomorrow—she'll know what to do."

"Pharaohs have often married priestesses in the past—so it's not unheard of—it creates a powerful alliance between court and temple," Kebi pointed out, "The priestesses of Abydos have been waiting for the rebirth of the divine: a saviour who will lead us out of darkness, like Horus several millennia ago. But I fear there are evil forces festering in the Temple and I don't know who we can trust— remember the chaos that was unleashed when Horus was born?"

Bentreshy shuddered at the thought. Seth, god of the Red Land, would be seething with rage if he knew about the child, and this time he would apply all his cunning to ensure the child was slain.

"Are you absolutely certain no one else knows?" Kebi questioned her friend, scanning the desert horizon beyond her garden, knowing the forces of Seth lurked behind the seemingly benign mounds of sand.

"I haven't told anyone else, I swear on the Knot of Isis. And I haven't suffered from morning sickness or missed a day of prayers, so no one would have cause to suspect. I didn't know myself until you confirmed it," Bentreshy assured her friend. She longed to tell Sety the news, but he was still in Thebes. He promised to return for the Harvest Festival in a few weeks' time and she hoped the Pharaoh would be overjoyed when he heard the news—and that he would see the child as a gift from Osiris, a blessing bestowed on all of Egypt. But what if he rejected her and the child—saw the whole affair as an embarrassment, one he wished to forget?

Kebi noticed her friend's anxiety, "Sety is an honourable man. He will do what's right. And it looks like the goddess is shielding you from harm; but all the same, we must be careful and amass the Guardians of Isis to protect you. In the meantime you should stay here with me until Teshen returns from work—he had to catch a snake at the carpenter's shop. Anyway, he knows a couple of soldiers and they'll see you safely home."

Bentreshy was grateful to have such a reliable friend—Kebi had the shrewdness of Seshet and the kindness of Hathor—and Bentreshy was certain her friend could outwit any malicious intent.

When Teshen returned from work he said he would round up two brawny soldiers, who played *senet* with him at the café. "I would trust these fellows with my life—you can tell a lot about a man when playing *senet*, how he places his chips and how he copes with bad luck—" Kebi interrupted her husband, "I'm sure Bentreshy is fascinated by your philosophy of *senet*, but it's time she got back to the Temple."

Teshen sensed the danger in his wife's voice and sprang into action: he rushed down to the café and whispered to one of the soldiers, then Bentreshy saw two men rise from their stools, their brown capes swinging from their shoulders.

Bentreshy kissed her friend goodbye and as they embraced she felt a chilling sense of foreboding, as if she'd never see her friend again. "I love you like a sister, you've always been the greatest friend to me," Bentreshy whispered, feeling a wave of sorrow sting her throat.

"Why all the melancholy—I promise you there's nothing to fear. I'm looking forward to being a God-Mother!"

Kebi watched her friend disappear into the night, the two soldiers by her side, and she couldn't suppress her feelings of foreboding. Bentreshy looked back at her friends sitting by the fire, engulfed in a nimbus of warmth; *if only I could hide away in their cosy domesticity, escape from my immense responsibility*...but everything will be all right when the Pharaoh returns, she consoled herself.

The soldiers left Bentreshy by the Temple gate and bowed graciously, the tall one whispering to her, "Goodnight, White Lady of Isis, say a prayer for me tonight—let me beat the general at *senet!*"

Bentreshy laughed at this comical request and opened the Gate of Isis with her knot-shaped key, then she scurried through the Temple grounds with a lighter step, enjoying the way the moonlight danced through the trees and the oranges glistened like copper orbs. The Temple grounds were bathed in ghostly silence, and she said a prayer to restrain her fear. *The Temple is a place of peace and Isis will protect me*, she repeated, quickening her pace to the House of Isis. Bentreshy tiptoed through the hall and into her room, careful not to wake Meryt. But Meryt was away in Memphis for a week, she remembered; *I am all alone here.*

She would go and see Inhapi first thing in the morning, she breathed into her pillow, inhaling the dreamy smell of lavender hidden in the linen folds.

Bentreshy awoke with a start: she'd slept in and missed her morning prayers! Why hadn't the attendants awoken her? "Silly girls, they'll get me into trouble," she moaned, splashing cold water on her face and sprinkling herself with jasmine oil. "That'll have to do, I'm afraid," she decided, rushing down the hall to Inhapi's Quarters, straightening her braids as she ran, and adjusting her turquoise collar.

To her surprise Inhapi wasn't at home, and the severe face of Priestess Woserit peered round the door. "What do you want, girl?" Woserit snapped, her eyes were red, as if she'd been to an all-night feast.

"I've come to see Priestess Inhapi—I have an urgent matter to discuss with her." Bentreshy stopped herself from revealing anything more, noticing the harsh corners of the woman's mouth trying to feign a smile—more like sucking on a lemon, thought Bentreshy, watching the woman's top lip concoct a grin. She seemed to change from severity to benevolence in the blink of an eye, like one of those lizards from the southern jungles.

"Inhapi will be delighted to see you, but she won't be back until midday. Sit down on the cushions and join me for a refreshment," she stroked Bentreshy's arm and poured her a glass of grape juice. "Now tell me what's troubling you, child," she said sweetly, evoking a sympathetic stance with all her efforts. Bentreshy stiffened, the sour grapes alerting her senses. "I must speak to Inhapi and no one else, it is a private matter."

Woserit raised her eyebrows in alarm, "The matter seems of great importance. I will see if Inhapi can be summoned immediately—she went home to her family yesterday on some urgent business, but as I said, she's due back by lunch time."

Bentreshy detected a flicker of fear in her belly; *it wasn't like Inhapi just to go off like that, without leaving word. But then I was over at Kebi's last night*, she considered, trying to assuage her mounting anxiety.

Woserit returned several minutes later looking jovial, her usual scowl softened with good humour. "You're in luck, Inhapi returned earlier than expected—apparently she's been in the Underground Library all morning, looking through the archives—something about a lost Book of Thoth. She has such stamina when it comes to old manuscripts—she'd be there all day if the servants didn't remind her to take lunch."

Bentreshy was pleased to hear the Priestess had been found, "I would like to see Inhapi immediately—this cannot wait."

"Well, I hate to drag her away from her studious revelry—you must go down and see her in the library. I believe you share a similar passion for old books."

"I love the old stories, if that's what you mean, but I am not as academic as Priestess Inhapi. I prefer to be outdoors, rather than confined to a stuffy library, especially an underground one, where the air is stale. I'm afraid I lack Inhapi's discipline."

Bentreshy wished she was meeting Inhapi in the garden instead of in this subterranean chamber. But she was anxious to see the Priestess—hopefully persuade her to go for a stroll in the garden. Bentreshy shuffled down the steep passageway to the Underground Library, her oil lamp flickering in the shadows. The tunnel narrowed

126

as she descended into the earth, passing scenes from the *Book of the Dead* as she stumbled along, the figures in the murals sinking into the Underworld. A strange way to decorate a passage to a library, she thought, fearing the tunnel would go on forever, her lamp growing fainter and the darkness threatening to swallow her. Then she finally came to an arched doorway with a crack of light by the floor and her spirits lifted above the gloom. She burst into the room and shouted, "Inhapi, you don't know how glad I am to see you. I was forced to sip grape juice with Woserit—what a grumpy old woman she is—although they say you're the same age, you'd never think it—" Bentreshy faltered, her eyes searching the room, suddenly aware the place was empty.

Inhapi!" she cried out, listening to the name echo through the columns and resound with a vacant drone. Then the door slammed behind her and her lamp went out, the room sealed in darkness. Her hands searched the stone surface, pushing against the impenetrable door. There must be a latch—it can't be locked, who would do such a thing? A wave of panic possessed her, like a fire burning her flesh, and for a moment she stood quite still, trying to separate reason from fear.

"Inhapi!" she called out, "the door has blown shut. I'm afraid it won't open—you'll need to light the lamp—" Then she heard a rumble of laughter in the distance; a vicious sort of laughter devoid of feeling, she thought, wishing it would cease. A light flickered in the back of the room, exposing the stone slabs, the unpainted columns. A figure stood before her: it was Master Amenkef in his long black cape.

"Where is Inhapi? I was told she was down here." Bentreshy glanced around the empty chamber; there was no sign of her mentor.

Amenkef nodded politely, his tight jaw concealing a grimace. "I thought you might be happy to see me, but I can tell you're only interested in seeing Inhapi. If only you could confide in me, child—I could make it easier for you. I am not here to punish you, Bentreshy. Just to learn the truth. It is paramount that you tell me everything. I can sway the others to be merciful—after all, it isn't your fault," Master Amenkef flashed his wily eyes, "But if you try and deceive me I will have no choice but to punish you—the Laws of Ma'at will demand it."

"I have done nothing wrong and I have nothing to confess. I am here to see Inhapi," she stated clearly, unnerving the priest once again with her composure. He knew the girl was praying to Isis, turning her terror over to the goddess and gaining relief from her fear. This fact unsettled Amenkef, and he called to the priest listening in the shadows. "Did you hear that, Master Kahotep? The girl says she has nothing to confess!"

The High Priest sniggered in the darkness, "And yet she is riddled with secrets—does she think we do not know about her clandestine affair?"

"Well, if you know my secrets then why must I confess?" Bentreshy overcame her fear, her indignation forcing her to speak.

Master Kahotep leaped out of the shadows, his tall frame towering with vengeance and his eyes white with rage. He dragged her towards a rectangular stone, her feet splashing through cold water.

"This is the tomb of Lord Osiris," he forced her to touch the stone. "Tell the truth before Osiris, or risk eternal damnation!"

She wondered if this was really the Lord's burial place—built on a stone island, Inhapi had told her, where the god rose from oblivion. It was hard to tell in the darkness, her mind clouded with fear. Then she saw the god's green face emerge from the stone shadows.

Do not tell them, my child . . . I will keep you safe. I will raise you up.

Raise me up—what does this mean—where am I going? She searched the Lord's malachite face, seeing the compassion in his eyes.

I won't tell them anything, she promised.

"Perhaps a night in the Confinement Chamber will make her more compliant. Take her away." Kahotep motioned to the guards who grabbed her by the arms and carried her out of the room.

Bentreshy felt their rough hands on her skin, pressing painfully into her bones, and they marched forward like soulless men, their unflinching eyes following the light in the tunnel, obeying the priest's command.

The journey through the tunnel seemed to take an eternity and Bentreshy lost all sense of time; they dragged her into the depths of the earth, twisting and turning so many times she had no idea which direction they were heading. She lost her footing several times and the men hauled her along the rubble, her feet scraping on the stones, the pain grinding through her ears. They finally halted by an arched doorway and she was thrown into a dimly lit cell, the air thick with dust, the stone walls secreting an air of indifference; she heard them bolt the door, their resolute footsteps marching away into silence. She watched the candle flicker in the chamber, the faint light clinging to the wall, fighting for its last breath against the encroaching darkness. The candle gave a final sigh of light before resigning its flame, and she cried out in anguish, the last remnant of hope sinking into the abyss. She'd never seen such pure darkness, and for a moment she stood stupefied, mesmerised by the sense of oblivion—as though being flung outside the world. The black hole consumed her mind and she stared into nothingness, unable to tell whether her eyes were open or closed. She tried to imagine the face of Isis, but there was nothing but a blank space, the heart of terror, and she feared that even the goddess was lost in this pitiless void. Bentreshy slumped to the floor, hugging her knees to her chest, rocking back and forth until she fell into a troubled state of sleep, and dreamed there were demons bouncing off the walls, and flying through the pit in dangerous sweeps, their twisted faces splitting into evil grins.

She opened her eyes and saw a malicious face towering over her, his nostrils flaring like angry bees, his flesh the colour of pond scum. The figure held a lamp to her face and she winced in pain, the white flashes of light stinging her eyes, like lashes from a whip.

Master Kahotep began to speak, "I hope the night in confinement has made you come to your senses. Are you ready to confess, my child?"

Bentreshy could smell the priest's sour breath as he bent over her. "Tell me who the father is." He rubbed her belly and her entrails recoiled, the foetus twisting in her womb.

"You want me to tell you who the father is—very well. On the night of the Fertility Feast I met a handsome boat builder from Byblos. I cannot remember the man's name. I confess I drank too much wine and lost my senses. I was caught up in the festive revelry, like everyone else that night. On such a night even a priestess can be swayed by the charms of a handsome stranger, and succumb to self-abandonment."

Master Kahotep sniggered at this confession. "You expect me to believe the father is a boat builder from Byblos?" he shook his head, "Oh no, my priestess. I think the father is somewhat more illustrious. Much more powerful indeed. A vizier, a judge, or a member of the Royal Family perhaps—a man of calibre, capable of inflaming the passions of a fair priestess." He stroked her cheek and she turned her head away in disgust. His face twisted into a perverse smile, "A prince or a king—now that is more becoming of a beautiful priestess—you'd spread your legs for a great man like that, wouldn't you, my pretty one—he'd get your virgin juices going!" Kahotep brushed his cold hands across her neck and slid his hands inside her robe, fondling her breasts with a lewd sense of pleasure. She struggled to push him away and he roughly squeezed her flesh. "What a pair of ripe peaches. I'll bet your royal lover had a delightful time with you!" He gave a callous laugh and pulled her robe open, his lascivious eyes feasting on her naked chest. He gave a licentious grunt, and she could see his groin bulging beneath his robe.

"Violate a priestess and you will be sentenced to death," Bentreshy found the courage to shout. The priest stiffened. Even this vile man knew about this sacred law, and the effect was like a cold shower. Just as he was straightening his robe, Master Amenkef entered the chamber with another priest.

The priests gathered in a circle, their robes drooping like broken wings. Bentreshy strained to hear their voices and caught someone asking, "So you're sure he's the father?"

"She hasn't confessed to anything but I'm sure it's him."

They caught a glimpse of Bentreshy staring at them and the priests stepped outside to finish their discussion in private, unaware of her exceptional hearing.

Bentreshy recognised Kahotep's hushed voice, "You know what this means if it is the Pharaoh's child and he decides to marry her. People will see the child as the reincarnation of Horus, the Holy Child of Isis and Osiris, and then the people would never rise against him."

"We'll have to get a confession from the girl—proof that the Pharaoh raped a priestess."

"The girl will never confess to that—she's the most obstinate pupil, never does as she's told." Amenkef informed the priests.

"Then we'll use whatever means necessary. With a bit of persuasion the truth will come pouring out of her—she'll be begging to confess,"

Kahotep's voice was cold and mechanical, like a metal blade cutting her skin.

Kahotep entered the chamber, the torchbearers illuminating his frame from behind, and she saw his face in a dome of light. The face was devoid of emotion or humanity, like a mask, she thought. Bentreshy was staring into a gaping hole, with eyes like splinters of stone. She tried to turn her mind to Isis, but the priest blocked her path with his sinister presence, and when she closed her eyes his black cape flapped in anger, subduing the light and filling her inner vision with fear and futility. She pushed through the dark matter, beyond the shadows to the world of dreams, where the doorway opened to the spirit realm. But the black mass was suffocating her under its terrible weight. Opening her eyes for a second, still remembering the radiance, the pathway to Isis; just a moment ago she'd resided in this warm place, a dome of light arched over her mind, the goddess protecting her from harm. She was alone now—expelled from the sanctuary; the emptiness in the room devoured her, drew her into its cold embrace.

Bentreshy detected a grazing sound like a bronze axe being dragged on the stone—the sound grew louder, piercing her ears with its metal shriek, sending shockwaves to her brain. Then she felt prongs poking her body, pricking her skin, the pain shooting to her nerve-endings. The agony rising in great obelisks, their sharp points piercing the sky; she cried out, her shrieks ringing through her head.

"Had enough, my child? Ready to confess your crime?" The voice sounded far away, as though filtered through a tunnel, but she recognised Kahotep's cruel tone, the mechanical sound of terror, remote and unfeeling, crawling though her nerve centre. They were trying to burrow into her flesh, thinking of the rabbits by the edge of the fields, digging their way underground. She felt like a warren; *I will offer them refuge from the world, they can hide inside my body, find a protective place away from the hunter.*

Bentreshy opened her eyes and saw Kahotep standing over her, a bloody pin in each hand, and he was breathing heavily, his shoulders heaving with exertion. What was the matter with him? His face looked pale, and she saw him retch, then he turned away and clenched his belly, holding his breakfast in place. He didn't have the stomach for this sort of thing, and still the girl hadn't confessed. He would have to be more brutal if he wanted her to talk—she had an unnatural ability to withstand pain. But he didn't want to spoil his next meal. He'd get the guards to take care of her, men who could get the job done without much fuss. Why should he make himself sick over the girl? Kahotep left the room and went to the bathhouse for a wash. After lunch he'd have his confession and could look forward to his afternoon nap, knowing that the Pharaoh's fall from grace was nigh.

Harp of Joy lay in the stillness; the silence was disturbing, like an augury anticipating a cataclysm. She examined her legs and noticed they were covered in small pinpricks, blood oozing from her skin like new shoots in the ground. She lifted her robe and found her torso was also covered in prick marks, the blood forming into tiny beads. The sight forced her into the depth of horror—this was only the beginning of her suffering—once those guards returned she would undergo unimaginable torture. Either that or she must denounce the Pharaoh—sign a confession that would see him ruined. What would they force her to say? That he had taken advantage of her—violated a priestess and left her pregnant?

Rubbing her bleeding arms against her robe she felt a solid lump buried inside her robe. What was it? she wondered; searching through the folds of linen she found a tiny phial tucked inside a pocket. She'd forgotten it was there, but it now seemed like a precious gem, rolling the alabaster phial round in her hand. Kebi had given it to her the last time they'd gone snake-hunting, reminding her, "One drop will work as an antidote against a snakebite and will save your life. But anymore will kill you dead."

Bentreshy struggled to open the lid with her trembling hands, her palms clammy with sweat. She pulled on the plug—not much time—the men were in the hallway, they'd finished their lunch and would be coming back soon. She finally opened the bottle and found a tiny obsidian blade attached to the cork, and made a slight incision inside her mouth. Her body shaking as she swallowed the liquid, wincing as it settled in her stomach, her *sekhem* resisting the force of death. Then she rubbed the rest of the liquid into her arms, the wounds absorbing the venom like healing ointment. She didn't want to die and yet she felt incredibly calm about the prospect, as if bracing herself before a cold bath, only to find the water was quite warm and scented with fragrant oils. Bentreshy closed her eyes and saw the cobra rearing above her, the snake coiling herself around her neck. "This may hurt a little, but then you will feel such peace, soon you will be in my immortal realm and no one can harm you," the snake told her, driving its fangs into the girl's soft flesh. *Oh human child, shed your mortal coil and follow me to the land of cobras. Where we drink divine poison and live forever!*

The men were coming down the passage now, their large frames resounding through the stone. She held her breath—wishing her breathing would stop and she could finally drift away from this world. She imagined herself as a cloud, floating over the hills, seeking the pure air above the peaks. Suicide was a crime against the *Ka*; she would have to atone for her misdeeds in the Afterlife. She trusted the Laws of Ma'at on Judgement Day would be kinder than the laws of men on earth.

The men pushed the door open with their beefy hands—their bovine nostrils flaring—they were great brutes with the strength of oxen, capable of savage cruelties. She saw them towering over her, and for a moment they seemed like statues; terrifying specimens yielding sticks and hungry for violence. She lay there in terror, watching the older man raise his cane in the air, trembling at the thought of the impending pain (remembering the fear of pain was almost worse than the actual thing), and she cried out as the cane struck her right foot. The guard continually struck both feet with his cane, the pain burning through her body, bringing the venom to life. Fear makes the poison race through the veins, she remembered, and then it grips the heart in a death lock. The poison mingled with the pain until she was seized by a great convulsion, her body twisting like a snake. A child floated past her with golden hair and spherical eyes, emitting sparks of light. "Good-bye, Mother. Do not mourn for me, I am going to be a star— look for me in the sky, my name is Sekhtey," he pointed to the yellow stars painted on the ceiling and in a flash he was gone, burning a hole through the stone.

Then there was no more pain, and she felt herself slither across the floor, a snake come to drink by the river; heat rising from her scaly skin, her body stretching into a tubular shape. Her skin was tearing at the seams, like a tall woman in a short dress, and she slid out of her old form and left it on the floor. She was transforming into her real self—a more flexible self capable of twisting out of her chains and slinking into the undergrowth unscathed.

She crawled up the ceiling and watched the men beating her body, the swear pouring into their empty eyes. And then they noticed the girl wasn't moving anymore and lay quite still. She couldn't be dead so soon—they'd only just started. Bentreshy watched the thugs shake her shoulders and the pink phial roll into a crease of fabric.

"She's dead," one of the men said in horror. The other man grabbed his arm, "We'll never get a confession out of her now—and you've ruined our chance of freedom. Now we'll never get back to Nubia."

"I've ruined it?—you were the one who wouldn't stop..." the men began to argue, and they were so consumed with anger that they failed to notice Kahotep and Amenkef enter the room.

Amenkef examined the girl's body: her skin was full of pinpricks and her back was bleeding where she'd been whipped; her feet bruised and swollen from the beatings.

"What have you done to the girl? You weren't supposed to torture her to death!" Amenkef turned on the two men; the magnitude of this crime was starting to hit him, fear rising in his intestines like typhoid. *If this gets out we are all doomed*, he began to panic, imagining the Pharaoh's wrath and how he'd blame them for the girl's murder. Even Kahotep looked uneasy and paced the room in an agitated state, clutching his hands and breathing heavily.

"Well, don't just stand there—take the body away and dispose of it," Kahotep motioned to the men, who were standing by the door in a senseless daze, their brutish faces splattered with blood. When they bent down to pick up the girl, a pink phial fell to the floor, their eyes drawn to the clinking sound of alabaster rolling on stone.

"What's this? Give it to me," Kahotep grabbed the phial from the guard's hand and held it to his nose. Master Amenkef had done a bit of snake charming in his time and he recognised the musky smell. "Snake venom, Master Kahotep—the girl must have taken a lethal dose of it." He breathed a sigh of relief—it wasn't murder after all, the girl had committed suicide to avoid a confession. She had sacrificed her life to save the Pharaoh. He couldn't help but admire her sense of honour, even though she'd made fools of them.

"Never mind how she died—the fact is the girl is dead. And without a signed confession from her we can't prove anything." A shadow fell over Kahotep's face, his shoulders sinking into frustration; his plan to denounce King Sety had been thwarted. The girl had ruined everything—and no one would rise against the Pharaoh—not unless he'd violated the Laws of Ma'at.

"It's no use sitting here in despair—we've got to devise a plan. I'm not going to be charged for this crime and I don't think you intend to be either," said Amenkef, his concise voice ringing with reason, his brisk tone awakening Kahotep from his despondent daze. He could always rely on Amenkef's practical nature, and despite being a bureaucrat, the man performed his duties with the utmost efficiency.

"So what is your brilliant plan, Master Amenkef—to bring the child back to life with one of your magic spells?" He couldn't resist mocking Amenkef, even though he was eager to hear his plan—it's just that the man could be so irritating.

Amenkef's face hardened, then settled into the cold stone; he hated being ridiculed by this brainless man—it was only through his cunning that he'd managed to rise in the ranks and align himself with powerful figures. Kahotep knew how to flatter and ingratiate himself to the higher ranking officials and it made Amenkef cringe with revulsion—that this perverse little man had become a High Priest! Amenkef refused to play that game—he couldn't bear to flatter those he deemed inferior to himself. He preferred to remain anonymous. He would sit in the corner and watch the others play their games; not once did they throw a glance his way, or notice his tight jaw curtailing his resentment. To them he was irrelevant. Yes he could direct a dance for the Mystery Plays, but he was still dull Master Amenkef, not much better than a public servant. Nevertheless, he was the only one with a plan. "We should bury the body deep in the desert and then join a caravanserai heading for the coast—I suggest we go to Canaan, where Prince Septah will give us refuge."

Kahotep agreed it was a good plan. "We could be out of the country by dawn—before they realise the girl is missing. Well don't just stand there—get a move on," he shouted at the guards.

Harp of Joy looked down on the gloomy room and saw four men arguing amongst themselves, their faces flat with fear. They hovered over a bruised body resembling a discarded robe, streaked in blood and dirt. At first she thought, how that poor girl must have suffered, tortured by those wicked monsters—but then realised she was gazing at her own her lifeless form, like a lamb asleep in a manger.

They wrapped her body in a hemp sheet and the guards carried her through the passage, to the west side of the Temple. The priests followed behind, the dark capes making an eerie procession through the night. Then they threw the corpse onto a wooden cart pulled by a black horse, and drove through the desert without a word. There was no one around, the priests confident there were no witnesses — they'd emerged through a secret tunnel leading them straight into the desert, where only jackals liked to roam.

Bentreshy followed the procession, skipping to keep up with their rapid steps. She didn't need to walk through the sand — realising she could leap into the air and hover over the surface like a bee. But she liked the way the sand tickled her feet, the grains rubbing between her toes like breadcrumbs, or ground corn. Thinking about food, she wondered if there would be culinary offerings at the funeral, tantalising morsels to feed the deceased and please the gods. Don't be silly — this burial would have nothing to do with honouring the spirit of the dead, or following religious tradition. They'd dumped the body on an old cart, without performing the sacred rites or the Opening of the Mouth ceremony.

When they came to a secluded spot Master Kahotep ordered the guards to stop the cart. "This place will do fine. No one will find the body out here. Now start digging," he shouted to the men, "Just make the girl disappear and we can forget about this unfortunate incident — then we can head for the caravanserai, have a hot meal." Kahotep was feeling the cold, the desert wind penetrating his cape, but it was more than the desert wind, he knew. He didn't like messy situations, or murder for that matter, and his hands were still trembling from the shock. The desert seemed to be taunting him with its vast mounds and ruthless winds, filling his lungs with dust.

They started to dig a hole for the corpse, emitting a faint grunt with every spade full of sand. Bentreshy examined one of the burly gravediggers: he was a stout man with muscular arms and legs, his hefty shoulders bent towards the ground. She could hear the man's heart racing with exertion, breathing in time to the rhythm of his spade. It wasn't easy digging through parched desert; the surface compacted with ossified particles. They were digging through a layer of human remains, a valley of bones…

Bentreshy looked up at the sky and saw the pale moon struggling to transmit fragments of light. There was something missing about the moon, it was incomplete, unfinished. It must be waxing, she thought, staring up at the oblong orb; it looked like it had been punched in the face, all swollen and out of shape. Then she saw a bright star surrounded by a green halo. It was Sekhtey, shining down on her from the heavens...*Do not mourn for me, sweet mother. I belong to the heavens.*

There was just enough light to see the Temple of Abydos in the distance, and the mud houses where the villagers slept, oblivious to the clandestine burial procession. The priests were facing east, beyond the Mountain of Offerings; the landscape looked so radiant in the dead of night, the desert drifting into the mountains, the gentle peaks merging into the mantle of sky. Her attention was diverted by the beauty of the night, the millions of stars like shiny grains of sand, and for a moment she forgot why she was here.

The men worked quickly—they'd spent their lives burying bodies, their profession moulded into their hands, their backs arched over the grave. When they thought the hole was deep enough the men nodded to each other and they slung the corpse into the hollow. Bentreshy watched the earth swallow the body, feeling a tinge of sadness for the corpse, laid to rest in an unmarked grave, without a proper burial. And then she remembered they were her remains, left to rot in obscurity, and she began to panic: *I'll never reach the Underworld without a proper ceremony. I'll be trapped on earth, wandering as an aimless spirit, haunting the locals with my ghoulish cries.*

The procession returned to the footpath, the gravediggers marching in silence, the priests quickening their pace, anxious to get away from the Mountain of Offerings where they'd abandoned the body to the desert. She watched them walking northward, until they shrivelled to flecks of dust on the horizon, and she was alone in the desert, the silence swallowing her in a purple mound.

8. Beneath the Sand
1936

Dorothy awoke to find a pile of papers on the desk, and she leaped out of bed, anxious to read the scribe's recent transcripts. What had become of King Sety and Bentreshy? she wanted to know; their love had been erased from history, subsumed by the desert strata. She began to read the rush of words dictated by the scribe:

I am here to tell you the final tale of King Sety, Men-Maat-Ra and Bentreshy, Harp of Joy . . .

Their union was condemned by a group of fanatical priests, scratched out like a stele proclaiming the wrong god. But a love like theirs cannot die, it lingers through the ages like the scent of jasmine on a barren bush, the perfume trapped in the dead twigs. Their essence remains forever, their voices echo through the Temple chambers and secret passages; their images rebound off the rocky cliffs and folds of sand, and emerge from the mounds of bones. The whole place is deep in bones—the bones of Narmer, Den and Djer, the earliest Pharaohs of Egypt; a place where Osiris brought peace and happiness to the people, and Isis raised them from the dead; where Osiris' followers built him a great tomb rising out of the primeval waters, where King Sety built a temple of worship and a palace of pleasure, as the two were inseparable to him. It was a time when pleasure was seen as divine, when earthly delights were a form of religious devotion. By indulging in carnal bliss, feasts and festive revelry, you were opening the portal to the gods, honouring the things they created.

Alas, there were evil forces in the desert land, creatures twisted with revenge and malice—they couldn't stand to see the people so happy, enjoying the wonders of creation. The primeval rage of Seth resurfaced from time to time, rising from the dark intestines and gestating in the desert, toxic gases burning the bushes to the ground. Take heed! It only takes one bad demon in the form of a mad priest or prophet, and the path to destruction is paved. The priest (who thinks he is a prophet) will make the girl confess, reveal the identity of her lover and the father of her unborn child. Seth will not allow the child to be born. Isis and Osiris had given birth to Horus, and the child had

138

overthrown him. A mere boy! Thanks to this fearless child Seth had lost his power and was forced to wander in the wilderness, where he did the odd bit of malice, but nothing more. The child of King Sety and Bentreshy would be equally troublesome, eradicating evil with their good nature and calling on the gods for assistance. And then the dynasty would start again, Seth seethed, imagining the power Isis and Osiris would possess, with such mortal connections on earth. But Seth had a few allies in the priesthood—they would take care of the unruly girl. And Seth would deal with the Pharaoh himself, he'd been longing to do battle with this pompous King, so adored by his people, just like Osiris. He'd show the people what a charlatan King Sety was, how he had fooled them with his grand schemes, his good looks and cunning charm; how he'd violated a priestess, forced himself upon a Daughter of Isis and left her pregnant.

The evil deal was struck: Amenkef and Kahotep waited until Priestess Inhapi had gone to visit her family and the King was safely back in Thebes. Then they locked Bentreshy in the seclusion chamber where she was forced to face her worst fears. She must denounce the Pharaoh, they said, tell the court he had violated her, and her life would be spared. But the girl was made of sturdier stuff and refused to confess, even after torture. For she knew the priests wished to depose King Sety and gain power for themselves. Once Prince Septah was crowned as Pharaoh, Kahotep would become the Grand Vizier and Amenkef the High Priest. She swallowed the poison hidden in her robe, the venom twisting round her nervous system like a cobra, strangling her life force. The girl let out a primeval scream, her sekhem fighting against this untimely death, and she uttered her last words on earth: "I would rather die than denounce King Sety, for Egypt will perish without her noble Pharaoh . . ."

Dorothy raised her eyes from the page, her face flushed, tears burning her cheeks. She had seen glimpses of this past life over the years, and now the whole truth had been revealed. The impact made her fall to her knees, and she lay on the floor writhing in anguish, as though she'd been kicked across the room. Dorothy lay there for several minutes, the past events colliding in her mind, three thousand years of history falling into place. Then she crawled back to the desk and reread the pages: it was like reading an old diary, having forgotten most of the events. Yet slowly the memories began to surface; a glimmer of the horizon in a sandstorm. The ancient symbols illuminated the darkness and brought an unbearable truth.

She ran her fingers over the loose lines and the words took shape in her mind, the truth unfolding like a deluge, turning from the unknowable into something frightening yet unfeigned. She was Bentreshy, who once danced in the Temple of Abydos; a beloved Daughter of Isis, praised for her beautiful singing and mystical nature, who brought laughter and joy to all who knew her. But not everyone appreciated her ethereal qualities. Master Amenkef said she was coarse and untamed, ruled by unbridled passions, like a wild horse that refused to be ridden.

King Sety found her untamed spirit intoxicating. Bentreshy was like Isis, he thought, able to bring the dead back to life. He'd grown weary of life, burdened by royal responsibilities and a loveless marriage. Bentreshy had incited his *Ka*, regenerated his body with joy and filled his heart like a reservoir. He'd felt his *Ka* reach out to her, as if seeking a place to shelter.

Their *Kas* had circled one another in a bird-like mating ritual, then moulded into one organism, like the process of alchemy, turning basic metals into gold.

The truth lay bare, unravelled by her own hand. Dorothy reread the passage about her love affair with the Pharaoh, how the priests found out and locked her up, then tortured her for a confession. She imagined herself rubbing venom into her wounds, performing her final ritual. The snake goddess Renenutet helping her escape from the mortal realm, protecting her soul through the Underworld, where she disappeared for three thousand years…

That night Dorothy wished the Pharaoh would visit her, she wanted to tell him she finally knew the truth about Sety and Bentreshy, a love story of epic proportions — but also just a simple tale about two lovers who would never abandon each other.

It had taken Dorothy nine months to decipher the events and she was left exhausted and bewildered, yet curiously illuminated; seeing the indiscernible awaken into truth.

That day Imam had come to his own moment of truth: he could no longer stand the dreams, the nightly visitations, the terrible obsession with ancient Egypt that left him isolated from his wife, stranded in the cold margins of history.

They sat eating their dinner in silence, and then Imam finally spoke, "I've been offered a teaching job in Iraq for a year, what do you think I should do?" He looked at her with pleading eyes, as if willing her to let him go.

"You should take the job, Imam, it's a marvellous opportunity. I'll stay here with Sety—it's best not to disrupt him at this age."

The job opportunity came as a relief to them both, although neither of them let on; they were terribly civil about the whole thing, she later observed. They had a practical plan: Dorothy would stay in Egypt (there was no chance of her leaving now) and Imam would work in Iraq. They would spend a year apart—lots of Egyptian husbands went off to work in other countries, it was quite common.

Two weeks later, Dorothy saw her husband off at the docks, waving and shouting from the shore, engulfed by a flock of weeping wives. Dorothy had been very gracious about the separation, agreeing to reassess the situation in a year's time. Standing on the dock she wondered why these wives were so distraught, when she experienced a secret sense of relief, like letting go of a dead weight…She expected Imam felt the same way, yet he'd kept up the pretence quite well, always appearing to be the dutiful husband. But they both knew the situation was impossible: she wanted to live in ancient Egypt and he wanted to hurl himself into the future.

"The first thing I'll do is move out of that insufferable neighbourhood," she vowed to herself, "with the colonial toffs, petits-maitres, prim gardens and hideous imitations of Parisian avenues."

It wasn't so bad, this having a husband in another country, she began to realise, with the freedom to do as she pleased, yet respected as a married woman, with legal rights and Egyptian citizenship. Dorothy would head for Giza, where her neighbours would be ancient pharaohs, pyramids and sunken tombs, where the past obscured the present in a layer of bone meal.

∧∧∧∧∧   ∧∧∧∧∧   ∧∧∧∧∧

One month later . . .
Giza.

Dorothy stared up at the Great Pyramid and felt her mind expand, as if trying to accommodate the massive structure. She could feel the sheer struggle in the stones, the workers' sweat and exertion; on a wider scale, she thought about the human struggle to create civilisations, forge buildings out of sand, draw meaning out of nothingness. Sety tugged at her skirt and let out a soft cry, reminding his mother of life's basic essentials. *The child is right: there's no use gaping at the pyramids when you've no roof over your head.* She had to erect the tent and then make the tea before it got dark. Ahmed had found this old military tent in one of the storage rooms, which Flinders Petrie had used on his Memphis excavations, the smell of his pipe smoke still trapped in the canvas. Dorothy spread the tent out at the foot of the Great Pyramid and began arranging the poles, flaps and endless folds of fabric, the ancient structure mocking her incompetence. She got herself in such a muddle, trapped under the canvas roof, wishing she had 200,000 pyramid builders to come to her aid, because that's how many men she'd need to erect this blasted tent!

"Get in there, you bugger!" she cursed the bent ridgepole that wouldn't stay upright, hearing laughter echoing behind her, as if the dead pharaohs were deriding her ineptitude. She followed the stream of laughter to the front of the tent and found a young boy grinning at her, his white teeth contrasting with his grubby face and gallabiya. "I never hear English lady swear—I hear men on digs swear many times, but never English lady!"

"Never you mind my cussing. If you're such a clever clogs show me how to put this tent up." Dorothy pointed to the tent and made the sign of the pyramid with her hands, which sent the boy into further fits of laughter, "You make great house, like pyramid."

"Yes, I appreciate your sense of irony but I need to get this thing up before it gets dark."

Gamal tied his donkey to the lintel and took hold of the recalcitrant ridgepole, and together they locked the poles in place, erected the roof and tied the guy ropes nice and tight. As Dorothy hammered the last tent peg in with a stone, the sun began to set in a sea of crimson, the sweat pouring down her face and filling her mouth with salt, and she felt an incredible sense of achievement, as though she'd just built a pyramid. Sety was sleeping in the shade, oblivious to his mother's triumph and the new addition to the pyramid complex which was to be their new home.

As they sat down to drink their tea, a little girl appeared out of the blue, surveying the tent with curious dark eyes, and then tracing the floral pattern of Dorothy's wide skirt. The girl had seen many tourists visiting the pyramid, but she'd never met a woman like Dorothy, wearing a pretty dress and bright lipstick, and yet preferring to live in an old tent instead of a comfortable flat in Cairo.

"*Ismak ey?* What's your name?" asked Dorothy, stroking the little girl's dark curls. She was a beautiful child, with a tiny perfect face, huge dreamy eyes and light brown skin, the colour of Demerara sugar.

"My name Lila and I am five," she said proudly, glancing at Gamal. "He my older brother—he nine years old." The girl was very talkative for a five-year-old, thought Dorothy, chatting away as her brother adjusted the tent flaps. Perhaps Lila could be a friend for Sety, she hoped; although he was only three he was quite articulate for his age.

"We live in the village. Our house has blue door with terrace on the roof—we sleep there in summer," she pointed to the mud huts in the distance, where her parents tilled their plot of land and sold their produce in the market. "My father also work on the dig—he find many treasures, now in museum. Have you come to work with the duktõr?" Lila wanted to know, seeing no other reason why an English lady would live on her own by the pyramid.

"That's the plan—I'll have to see what happens. One step at a time." *The truth was she didn't know what she was doing here—she'd arrived on a whim, making it up as she went along.* She glanced at the pyramid base, the large slabs polished with human sweat. Tomorrow she would visit Dr Hassan, show him her sketches and ask him for a job.

Sety woke up and began to cry, as if sensing his mother's anxiety. "We have some visitors, Sety—this is Lila and Gamal—they've come from the village."

Sety eyed the two children with astonishment; having spent most of his time with adults they seemed like a rare species to him, their small frames a welcome change from the towering grownups. "You come sit down, you eat supper with me," he told the children, scanning his mother's face for approval.

"Of course they can eat with you—if you don't mind sharing your supper." Dorothy had bought some kushari in the café, and she divided the lot into three small bowls; the children ate the lumpy leftovers without complaining, too busy chatting and playing with the marbles on the mat.

When it was getting dark the children reluctantly got up to leave. "We come again, Sety. Next time we play hide go seek—with pyramids many places to hide," Gamal promised, lifting his sister onto the donkey and then gracefully leaping onto the beast's back. Once the children had gone home and Sety was tucked up in his camp bed, Dorothy was left with the silent majesty of the pyramids, the lonely stretch of sand filling her with a sense of imminence; impending adventures looming on the horizon, forging out of unknown shapes.

The pyramid complex stretched for several miles, mostly hidden under the sand and drifting into desert wilderness. There were the main pyramids of Khufu, his son Khafre, and grandson Menkaure, and there were countless smaller pyramids housing the queens, royal wives and their numerous offspring. There were mortuary temples, mastabas and hidden causeways connecting the temples to the pyramids, sacred boats buried in pits—and who knows how many tombs and pyramids lay beneath the sand, all waiting to be rediscovered.

"With a bit of luck I'm going to be part of it all, unearthing the ancient wonders, liberating the past from obscurity." She felt a wave of excitement, and ran through the sand in a rush of high spirits. Dorothy looked out across the valley, the whole complex bathed in purple moonlight; the dark stones rising out of the earth, pointing towards the stars. The three pyramids descended along a southwest axis, all aligned with the North Star. Each pyramid 8.5 degrees west of magnetic north. Finding the illustrious North Star, her eyes drew a line through the sky down to the pyramids. She took a deep breath, inhaling the wonder of it all. It was an incredible engineering feat, even by today's standards—and yet the ancients did this thousands of years ago (the Egyptologists said the pyramids were about 4600 years old, but she sensed they were much older...)

Her vision drifted away from the pyramids, the valley resembled a sea of amethyst, the desert stretching into purple eternity. The mounds of sand drifted to the Nile, turning from arid ochre into lush green, twisting towards the sea in a spiral of life.

Back at the tent, Dorothy crawled into her camp bed and lay listening to her son's somnolent breathing, his blanket wrapped round his chin. She closed her eyes and could see the valley temples rising from the sand, the granite pillars sparkling in the dawn, the perfectly intact Temple of Isis traced in pink mist. She felt a surge of warm air fill the tent, like the first rays of sunrise. *He is here. King Sety, Nisou-Beti.* Sensing his presence next to her, his breath flowing into her, the warmth of his body radiating through her being. *"Nisou, my love, you've come back to me."*

"I will always come back to you. My soul cries out from the darkness and I must find the light, radiating from your being."

They lay together swathed in warmth and love, their bodies melting into an indistinct shape, and then dissolving into an ocean of bliss.

When Dorothy awoke the next morning, his love surrounded her like the early mist, hovering over her being. Each morning the mist wrestled with the heat of the sun; the force of daylight evaporating the nightly vapours, leaving only a faint essence of this dark world.

Dorothy drank her black tea while she listened to the radio, and Sety ate his millet porridge in silence, watching a beetle emerge from the sand like a corpse rising from the grave. Then she washed the dishes in a tin bowl, using sand to scrub the burned porridge from the pot.

"Now it's time to get mummy a job, habibi. Let's go and meet Dr Hassan." She lifted the child onto her shoulders and marched across the plateau towards the archaeological dig. Dr Hassan would never forget the first time he saw Dorothy walking over the sand barefoot, her determined steps coming straight towards him, destined to make his acquaintance. Despite her confident air, she was sick with nerves, her stomach flapping like a cave full of bats. The desert magnified her sense of urgency, her will to survive; the barren earth mocking life's essentials. She spotted a man of medium height wearing a panama hat, a white shirt and black trousers. "That must be him," she whispered to herself. He had a commanding air about him, the way he stood silently watching his team, mapping out the area with an intense gaze; approaching the man she felt her chest tighten, her heart accelerate. "Are you Dr Hassan?" The man nodded to her and kept one eye on his dig.

"I am Madame Bulbul Meguid—but you can call me Dorothy, if you like. I have come to enquire about a job. I can do sketching, collating, writing, even secretarial work—but I would really like to work as a draftswoman." She was saying too much, words tumbling out of her mouth. The professor looked up when he heard Dorothy's credentials. A draftswoman—he'd never heard the term, and he mulled the concept over in his mind. Dorothy handed him the sketchbook and he began flipping through the drawings; a flash of pillar, a rush of mural, statues flying off the page; enough to see the lady could draw exquisite images and that she'd captured the spirit of the objects, making them seem alive. "These are very good. Leave your portfolio with me—if nothing else I am in need of a temporary secretary," he told her, "I'll discuss your employment with my team," he added, not wanting to appear too eager.

"Very well, Dr Hassan. I'll be in my tent, if I'm not roaming the desert—I'm usually back by midnight." Dorothy called to her son who was playing in the rubble, sifting through some fragments of pottery.

Later that evening Dr Hassan thought about the English lady in the red and white dress, carrying her portfolio under her bare arm. Hardly the right attire for an excavation. But how could he refuse to hire her? She was an excellent draftsman and seemed desperate to work. And the lady didn't seem to care about money, as long as she had enough to live on. Besides—Dorothy could help him with his writing—a good English editor was hard to find these days.

Two days later Dr Hassan paid a visit to Dorothy's tent. "I hope you can start right away," he enquired, dropping his pretence of nonchalance. "I need someone to draw a plan of the tomb I've been excavating," Dr Hassan shuffled through his folder and stared gravely at his crumpled notes, "and to catalogue my research as it's in a terrible mess."

"Of course I can! I can start today if you like," she replied, leaping out of her folding chair. The professor stepped back, startled by her enthusiasm. "No, today isn't convenient. Come to my office tomorrow morning—I like to start work at seven o'clock."

She would soon realise that Dr Hassan was a rather earnest, academic man with the demeanour of a grand vizier at the court of Khufu: he was fastidious, punctual and expected his staff to maintain his meticulous standards. Despite his serious manner, he was a man who could recognise talent and displayed a generous spirit towards his protégés. He was amazed by Dorothy's drawings of tombs and temple reliefs, by the accuracy of her work and the fine attention to detail. These drawings were the work of a dedicated mind, he knew, one who understood the beauty and subtle magnitude of ancient Egyptian design.

Dorothy glanced round the professor's orderly study with the rows of books and periodicals, the coloured folders labelled and filed in alphabetical order and she felt a tinge of anxiety—neatness wasn't her strong point—thinking about her untidy flat in Cairo and her husband's disappointed face when he came home to a pile of dirty dishes and clothes. "I'm not the tidiest of people, but I am prepared to learn," she promised, trying to sound efficient; she'd be filing ancient manuscripts and artefacts from newly excavated tombs—a far cry from sorting out the washing.

It transpired that Dorothy was the first woman to be hired by the Egyptian Antiquities Department. "Mummy is making history," she told her son, as they huddled by the fire for warmth. "Mummy making history," Sety repeated, shivering under his woollen blanket. She would have to get some thicker blankets—the desert could be surprisingly cold at night, even in the heat of summer.

When Sety had fallen asleep, Dorothy sat by the fire burning the dried stalks she'd bought from Lila and Gamal. She let her mind trace the contours of the Great Pyramid, the moonlight outlining the elaborate structure, illuminating the obscure patterns in the stones. It was the most complex, intelligent construction human beings had ever produced...it was a leap of consciousness made tangible, like a dream catcher snaring the divine and turning it into stone. The creators were bringing heaven down to earth, grounding it in the here and now. Dorothy's mind was giddy with sleep, the shapes swirling into strange shadows under the moon's gaze. She drifted off to sleep, the colours leaping out of the pyramid: gold, silver, purple incandescent rays; the smell of sweat, the sound of workers spitting out sand.

∧∧∧∧∧ ∧∧∧∧∧ ∧∧∧∧∧

After weeks of administrative work, cataloguing books and filing papers, Dorothy began to feel like a permanent secretary. She was so relieved when the professor finally invited her to the dig to make some sketches of the tombs. She began by copying the tomb of Ra-wer, High Priest of Heliopolis in the reign of King Nefer-ir-ka-Ra. She loved the story of Ra-wer who'd once been the King's barber and rose through the ranks to become a man of status. Dorothy scrambled into the dim tomb, following the light reflected by the worker's mirror, bouncing light into the far crevices, just as his ancestors had done in the Old Kingdom. As her eyes adjusted to the faint light she was struck by the beauty of the statues and the intricacy of the tomb's layout. She traced the carvings with her hand, feeling the symbols awaken under her fingers, their power drawn into her skin. The image of Ra-wer looked towards eternity, his serene face rising out of the wall, the shrine surrounding him in a circle of divine approval.

She sketched the family of statues: his father Ity-sen, his mother Hetep-heres, and Ra-wer with his knee-high children either side. No sign of the children's mother—Dorothy made a note of this to ask about later. The statues were broken and their heads were lying in the rubble, but when she closed her eyes they became complete, a portrait of a loving family beaming from the Old Kingdom. Opening her eyes again she began to notice subtle details: the mother's right hand round Ra-wer's waist, his daughter's left hand holding his calf. Dorothy noticed the way Ra-wer's tunic sagged slightly round his belly, a sign the priest had a middle-aged paunch, she laughed at this notion—he was probably quite the porker, enjoying the unexpected luxuries bestowed upon him by the court. *Ra-wer the sun-priest is strong, and rather plump!*

The family of statues were going to the Cairo Museum. Dorothy would miss their presence—but she knew it was for their own safety, to prevent grave robbers from selling them to a private collector. At least the family would be staying in Egypt...

Dorothy began copying the hieroglyphs below the statues, her pencil forming the ancient symbols, the lines leaping out at her, like fish jumping from the river. Inscriptions and images put to sleep for 4,500 years, she reflected, entombed in sand and slowly forgotten. And now these figures were waking up after four millennia, the figures still radiant, their eyes shining with eternal clarity. Drawing the Pharaoh's image, she became aware of a sweet smell, like honey and sandalwood, with a hint of smouldering pine resin. It was unlike anything she'd smelled before and yet it was strangely familiar, teasing her memory, hinting at the invisible. The aroma was somehow linked to the past, to the memory of the place—perhaps Ra-wer's memories, she mused, sketching furiously, trying to capture the smells, the essence of his life entombed. She felt like an embalmer, preserving memories with her sketch paper. Then she'd take these images out of the graves and into the sunshine, where people could marvel at their beauty, become acquainted with the souls of the dead. The excavators were also resurrecting the dead, she noted, their trowels like surgical implements restoring people to life. Dr Hassan was like Dr Frankenstein: he'd discovered the tomb of Ra-wer and given him life again. And what a man they'd resuscitated, thought Dorothy. Born into a life of humble obscurity, he managed to become the barber to the pharaoh. Dorothy imagined the barber shaving the king's face, careful not to cut his royal skin, then shaving His Majesty's chin before applying his false beard. She imagined the obsidian blade in the barber's steady hand, scraping the pharaoh's jaw with mindful strokes. All the while he chatted to the king and soon became his trusted confidant; cutting the pharaoh's locks and fashioning his way into the royal court. He must have been a great storyteller and a great barber for that matter for he was promoted to the position of High Priest of Heliopolis, the illustrious ancient capital of Egypt. There was evidently social mobility at that time, and if you had talent you could move out of your station, unlike in England, where a person of humble origins would never rise to such a position. Imagine a barber from Plymouth becoming Archbishop of Canterbury! she laughed out loud, a wave of cackles bouncing down the passageway. The man outside began to shake the mirror, sending the light spiralling round the tomb, "You OK, Sitt Meguid, you OK?" the man's concerned voice echoed through the tomb.

"I'm all right, Mahmoud. I'll be finished here in a few minutes." Dorothy put the finishing touches to her drawing, and then she closed her sketchbook and let her eyes linger over the murals, the soaring images of Ra-wer filling her with fear and wonder. There were hundreds of statues in this tomb, splendid figures emerging from the walls, others lying in dismembered heaps. She knew these statues were more than pleasing objects: they were the sacred houses of the *Kas*. If a mummy began to rot away the *Ka* could take refuge in the statue, an essential mediator between this world and the next.

149

Dorothy emerged from the tomb covered in a film of dust, her eyes blinking in the harsh sun. Dr Hassan was working outside the tomb, ordering his team to clear the sand to the foundations. Dorothy watched the professor brushing off a stone inscription, making gentle strokes with his tiny brush, as if handling a delicate flower. He worked with a precision she'd never seen before, sealing off a rectangular area and brushing away every grain of sand, careful to analyse every stratum, every formation, no matter how insignificant it may appear.

Dr Hassan looked up from the dig and saw Dorothy sitting on a stone, her son sleeping on the mat by her side. Her face was glowing in the sun and her brown nose was covered in freckles. Hardly the best conditions for an English lady's complexion—he would remind her to wear a hat. He thought about his wife back at home, sitting on the shady veranda sewing her tapestry. She prevented her skin from darkening in the sun and always sat under an umbrella, but English ladies didn't seem to value their pale skins—they were obsessed with suntans.

"You were down in the tomb a long time. We were beginning to worry you'd slipped down a shaft," the professor remarked, pulling up a chair next to her, "Can I have a look at your sketches?"

Dorothy handed him the sketchbook and went on stroking her son's hair while he slept. "They're not finished yet—they need some fine tuning, but you're welcome to have a look."

Dr Hassan dusted off the cover and began flipping through the pages. He was stunned by what he saw: the lifelike figure of Ra-wer with his family, and a precise replica of the tomb sketched from every angle, in minute detail. "You have a fine hand, a unique ability to capture the essence of a place. These are remarkable sketches, Dorothy. Keep this up and I may use them in my next book," he smiled awkwardly; giving praise was rather difficult for him, Dorothy could tell—he was obviously more accustomed to correcting people with his critical eye. He stared at the drawings for a moment: the dimensions were uncanny, he observed, as though she'd spent hours at a draftsman's table, the figures full of movement and life. And yet Dorothy had drawn them in an unlit tomb...

Dorothy spent the next few months drawing the tombs, wall scenes, statues, and every shard of pottery uncovered by the archaeological team. She'd never been happier, crawling around in the tombs, her face perpetually covered in dust, like pancake makeup. "Who needs foundation when I have this natural powder, made from ochre and bones." She would bottle it and call it *Tomb Powder: for an Egyptian Queen's complexion. Guaranteed to give you a golden glow.*

One day Flinders Petrie paid them a surprise visit on his way to Palestine. He spent the afternoon walking round the Great Pyramid, satisfied with his previous calculations. Dorothy watched the old man circumnavigate the pyramid, his long beard streaked nicotine yellow.

"I hope he doesn't want his tent back," she began to worry—but then she remembered he preferred to sleep in a mastaba. Flinders nodded to her as he approached the tent and he sat down on a rectangular stone. "Dr Hassan showed me your drawings of the tombs—could have done with you in Gurob."

"Thank you, sir. I've just put the kettle on for tea—I'm afraid there isn't any milk."

The professor drank his black tea and then wandered back to the Great Pyramid, his old mind sharp as obsidian, still measuring the stones.

∧∧∧∧∧   ∧∧∧∧∧   ∧∧∧∧∧

In the evenings Dorothy sat around the campfire with the team, roasting lumps of chicken, onions and aubergines. The men drew a sigh of relief when Dr Hassan packed his tools away and took the carriage back to his flat, where he spent quiet evenings with his wife, reading a book on the terrace and drinking mint tea. Everyone had great respect for Dr Hassan, as he was one of the first Egyptians to rise to prominence in the field of archaeology. He was a brilliant Egyptologist who'd excavated some of the most important sites in Giza: the sphinx, numerous mastabas, the shaft under the Great Pyramid—but his finest hour was the discovery of the Fourth Pyramid. This pyramid was built by King Djedefre, one of Khufu's sons. It was a remarkable discovery as the pyramid was located on a hilltop in Abu Rawah, several kilometres from the three main Pyramids. As it was a modest pyramid, Dr Hassan suggested that Djedefre had come to power as an old man and hadn't had time to complete a massive building project. But Dorothy heard he'd murdered his older brother to be next in line for the crown—if true there was a bit of Seth about him, she thought; rumour had it Djedefre had fallen out with his father Khufu, and later, when he became Pharaoh, his people turned

151

against him. But Dr Hassan said that was the stuff of myth and that there was no evidence to prove it. Still, it was very mysterious — why Djedefre built his pyramid so far away — deliberately distancing himself from his family.

The team were so in awe of this eminent professor that they didn't dare put a foot wrong, and Dorothy thought they behaved like frightened children in his presence, trying to impress the Pharaoh with their good behaviour. Mustafa Sahal, a student from Cairo had recently joined the dig and he seemed to lose his nerve whenever Dr Hassan approached him, forever mislaying his notebook and dropping his tools in the sand, his palms clammy with anxiety. But once the patriarch had disappeared over the desert in his caleche Mustafa began to relax; the staff members filled their tin mugs from the secret keg of beer and raised a toast to the end of another successful day; the fragments of pottery and bones spread out on the table as recompense for their sweat and labour.

Laurie Jackson had found a tiny alabaster figurine of Hetepheres and placed it in the middle of the table, looking quite pleased with himself. "A bloody good find — even Dr Poface was impressed. A bloody great find." Laurie was an Australian archaeologist in his late thirties, a leading expert on amulets, although he was more famous for his bad language and cultural faux pas. He had light brown hair and a boyish face, his grey eyes darting with mischief. He came dressed for the Australian outback: he wore a battered cowboy hat and rough leather boots bearing the scars of a crocodile attack, his khaki trousers bulging with knives and tools, ready for any emergency.

He noticed Dorothy had an uncanny ability to find Bastet figures, and that afternoon she'd found an exquisite blue cat carved out of lapis lazuli, and he insisted she placed it next to his Hetepheres figurine. Laurie had never seen a cat like it, he claimed, "Well bugger me, Dorrie! What a bloody great find — ya make the rest of us look like dongas!" Laurie's face glowed with enthusiasm, unaware that his stream of expletives had echoed through the camp, reaching the sensitive ears of Dr Hassan and making him cringe with displeasure. Peter Wallis sniggered behind his boat sketch — Laurie made the rest of them look like angels. Besides, he couldn't understand Laurie's fascination for cats — Peter had a thing for boats instead. In fact he'd just finished his PhD on boat pits from the Old Kingdom. His dark hair and long face made him appear rather sullen, even morose at times, but Dorothy discovered he was a kind-hearted fellow with a passion for sacred barques travelling to Amenti, and gradually the warm sun melted his reserve.

Dorothy sat in one of the camp chairs drinking a mug of lukewarm beer, enjoying the yeasty saliva in her mouth, blending with the chalky dust and forming a creamy substance much like fresh dough. After several sips her dry throat began to clear, like a wadi after the rains. Mustafa sat next to her sipping his beer, his worries visible on his young face, making him appear suddenly older. "I need Dr Hassan's approval, my future plans depend upon it," he confessed to Dorothy, "I need a recommendation from the professor so I can study for a PhD—that's why I must impress him, but I think I have failed terribly."

Dorothy felt sorry for the poor student and tried to increase his confidence. "Your brushwork is very good and you keep meticulous notes. Yes, you're a little clumsy sometimes, but that's just nerves. Dr Hassan will give you a good reference—he may seem formidable but he is a decent man—you will get that scholarship, I'm sure of it."

Mustafa forced a smile and seemed encouraged by this news. "You are a kind lady, Dorothy—you give me hope." He took a gulp of beer and leaned back in his chair, the warm fire and friendly people elevated his spirits, his fears of Dr Hassan retreating into the flames.

After sunset and evening prayers, the local men returned with baskets of food for the staff, their wives and children following in a colourful procession. Gamal and Lila played hide and seek with Sety, scampering through the sand like scarab beetles. Their father Samir had spent two seasons on the digs and he knew when to use a spade or a trowel, and all about the various brushes, thanks to Dr Hassan's instruction. He saw no reason why locals couldn't do these more specialised jobs, even if they were illiterate.

With the animals safely in their pens and the stalks piled high for the morning fire, some of the village women joined in the feast, bringing plates of spiced couscous, ta'amiyas and pastries to sell to the hungry workers. Lila's mother Hasna squatted by the fire, dishing out her fatiras, corn fritters and bean stew. She handed Dorothy a fatira, the warm bread sticky in her hand.

"*Shukran—kwayis*—it's very good." she noticed Hasna's nimble fingers, used to weaving, sewing and kneading bread, her delicate features and large brown eyes that seemed to leap from their sockets.

153

Dorothy let the tasty food settle in her belly, the beer warm her veins, and she stared up at the star-filled sky, Nut's frame arching across the horizon. The squeals of laughter, the flow of Arabic and English filtered through her senses, the burst of song and cymbals rousing her to dance. Dorothy leaped to her feet and began an improvised belly dance, her hips swaying to the sound of tambourines, cymbals and flutes, and soon the women and children joined in, performing a local dance of celebration. The children gathered round Dorothy's flowing skirt, the folds spiralling like a whirling dervish and together they performed an Egyptian dance in the desert, the pyramids as their stage set, pointing to the sky and calling on the gods to witness this expression of joy.

Sometimes she thought of her old life in England, *if my teachers could see me now*, she smiled to herself. Thinking about the women she knew in England, working as secretaries or seamstresses until they got married. I couldn't do this kind of thing back home, and I certainly couldn't live in a tent—it wouldn't be socially acceptable... She looked around at her colleagues and wondered why they accepted her. These men seemed to appreciate her knowledge and enthusiasm; archaeology bonded them together, and it went beyond gender, nationality, or anything else. *Maybe if you just go ahead and do things people accept you.* The beer was loosening her mind, leaping from thought to thought like a hare in the desert. "I'm awfully fond of you fellows," she gushed, words blurring into emotions, "for the warm showers—the warm beer, and warm stew for Baby Sety when I'm down in the tomb..."

The men laughed at her tipsy confession and passed her a cup of sobering tea. Then Laurie and Mustafa guided her back to her tent. "You'll feel better in the morning, me lidy," said Laurie, his Australian accent giving her the giggles.

"G'night, mite," she replied, rolling onto her camp bed, "May Isis guide you through the rough seas."

When everyone had retired for the evening and the desert air descended into an eerie silence, Dorothy stumbled out of her tent and lay under the stars, feeling the universe expand under her gaze and the moon swell with the rhythm of her heart, pumping in her breast. Her head began to clear in the crisp air and she felt herself transform, her body becoming lighter, her senses filling with light. Standing up to greet the sky, her body like the sea, drawn by the moon. She turned her face to the silver orb, aware of its intangible influences: causing the earth to spin, the tide to flow, and although the process was invisible to her, she felt its dizzying effects, omnipotent and invincible. Her limbs felt feathery, floating with a curious sense of weightlessness, her skin radiating pink and gold streaks of moonlight. She saw a figure coming towards her, his blue robe suspended on the horizon, as if fashioned out of the firmament, cut from the fabric of the sky.

"Nisou, my love," she whispered, her excitement rupturing the stillness, sending ripples of anticipation through the night.

The wave of passion was like a raging torrent carrying him downstream, and he drew her towards him, her body opening like a window, filling his lungs with fresh air. Dorothy kissed him, her lips trembling with longing, seeking the refuge of his warm mouth and she inhaled his sweet breath, his life force travelling through her lungs. Who witnessed their kiss? The falcon saw it from the dark heights and carried it to the lonely hills. The stars and the moon saw their tender caresses and carried them to the far corners of the cosmos, the jackals and wolves heard their gentle cries of passion, taking them through the underground caverns.

"Follow me, I want to show you something," King Sety turned towards the Great Pyramid and Dorothy had to run to keep up with him. He held her hand and helped her onto the first set of stones.

"Do you think you can climb to the top?"

She nodded, "I've climbed it before, but I can't remember when."

He laughed, "Yes, I expect you have, during the three thousand years you circumnavigated the universe, eluding even the gods."

They climbed to the centre of the pyramid and traversed along the east side where Dorothy could make out a slight indentation in the rock. King Sety bent down and used all his might to push the stone aside. He stood panting for a moment and then scrambled towards the gap.

"Let's go inside." He took her hand and pulled her onto the ledge, his fingers locked over hers. His hand felt smooth and supple, his skin bathed in soft moonlight. The narrow entrance emitted a blue light and Dorothy noticed her nightdress glowing in a stream of indigo; she was standing in a spotlight on a stage, yet the stage was so immense you couldn't see the theatre, the limelight shining from an endless sky.

They were inside the tunnel now, heads bent, feeling their way along the narrow passage that turned right and then left in a geometric pattern, the blue light showing them which way to turn.

"This is a secret passage. People have forgotten about it because it's been hidden for thousands of years. When we arrive at our destiny, you will understand why."

The tunnel began to widen, the light fading from blue to purple and then into a golden pink, and Dorothy looked around in amazement, feasting her eyes on the most beautiful murals she'd ever seen. There were images of birds and cats drawn in exquisite colours and designs, and trees laden with fruit and flowers. The reliefs were so lifelike the figures appeared to be frozen in the walls, with their supple skin, the fluids still pumping through their organs. Instead of blood their bodies flowed with colour, applied by the artist's brush and skilfully brought to life. The figures advanced in a joyful procession, cavorting with Osiris and Isis, the bird-headed Horus and the jackal-faced Anubis, left foot forward, heading towards the future. Dorothy felt part of this great procession, emerging from the shadows. *That's what the figures are trying to tell us: we are you—we are everybody and we are all evolving. This is the human race and here is your procession, from the darkness of the cave to the colours of creation.*

How extraordinary, she thought, that I hadn't realised this before. And just as she was considering the enormity of this evolutionary journey, she stumbled into an offering table, scraping her knee on the granite surface. Looking around, her knee throbbing, she observed a vast temple, with columns and carvings more spectacular than Karnak, and almost lost consciousness, as the sense of awe was like a blow to the head and for a frightening moment she thought:

I must be on the other side of the world...

The Pharaoh embraced her in his arms; she felt herself cave into his body, his frame tightening around her like a cobra.

"Don't be afraid, my love, we are in the Secret City."

She looked around in wonder, "I've never heard of this place. How did they manage to keep it a secret, considering it's right under the Pyramid?" It was like trying to keep Paradise a secret when it was in your back garden.

156

"People easily forget what they cannot see on the surface. And once they lose sight of the entrance, they end up denying its existence altogether." King Sety stood on a stone slab, a moment of sadness darkening his mood and he cast his eyes down the deep channel, as if hurling his sorrow into the hidden crevices.

The Secret City had once housed the Mystery Schools, where young priests and priestesses were initiated into the arcane mysteries and were taught the ancient wisdom, so that one day they would emerge from the underground and bring their great knowledge back to earth.

"People believed the priests of the Secret City were blessed with supernatural powers as they had learned to navigate through the caverns of the Underworld and could control the nature of good and evil."

Dorothy followed the Pharaoh through the labyrinth of natural caverns, which the ancients had turned into an extraordinary community, intricately planned with temples, schools, shops and villages. Passed mud houses painted in shades of yellow, red and blue; workshops, stables and bakeries, where the golden loaves lay entombed. There were complex irrigation systems, waterways and rivers leading to huge lakes, and at the edge of a blue lake they came across a whitewashed palace decorated in geometric patterns and spirals, like a giant's torso covered in tattoos.

They were below the bedrock of the Nile, heading towards Cairo, he said; Dorothy leaping over fallen friezes and severed statues in order to keep up with the Pharaoh's pace, who seemed desperate to get to his destination. Finally they stopped outside a small temple decorated with figures of Isis, Nephthys and adoring priestesses offering jars of wine and incense. There was something astonishing inside this temple, she could sense it, her heart leaping like a salmon. She followed him through the temple entrance, and they walked through a series of chambers, each one smaller than the last until they arrived at the last chamber, which was so small they had to duck their heads through the passageway. They stood in complete darkness, feeling the intimate space leach into their beings, and after a while Dorothy imagined being back in the womb, the cherished space that was both oppressive and bountiful. She was in a tiny cocoon that housed the seeds of the universe and sensed the energy even in the darkness, pushing through the tight enclosure, searching for the light.

She heard King Sety breathing beside her, a gentle wheezing of dust, stone and pigment; lungs struggling for oxygen.

Listening to their laboured breaths, Dorothy noticed a dim light flickering next to her. The light grew brighter; King Sety was holding a spherical ball that glowed in his hands, revealing the dark blood in his veins. The chamber shone in a myriad of colours, his face splashed in green and gold light, eyes staring in unfathomable wonder. "This is what I wanted to show you: The Ball of Thoth," he handed her the crystalline ball and told her to stare into the centre. She was surprised how sturdy it was, yet so delicately created. She examined the ball for a moment, amazed by its intricacy. "There are hieroglyphs inside— hundreds of them, and they seem to flip over like pages when I read them."

Sety nodded auspiciously, "It's one of the unsolved wonders of the ancient world. They say a priestess created it after a dream. In the dream Thoth told her how to build the spherical ball containing the mysteries of the universe: the wisdom of Thoth and Seshet."

Dorothy stared into the ball and let her mind sink into the inert crevices, her subconscious mind awakening and dragging with it a cauldron of dreams, where flights of fancy spin their own wings. The symbols spun round the ball and when she'd read them they disappeared and a new set of symbols appeared, as if she'd willed them to appear. The ball of light seemed to be working with her subconscious mind, communicating telepathically, the hieroglyphs forming as she mentally requested them. Her mind raced through the *Book of Thoth* and the *Wisdom Texts*, and she caught glimpses of enlightenment, shot through the shards of light.

Atum exists in the primordial waters of Nun. He evolves out of the intangible, yet he is not invisible to those who see . . . You are the glimmer in the heart of the flame, you emerge from the fire as a self-creation . . . Nut is your mother, the Mistress of Heaven. Her limbs spread across the sky and shelter you from harm. At night she swallows you in her mouth and every day she gives birth to you at sunrise. The stars are her words. Oh Mistress of Heaven. Listen to her words and you will hear the language of the cosmos . . .

Then the words became blurry and Dorothy strained her eyes to read, *"Their words are lost in their books . . ."* the letters were shrinking into the ball, *"but the path below the temple is open . . ."* and when the words had vanished into the opaque glass, King Sety gave her a few gentle nudges, "It's time to go. We must emerge from the City before dawn." The golden flecks of light had faded from his eyes and the crystal globe was growing faint, the chamber sinking into dark confinement. Dorothy felt her conscious mind returning to prominence, her land of dreams banished to the murky Underworld.

They emerged from beneath the Sphinx, the reclining figure of Horus guarding the Subterranean City with his omniscient eyes. *Your secret is safe with me, child,* he appeared to say. The Sphinx had been sitting there for thousands of years, the entrance to the Secret City right under his paws, and no one seemed to notice! This was the true riddle of the Sphinx . . . it was one of life's great riddles: that the Underground City was still veiled in secrecy; the Sphinx a silent beacon in the sand, and nobody saw what lay beneath. Mesmerised by the awesome power of the statue, people saw no further than the Sphinx's bewitching gaze.

Dr Budge had told her the word "sphinx" came from the Greek verb *sphingo*, meaning *to strangle*. The Greeks thought the Sphinx was female and that her purpose was to interrogate weary travellers and test their wisdom. "Which creature in the morning goes on four feet, at noon on two, and in the evening upon three?" The Sphinx strangled anyone who gave the wrong answer. But Oedipus solved the riddle, "The answer is man: he crawls on all fours as a baby, then walks on two feet as an adult, and walks with a cane in old age." The riddle finally solved, the Sphinx threw herself from the cliff and died. Other versions said she devoured herself once the riddle was discovered, her mystery destroyed. But King Sety said the Sphinx was older than any of these myths—the primordial guardian of man.

Dorothy crawled into her tent and heard King Sety whisper, "Sweet dreams, my Lotus Flower. I'll see you again soon."

Dorothy soon fell asleep and dreamed of multicoloured caverns, with silver lakes and temples clinging to the subterranean shores. When she awoke her feet were covered in red clay, her nightdress torn and stained with the same red earth. She'd been sleepwalking again and she'd banged her knee badly. Rubbing her wound she recalled her astral dream of climbing the pyramid, (a dream so realistic she had the scars to prove it) and the blue light that had beckoned them into the Secret City. "I will find out more about this Underground City," she vowed. She'd ask the archaeologists if they knew anything about it. "I'm sure Dr Hassan would say it was a foolish notion, based on legend and fuelled by Western cranks."

When Dorothy awoke from her astral dreams a pink mist permeated the landscape, the morning light smothered by a mantle of shadows. She allowed the psychic dust to settle, forming a soft film over the desert. Everything seemed slightly altered, as if wearing the wrong spectacles, the world appearing out of proportion. Her nightly travels left her with an ethereal residue and she was glad to have such physical work at the tomb, as it brought her back to the tangible world; her fingernails clogged with red sand, grounding her to this very place.

Baby Sety was sleeping soundly, his nose squeaking as he inhaled. Dorothy examined the child and saw his nostrils were full of dust. "I will take him to the water pump later, give him a good scrub in the tin bath." A bath would be lovely—she'd forgotten what a proper bath was, with warm water and a thick bar of soap to make a rich lather. Dorothy poured the water from the jug into the ceramic bowl and splashed cold water on her face—that would have to do—she would have a shower at the camp after work. Being the only woman on the dig had its advantages: the men usually let her shower first, treating her to warm water heated by the sun.

She opened the tent flap and staggered into the morning sun. It was six am and the sun was trembling through a veil of mist, sending streams of muted light down the pyramids. It was a remarkable sight: the top of the Great Pyramid lost in a gold cloud. She lit the Bunsen burner to boil water for Sety's porridge and her morning cup of tea. Looking up at the misty pyramid she saw a slight indentation in the eastside, one third of the way up. How strange she'd never noticed this before, or that no one had ever mentioned it. She looked down at her grazed feet, still stained with red earth, even after a thorough scrubbing.

Dorothy heard Sety crying inside the tent and then he poked his little tear-stained face outside, wailing and squinting in the sun.

"No need to yelp like a jackal, habibi. I know you're hungry and your breakfast is ready."

She picked the child up in her arms and covered his belly in kisses, his cries turning to squeals of laughter. She cradled him in her arms, feeding him the millet, mashed bananas and honey. And with his belly full and good temper restored, mother and child set off for the site.

"Time to dig up some bones, habibi," she told the child, carrying him on her hip across the sand, his face bouncing with joy. The child loved to crawl amongst the ruins, picking up shards of pottery and bones, and shouting, "Mama! I found a treasure!" proudly passing the object to his mother. Often she was inside a tomb when the child made one of his discoveries, and the fragment was passed from digger to digger, finally reaching Dorothy underground. "Great work, Sety—now find mummy a golden goblet and you'll make her a rich lady!"

The workers took turns minding the child and listening out for his notorious wails of hunger, the only time the child made a fuss, and then a fellah would track Dorothy down, and reel off in breathless Arabic, "Sitt Meguid, baby is hungry—he cry, *'ana ga'an!'* "

When Dorothy finally emerged from the tomb she found her son sitting under the tarpaulin with the fellaheen, tucking into a communal bowl of stew.

"*Ta'mu kwayyis*—it tastes good," then Sety looked at his mother and started giggling, "*Omm awi wisikha*—mummy is very dirty!" The whole team erupted into laughter.

"Yes, mummy is covered in dirt and cobwebs—*awi wisikha*." Well at least the boy was learning Arabic . . .

When Lila and Gamal finished helping their mother collect firewood, the children played with Sety outside the dig tent, and he disappeared in a swarm of village children, who'd adopted him as their little sibling. Dorothy was grateful to be amongst such caring, friendly people, who perceived childrearing as a communal responsibility and there was always some kind neighbour to see to Sety's welfare. Not once did anyone criticise her parenting skills, or chastise her for being a working mother. Imagine the kind of flack I'd get back home. I know what my mother would say, she laughed to herself, watching her son play amongst the piles of pottery, his face smeared in five-thousand-year-old bone dust.

She walked through the necropolis, the fragments stirring old desires; the place was now a ruin, like her forgotten memories. *But it hadn't always been this way. She held a shard of pottery and felt the past come into focus, her memories emerging from the rubble. The first time she'd been here the place was bathed in beauty and colour. The necropolis was filled with exquisite mortuary chapels and the villages teemed with life. There was an artisans' village with*

*pretty white houses and workshops where the artisans chiselled their
sculptures and painted fine motifs on papyrus.*

"Hey Dorothy, what's that piece of pottery you got there—must be
bloody marvellous the way you're drooling over it!"

Shaken from her reverie she looked up to see Laurie Jackson
grinning at her, his face caked in red dirt.

"Just a piece from an offering jar, but it got me thinking . . . I was
wondering where to sketch those funerary jars—perhaps inside the
tent, if Dr Hassan is busy in his library today." Dorothy stared at the
fragment: in archaeological terms it was nothing special—and yet
the piece had stirred something mysterious within her. For a moment
she'd seen things whole: recollected and reconstructed. Isn't that
what these archaeologists are trying to do? Unearthing, retrieving
ancestral memories and reconstructing the glory of the past . . .

Dorothy cast the shard aside and climbed down the ladder into
the excavation site, soon immersed in a cloud of dust. The locals
were carting buckets of rubble up the slope and arranging them in
neat rows, their scarves pulled up to their eyes and their gallabiyas
dirty and frayed. Samir and Abdul were busy with their brushwork,
methodically cleaning a frieze from the recently discovered chamber.
She was impressed by their delicate brush strokes—they were
obviously glad to see an end to the backbreaking work, digging and
hauling buckets of sand.

She'd also done a lot of digging lately and was beginning to realise
that an Egyptologist was both a manual labourer and an academic—
and it helped if you were also an artist, historian and fantasist,
capable of imaginary flights (Dorothy had no trouble with that part).
After several months of working in the tomb, she'd learned to dig,
scrape, screen and brush according to Dr Hassan's exact guidelines.
She knew how to map out a site with gridlines and trenches, dividing
the area into five metre squares and marking each segment with
cord lines. Dorothy also drew the survey maps and site diagrams so
everyone knew where they had to dig and shift the debris.

Even Dr Hassan enjoyed a bit of digging and if anything important
was found, like a statue or a coffin, the workers would shout, "Dr
Hassan, come quickly, roll up your sleeves!" Then the professor
would rush down the ladder and start digging just like a fellah, his
brow caked in sweat and grime. There was something primeval about
unearthing a great artefact and Dorothy loved this experience almost

as much as drawing. Her body grew strong, straining under the weight of granite and limestone, and her skin turned light brown, darkened by the sun and the ochre sand. She grew fond of her rough hands and feet, the desert under her fingernails; the earth had permeated her body, shaped it to its will. She felt part of the terrain, the bones and the artefacts, emerging from the tomb at sunset, a woman carved out of stone.

After a hard day's digging the workers gathered outside the big tent and shared a communal supper of rice, ta'amiyas and vegetable stew. Today the team were in a bit of a slump because the Family of Statues had disappeared, and rumour had it the Family was destined for America, where they'd be separated and sent to various museums. Dr Hassan was enraged when he heard the news. "They promised me the statues would stay in Cairo. After all these changes in policies, tougher regulations—and they are still robbing our treasures!" He was angry with the Egyptian Antiquities Department, too, for letting King Farouk and Western markets get away with it, for being seduced by foreign money.

The next morning Dr Hassan returned to the dig with an armed guard. "This is Tarik. I have employed him to watch the tomb at night, and to shoot anyone who tries to steal the treasures," he spoke in a grave tone, the team silent with fear, but Dorothy detected a glint in his eye, and she knew his heavy tactics were aimed at deterring potential thieves. "We have tracked down the statues, and I am doing everything in my power to see them housed in the Cairo Museum—and to ensure there are no further thefts."

After his terrifying speech, Dr Hassan suddenly lightened his mood. "Now that's clear to everyone, I have some good news to tell you. We are expecting an important visitor tomorrow—Dr Reisner is coming to see the new discoveries," the professor stated with an air of veneration.

"You mean *the* Dr Reisner? The one who discovered the tomb of Queen Hetepheres? Dorothy enquired. "The man has found more tombs than anybody," her eyes alight with admiration." She'd read all the professor's essays and found them a great source of inspiration.

"Precisely. *The* Dr George Reisner," he said with equal reverence. "And I would like you to be present, Dorothy, as I will need you to take notes—and write a short summary of the dig for the professor."

Dorothy was thrilled at the prospect of meeting the eminent Egyptologist, who, like Dr Petrie, had taught the world so much about excavation work. "First Petrie and now Reisner—life can't get any better . . . But I hope I can keep up," she worried, "I don't want him to think I'm an amateur..."

When the staff had finished the dishes and cleaned the camp area, Abdul, Samir and his wife Hasna joined Dorothy round the campfire. They arrived just as the stars were beginning to emerge from the sky, shining like a diamond-studded canopy. They sipped their hibiscus tea and gazed at the night sky, as if they were watching a movie screen. Dorothy raised her cup to the heavens, "All the famous stars are in this one: Orion, the Great Bear, the Little Bear... performing just for us!"

"On such a bright night, Sitt Māt is sure to make an appearance," Samir shivered, obviously frightened by this woman's presence.

"Who is Sitt Māt? She sounds like an *afreet* to me," Dorothy laughed, "surely you're not afraid of an *afreet*, Samir."

"We call her Sitt Māt: Lady of Death, because people die after they see her. They fall down big hole, break their neck."

Dorothy had seen a ghostly figure wandering near Campbell's Tomb. "The lady seems friendly enough, quite a gentle soul really— it's the living you have to watch out for! *Afreets* just want a little attention, and a bit of common courtesy goes a long way."

Samir stared at Dorothy incredulously. The Ingiliziyya sounded like she had first hand knowledge of *afreets,* and she didn't seem frightened in the least.

"She is dangerous *afreet,* Sitt Meguid, and after seeing her people so scared they fall down tomb. We all believe evil lady take them to death."

Dorothy tried not to laugh at the man, knowing the villagers were quite superstitious and often consulted a witch doctor, believing they were possessed by supernatural beings. She'd spotted Sitt Māt the other night, strolling round the pyramid plateau, when the moon cast dark triangular shadows across the sand. The figure wore a transparent robe, like an ancient Egyptian, her long hair braided with glass beads. Sitt Māt had approached her with a nervous titter, and when Dorothy didn't run away the lady looked surprised, her laughter getting louder with every step. The ghost meant her no harm, but her laughter was infectious and Dorothy was seized by a fit of giggles, which seemed to please the lady. The *afreet* is like Bes, thought Dorothy, reminding us of the funny side of life. *Life, the cosmos—it was all a big joke; what a comedy of errors, what a giant farce!* Perhaps Sitt Mãt was trying to remind us not to take life so seriously and to enjoy the comic moments. But the irony was people were responding in blind fear. Sitt Mãt led them to the tomb so they could look into the abyss—to remind them of death and the importance of enjoying life. And what did they do—they fell into the deep shaft, driven by their own fears.

Walking back to her tent, Dorothy felt incredibly alive, the night air sharpening her vision, the smells and sounds pulsing with nocturnal energy. She realised this was the happiest time of her life, and for a moment she stepped out of her body, seeing herself walking through the sand, her skin opalescent in the moonlight. How odd, she thought—most of the time we're only aware of our happiest moments after they've passed, when we're reminiscing—and here she was looking down, watching herself on a screen . . . seeing her joy, her good fortune, the wonder of it all . . . being in this mythical place, surrounded by our greatest creations. She was living at the foot of the ultimate human achievement, the Great Pyramid—and to think she'd been living in Manya el Roda only six months ago. Dorothy thought about the suburbs with the insufferable colonials, feeling trapped and misunderstood. And now here she was fulfilling her dreams: discovering the treasures of ancient Egypt, walking barefoot through the desert, listening to jackals howl at the full moon, and laughing with an *afreet*. But best of all, His Majesty was visiting her regularly—he'd taken her on a wonderful journey through the Great Pyramid to the Secret City. "If I have the chance tomorrow, I'll ask Dr Hassan about the Secret City . . ." and then she fell asleep on her mat, dreaming about the underground metropolis with the crystal lakes and golden temples.

"Mama, wake up, you need costume," Sety pulled on her sleeve; someone was dragging her out of the silver lake . . . "You need costume for tomorrow."

"What do you mean, habibi—what costume?" Then she remembered the important occasion tomorrow. "Silly old mummy falling asleep in the sand—and I haven't got my clothes ready for morning."

Sety led his mother inside the tent, where several dresses hung from the ceiling like mismatched curtains. "Luckily I have one clean dress left," she told Sety, who was now busy eating pistachios. "Mummy should wear white dress with the big sleeves, like a cream cake," he suggested through a mouthful of green nuts.

"Don't you think it's a bit fancy for work? And I think it needs a wash—what do you think of this one?" She held the yellow and blue dress against her body; Sety shrugged dispassionately (obviously preferring the white one), and went on chewing his nuts, chuckling and talking to himself. He was now three years old—he'd been eating solid foods for a while now, yet he would keep the nuts in his mouth for ages, until his baby teeth had mashed them into a pea-green paste. At first Dorothy was afraid the child may choke on the nuts, but seeing how thoroughly he macerated each mouthful, she put aside her worries. The child sat on the floor methodically chewing the nuts and playing with his wooden animals, which gave her a chance to finish her sketches and write up the field notes for Dr Reisner.

Dorothy and Sety took the bus to Dr Hassan's house in Cairo. She read through her report on the bus, hoping Dr Reisner would approve.
I hope he doesn't think I'm an impostor . . .

"Habibi, it sounds like a busy day spent indoors, so you'll have to amuse yourself with your toys and books, and be on your best behaviour," Dorothy explained to her son, making sure to pack his building blocks and an extra bag of pistachio nuts. "I'll be on my best behaviour, too, as I'm meeting a famous Egyptologist called Dr Reisner."

Sety chuckled playfully, "I play dominoes with Omar, and when I win he cries and then we build a pyramid with our blocks and forget all about it." Sety loved visiting Dr Hassan's house as the rooms were full of interesting artefacts and the professor gave them a box of ancient figurines to play with. Sety was an affable child and seemed to know when important people were present and a sense of composure was required.

Madame Hassan led Dorothy into the library and poured her a glass of lemonade while she waited for the professor to finish his breakfast on the terrace. She was an attractive woman in her late thirties, with a slim figure and graceful movements. Madam Hassan wore a blend of French and Eastern fashion, which Dorothy admired, and it was evident she was a well educated lady, with her own ideas. "I share my husband's love of ancient Egypt, but not his love for excavation work. My passion is for murals and tapestries," Madame Hassan confessed, turning Dorothy's attention to a wall hanging.

"That's very fine needlework," Dorothy could tell, studying the intricate details of the Battle of Kadesh, with Rameses triumphant in his chariot. Madame Hassan smiled graciously, "It gives me something to do when I'm at home with my son—embroidery was a great comfort to me throughout my pregnancy. Men don't realise how confined women can feel," she sighed, staring towards the door, hearing her husband's footsteps down the hall.

"It can be difficult at times—having a family and following your own interests," Dorothy replied in a low voice, "but with my husband away I only have my son to think about, and he seems to accept the life I've chosen, at least he never complains!"

"Children are so flexible, unlike their fathers they can adapt to a variety of situations. You are lucky with Sety—he is such a cooperative child."

Talking to Madame Hassan, Dorothy realised how much she missed female company. On the excavation site she spent most of her time with men and had grown accustomed to the male point of view, the directness of their speech and their masculine mannerisms. When in the rare company of women, she found herself seeing them as men do, surprised by their soft curves, gentle features and melodic voices, bewildered by their feminine ways. Being on the dig day in day out, she was used to seeing hairy faces, large rough hands and hearing deep voices—the sight of delicate hands and soft skin seemed to belong to a foreign species. Sometimes Dorothy had to remind herself she was one of them . . .

Just as she was contemplating the peculiarities of gender, a large lady burst into the room, followed by Dr Hassan. "Sorry we're late, darling. It takes us all morning to get ready these days, but we're here now, so the professor will have a look at that book proposal, if it's ready." The woman was called Miss Perkins, Dr Reisner's trusted secretary. She spoke in a man's voice, with masculine conviction, and yet her body was a mountain of female flesh, her face powdered, lips painted red. "Dr Reisner will be here in a moment—he stopped to admire one of your vases in the hall."

Dorothy was mesmerised by the imposing figure of Miss Perkins and failed to see Dr Reisner standing behind her, a frail figure clutching his cane. He was partially blind and paralysed down one side of his body, but his love for Egyptology eclipsed his failing health. "I'm anxious to hear about Ra-wer's Tomb—I hear you've found some remarkable statues."

When Dr Reisner started talking about ancient Egypt, his energy and passion returned and there was no sign of the frail old man Dorothy had met that morning. She sensed his devotion to Egypt included an esoteric dimension—perhaps being closer to death made him more intuitive. But he was hardly going to reveal this mystical side to Dr Hassan, who counted on his sound scholarship and rational approach.

How privileged she felt, listening to the doctors reminisce about their first discoveries in Giza and Saqqara and the many tombs they'd excavated; they argued over the age of the pyramids, the mysterious water marks—were they evidence of a primeval sea or flash floods?

Dorothy's knowledge of ancient Egypt seemed to impress Dr Reisner, and he was amused by the way she chatted about the pharaohs, referring to Sety I as "a wonderful man with an artistic flair"—and Rameses II as "a chip off the old block"—but sometimes Rameses got carried away, she admitted, "he lacked his father's subtlety."

"Dorothy has a vivid imagination, Dr Reisner—I think she should write these observations down—they would make a good novel," interrupted Dr Hassan, wondering what Dr Reisner would think of her flights of fancy, speaking as if she'd known the royals personally.

"In archaeology it's important to have a vivid imagination— it helps you envisage what life could have been like, and this can lead to interesting connections, original theories. Some of these academics are blinded by their own pedantry—they could do with a bit of reverie."

Dorothy was encouraged by Dr Reisner's broad-minded approach. "Speaking of new theories, there's a rumour about a Secret City underneath the pyramids, and that this city was once used to initiate the priests into the Esoteric Mysteries." She wondered what the professors would make of such a notion. Dr Hassan hesitated before replying, "It's a theory I have been studying for some time, and I've come to the conclusion the theory may be true." She was surprised by Dr Hassan's response and urged him to continue.

"We discovered several shafts that lead to underground tunnels and chambers, but I can't confirm how extensive they are or what they were used for. The problem is the existence of the Secret City has been denied by the Egyptian government and any excavations beneath the pyramids have been forbidden." He stared at Dr Reisner furtively, wondering what he knew about the Secret City.

"They say it's dangerous to open up the tunnels as the pyramids may collapse," Dr Reisner gave a wry smile, intimating he was sceptical of this claim.

"It seems more likely the government has found something they don't want people to know about—like evidence of an advanced society, with technology far superior to our own," Dorothy replied, thinking about the Ball of Thoth, the waves of light and words.

"I have been denied access to the shaft, so I'm afraid that's the end of it. We could sit here all day making assumptions, but we've got work to do—we must concentrate on the Tomb of Ra-wer. Dorothy, I'd like you to read Dr Reisner the field notes and the summary you wrote on the excavation," Dr Hassan spoke in a formal tone, eager to return to rational scholarship.

Dorothy rifled through the pile of papers. *I should be more careful what I say—they'll think I'm one of those crackpots who believe the pyramids were built by Martians.* She cleared her throat and started to read the summary:

"Excavations at Giza: the Tomb of Ra-wer. This Fifth Dynasty tomb is a vast and complex structure located to the south of the Sphinx. The tomb belonged to Ra-wer, barber to Pharaoh Nefer-ir-ka-ra, the barber who later became High Priest of Heliopolis. The team discovered over one hundred limestone statues of Ra-wer and his family members, many of them still intact . . ."

In this land of dust and bones, the most famous archaeologists gathered by the tomb, like illustrious vultures cleaning the remains...

When Dorothy returned to her tent she found a letter had been slipped through the flap. The letter was from Imam; he said his teaching post had been renewed and that he would be staying in Iraq for another year. He talked about his cousin Sana, and how she'd been a great support to him lately . . . "I know it's rather sudden, but I am hoping you will agree to a divorce . . ."

It was all a bit of a shock, and Dorothy poured herself a brandy. Perhaps divorce was the best solution, she reflected—they already lived separate lives. Once the news had sunk in, she began to feel relieved—at least Imam hadn't asked for custody of their son—and she could stay in Egypt . . .

Later that evening Dorothy slept outside the tent, gazing up at the stars she joined the dots together and made patterns in the sky—a lion, a man carrying a staff . . . a pyramid made out of stars . . . On earth the pyramid started with a mass of blocks ending in a pinnacle, the large foundation shrinking to a pinprick as it ascended . . . but from the sky it seemed the other way round: starting with the point, a particle of dust and then expanding outwards through space (just like a star).

The three pyramids mounted on the plateau, a mirror image of Orion's Belt: the Nile the Milky Way, the celestial river of Ra, who travelled to his rebirth . . . and Dorothy asleep in the sand, dreams shrinking to a pinpoint, then magnifying into unconscious chambers, small, big, light then dark, music then silence. . .She went backwards, before the pharaohs, before Egypt . . . *If you go back far enough in time, you come full circle...you go beyond the past and there you find yourself three thousand years from now . . . the past becomes the future.*

9. Pega-the-Gap
1290 BC

Bentreshy found a crevice in the rocks and nestled into a blanket of sand, waiting for the dawn to come. Perhaps this was her life now: to wander in the desert, neither dead nor alive, to hover like the morning mist, suspended between this world and the next. She watched the sun rise and surreptitiously light up the sky. She had time to watch it happen—there was no rush to get to the Temple for morning prayers, or remember her amulets and jars of incense. The sun was over the horizon now, spraying shafts of light across the sky, like great staircases ascending to heaven. As the morning progressed the stairways began to fade, melting into gold streaks—for a moment the shafts turned yellow and orange, with a hint of silver round the borders—then dissolved into a pale green sheet. As the sun cut loose from the fields she watched the colours seep through the sky, like water soaking through fabric, the whole backdrop painted turquoise.

People were coming out of their houses, strolling round the market with their hemp bags; the priests wandering through the courtyard, their feet shuffling with deliberate steps, their minds lost in meditation. There was a faint sound of music and a girl singing. Was that a scent of jasmine in the air? Bentreshy turned away; it didn't matter anymore, I am no longer part of it—and yet she still had a vivid impression of the place, the music, the flowers, the morning incense burning in the brazier.

She ran through the desert towards the Mountain of Offerings and slithered into the gap in the rocks. She'd be safe here, away from the bright sun and the force of human activity. People led such hectic lives, what with their rituals, their ablutions, their temple duties and daily chores. She closed her eyes and concentrated on the darkness, the painful memories slipping into the shadows. There were a few scars on her body, but she was free from pain. No nerve endings screaming in her brain, no receptors burning in agony. She inhaled the silence and crept further into the crevice where the light couldn't penetrate. Her fingers traced the purple veins in the rock; flecks of silver, pink and black. How extraordinary it was, this cleft in the mountain, she noted, the colourful lines interlacing with such symmetry.

171

From the mountaintop Bentreshy watched her friends cross the field and head towards the Temple for midday prayers. It was comforting to see that life carried on, as if this terrible deed had never happened. If only her friends could linger in this blissful ignorance and never know the truth. But it was too late: Kebi was already on the trail, instinctively following the scent. Crossing the garden to the House of Isis, wondering why her friend had missed prayers again. She hadn't seen Bentreshy for two days now—not like her to hide way, even in her state. I'll go and see Inhapi, she decided, find out what's going on. Inhapi would understand and offer Bentreshy protection—she'd see the importance of such a birth and how it would bless the Temple.

Inhapi was sitting in her study reading a book of poetry, her shoulders caved into her chest—she looked remote, anxious even, eyes lowered beneath her brow, as though burdened with too many responsibilities. She looked relieved to see Kebi and jumped out of her chair, her book slipping to the floor, but she didn't seem to notice.

"I'm so glad you've come. I'm worried about Bentreshy—have you seen her? I think something's been troubling her."

Kebi looked alarmed, "I thought she was with you. She went to see you the other night—she had something important to tell you—she needed your help."

"I've been visiting my family. I only got back this morning . . ."

Kebi's face went ashen, "Master Amenkef . . . Master Kahotep—if they know the truth, her life could be in danger."

"Know what? You must tell me, Kebi—what's happened?" Inhapi gripped the girl's arm, as if to shake the truth from her. She felt the woman's fingers press into her flesh, her hands unyielding and for a moment Kebi was frightened of her, knowing the priestess demanded answers.

"Bentreshy wanted to tell you...about her relationship with King Sety—it wasn't just at the Festival of Osiris. They've been meeting secretly, and now they've fallen in love—they cannot bear to be apart. She should be telling you this herself—it's not right for me... oh, I don't know what to do—Bentreshy is pregnant—and now she's disappeared. I shouldn't have let her go home on her own— but I thought she was going to see you," she cried, turning towards Inhapi, feeling such tenderness radiating from the priestess, arms

172

wrapped around her like tentacles, pulling her into a private space. Kebi detected strength and determination in that intimate space, the priestess gazing wistfully. "I dreamed about this, so the prophecy is true . . ." Inhapi whispered under her breath.

"We've got to find Master Amenkef," she decided, gently pushing the girl from her bosom.

"Summon the guards—tell them it's urgent," Inhapi signalled to the servant, throwing her cape over her robe and pacing the room with bold steps; she was transforming into a powerful figure, a priestess warrior. She sensed danger, had an instinct about it, there was a certain smell in the air—the slight odour of sweat, the harshness of metal. A strange scent—just enough to sharpen the senses and alert the mind to the impending peril.

Kebi followed the priestess down the hall, Inhapi's cape obscuring her vision so she couldn't see where they were going; feeling like a shadow trailing in the woman's footsteps. A convoy of guards walked behind them, their grave steps booming down the passage, rousing Kebi's fear of what might happen—and even worse—what awful event had already come to pass . . .

They stopped outside Amenkef's private chambers and Inhapi knocked on the door, when there was no answer she motioned to a burly guard who rammed his shoulder against the door. The door swung open to reveal an empty room, the hollow sounds bouncing off the bare walls. There were a few clothes on the floor, an empty box lying on the bed, the remnants of a hasty departure. "Find his servant, ask if anyone knows the priest's whereabouts." Inhapi paced round the room trying to pick up clues, her sharp eyes inspecting the few remaining belongings. "He's taken his scrolls, his *Book of the Dead*, and his scribe's palette is missing."

Where was he off to in such a hurry? Kebi wondered, and could he have taken Bentreshy with him? What did he want with her? she dreaded to think.

They marched back to Inhapi's chamber in silence, Kebi filled with remorse and fear. She thought they'd have some news by now—that Bentreshy had run away—perhaps she was on her way to Thebes to be with King Sety. That's what Kebi was hoping for, as they made their way back to the courtyard: Bentreshy had taken a boat and was sailing up the Nile, hoping to get to Thebes in two days. But it was dawning on Kebi that the truth was far more sinister, the feeling of

173

doom tightening round her heart, the way she'd seen a snake crush a mouse.

The chief guard returned to Inhapi's chamber, his face lined with anxiety, "Kahotep and Woserit have also disappeared—they've taken some belongings and their travel bags are missing."

"I must warn the Pharaoh. Send the fastest messenger to Thebes—tell him King Sety must come immediately. Make sure he gives the Pharaoh this letter." Inhapi sat down and wrote with a feverish hand, warning the Pharaoh of the impending insurgence.

Poor King Sety, thought Bentreshy, he doesn't know the terrible truth. She imagined him sitting in his lavish palace, sinking in the lap of luxury. If only he'd come—why didn't he come for me? How incompetent men are, unable to save the ones they love. But I shouldn't berate him—he will do enough of that himself—I must pity him for the misery he's about to feel, for the remorse that will rule the rest of his life.

Bentreshy climbed to the top of the Mountain of Offerings and waited for the Pharaoh's barque to sail up the canal, each day a sign that his ardour was growing weaker; his love half-hearted. "Don't be silly—it takes at least two days to sail from Thebes, even with a passionate heart."

"Look, here he is—he has come at last," wondering why she was whispering, with only the wind and sand to hear her words. She gazed down from the mountaintop, watching the Pharaoh jump off his gold barque and march up the steps to the Temple, his feet resonating with purpose. It was like watching a play at the festival, the main actor commanding the stage with his heroic stance, captivating the crowd with his pathos, his tragic beauty.

"I love you, King Sety!" she shouted, as if calling from the gods. Just like a swooning fan appealing to her idol, hoping to get a glance of recognition. *He can't hear you, you silly girl.* She slid onto her stomach and peered into the abyss, the inaccessible space between this world and the next. She saw a phosphorus ether rising from the ground. *If I jump down I will rebound straight back up, like falling onto a linen sheet. It was like trying to break into the inner circle at the Temple, out of reach to the uninitiated. I was admitted to the circle—but now I feel like an outsider, calling from the balcony of the Otherworld, unheard, unseen.*

She watched the action from the summit, wondering what the hero would do next. She wasn't one of the Divine Ones, she couldn't influence the outcome, not yet. And what about the story so far? The hero left his lover and went back to his palace, promising to come back soon. But he didn't consider the dangers, didn't imagine people would wish to do her harm. He made a fatal error and now the girl was missing. Or perhaps he knew the dangers but had failed to act, paralysed with fear and self-doubt. It was like watching the Passion Plays, when Isis was looking for her missing husband. Unlike Isis, who still believed her husband was alive, the audience knew how the story ended. Bentreshy couldn't bear to watch, covering her eyes with her hands, peeking through a crisscross of pink membrane (she knew how it ended).

The priests' chambers were ransacked, men pressed against the wall with coarse hands. "Master Hbari, your life will be spared, only the guilty will die," the guard told the young priest. Soon Hbari began to talk, his confession falling like leaves from a book, unbound. "The rebellious priests have fled to Canaan, they hope to raise an army against King Sety and put Septah on the throne, a descendant of Thutmosis I—who some believe is the rightful heir." Oh what a devious plan, such heresy will be the death of them! But where is the girl—the priestess Bentreshy—surely that's why the King has come! He will find the girl. Leave no stone unturned.

The tragedy was unfolding before her eyes. How she pitied human beings, the way they were unable to step outside themselves. If only they could be an observer for a moment, hover like a ghost over their own mortality, then they would see...Perhaps then we'd be more careful of our actions—or perhaps we'd never act at all, being aware of the pain we may cause could render us impotent. But the Pharaoh did act—he gave orders to search every house, every chamber, to sift through every grain of sand in the desert.

Of course Sety's trusted guards found the men responsible. They were ambushed on the way to Canaan: Kahotep, Amenkef, Woserit, and a few loyal followers, dragged from their tents in the middle of the night, their heads blurry with sleep and nightmares. But they were soon to realise no nightmare was greater than the Pharaoh's revenge...

At times Bentreshy was glad to be up there on the hill, removed from it all—the terror, the violence, the human need for revenge. *But if I was down there that would mean I was still alive, and none of this would be happening...At least he's searching for me, and if they find me I'll be given a proper burial, and then I can begin my journey to Amenti, instead of spending my life on this mountain, hovering in this no man's land . . .*

The Pharaoh's retribution was monumental, his vengeance equal to his passion. Bentreshy couldn't stand to see him so full of hatred, his eyes hardened into callous shells, his heart a pickled egg, shrivelled into bitterness.

The priests were beaten and bludgeoned, their flesh oozing like split figs; the truth was ripped out of them: *"Yes, we interrogated the girl, roughed her up a bit. But we never meant to kill her. In fact she was already dead—poisoned herself to protect King Sety—we have the empty phial to prove it. Our only chance was to escape to Canaan—we knew Septah would take us in . . ."*

The criminals were impaled in the desert, not far from the girl's makeshift grave. ... They faced the midday sun, their torsos writhing on the wooden stakes, the vultures circling over the hills. Bentreshy looked down at the raw bodies, like slabs of pork roasting on a skewer; Amenkef, Kahotep, Woserit and the two guards howling like wounded hyenas, crying out for death. She pitied them their agony, the pain rising through their entrails, piercing the body with arrows of torment.

The priests told Sety's guards where to find the body—the last decent thing they'd done on earth. The grave-diggers exhumed the sack from the ground and slung the body onto the cart, guiding the horses back to the Temple. As they carried the body into the mortuary chamber, Bentreshy realised she was witnessing her own salvation: the ritual that would lead her to Eternity. *But you're not out of no man's land just yet. There's the Opening of the Mouth Ceremony and the Hall of Judgement to face. The Scales of Justice could still tip towards damnation.*

The Pharaoh had given instructions for an elaborate burial, with sacred water to cleanse Bentreshy's body, the finest natron and linen to preserve the mummy. The embalming process lasted seventy days and nights—just like a royal! And the Pharaoh offered the embalmers a box of amulets from the Royal Chest: eyes of Horus, scarabs and ankhs were placed freely within the folds of linen, to counteract the demons who may try to claim her soul.

The funeral was an impressive affair, with professional wailers tearing at their clothes, the priestesses walking with dignified remorse. King Sety led the procession through the desert, dressed in his mortuary leopard skin robe, his forlorn face hidden by the mask of Anubis, his broken heart strengthened with a gold scarab. She couldn't have asked for a better send off—her friends weeping and pulling on their hair, just like the professionals, but with real heart-felt emotion. Kebi was in a terrible state—she'd lost her best friend, her sister, her ally—eyes puffy with sorrow, her face smeared with dirt and tears. Poor Salidji, weeping her blind tears, muttering lamentations no one else could understand. Inhapi was like a mother who'd lost a child—her grief numbed by disbelief, a maternal refusal to accept the death of a child. *She was like a daughter to me,* Inhapi cried, *my protégé, my brightest star. Why was she taken from me—so young, so talented, her life only just begun . . .*

All this outpouring of grief—how people must love me! Bentreshy began to feel a little brighter, better than she'd felt in weeks, her malaise lightening into a muted optimism. If only people knew I was safe and free from pain. They spend all their time praying to the gods, performing the rites and yet when it comes to death they are inconsolable. Did they think I was a damned soul, twice dead, my heart eaten by the demons, never to reach Eternity? If only I could tell them—death is more forgiving than that. I may not be in Amenti but I can wander freely through the desert, scale the Mountain of Offerings and sleep in the legendary Pega-the-Gap. How I wish I could tell them: I am ready to begin my journey through the Underworld—all they need to do is utter the spells from the *Book of the Dead*.

The attendants carried the coffin to the awaiting tomb and Bentreshy was happy to know she'd be buried next to Nubiti. The tomb had been reserved for an elderly priestess called Nithotep, who kept resisting her cue to die, each time bouncing back to life at the last moment. All the priestesses built their tombs in this cemetery; Inhapi's tomb was nearly finished, she noticed, although it would be another two decades before the priestess would inhabit her House of Eternity.

Sety would be buried in the Valley of the Kings in Thebes, Bentreshy imagined. If only they could be buried together, two mummified lovers preserved for eternity. But it was too late. Her body was being buried in Abydos, the tomb sealed inside the final chamber, the fresh sand sprinkled over the footsteps, as if no one had been there.

People lived such muddled lives, flitting from one situation to another, never knowing what would happen next—they were such ignorant creatures, unable to control their destinies. Why couldn't they see the face of evil?—Kahotep, Amenkef, and their rotten followers—the Pharaoh's very own priests! How ridiculous people were with their prayers and rituals, their lavish funerary processions. How the gods must pity them.

Bentreshy wondered where the fallen priests had got to. Were they somewhere in this interim wilderness, this dividing line between this world and the next? When darkness came she was frightened of bumping into them, finding them huddled in the rocks; they too needed a sheltered place for the night. She heard the jackals cry and imagined it was Kahotep and Amenkef, their impaled bodies clawing their way up the mountain. But their remains had been cut into pieces and fed to the crocodiles; their false hearts sliding off the scales and down the reptilian throats. A rat scuttled across the rocks, pausing for a moment to glare at the human intruder. Bentreshy kicked up a cloud of dust with her sandal and the rat disappeared into a hole. He reminded her of Amenkef, with his glassy eyes and twitchy manner. The crevices were home to many creatures: snakes, lizards, rats and spiders, the deep cracks appealing to those with a covert nature, who wished to slip away from the mainstream.

10. Another War
Giza, 1939

During the summer months it was too hot for excavation work and the foreign Egyptologists took refuge in the Northern climes, driven into temporary exile by the insufferable heat. There was no chance of Dorothy leaving Egypt, so she decided to move into a house in Nazlet el Samman, which had spacious rooms and a large balcony built in the Ottoman style. The house had once been the Pasha's guesthouse, and in the last century it would have been a prestigious place to stay, with its latticework, archways and Turkish ceramics, but the guesthouse had fallen into a state of neglect, the paint peeling off the walls, the wooden architrave bleached by the sun. With the fall of the Ottoman Empire after the First World War, the Pasha had lost his authority, his great house and his influential guests. The guesthouse had been divided into two flats and Dorothy lived on the top floor, but as no one was living downstairs she turned the place into a refuge for stray animals: home to two old dogs, a donkey and a goose. Various cats lay around the place like feline pashas, waiting for their next meal with an air of self-importance.

Dorothy loved the ancient village with the tiny streets, leading her into remnants of the Old Kingdom, like the stone well dating from Khufu's time. "Not having running water has its good points," she told Hasna, "I meet the local women by the well and get to hear all the gossip, how else would I know who has the laziest husband and which one snores the loudest?"

"Well, you know I have messiest husband in the village," Hasna complained, "he bring home pottery pieces and bones from the dig and piles them on the table, he always leaving a trail of dust behind him." Hasna's family lived just up the road and they treated Dorothy like one of the family, caring for Sety as one of their own.

"Mamma say our blue door is always open to you," said Lila, sitting in Dorothy's overgrown garden.

"And you are always welcome in the Pasha's courtyard," replied Sety, happy the girl was a regular guest.

Dorothy liked the decaying grandeur of the house and the ornate balcony with the stunning views of the pyramids. The house had no modern comforts or electricity, but by now Dorothy was used to living without these luxuries.

"We are important guests of the Pasha," she reminded her son, imitating a pompous sultan. They danced around the splendid room dressed liked Ottoman effendis, wearing pantaloons, wide sashes and bright turbans. Sety loved to play these games and had a talent for the dramatic, his five-year-old frame prancing around like a haughty midget, acting out scenes from the Arabian Nights. "I am the First Kalendar, Son of the King. Step back and let me open the tomb!" Sety demanded, wielding his sword and pretending to pry the lid off the coffee table, his oriental coffin.

Sety spoke fluent Arabic and English and was a great reader, although he didn't go to school. Dorothy thought of the miserable time she'd had at school—the boy wasn't missing much. She'd gained all her important knowledge from reading books and talking to wise people. *Sety was surrounded by ancient history and eminent scholars, what better education could that be?* Dorothy knew her husband would disagree (he was a teacher, after all) and when he returned from Iraq he would expect the child to go to school, she imagined. Imam wouldn't see the charms of Nazlet el Samman, its caring community, gentle people and ancient dwellings. He'd only notice the scruffy mud huts, the outdoor kitchens and latrines, the breeding grounds for disease.

Despite her grand bedroom, Dorothy preferred sleeping close to the earth, feeling connected to the bones lying below, and the ancient civilisations compressed into the desert strata. She was drawn to the dark desert where the mounds of stillness would lull her to sleep. Then she'd find a temple doorway half covered in sand and lie down in this serene portal to the gods, and sleep like the dead.

One night Dorothy lay in bed listening to the creatures of the night and imagined the great canopy of stars above her head, a huge orchestra reverberating with strange sounds. The cosmos was far from asleep and she felt compelled to fling herself into its orbit, catch the meteorites shooting through the sky.

She strolled through the desert, the cold sand sifting through her bare feet; her mind was wide awake, receptive as the nocturnal creatures hidden in the darkness and she felt compelled to run with them, knowing every sensible human was curled up in bed and the

180

world belonged to her. At night she felt like a different person, the transformation occurring in the shadows; her body getting lighter and her instincts more acute. She lay down in the sand, her blue nightdress spread out like great wings. The indigo sky looked immeasurable, and she held her breath for a moment expecting to fall into the abyss, the cosmos rushing past her like a blue dome. The stars were bright and in their billions, falling like snowflakes from the sky; she remembered being a child and trying to catch the snowflakes in her mouth—big white diamonds which looked like shooting stars. Lying motionless in the sand she saw three shooting stars streak across the sky and then fizzle out, leaving a milky trail in the darkness. She spotted the Little Bear and recalled how the adze was made in the shape of this star formation; the instrument used to awaken the deceased to eternity.

Her head spinning with meteorites, the cosmic tapestry overflowing in her mind, she was suddenly weightless, invisible, her physical form evaporating like a shooting star, leaving an ethereal essence behind. She felt luminous, her body capable of great feats, streaking across the sand like a beam of light, her energy radiating with the power of Sirius. Dorothy walked towards the Sphinx and knelt down before the mammoth paws, staring into the lionesque eyes. King Sety had once told her the Sphinx was an image of Horus and not Khufu, as most people believed. The Sphinx was much older too, built long before the pyramids, when the constellation of Leo was rising. As she meditated by the figure, she knew the Pharaoh was right, feeling the spirit of Horus hovering over her, inciting her *Ka* to take flight. *Horus is my untamed self.* Dorothy was in search of this untamed self, her Leo spirit rising beyond the material boundaries. She was struggling with her human form, trying to free herself from social expectations; the domestic role she'd tried to play, her failure as a wife...She'd squeezed herself into a tight tunnel, but somehow she'd managed to crawl her way out and learn to breathe again. She stared into the Sphinx's incisive eyes. Horus was at once bird and lion. He could manifest himself in many forms. His reclining image was there to remind us that we, too, were multidimensional beings and could transform ourselves at will.

Help me transform myself. I have struggled for thousands of years. Help me return to Amenti. Dear Horus . . .

Dorothy began chanting strange words she didn't understand, and yet they seemed to make sense, like singing a love song in a foreign language. Relaxing her mind the words became clearer and she started to understand their meaning: *I set sail through the flames of creation, I travelled over the ocean to the first island, and there I met the first god, Atum, about to cast his original creation.*

Dorothy threw off her nightgown, the cool air embracing her body. She stood before the figure as her naked, true self, feeling herself expand before this human face of the divine. Horus was telling her, *You are at once human and divine.*

She kept mumbling the chants until early dawn, unaware that she was being observed by two furtive figures wrapped in black shawls. Nazirah let her shawl fall from her face, whispering to her sister, "*Sahra, miin di*—who is that?"

"*Da Sitt Meguid.* What is she doing here?" She has no clothes on! *Da mish kuwayyis*—that's not good. She will awaken the dead!"

Sahra realised her sister was about to approach the naked figure and grabbed hold of her arm. "The Ingiliziyya appears to be in a trance. Look how her body shakes, and listen to the strange spells she is saying. *Na ooso billah!*—May God protect us."

It wasn't unusual for Egyptian women to pray in the nude—even the most devout women prayed this way, believing it brought them closer to God. Of course they always did this in secret and never in front of their husbands.

The two sisters hid inside the Temple of the Sphinx and peered over the crumbling wall, watching Dorothy place incense and water by the lion's feet, and then chant some more spells. Nazirah had never seen a foreign lady do this before, and certainly not in the nude. Although she'd chatted to Dorothy in the market, Nazirah agreed it wasn't wise to approach her in this altered state. She caressed her pregnant belly—she'd had another bad dream about the child, born with seven fingers on each hand.

"You don't want people to know you are out at night traipsing round the pyramids. And who knows what that foreign lady is chanting? She could put a curse on your unborn child." Sahra didn't trust the Europeans.

"This Ingiliziyya is different. She's not like those silly tourists from Cairo. She lives like one of us and even collects her water from the well. Yesterday she chatted to me in Arabic." Nazirah recalled her encounter with the woman and how she pacified an angry snake, and sent it crawling back to the undergrowth.

182

"You see what I mean, sister, she uses magic. She's a djinn."

Nazirah rolled her eyes in frustration, "And what are we doing out here? We are asking for magic to protect my baby," she began to cry and clutch her abdomen, fearing a demon had possessed her womb. She stared up at the Sphinx with pleading eyes, "Abu el-Hol, Father of Terror. Please help my child." She felt drawn to the figure, not knowing why. Then the Sphinx whispered a reply, *"Rasheed . . ."* He seemed to be calling to the unborn child.

"The baby must be a boy, Abu el-Hol is taking care of him—he called him Rasheed! My child will be all right, Alhamdulillah." Nazirah fell to her knees and wept for joy.

"Keep your voice down, that Ingiliziyya will hear you. Who knows what trouble she could cause you, ya Allah," warned Sahra, pulling her sister onto her feet. But it was too late—Dorothy stopped chanting and turned to face the two women, gazing at them intently, as if she knew their intimate secrets. Sahra cowered behind the crumbling wall, fearing the English lady's evil eye, wishing she'd ignored her sister's pleas and stayed in bed. But Nazirah wasn't afraid and could sense the woman wanted to help her. *Perhaps she's a medium who can talk to spirits.*

"Misa il khayr. Lovely night for it," Dorothy smiled, her teeth flashing in the moonlight.

"Misa 'in noor. Yes, lovely night for it." *For dabbling in witchcraft and spells.*

"I haven't got any clothes on," Dorothy laughed, breasts bouncing as she walked towards the woman. She sat next to Nazirah in the sand and casually slipped her dress on. "I see you also pray to the Sphinx—Abu el-Hol. I'm glad to see he's still being honoured."

"Oh yes, many women pray to Abu el-Hol—when they have trouble with their husbands or pregnancies. He understands everything. I ask for his protection and he gives me peace of mind."

Sahra finally crawled out of her hiding place, having decided the Ingiliziyya wasn't going to give her the evil eye. The three women gazed up at the stars and soon fell into a deep sleep, lulled by the humming sound of the wind, the Sphinx whispering his eternal secrets.

When Dorothy awoke the two women were gone, their soft imprints visible in the sand. Her son was lying by her side. "The ladies went back to their village, they're scared of afreets—the thin lady is even

183

scared of the Sphinx," he laughed, nuzzling into his mother's neck; she wasn't afraid of afreets or sleeping in the desert. Sety was used to his mother sleeping outdoors—she was usually snoozing by the Sphinx or the entrance to a tomb, and when he poked his head out of the tent he often spotted his mother wrapped in a blanket, her hair protruding like blonde tentacles. She kissed her son's forehead and wrapped her arms round his waist. "Let's go over to the dig— breakfast should be ready by now. It's too hot to be lying out here, even at six am." They made their way over to the mess tent, the smell of warm bread, scrambled egg and fuul wafting over the desert, taste buds rising with the sun.

Dorothy spent the summer months collating the artefacts they'd found over the winter-spring season and storing them in wooden cases, ready to be taken to the Cairo Museum. One morning Dr Hassan handed her a strange object, "What do you make of this?"

She turned the stone object over in her hand, her fingers tracing the carved notches. "It's a curious little specimen. At a guess, I'd have to say it looks like part of a pulley. Why do you ask?" She handed the object back to the professor, who couldn't suppress his pleasure, his earnest face breaking into a rare smile. "This little stone has just caused a furious debate: did the ancient Egyptians use pulleys or ramps to build the pyramids? Most Egyptologists cling to Diodorus' erroneous notion that they didn't have pulleys back then, and that they dragged the stones along ramps." The professor held the artefact up to the light for inspection, "However, this little stone suggests they could have used pulleys and raised the blocks using ropes and counter weights."

"Of course they had winches and pulleys—the ancient Egyptians were very advanced people and the pharaohs had the best engineers in the world. Each pyramid stone weighed around fifteen tons and had to be carved to perfection, but they had an endless supply of workers and plenty of time—they didn't care how long it took to finish things—what's a few decades in the face of Eternity?" Dorothy loved to take part in such debates, but was careful not to sound too whimsical, making a point of using academic rhetoric to give her ideas credibility, as if they'd come from a book.

The archaeologists loved to argue over controversial theories and one day she found herself sitting in Selim Hassan's library discussing the ceremonial uses of the sacred boats with Dr Junker.

"Of course, the great barques transported the deceased pharaohs and their queens to Abydos. They stopped off at the Valley Temple at the edge of the river—that's where the dead king met the gods. The religious ceremonies were held inside the great hall and then the king was ready to travel to Amenti in his sacred barque."

Hermann Junker looked at her in disbelief, "And how do you know all this, Dorothy?"

She'd said too much, struggling to recall a book on sacred boats—one she might have read—something by Dr Budge . . .

"Dorothy is deciphering some pyramid texts in her spare time—she's learning a great deal about the funerary practices of the Old Kingdom, and she's enlightening us all." Dr Hassan gave her a furtive wink, as if to say, "Don't let the old pedant catch you out." He was beginning to understand her intuitive knowledge, and despite her ethereal tendencies, she was becoming a proper scholar.

Dorothy caught a glimpse of herself in the mirror by the door: her face tanned ochre, her sun-bleached hair braided down her back. She looked like an Egyptologist: her brows knotted over an artefact, her eyelids heavy from squinting in the sun and her jaw settled into a ponderous mould.

When Imam returned from Iraq, he also noticed Dorothy's transformation: from chubby suburban housewife to female adventurer, her body taut and strong, her mind decisive, teeming with new ideas. Imam had also changed: he seemed more settled, comfortable in himself, dare she say conservative? His face had filled out, thanks to his new wife's lavish cooking, his girth responding to the comforts of family life.

They met for lunch by the Cairo Museum and sat in a quiet corner by the window. This is all very grownup, Dorothy thought, with the civil conversation and well-cooked vine leaves. But when the lamb stew arrived Imam's his face began to darken, the light fading from his eyes; he was struggling with his conscience, his gaze darting round the room like a fox. He said he'd come to some important decisions about the future. "It is time the boy went to school. Soon he will be six years old. My wife and I can provide a good home for him, where he will have stability, brothers and sisters—he will have all he needs," he faltered, feeling a sense of guilt and remorse, hoping Dorothy would understand what he was trying to say: her nomadic existence was no life for a child.

The thought of losing her child suddenly filled her with despair. "How does any mother give up her child?" Dorothy asked him, her voice caving into grief. *Even to offer him a better chance in life.* She feared this day would come and now it was upon her, like Armageddon.

"I know this is a big shock, a big decision for you, so I will give you time to think about it. I know you will do what's best for the boy." With the meal over Imam kissed her forehead, placed some money on the table and left the restaurant, his polished shoes resounding with determination.

What was she to do? Legally she had the right to keep the boy until he was seven, but then Imam could demand to have the child. Dorothy wandered through the park, trying to focus her thoughts, but instead she was seized by a growing sense of doom. Everyone else seemed to be possessed by the same torment, as though a reflection of her own despair. "Isn't it terrible? I never thought I'd live to see another one," one woman cried, her brow creased with worry.

"Isn't what terrible?"

"Why the war, of course. England has just declared war on Germany. Haven't you heard?"

Dorothy had been sitting in this park for several hours, isolated by her own despair. She looked round at the English couples strolling with their children and pets, their grave faces seemed out of place; a blemish on the photo of perfect happiness. "All British subjects have been advised to return home. I don't know what we're going to do—we've just let our house in Southampton."

The world is crumbling, she thought, I am losing my son and Britain is at war again. She remembered the last war and how the British Museum had been closed, and excavations ceased for several years. What a blow to archaeology, she muttered bitterly. Bombs destroying the temples and tombs, without a thought for the ancient civilisations they were erasing. *It was bad enough they were destroying their own civilisation, but must they destroy the past as well?*

Dorothy took a cab to the Hassan residence where her son was happily playing with Omar; she saw his innocent face, oblivious to the tragedies in the world.

Madame Hassan poured Dorothy a cup of tea, her deep eyes filled with tears. "Only a mother can understand your pain right now. But if there is to be a war, then maybe it's best for the boy to be far away from it all. He will be safe in Iraq. Egypt is bound to be dragged into this messy affair, what with the Suez Canal. I expect the European empires will be fighting over it soon enough."

Madam Hassan was right about the boy, and little did she know how prophetic her remark about the Suez Canal would be. With Britain at war, Egypt was up for grabs and whoever ran the Suez controlled the wealth flowing from Asia to Europe.

Dr Hassan was unruffled by the impending German invasion. "Don't you worry, Dorothy. I have no intention of ending the excavations. We have a busy season ahead: I plan to excavate the boat pits and clear the area next to Khufu's pyramid. I have a feeling there's another pyramid hidden under the sand."

The season of '39-40 turned out to be the busiest season ever, as most of the archaeologists had returned to Europe and America. Despite the shortage of staff, Hassan's team excavated Khufu's mortuary complex, the numerous temples and mastabas scattered over the Giza Plain. Dorothy did the work of four people: digger, collator, archivist and secretary. She didn't complain though, as it took her mind off her son. She could still see him in his little grey shorts and blazer, hugging him goodbye for the last time, squeezing him tightly, his soft cheeks squashed up against her face, her heart sinking with sorrow.

No, this wouldn't do, she scolded herself. She mustn't become maudlin and wallow in regrets. Sety was happy in his new life. He lived in a lovely villa and went to a good school, he informed his mother in his letters. There was no need to worry about him; he was far from the war.

Not that anything had happened, except a huge influx of British soldiers which the locals said was good for business. They replaced all the expatriates who'd returned to England, so it hardly made a difference as far as Dorothy could see. The good news was many of the awful colonials had left, like the Scammells, who feared the

Egyptians might back the Germans. The only Germans Dorothy knew were eminent scholars like Hermann Junker and George Reisner (and he lived in America). But she supposed they were hardly a fair reflection of German society, who seemed rather fond of fascism these days. Dr Junker hated the Nazis and said he would rather live in a sewer in Cairo than return to his homeland while Hitler was in power.

As Dr Hassan was often busy with his heavy workload and teaching duties, Dorothy found herself running the dig and directing the small crew. Samir and Abdel had been promoted to supervisors, as they'd learned how to manage a dig, and they were left in charge when she went to Cairo. With the absence of professional archaeologists, she trained a few of the fellaheen in the art of excavation procedure. A young digger called Ahmed became quite handy with a trowel and never broke a single artefact, unlike some of the clumsy 'experts' Dorothy had worked with.

She was so excited to be working on the boat pits, crawling inside the long burial trenches that once housed the stellar boats, the sacred vessels that transported Khufu through the Underworld to Amenti, following Ra's nightly journey towards the rebirth. So far they'd discovered five boats. Why five? She supposed it had something to do with the four cardinal directions, so the *Ka* could travel in any direction, the King's body following behind in the fifth boat. Let's hope he follows the right one, she thought, or he could end up in the North Pole!

One of the boats was well-preserved, having been hidden in the sand for over four thousand years. She made sketches of the long curved bow, the cedar wood frame stained a deep brown, conserved by the dry desert. She loved the preservative qualities of the desert, the boats hermetically sealed in the sands of eternity.

From the archaeology Dorothy surmised the boats were highly sophisticated: more like ships on the high seas than ceremonial boats. As though the ancients knew about oceanic navigation, knew the kind of ship they'd need for such an expedition . . .

To think these ancient wonders had only been known to us for about 140 years, with Napoleon's expedition into Egypt—and if it hadn't been for Champollion the hieroglyphics might still remain a mystery. For thousands of years this culture had lain in waiting, their achievements forgotten over time. Just like Harp of Joy, she thought, who'd waited for three thousand years, her love for King Sety buried beneath a layer of silence. Everything was being unearthed now, freed from their tombs. The inscriptions deciphered, the statues returned to the sun. Although the mummies and artefacts belonged to an ancient world, they seemed reborn, as each day a new discovery was made, the relics bursting from the graves and demanding to be identified.

There was growing talk that the war would put an end to the excavations. Dr Hassan slammed his book on the desk, "I won't hear another word about shutting down the site. This is not Egypt's war— and yet Europe insists on using our desert as a battleground."

Dorothy read the newspaper headlines: "Mussolini has landed in Egypt. Italian troops are advancing along the Mediterranean. They have set up a military fort at Sidi Barrani and are preparing for a full invasion."

"They're on the route to Alexandria," she realised; the war was like a sandstorm gaining momentum as it swept through the desert, about to suffocate the inhabitants.

In this state of emergency the soldiers left their Arabian sweethearts, the dance halls, the oriental nights of pleasure, and set off to fight the Italians. The Allied forces were outnumbered, but they managed to surround the Italian troops and cut them off. Dorothy followed the drama in the Cairo Times: After several weeks of fierce fighting, the Italians were finally beaten by Allied forces, and Mussolini began to withdraw their troops. The British rejoiced at their victory, and the city of Cairo was once again crawling with boisterous troops, delirious with success, filling the streets with their feral enthusiasm. They celebrated in the dance halls, clubs and bars, and the smell of hashish snaked its way through the souqs, all the way to the posh mansions along the Nile.

But Dorothy sensed the victory was to be short-lived. Rommel had invaded Tripoli and she knew it was only a matter of time before the Germans invaded Egypt. "They have defeated the Allied forces in Libya, so we must prepare for the worst," she told the diggers.

The European troops were busy dismembering bodies in the desert while Dr Hassan's team were in the business of putting things back together. But how could they protect the past from modern bombs and tanks that could crush a temple into the dust?

She heard people say, "The war won't last more than a few weeks." But that's what they'd said about the last world war, she recalled, and it had lasted four years. How quickly they forget. Dorothy could sense the ruthless resolve of the Nazis—they were like the Christianised Romans, hell bent on destroying the pagan religion, the ancient culture and language of Egypt. The Nazis were on a similar mission to conquer and eradicate cultures they thought inferior. They ploughed their way through Europe, then North Africa, tyrannising countries as they progressed. And now they'd set their sights on the Middle East, India and Asia . . .

Dorothy realised some Egyptians struggled to choose a side in this war, as there were many Germans living in Egypt and they were no worse than the other Europeans. And the Germans were giants in the field of Egyptology: Carl Lepsius, Georg Ebers, Adolf Erman and Kurt Heinrich Sethe—they'd all done pioneering work and made remarkable discoveries.

"Did it matter which side we choose?" Mustafa asked her, with anger in his voice. "This is a European war. We have been dominated by colonial powers since the Greeks, this war is just another form of colonial power. Why bring this war here?" He was annoyed the Cairo Museum had been closed and his university grant put on hold.

"They are fighting for the soul of Egypt, and whoever controls Egypt controls the Eastern world. I understand your resentment, Mustafa, but the Nazis must be stopped—they are ruthless thugs—far worse than the British," she informed the young man.

The Wafd government had agreed to support Britain, with the promise of full independence after the war, Dorothy heard; but Germany also promised Egypt independence if they were loyal to the Germans—no wonder people were confused about which side to support.

Although Egypt was technically neutral, everyone knew the British were in control: Cairo was a major army base for Allied forces and Alexandria harboured their naval fleet—but the main artery was the Suez Canal. The Suez brought the riches from India and the Orient: tea, textiles, ivory, gold and opium, and made Britain the wealthiest and most powerful empire in the world. In 1936 Britain and Egypt signed a treaty which gave Britain the right to protect their interests

190

in the Suez Canal. And in return, Egypt was given greater freedom, but they were still controlled by Britain.

"This treaty gives the British the right to station troops wherever they like—all they have to say is they are protecting their interests," Mustafa grumbled, passing Dorothy a case of artefacts. He was now Dr Hassan's research assistant, since most of the European academics had returned home. At least that's one good thing to come out of this war, she concluded.

Apart from the Allied troops in Cairo, you wouldn't know there was a war on. Except that there were young men from the far corners of the empire, all dressed in smart uniforms and bursting with enthusiasm. Dorothy heard them talking in the café, "I doubt we'll see any action, stuck out in the desert," one soldier remarked. He wanted to kill some Gerries and it was doubtful he'd get the chance out here, he complained.

"I'm quite certain the Gerries will invade Egypt. They've already invaded Libya, and Egypt will be next," the general replied. "Don't worry, son, you'll see some action, you'll get your chance to be a hero."

Dorothy returned to Nazlet el Samman feeling dismayed by the talk of invasion and the reckless young men, like a pack of lions waiting for their prey. She remembered the First World War and the devastation: the bombs, the fear—the chaos it had caused her adolescence, the way it had interrupted her life and put an end to her trips to the British Museum. She threw herself into her work to forget the war and spent long hours at the excavation site—they were clearing a new pyramid, although Dr Hassan wouldn't let anyone call it a pyramid, "We cannot make suppositions until the entire area is cleared, so let's not jump to conclusions. There is evidence of a large tomb, but a scientific analysis is incomplete at his time."

"He can be so pedantic," Dorothy grumbled to herself—but unfortunately he was right. Most of what they had was speculation: there was an air of mystery about the 'pyramid' and no one could agree why it had been built. Dr Reisner had begun clearing the site thirty-five years ago, but he'd never completed the task.

After work the crew sat round the fire drinking beer and discussing the mysterious tomb. Dorothy had her own theory, "It could have been built to house the pharaoh's *Ka*, his immortal double."

191

"What a megalomaniac that bugger must've been—he builds a second tomb just for his alter ego!" Laurie laughed at the idea, lying back in the sand and telling jokes between sips of beer and hoots of laughter. He was one of the few Westerners who'd stayed—he said he wasn't afraid of Nazis as he knew how to handle vipers and snakes. In this atmosphere of merriment the conversation turned towards the spirit world and Dorothy took delight in hearing otherwise rational people talk about ghosts they'd seen, and strange incidences near the pyramids.

"The other night me and the boys had just finished taking pictures in the Great Pyramid when I realised I'd lost my penknife," Laurie began his story, poking the fire with a stick, the sparks soaring like fireflies. "I always keep it clipped to my belt—so I go back inside the Pyramid and start searching the passageways, when suddenly I hear the top of my rucksack flapping by the entrance to the King's Chamber, and I spring into action, thinking I'm being robbed. But there's no one around, and yet my rucksack is going nuts, as if some crazy donga's opening and closing the zipper, and yet there's no one around. Then I look inside the unzipped pocket and find my penknife. I was so stunned I nearly fell over—and then I grabbed my rucksack and got the hell out of there."

"It was Khufu coming to your aid, he can be very helpful," Dorothy pointed out, "he found Dr Hassan's trowel the other day. We followed a sequence of scratching noises and there was the trowel, scraping against the limestone wall, suspended in the air."

The men looked at Dorothy in awe, and then burst out laughing. She knew they had trouble dealing with the world of spirits, but after a few beers their rational defences were subdued and they caught a glimpse of the invisible realm.

The moonlight fell upon the sand in buttery swirls, the soft light moulding its way over the pyramids. What a wonderful evening to discuss the spirit world, she thought; despite the men's scepticism they gathered round to listen to the ancient tales of magic, about *afreets* turning themselves into black dogs, giant birds and ghost boats flying through the sky...

"Oh, the British and their ghosts. They have such an affinity with the supernatural world and yet they call themselves a Christian country. Not that I'm a Christian—to be honest I think it's a load of old bollocks. I'd much rather believe in a Black Dog." Laurie was on to his fifth beer and found the black dog cult very appealing, and he started to draw a canine head in the sand and howl like a jackal.

Samir made a grimace when he heard the jackal sounds and held his belly.

"It's only Laurie messing about—they aren't real jackals," Dorothy assured him, seeing the man's distress.

"I not worried about jackals—I have bad stomach ache since this morning," Samir winced, rubbing his abdomen.

"I know an ancient Egyptian spell to cure such ailments. Will you be my guinea pig?" she asked, hoping to practice her magic skills.

Samir nodded, "Anything to take away pain."

"Excellent—I will use a remedy from the Old Kingdom—it was even known in pre-dynastic times." Dorothy took his hand and led him towards the fire. She drew a quick picture of him and added several dark spirals where his pain originated. Then she burned the paper in the fire and collected the ashes in a glass. She filled the glass with water and gave it to Samir. "You must drink this in one gulp and soon your pain will disappear." And sure enough, an hour later the man was feeling much better and drank a mug of beer, forgetting all about his stomach ache.

The fellaheen had no trouble accepting these spells, as they believed *afreets* inhabited the desert. Samir made a point of telling these foreigners it was no laughing matter. "There are good *afreets* and then there are wicked *afreets*. And sometimes there are angry *afreets* and they cause terrible destruction. The *afreet* who makes *khamsin*, sandstorms, is called Gaber. When I was a child and my father argued with my mother, there was mighty *khamsin* and when we wake next day our house is buried in sand, right over roof. We dig our way out, like in tomb. My father so scared, he promise to Gaber el Afreet he never shout at my mother again."

The crew came to accept this occult side of the locals and their avid supporter, Dorothy, who knew the ancient spells and talked to cats as if they were old friends. They associated her use of magic with folklore, the way an anthropologist studied the tribal customs in order to understand the locals better. Although in Dorothy's case it wasn't research. *But how could I tell them that I've lived here before, and remember things when I enter the tombs and temples, the spirits whispering their secrets from inside the stones. Let them believe I'm a fine scholar—it's easier for them to accept my information comes from books and working with Dr Budge.*

If they only knew! The astral travel, the materialisations, the double self—they would think I was crackers, they'd lock me up! Maybe one day people will read my diaries and the rest of the world will know the truth. Of course they will try and suppress it because I am living proof that it is possible to reach the spirit world, to burst through the membrane separating this world from the next.

She hoped one day to entrust her journals to a faithful friend, but who could she trust? And who would understand her relationship with King Sety?

One night the Pharaoh came to her in a dream, and he warned her about the growing danger. "The powers of Seth are festering in the desert and soon the forces of evil will cause untold destruction. But have no fear, my Lotus Flower, I will watch over you."

If only Ma'at could restore harmony . . . the world was slipping into chaos—most of Western Europe was occupied by Germany, and British forces were struggling to stop the Nazi machine from taking all of Europe . . .

She felt Nisou's breath pass through her body, giving her strength and reassurance. He lay beside her until dawn and then faded like the North Star, shrinking into daylight.

The next morning Dorothy arrived at the dig to hear the terrible news: the Germans had finally crossed into Egypt. The crew huddled round the wireless to hear the bulletin: *The German troops have gathered at El Alamein, just 150 miles from Cairo. Allied forces are gearing up for the fight of their lives . . .*

"It will be a fight to the death: to determine who will rule Egypt and all of Asia," Mustafa concluded, resigning himself to siding with the British, "it's a case of the lesser of the two evils," an expression he'd learned from Dorothy, when deciding Egypt's fate.

"The British may be pompous and self-righteous and consider Egypt part of their empire, but you know where you are with the British," added Dr Hassan. "The Nazis are a different story. They believe in eradicating whole nations, whole civilisations. They are a new kind of invader, and you can be sure they hate Muslims as much as Jews." That's why Egypt had to side with the British, he decided, because despite their supercilious ways, they still stood for civilisation (and in this case Dorothy agreed with him).

Others were not so sure. There was a young officer called Gamal Nasser who believed that the Germans would help liberate Egypt from British rule. He told people that if Germany won the war they would ensure home rule for Egypt.

"Don't believe a word of it!" Dr Hassan protested, "the Nazis will put us all in concentration camps, including Nasser."

El Alamein was turning into the bloodiest battle in North Africa. Rommel employed all his military power to conquer Egypt, and at one stage he appeared to be winning. The British were exhausted and demoralised by their defeat in Libya—and then they had to face the fact that Rommel had more troops and superior tanks.

Dorothy scraped the tomb wall with her trowel as she listened to the radio, thinking of the soldiers suffering in the desert, killing each other under the blistering sun, their faces caked in dust and blood. At these moments she felt Bentreshy step out of her body, and she was back in ancient times; King Sety telling her about the trouble in Libya—some hostile tribe disrupting the trade route. And then there were the Hittites, bent on ruling the world. King Muwatallis wanted his empire to be as powerful as Egypt—he was tired of living in her shadow—he wanted to be a great ruler in his own right, mightier than any pharaoh.

What had they learned in those three thousand years? Dorothy wondered. Back in the 19th Dynasty, Egypt was the mightiest empire on earth, but not everyone was happy with their omnipotence. Despite the skirmishes in Sety's reign, the warmongers never invaded Egyptian soil. Egypt remained a land of peace, secure in her unchallenged glory. How Dorothy yearned for this glorious past, this idyllic sense of permanence.

The present war was turning civilisations into rubble—the great European cities were being destroyed, and yet the pyramids stood in defiance, the tombs preserved beneath the sand; the stone remnants of an advanced people, their bodies still intact, waiting for the resurrection.

Dorothy sought refuge in the Old Kingdom tomb, crawling her way through the sand-filled tunnel, like a vole seeking the comfort of the underground. She wanted to protect herself from the living—the British, the French, the Italians, and now the Germans—wanting to strip Egypt of her riches and grind her into the dust. "Egypt should never be ruled by anybody!" Dorothy shouted down the passageway — why couldn't Europeans understand this? Her mind was giddy with darkness and lack of oxygen. "I am against all forms of colonial rule," she asserted, making her political position known to the mummies and any spirits in the Underworld who may be listening.

Back in Cairo she made a point of telling the troops the same thing. "This war will put an end to the great empires of Europe, just you wait. By the time this war is over people will be so sick of empires. They won't buy it anymore. How can Europe stand for civilisation when they are bombing the hell out of each other? And how can the colonised countries look up to an empire that is set on destruction, their beautiful achievements bombed to oblivion and left to crumble into dust."

The troops were shocked by her apparent disloyalty to the British Empire; by her dangerous honesty. Dorothy didn't blame them. Most of them had never been away from home before. They had no idea they were simply pawns in the empire's game. Of course she wanted Britain to beat the Nazis, but once the war was over she hoped they'd give up their control of Egypt — perhaps the war itself would bring an end to colonial rule . . .

Dorothy met a young Maori called Mikaere, wandering round the Cairo Museum while his mates smoked shisha in the café. He said he'd joined the army to get away from his domineering father. "He expected me to take over the family boat building business, so I joined the army instead." He looked around at the ancient relics, wishing he could come here every day, instead of fighting in the desert. Dorothy detected a wild nature within him, the New Zealand landscape emerging from his body: his short hair growing in spirals like budding waves; his broad nose, full lips reminded her of a lush wilderness, untouched by colonials.

Mikaere told her about the awful battles at El Alamein and how thousands were dying on both sides, the sand a pool of blood. "And then we are let off for the weekend and come to Cairo, where we go to the dance halls and bazaars, and you'd never know there was a war going on."

It was enough to turn someone insane, thought Dorothy, living a life of intense violence for weeks on end, and then arriving in this

196

city of pleasure, with belly dancers and Turkish baths, with enough money in their pockets to satisfy their wildest fantasies.

"It's not going very well," he admitted, "I don't think we can beat the Germans under General Auchinleck. Rommel is a superior general, all the troops know this is true, and it is bad for morale."

"So you think we could lose this battle?"

Mikaere nodded woefully, "There is a possibility."

Dorothy realised the terrifying repercussions of losing this battle: German tanks could be in Cairo in a matter of days and they'd have the place surrounded. And they would hang a swastika over the Great Pyramid as they had over Freud's house and the Parisian landmarks. All British expats would be taken as POWs. But I am an Egyptian citizen, she reminded herself, her passport said "Bulbul Meguid." All she'd have to do was wear a scarf and gallabiya, and the Germans would never notice her.

By August the Allied forces at El Alamein were getting desperate. Churchill decided to recall Auchinleck and put General Montgomery in command. Montgomery had never fought in the desert before and yet the troops trusted him. He was an instinctive leader who looked for the weaknesses in his opponent and moved in for the kill. He realised Rommel was running out of supplies and that he was hemmed in by the desert. It was only a matter of time before this desert fox felt cornered and tried to run for cover—under extreme anxiety the fox would feel trapped, he would lose his nerve, his direction. The Allies, on the other hand, had access to supplies in Alexandria and the Suez Canal.

Three months of bloody fighting ensued, the desert covered in tanks and shrapnel, littered with mines and unexploded bombs. The bombs that did explode left huge craters in the sand, and sometimes Mikaere believed he was fighting on the moon.

The desert became a red sea, with 25,000 German and Italian troops killed, and 13,000 Allied troops. Rommel had no choice but to withdraw, slinking back to the lake of fire. Mikaere had never seen such human carnage, so many dismembered bodies and pools of blood (he was only twenty-three). The earth was so dry the blood refused to sink into the ground and formed rock pools fit for Dracula's garden, bubbling like thermal arteries.

In the aftermath of such horror (it didn't feel like victory), Mikaere was given weekend leave. He found himself in the streets of Old

Cairo, with snake charmers, whirling dervishes and spices that made his eyes weep. He spent an afternoon in the Al Khalili bazaar where he bought an Ottoman style coffee pot and an ornamental birdcage, and after smoking the shisha pipe and several glasses of mint tea, he headed for the Cairo Museum. To his surprise the Museum was open, and when he stepped inside he saw several people mulling around the artefacts, taking notes and the odd illicit photograph, as if the war didn't exist. Perhaps the war was all a nightmare and he'd suddenly awakened into a time of peace. But then he spotted two Allied soldiers wearing the same dusty uniform as himself, and his heart sank into recognition, as he recalled the vile reality. He ran upstairs to the Tutankhamun chamber and stood beside the gold death mask decorated with jewels and amulets. His body had survived for over three thousand years, lovingly embalmed to last for eternity. Mikaere thought of the dismembered bodies in the desert, men who would never be buried whole.

The two soldiers followed him into the chamber and he felt himself retreat. He didn't wish to speak to them and yet they insisted on being friendly. "Great mummies they got here, aye, this one reminds me of my last girlfriend."

Mikaere forced himself to smile; he was a long way from home, perhaps he should make some friends. The soldier's name was Sean Rankin, an engineer from Bristol, celebrating his thirtieth birthday. He had reddish blonde hair and an open, almost vacant face, his mouth forming a fixed grin, sometimes a sneer or a grimace. The other soldier, Raj Malhotra, was a Hindu from Delhi, and he looked as embarrassed as Mikaere, wondering how they'd ended up with this vulgar man.

Despite his crudeness, Sean had his finger on the pulse—he'd heard about a tour that took you round the pyramids, led by an eccentric English lady who also gave lectures on ancient Egypt. "It's supposed to be a real laugh and some people say she has magical powers—that she dabbles in witchcraft, but I don't believe it. Anyway, the fellahs that been say she's a scream. I'm going tomorrow if you want to come along."

Although he found Sean rather offensive, Raj agreed to go on the tour with him. He was intrigued by this English lady who brazenly traipsed round the pyramids in the middle of a war, and he decided he had to meet her.

Through her tours and lectures Dorothy met the Allied troops from Britain, Canada, Australia, New Zealand and India, and she began to realise the expanse of the empire, when people from far away lands were willing to fight for the Mother Country. They were often a mismatched group, but that's what happens in war, the most unlikely people are thrown together. She could tell by their eyes that they saw Egypt as one giant war zone. They knew only death and destruction. She wanted the soldiers to see that Egypt was more than a battle in the sand and a belly dancer in red sequins. She wanted to awaken something in them: a love of ancient Egypt, beyond the horrors of war.

They piled out of their trucks, their minds ravaged by daily death, walking like headless statues in the blistering heat. Their eyes were like broken gems, their sparkle reduced to dull a stare. Dorothy remembered the soldiers who'd returned from the last war, shell shocked and frightened of everyday life, startled by a squirrel in the park. That was the true horror of war, she thought, turning young men into feeble old men, before they had a chance to live. She sensed the atrocities they'd witnessed, smelled the burned flesh of their comrades who lay decomposing in the sun, their corpses licked clean by jackals. These lads in the trucks were the lucky ones, who'd managed to dodge the bullets, their lives random as grains of sand. They were in Saqqara, where the deceased triumphed over death, the desert littered with the earthly dwellings of the royal souls.

The three men stood in the sand watching the suntanned woman in the floral dress, waving her bare arms as if in distress. They were quite used to distress signals—it was the friendly greetings that threw them for a loop. This woman wasn't in distress—she was calling them over to start the tour, she was bursting with enthusiasm, a sentiment they'd forgotten. It's the Maori from the Museum, she realised, but she wouldn't let on—he was supposed to be buying supplies in the market and yet he'd sneaked off to the Museum . . .

She greeted them with a kiss on both cheeks, her face smiling, eyes squinting into the sun. "We are lucky we can still come here—most of the desert excavations have been stopped, thanks to this bloody war. Yalla, let's get on with the tour. We just need a bit of baksheesh for the guards and they'll turn a blind eye—they'll go play backgammon and we'll have the place to ourselves." The idea gave

199

her a thrill, the thought of exploring the ruins without any officials around. The site was usually crawling with Egyptologists and now it was completely deserted. And there were no Europeans trekking over the sand dunes to see the sunset—the desert returning to the Berbers and their camels. Dr Hassan had been forced to close the dig after a bomb had been found nearby. "You know, the bomb never exploded. The spirits were protecting the ancient monuments—they're encased in powerful magic," Dorothy believed. All the same, Dr Hassan decided it was safer to write his literary opus until the war was over.

"The area is probably full of mines—I don't think it's safe," Sean warned, scratching the surface with his boot.

"That's ridiculous. I come here all the time and I know the area is quite safe—the Germans have no reason to bomb the tombs. But if you're afraid you can always wait for us by the truck," Dorothy suggested, strolling off ahead.

"She's crazy," Sean concluded, spitting in the sand; the woman may know a lot about Egyptology, but she knew nothing about the war, he grumbled. It wasn't surprising that the excavations in the Western desert had all ground to a halt, due to the thousands of mines the Germans and British had buried under the sand.

"The excavations at Saqqara and Giza should not have been stopped—they're nowhere near the conflict," Dorothy insisted—in the face of such barbarity it was vital for them to continue—they reminded people of civilisation, when their own world was crumbling. "As long as I can take people round the pyramids I will continue to do so—and if they bomb the place, well, I can't think of a better place to die."

Raj could see Dorothy was no ordinary woman: she was both obstinate and courageous, and he didn't know whether to admire her or fear her. What was she doing in the middle of a war, taking people round the tombs and temples, like some demented tour guide in Hades.

"Quite simple. I need the money," Dorothy replied, marching on ahead of him, leaving him to chuckle to himself. This woman was a force of nature, Raj decided, with a wit as sharp as a bayonet. And he knew it was more than the measly tips from the soldiers that kept her here: she wanted to show them the ancient Egyptian wonders, the sublime creations, as if built by her beloved relatives.

"I want them to believe in something greater than this sewer they're in," she explained to Raj and Mikaere. "I see these men coming from the front, and I think, they need something to believe in—that civilisation will continue and will outlive this hell they're in. Right beneath their feet lies one of the oldest civilisations, virtually intact. And I want them to think, there's hope for us yet."

The tour began with the Step Pyramid of Djoser, the pharaoh who ruled from about 2635-2610 BC, Dorothy informed them. "He was a wonderful king—probably the best pharaoh of the Old Kingdom. During his reign humanity reached new heights. He had the good sense to employ Imhotep, the architect who designed the first great monument on earth—the Step Pyramid. He designed the building with six mastabas, one on top of the other, getting progressively smaller as it ascended, and forming a unique pyramid structure." She gazed up at the building, eyes resting on the final mastaba. "As you've probably noticed, these pyramids are much different from the ones at Giza. They are hundreds of years older. The shape had to do with their philosophy of the soul's journey to Amenti. The pharaoh travelled from the burial chamber through the antechamber which they saw as the horizon. Once the pharaoh was safely in the antechamber—the horizon, he was ready to make his ascent to eternity; to rise as high as the sun."

The place was a huge complex of temples, tombs, palaces and courts, and Mikaere had the sense that it was still alive...He was mesmerised by this English woman and the six mastabas leading to eternity. Only yesterday he'd been trudging through the desert on a manoeuvre, the sand a thin veil between his forces and the enemy. And now he was walking through a different coloured desert, with rich shades of ochre, with tombs, temples and courtyards, where a great city once stood; where a woman now walked barefoot in a floral dress and reminded him of joy.

He could see the entrance to the temple sticking out of the sand, hinting at a deeper world below. He got down on his knees and began digging, desperate to find a way inside the hidden wonders.

Sean rubbed the sweat off his face, his red skin prickling in the heat. "Have you gone mad, old boy? Dig any deeper and you'll end up in Australia. Well I've seen enough tombs for today—I'm going back to the truck for a beer. I'll see you devils later."

201

They were all relieved when Sean wandered back to the truck, the cloud of cynicism evaporating into the air. Raj and Mikaere crawled inside the temple and tumbled into a large chamber covered in exquisite murals, untouched for thousands of years. They gazed at the beauty in silence, and they were both thinking the same thing: how this culture could produce such wonders in the sand, when all their generation could do was destroy things.

Then Dorothy led the men through the pyramid, along the labyrinth of tunnels, chambers and galleries that measured six kilometres in length. They found themselves in the King's burial chamber with the granite sarcophagus, although his mummy had been stolen by ancient tomb robbers, along with his cache of treasures for the Afterlife. The robbers left the 40,000 stone vessels—Djoser's immortal offerings, but the vessels were all empty. The five pointed star was still visible on the ceiling, identified as the North Star, significant to the Pharaoh as it never sets, a symbol of rebirth and royal eternity... On the walls there were symbols of the Dog Star, the sun, and the worship of Osiris. The hieroglyphic texts described how the Pharaoh became one of the eternal stars next to the North Star. Djoser voyaged in his sacred boat and joined the sun god, crossing the astral ocean of night into day.

Dorothy stopped before a series of symbols and shone her torch onto a particular passage. "You see here. The Pharaoh experiences the same fate as Osiris: he goes through death, chaos, and then he journeys through the Underworld, uttering the protective spells to save his soul. Osiris offers him resurrection—he travels from the netherworld to heaven without peril, shifting from dark to light, night into day."

Mikaere shone his torch into a dark crevice, illuminating some brightly coloured symbols. Perhaps that's what we're doing in this land, he thought, stumbling through day and night, descending through the darkness, in search of the light. This ancient land was both heaven and hell.

"The pyramids at Saqqara were built differently from the later ones at Giza," Dorothy pointed to the wall, "you will notice that the main burial chamber leads through to an antechamber. The pyramid was a replica of the material world—the burial chamber as the earth, the antechamber as the horizon, and the Pharaoh's exit from the pyramid as his final ascent to eternity. The Pharaoh travelled from the physical to the celestial; his destiny to resurrect at dawn, to rise as high as the sun. But there's so much more they're trying to tell us —that we too are capable of rebirth—that this place is also for the living." She had the sense they were more like temples than tombs, portals to the beyond, once used for initiation ceremonies to reach the gods.

Mikaere would later say, "That afternoon I was awakened to the ancient magic. I came out of the darkness." He didn't expect the other soldiers to understand and he received a terrible ripping for it, and he was the butt of jokes for weeks to come, but he didn't care: he had entered a hidden temple, he'd dug through the sand and found humanity buried underneath. He'd found something timeless, a belief in gods he'd never heard of until that momentous day in Saqqara. And Raj had felt it too, standing in the dusky temple, his shoes full of sand; he was drawn to this sense of eternal, when his own world had become so transient, so mechanical. Life made cheap, human lives reduced to rubble.

On their next weekend leave, Raj and Mikaere arranged to go on another tour with Dorothy—this time to Giza and without Sean Rankin. They waited in the sun, enjoying the rare silence—they'd grown used to the hum of tanks, the bellows of army personnel.

Why are we fighting in this war?" Mikaere suddenly wondered, looking at Raj for an answer, who was four years older and seemed to know how the world worked.

"Freedom." Raj cleared the sand from his throat, "To free Europe from tyranny."

"But Egypt isn't free, neither are half the countries who are fighting to save Europe." They were all governed by the British Empire.

"Think of the war as a swarm of locusts—we've been invaded by millions of locusts and we are here to stop them before they destroy our world." Indian crops had been wiped out by locusts on numerous occasions, causing famine and death—and in ancient times locusts had overthrown pharaohs and caused social collapse—the great Plague of Egypt. Raj imagined the Nazis like green locusts in their khaki uniforms, great black eyes peering out from under their helmets; a greedy multitude bent on destroying the land.

"Hindus believe in reincarnation, right—do you think you've been here before?" Mikaere's mind was moving away from locusts; he had nightmares about them as a child, dreaded green aliens invading from Australia. He wanted to talk about the spirit realm, out of reach to locusts.

"I believe we come back many times until we get it right. In my past life I was a teacher in the court of Chandra Gupta I in the 4th century. I wrote poetry and taught the princes how to read. That's all I remember." As he spoke Raj envisioned a great palace carved into the mountainside, hidden by a festoon of blue mist.

"I have a recurring dream about running through the forest with a tribe, my face is painted in strange patterns—then I am wading in a green river and I feel so happy and alive," recalled Mikaere, drifting into silence. He saw a figure on the horizon: a woman in a green and white dress floating over the desert, a Bedouin scarf flapping round her shoulders, her breasts bulging like sand dunes, threatening to burst their cotton boundaries. Mikaere gazed into the soft mounds and felt his loins awaken into desire, a feeling he'd forgotten since the long months of fighting; his desires urging him into the wilderness. This sense of tenderness was unfamiliar to him—he'd become used to pain, the struggle to survive from day to day. His body had become a meticulous machine and now it was melting into human passion, and he stood trembling with longing.

This woman was more than just an enticing female body—she had shown him a hidden world; she told him about the sun god Ra who died with every sunset and was reborn each morning, and she taught him how to harness the god's energy by chanting the old prayers. She knew strange things about the stars, and where the hidden entrances to the temples lay buried in the sand.

Dorothy showed them the remnants she'd found in the tombs: the skulls, bones and amulets that no one had seen for thousands of years. "These handsome heads are four thousand years old," she spread the skulls out on the sand, proudly displaying the family she'd unearthed. She made a point of showing these skulls to all the visitors and seemed oblivious to their horrified faces, or perhaps she delighted in seeing their repulsion. Sean thought she was macabre and told them she was off her rocker—but Mikaere and Raj didn't think so. She saw life in these dry bones and splendour in the finely shaped craniums. Raj held one of the skulls up to the sun and couldn't help thinking of his fallen comrades, their severed bodies buried in the sand; flesh like tomatoes drying in the sun. They would lie desiccated in the sand alongside the millions of bodies, since the area had become a desert about 5500 years ago—before this time the land had been a verdant savannah, a regular Garden of Eden, and human settlements had flourished there for thousands of years. What would the ancients think of the newly deceased corpses lying in pieces beside them? It would have been the greatest dishonour to die in such a way, left to wander the Underworld in fragments, with no hope of finding their way to the Afterlife. The body had to be intact to make its journey to the eternal realm. Their limbs would have to be found and their bodies reassembled, just as Isis put Osiris back together so he could resurrect as a god. Raj felt ashamed when he thought of his fallen comrades and sensed the ancient spirits looking down on the desert in horror, mystified by the foreign bodies lying in scrap heaps, with total disregard for funerary customs. He thought of the ancient bodies that probably died of natural causes, buried in honour, and in proper tombs.

"In her glory Egypt had been a land of peace—it's an insult having these degenerates fighting over her body," Dorothy told them, "you know, Egypt created the world's first Peace Treaty, with the Hittites, which you can visit in Karnak." And now two foreign armies were knocking the shit out of each other, Raj thought to himself. Egypt had nothing to do with this conflict and yet her fate depended on the outcome.

Back in Cairo life went on as usual: soldiers, traders, shoeshine boys and camel drivers, "You want see pyramid—very big, very old!"

The soldiers had money in their pockets, and they spent surreal weekends on leave trawling through the bazaars, lured by gold, silk and spices, a pretty face with dark eyes. They were the most beautiful women the men had ever seen, with the most striking features. The women came from the exotic corners of the former Ottoman Empire: Asia, Europe and Africa, with gemstone eyes, skin the colour of the desert as it journeys from light to dark. There were belly dancers in Turkish costumes, peeking over their veils in the smoky hash dens, and they beckoned the soldiers to slip their notes into the sultry folds of fabric, with the promise of heavenly rewards. And the local young men were equally beguiling, with their perfectly aligned noses, gentle eyes and hair like a raven's crown.

The soldiers flocked to the seamy bars and nightclubs, which resembled sultans' palaces, with Turkish divans, Persian carpets,

205

and tables inlaid with mother of pearl; eastern delights to seduce the amenable foreigners. They'd never seen such opulence, or experienced such an assault on their senses, their eyes drowning in Oriental colours and rich patterns—unlike anything these Christian boys had seen back home. Religion, art, beauty, sensuality—it was all one and the same. It made them think how dowdy English churches were by comparison, with their rigid pews and cold stone floors. The protestant faith seemed rather anaemic, as if all the blood had been drained from its body. The mosques in Cairo were a spiral of light and beauty, places to dream in, where one lay down on plush carpets and stared into infinity. Raj identified with the religious sensuality as it reminded him of the Hindu soul and how it was reflected in the architecture. He felt at home here, Cairo reminded him of Bombay, with its great helix of humanity, swept up in a vibrant dance, a sequence of life's opposing elements: pain- pleasure, beauty-ugliness, rich-poor.

The soldiers spent decadent nights drinking and dancing until dawn, sleeping with exotic beauties and smoking hashish after breakfast. Just like in the Arabian Nights, where travellers indulged in fabled pleasures. Mikaere never believed they were true until he'd spent an enchanting night in Cairo: an old beggar led him through the labyrinthine streets of the bazaar, and there he met a dark beauty with green eyes, wearing nothing but a red veil. They danced all night while troubadours played Arabic love songs, until their hearts and loins ached with desire. The beauty lured him into a Bedouin tent and they lay on cushions smoking hashish from a water pipe, and made love until they heard the first call to prayer.

And then it was back on the front line come Monday morning, shooting at the Germans, the bombs kicking up the sand, artillery exploding like fireworks, the desert sky like a stained glass window, the sand a sea of blood.

∧∧∧∧∧ ∧∧∧∧∧ ∧∧∧∧∧

How strange it was to ride around the pyramids on a mule, when only hours ago Mikaere was ploughing a tank through the sand, shelling the enemy with a storm of bullets; he'd advanced like a bull in the plaza de toros, stupefied by the loud explosives, not knowing if he'd been hit, or if he were already dead.

206

The next weekend on leave Mikaere and Raj met Dorothy in Giza for another tour: this time round the Great Pyramid. Dorothy appeared like a ghost on the horizon traipsing over the sand with her childish bounce; she was barefoot, her tanned legs striding with confidence, as if she'd always lived here, as if her limbs had grown out of the sand dunes.

Raj could see she was at home here, like a desert fox sniffing her territory; her brown body shaped by the landscape, her hair bleached by the sun. The folds of her floral skirt rose above her knees, revealing a pair of muscular legs, and he knew she'd walked every inch of this place, marking her territory and claiming it as her own.

"Good morning fellows—glad to see you're still in one piece!" she greeted the soldiers, bending down to pick up a piece of bone, "Not like this poor fellow." Hearty laughter all round, relieving the agony—three weeks of death and desolation. Dorothy led the men round the pyramid, blinking in the harsh sun and pulling her hat over her brow. The soldiers stared up at the Great Pyramid and shielded their eyes, as if they were imagining the whole thing, like the mirages in the desert beyond the enemy line; a promise of hope, of new landscapes. The men treaded gingerly through the sand, their feet used to checking for mines. The men had just come out of the Underworld and they stood dumbstruck before the pyramid, too big to absorb with their war-torn eyes, trained to focus on minute targets, their vision narrowed to a pinprick, shrunken to a single purpose: to destroy a chosen target. And here was the Great Pyramid rising out of the sand, filling the sky and drowning their conical eyesight, forcing them to use their peripheral vision so they could perceive infinity. And Dorothy, calling them forward; she lived in a wider space, her senses capable of absorbing a vast landscape.

"There were great processions here in ancient times, like on the Vernal Equinox, the summer solstice and the Heb Sed, when the Pharaoh ran and danced before his people, to prove he was fit to rule, and that he had the blessing of the gods."

And now there was a procession of soldiers trying to find a lost civilisation; their forgotten selves . . . Mikaere thought of the war as a procession of tanks and artillery, a festival of death without a rebirth. Seth had had his way at last: the Lord of the Desert, destruction and chaos had come back to rule. The Red Land was a sea of blood.

Where was Osiris, their resurrection? The Green God came in many disguises, Dorothy told them. One day Osiris would return, and with him a Renaissance would follow.

"Now—would you like to see the oldest religious text ever found?" Dorothy asked the men, seeing the excitement growing in their eyes.

"Out here in the desert? Of course we'd love to see it!" the men replied, captivated by Dorothy's description of this original scroll. They hopped in the truck and Mikaere drove along the dusty road to Saqqara, the landscape bulging with unexplored temples and tombs.

"The inscriptions you are about to see were discovered inside the pyramids—their walls read like a book, describing the journey to the Afterlife. Maspero found these funerary texts in 1880 in the pyramids of Unas, Teti and Pepi II. He named the hieroglyphs the *Pyramid Texts*. The texts were written from the time of Unas in the 5th Dynasty to Ibi in the 8th Dynasty—inscribed in the tombs of pharaohs and their queens. Kurt Sethe completed the first thorough translation of the texts—a great Egyptologist and philologist, and German of course."

The men winced at this Germanic reference. They thought of Rommel and Hitler. How could they belong to the same race as these illustrious scholars?

"Kurt Sethe devoted his life to the *Pyramid Texts*—he proved to the world they were the oldest collection of religious inscriptions, the first bible, if you like. They recorded ruminations about the Afterlife and the pharaoh's journey to Amenti. Later on the texts were copied onto papyri and anyone could buy them for their own funeral, provided they had the money of course."

Dorothy motioned to the men to open their wallets, "A couple of pounds should do it—and the guard will go for tea."

The guard grudgingly took the money, feigning a struggle with his conscience.

They walked across the desert unhindered and stopped before a tomb entrance buried in sand. "This is it—the tomb of King Unas of the 5th Dynasty. We started excavating it last season and found these wonderful hieroglyphs—but now it's closed . . . well lads, let's start digging."

After clearing a path, they descended the tunnel inside the pyramid, crouching for what seemed like an eternity, passed the vestibule and antechambers to the burial chamber below. Finally they were able to stand up and witness the extraordinary hieroglyphs painted in blue symbols. "Here they are: the first corpus of spiritual chants in the world, they lay untouched for thousands of years—Maspero was the first to see them again—imagine his excitement!" Dorothy read the blue words:

White-crown goes forth,
She has swallowed the Great;
White-crown's tongue swallowed the Great,
Tongue was not seen!

"It's quite a complex inscription: the white crown is Upper Egypt, conquering the red crown of Lower Egypt, uniting with the cobra goddess Wadjet, often represented as Lower Egypt," she explained. "This verse was later used as a spell to charm snakes: the cobra swallowed, or tamed by the snake-charmer."

Raj was amazed by how quickly Dorothy interpreted the arcane symbols, uttering the prayers in ancient Egyptian, as though speaking in her mother tongue.

Ra-Atum, this Unas comes to you,
A spirit indestructible,
Who lays claim to the place of the four pillars!
Your son comes to you, this Unas comes to you,
May you cross the sky united in the dark,
May you rise in lightland, the place in which you shine!

They stood in silence contemplating the ancient litany; the flight from mortal being into divine essence, the journey from death to resurrection played out on the sacred walls. "But it's also about our own journey on earth," Dorothy believed; the death of the old self and the dawn of our eternal being, the place in which you shine.

When they emerged from the pyramid the sun was hovering over the hills, balanced like an orange beach ball. Mikaere watched Dorothy clamber over the ruins, she seemed to change before his eyes—walking across the sand as if floating on air, flitting from one tomb to the next; transforming from an English woman into someone else. Someone with a lighter gait, suddenly more playful, more childlike, bouncing around as if she owned the landscape. But it was stranger than that: it was as if the landscape owned her, the way the sand clung to her toes and the sun danced upon her skin in familiar patterns.

She turned to face the soldiers—within their joy she suddenly felt a spear of sorrow—she saw the war in their faces, dragging the horrors with them, even through this desert of benign spirits. She saw them with a child's eye: the way a child pities an adult for being grownup, for losing their exuberance; the blinkers upon their imaginations.

These men had been moulded by the military world, hardened by their conflicts. But as the men moved from chamber to chamber, emerging from darkness into light and following the path to eternity, Dorothy noticed their faces open into wonder, their terrors evaporate in the heat, like a wound healing in the sun.

"We will come again when we're next on leave," Mikaere kissed her on the cheek. "Thank you for showing us round—you know, we live for these tours," Raj admitted, wishing he could stay here with this adventurous woman.

"Next time I'll show you the boat pits—and maybe the shaft underneath the sphinx..." She would lead them into the invisible realm running alongside our own. It was quite easy for the present to evaporate in this land. If people could only see into the beyond, into the pharaoh's world, she wished, like when she slipped into a trance-like state and could see things as they used to be: the temples covered in limestone and gold, the gilt and fresh paint on the murals, the great avenues laid out in intricate paving stones, the granite statues aligning the pathways to the gods, and the magnificent gardens with their vibrant splashes of colour. Dorothy usually entered this other realm at night or just before dawn. She would rise and perform her ablutions, and then go to the Temple of Isis to pray.

Later that night she carried a jug of fresh water and a bowl of incense, walking through the failing mist, past the pyramid of Queen Henutsen to the ancient temple. Dorothy stood chanting by the figure of Isis until she felt her present form dissolve like honey in hot water, and when she opened her eyes she saw the freshly painted walls and flawless statues, without the ravages of time. She felt herself reassemble—become liquid and then solidify into a more arrant form, with canine senses and feline vision. She was seeing through the eyes of Harp of Joy: the incense rising in purple spirals, the drums and sistra vibrating through her pelvis and causing her hips to sway. *He is here, she sensed; Nisou breathing in the air and exhaling through the pictures on the wall.*

He is in her orbit now, his shapeless being coagulating into a solid mould. *Without her there is only chaos.* He inhales her breath and feels the blood begin to flow through his body, filling his vacant organs. Within her small frame lie the seeds of renewal, like the flutter of a butterfly's wings generating the universe. A swarm of emotions seep through his body, and he cries out, unaccustomed to the intensity of human responses. He is trying to remember being human, what it's like to live in the flesh: to breathe with lungs, to have internal organs and to nourish himself with food and water.

Nisou touches the girl's flesh and it rises with each breath, like bread leavening in the sun. He knows she is struggling too, trying to navigate through three thousand years of memories, trying to manoeuvre from one self to another, and yet the signs on the map are written in a foreign language, and she is terribly lost. In one memory she is waiting for the flood, darting through the sand like a desert hare, dancing through the streets in a religious procession and calling Osiris to rise from the dead. Then she is watching a film about the history of civilisation: the mighty temples decaying and sinking into the sand; the mummies resting in their tombs, and over time, shrivelling into their bones.

The desert is the great ruler of Egypt, a gritty membrane concealing the surface, obscuring man's mark. I am just a footprint, Dorothy realised, a footnote in the sand. But the desert can also be accommodating: it is possible to see footsteps that are thousands of years old, and the wheel marks of Rameses' chariot charging through the desert, to conquer the Hittites; the trail of German and Allied tanks zigzagging across the sand, quite visible from the air. They are the great scars of history; whip lashes across the back that never disappear. Or like a rough canvas, thought Dorothy, with bold streaks of colour that can never be painted over.

Dorothy would return to that time, when temples pushed back the sand and gardens grew out of the barren wilderness. She would will the stones back to life, breathe new life into their insensible forms. She would move them with the strength of her arms, and then turn her sweaty palms to the sun in prayer, invoking Ra to witness her deeds.

She would call to the old gods, as people used to do in this land, but now seldom do. She would raise them from the dead, with her invocations and irresistible spells. *I will raise the Temple from the rubble, complete the self I disassembled. And once my task is complete my spirit will fly to you, as a free entity, of pure light and radiant energy. A laser beam of creation, able to transmute into any form.*

Bentreshy and Nisou watched the world spinning like a child's top and they stretched out their hands to make the universe stop. They stepped into this suspended world, when the temples belonged to Isis and Osiris and the earth radiated with their irrepressible love for all of creation. Bentreshy and Nisou were the manifestation of this divine love and they walked into the centre of the cosmos, suspended in sensual bliss, so powerful even the gods bowed before them.

Bentreshy wore a translucent white robe, like a layer of cobwebs spun by a celestial spider with a sense of beauty. Her hair hung in intricate braids round her shoulders, her eyes shining like crushed cobalt.

Nisou wore his royal tunic and headdress, his blue cloak draped over his shoulders. "It's time, my love. I am taking you to the Feast of Amenti. But to get there we must travel through the Underworld, and I'm afraid we will encounter demons and man-eating beasts along the way, crocodiles and wily serpents, not to mention the hippopotami that love the taste of human heart. So you must stay close to me. Remain focused on the Feather of Ma'at and the purity of your heart will guide your path. Do not let fear or self-doubt enter your mind, as the demons will seize this moment of weakness and strike you down."

Bentreshy drove every ounce of fear from her mind and waited for the last drop of doubt to evaporate, and then she turned to Nisou, "I am ready for the Underworld."

She focused on the white Feather of Ma'at and held onto Nisou's hand. They walked through the tunnel entrance and down the steep incline towards the swampy heart of chaos. They passed crocodiles with gaping jaws, bottomless caverns with jagged teeth, and hippos with fat mouths that opened and closed in anticipation of pink flesh, salivating at the thought of a soul straying from the path. They walked along a narrow trail above a steep chasm, and Bentreshy realised how easy it would be to lose one's footing and tumble into the waters of chaos. As they walked along the path they encountered flying demons

212

with great wings and snakes rising up with red tongues hissing in their faces, but Bentreshy concentrated on the white feather and the beasts melted before her eyes. All she had to do was keep focused and never flinch. Soon they passed through the abyss of demons and came across a tranquil river that shone like a streak of onyx, and Bentreshy knew this black river would lead them to safety. They stepped aboard a long wooden ship and set sail for the Feast of Amenti.

Dorothy awoke from her astral travels feeling exhausted and slightly ill. Her body felt stiff and heavy, and she couldn't fit into its cumbersome form. She tried to settle into her present shape as Dorothy, but she could feel Bentreshy's solid persona, like water seeping through paper and creating its own design.

Dorothy prepared the morning porridge and tea outdoors, shoulders stooping under the saggy awning. She sat on the wooden stool, her arms resting on her knees, her bare feet warming in the sun. Despite the passage of three millennia, the setting hadn't changed—she still had an outdoor kitchen with a large stone oven and open fire to cook on. Then she lay in the hammock watching the women over the road arrange the bread on the wall, leaving the round loaves to rise in the sun. She saw Nazirah pick up the ewer and pour the water into her sister's hands, who began washing her face and neck. Nazirah had recently given birth to a healthy baby boy called Rasheed, thanks to the Ingiliziyya and Abu el-Hol, she claimed.

As the days followed it seemed the past was getting stronger, encasing the present in a dusty shrine. Ancient Egypt was no longer a past memory to her, it was becoming the main venue, echoed in the landscape and local characters. And Dorothy was attached to this place, the part she played directed by memory and emotion. The ancient gods were calling to her: the morning fog hugging the temple walls, the tongue of Anubis whispering her name in wet circles; Isis enshrined her in a veil of mystery, and her ancient lover haunted the passageways of her mind.

There were echoes of her past life everywhere, like the remains of a great feast, the discarded scraps hinting at the former splendour. Market day was full of such echoes, and she loved to sit in the outdoor café listening to the melodic voices, recalling the folksongs of long ago, when Egypt was the centre of the civilised world.

213

After a long day revising Dr Hassan's manuscript, Dorothy wandered through Cairo's old quarter, where the Europeans rarely ventured. In this world of scented labyrinths she inhaled the dark mysteries, her head swimming with strange voices, a verbal collage of Eastern languages: Arabs from Syria, Lebanon and North Africa, a mysterious medley from the Black Sea; Armenian, Turkish and Greek voices echoing through the souqs. There were Jews who'd come from Anatolia and the isolated pockets of the Eastern world, and they spoke a strange kind of Hebrew that was jumbled with Russian, French and Arabic. Like in Bentreshy's time, she thought, when people collided in this land of opportunity, drawn to the seductive aura of the place, this great caravanserai of life where dreams revealed themselves behind the lattice screen.

Dorothy loved the earthly delights of the city: the spice markets, the gold shops, the endless souqs, the musicians playing heavenly music, and she would be lured into the dark crevices where the Hebrews, Ethiopians and Babylonians once lived; where Jesus fled down a passageway to safety, where the cobbles trembled with Nazarene footsteps. She had also seen the twisted face of misery in the eyes of the lepers, beggars and cripples who lined the streets like gaping wounds, waiting to be healed by an unforeseen saviour. The brothel paraded their women outside the dark entrance to the gaudy paradise they promised. Young girls dressed in belly dancing costumes, their faces painted like showgirls. It turned her stomach to hear them calling seductively to the men passing in the street—the girls would never find their paradise with them. Behind the half-closed doors she heard the howling laughter of the deranged and the piercing cries of lost souls. It was hard to distinguish between pain and pleasure, human and animal, as the primal noises mingled into one communal voice.

Sometimes the sound of these mad beasts echoed through the privileged parts of the city and assaulted the European sensibility. On occasion the underbelly would rise to greet the smiling faces of the fortunate, and it was a rude awakening. Dorothy saw a well-dressed English couple emerge from a carriage only to be confronted by a decomposing dog, the remains of a poor family's feast. She saw their appalled faces, realising what they were witnessing, their noses coming to terms with rotting flesh, excrement and urine; the pervading aromas of the disadvantaged. Perhaps what upsets them most, Dorothy later pondered in the café, is the fear of losing their own privileges and ending up in such misery. The fear in their eyes was like a physical attack, and she'd seen this expression on many colonial faces; they'd stepped into a horror show they didn't want to see, upsetting their agreeable world (and they would need several gin and tonics to lay the ghosts to rest).

As she left the café Dorothy noticed the young English woman who'd got out of the carriage earlier. She wore a green twin set and matching shoes, and looked rather pale in the afternoon sun, with her big white hat. She began chatting to Dorothy in an anxious rush of sentiment, expressing her dismay at the poverty and filth. "I have never seen such misery, and to think these poor children have no shoes. It is truly frightful to see." The woman made a great show of being horrified and placed her gloved hand over her mouth, shaking her golden curls in alarm.

"Just because you don't see it, doesn't mean it goes away. Don't you think we should have the courage to face them—I mean, at least acknowledge their existence?" Dorothy looked round at the barefoot children coming towards them, wearing ragged gallabiyas and shouting in Arabic. The woman looked embarrassed, "Perhaps you're right. It's not very Christian of me to turn away. They are all God's children."

"Allah's children," Dorothy muttered to herself, watching the English lady fumble through her purse and give the children a handful of piastres, her face flushed with charity. Then she stepped forward with a sense of excitement, "There's my husband across the road—I see he's bought a carpet." She waved to the man in the white suit, his servant bending under the weight of the Persian carpet. She rushed across the road, tiptoeing round the lumps of mule faeces in her apple green shoes.

You couldn't live in Egypt and avoid the misery of life. If you wanted a Persian carpet you had to venture into the old quarter; you had to endure a little stench. You couldn't have one without the other: to see the beauty you also had to experience the suffering. No animal understood this better than the camel, thought Dorothy. The camel represented perseverance and dignity in the face of degradation. No other animal had to endure such pain and misery as the camel, and yet he bore it with a noble resignation. She'd seen a camel whipped and then beaten with a cudgel—all because its leg was stuck in a grid and it was blocking traffic. She'd watched in horror from the train, unable to get off and intervene. The poor camel was eventually shot and dragged away, and yet even in death he exuded an air of majesty; a humpback Christ figure who wouldn't be broken.

Dorothy took a caleche back to the village and then walked to her house through the quiet streets, the old men at prayer, the women and children rounding up the animals before dark, the fellaheen carrying their archaic tools. She passed the mud houses with their painted walls, the sound of bare feet running down the sun baked street. She watched the women coming in from the fields, leading their cattle and children to the safety of home. There was something feral, unleashed about these women, despite their enveloping robes. She sensed something creeping, rising behind the dark veils.

11. The Underworld
1290 BC

Bentreshy awoke inside the pink foetus of dawn, eyes squinting in the blade of light piercing the cave. She was surprised to find her body was intact—even after the disembowelling and the jagged incisions made by the embalmer. She examined her body: no sign of any wounds, just a few old scars. Perhaps she'd dreamed it all and now she'd awakened into her real self, one that knew no physical pain. The torment may have stopped, but she was haunted by the memory, imprinted on her like a bas relief: the priests with their torture devices, the pain they'd inflicted in order to get their confession—but she hadn't said a word . . . *And the body I am in now—is that just a memory of my human form? In the aftermath of death, have I recreated my own image—given birth to myself?* What a strange notion, she thought, to spring forth from my imagination. Master Amenkef would say that was carrying her reveries one step too far. But he was dead now too, impaled and left to rot in the desert, his bones picked clean by vultures, and gleaming like polished limestone.

Where am I? Bentreshy doesn't recognise this strange landscape. She huddles in a small cave in the rocks surrounded by sea, where there is no land to call an Empire. Everywhere there is water and waves of chaos, churning in great swirls of black, purple and blue. A band of mountains forces its way out of the abyss, the jagged peaks tearing through the sky. It's a precarious existence in this vast sea, where every patch of land is precious and creatures cling to its shores.

"I once lived in a land where things were the other way round: where the world was a vast stretch of sand and stone, as far as the eye could see, and there was only one river to nourish a surprising multitude of life forms." This image of her former home now seems like a dream, and she can hardly believe it once existed. She remembers the old men who talked wistfully about the past, and no one believed them because it was so far removed from the present, so far-fetched.

Bentreshy can't believe her eyes: all this water and no Fields of Reeds or papyrus plants. This must be the beginning of the universe,

217

when all was primeval chaos, before there was a land called Egypt. Back then there was nowhere to plant a crop of wheat, just a few tall peaks offering a refuge from the abyss. She recalls the old tales about the mound of creation: how the god Atum had risen from the dark waters of Nun and created his progeny from his own semen. Once the universe was created the other gods came on the scene: the sun god Ra produced light, Geb created the earth, and his wife Nut gave us the sky. Ma'at created a state of cosmic harmony, her scales perfectly balanced between order and chaos.

Every year when the flood came, the people were reminded of the beginning of time, when everything was chaos and there was only water and sludge, and shapeless beings were moulded out of the mire. Their lives were suspended between order and chaos: the annual flood and ensuing droughts, the light and dark skies, the birth and death of human life.

Harp of Joy steps gingerly along the summit's path, crawling out of chaos. She heads for the highest peak in the distance, towards the western sky where the day has ended. A red sky at sunset signifies the chance of a new dawn. She pulls herself over the steep cliffs, her heart pounding in her ears; she is hot, then cold, scorched by the harsh sun and then frozen by black clouds. The weather is unpredictable here, in a constant state of flux. She is unaccustomed to such climatic extremes. Even the creatures are strange to her, and when she stops to catch her breath flying beasts descend upon her, pecking at her face. She fights them off with her fists and curses; she struggles to remember the spells from the *Book of the Dead*:

I curse you flesh eating demons!
My Ka is free from malice and wrong-doing,
I am destined for the land of the Shining Ones,
Return to your feast of evil delights,
My heart is pure and no good to you,
Devourers of rotten organs and all things putrid!

The spell doesn't sound right, but as she utters the words a beast flies over her head, skimming the top of her crown with its black claws, then loses impetus. Strands of her hair dangle from the bird's feet, which she'll use to line her nest and then give birth to more winged monsters.

The weather has cleared up; the water is like a sheet of blue faience, the sky a mirror of eternity. Bentreshy continues up the path, the crag getting more narrow and slippery the higher she goes. She falls flat on her face, her legs dangling down the ravine, her hands grabbing the shapeless mud. She slides down the ravine, the clay tickling her belly; her fingers form a wavy trail, like snakes racing to the river. She remembers falling as a child, the rush of fear like bare feet running on hot sand. Fear that drives human consciousness out of chaos. The fear she suffers is less intense—it is only the memory of fear, like a mirage in the desert, hinting at what might be. She descends towards the water, her body slimy as an eel, the sludge sticking to her body in loose folds. She hits the water with a splash, oceans parting into waves, and she cries out, "Help me!"

She sinks beneath the surface, her voice strangled by the swell. Bentreshy is an intruder and yet the water accommodates her, quickly swallowing her up. But the water isn't very deep and her feet lodge themselves in the silt. She twists and turns, burrowing deeper into the bog, pushing her way through the amorphous mass. She breaks through the membrane, her gaping mouth a black hole. The water is warm, bubbling like fermented barley, and it's a whirl of colours: red, purple and black, with flecks of ochre spinning into bright waves. She doesn't remember the Flood like this—there were fields of dark blue water and at sunset the surface turned to liquid gold, enough to fill a million vessels (but never such unusual colours as these).

Floating in this warm, multicoloured water she forgets her fear. She can swim like a fish, feet flapping as if they are fins. *Am I a fish, or just a memory of a fish . . . she doesn't know. I imagine a fish wouldn't question its existence; it swims, breathes through its gills, it opens its lipless mouth in search of plankton.* She suddenly feels a sense of urgency—the life of a fish is precarious—there is always something bigger wanting to eat you. She hides inside a crowd of bulrushes, feeling safe behind the green soldiers; no one dare eat her now. As a child, Horus hid inside the bulrushes and his enemies never found him, and much later, another famous child would hide in the bulrushes and when he grew up they would call him the Messiah.

Surrounded by the shield of bulrushes she starts to relax and enjoy the leisurely manner of the fish. In this amorphous form memories return; you have time to reflect in this blue world . . . the ideas are free flowing, pliable as soft clay.

"I suppose I'll have lots of time to think, now that I've left the earthly world. But it's no good, I'll have to keep moving or else my gills will fill with water." Being so malleable has its downside: you absorb water better than a sponge. Bentreshy talks out loud, as if the rocks and plants understand her words. In this strange landscape she feels the need to make connections, to join the dots together on the map; to know where the world begins and ends. If only she could find a community of friendly creatures, then things would make more sense. Just to be able to say things like, "Look at the way the sun glimmers on the water, isn't it wonderful?" To comment on how the clouds turn pink, the sky sinks from blue to black; to have the beauty confirmed by others, to help make it real. But Bentreshy is not alone. In the open sea there are big creatures with gaping mouths and sharp teeth, and they open their jaws like caverns of death, glistening with stalactites. She doubts they wish to enjoy sunsets with her.

She must get herself out of this dangerous place, away from the jaws and the rapacious dead eyes.

"I should recite a spell, but which one should I say? I once knew the *Book of the Dead* backwards, but now it's all a blur." Harp of Joy opens her mouth to utter a spell, but nothing makes sense. She has the mouth of a fish, her tongue is like a slide and it has slipped down her throat. The words come out in air bubbles, floating to the top and then popping on the surface: *I have gained power over my limbs, I have gained power over my mind and Ka. I will live for eternity with the Shining Ones.*

But Bentreshy has no limbs and her mind has turned to jelly. She hears the words in her mushy head, booming like thunder, her pelagian body lunging forward, a fish flying without wings.

Something is happening to her—her form is growing heavier, fins turning into flippers, her fish mouth growing into a snout. "Who am I now?" She thinks of all the animals that can swim under water: crocodile, hippo, otter, frog and snake. She doesn't recognise her own form.

I've become a platypus, she realises. With four limbs, flipper-feet, a tail, and a nose that can smell the dank mud. She's on dry land now, washed ashore by the tide, an exile from the Flood. Standing on four legs she shakes the water from her hair and heads for higher ground. She turns her back on primeval chaos and starts to climb the mountain along the narrow path. Her feet are nimble, jumping from stone to stone with the instinct of a cat, fingers like claws clinging to the rocks, toes digging into the mud.

When Bentreshy reaches the pinnacle she stands on two legs and surveys the landscape, surprised to see a figure on the next hilltop, waving like an old friend, or like her mother, calling her in for dinner. The figure is wearing a light brown robe, the colour of the rocks; materialised out of stone, a boulder cast loose. She looks like a young woman, the way she bounces over the hills, but her face is lined with wrinkles, older than I first thought, Bentreshy admits, assuming the Eternal Ones would have flawless skin, like in the murals. If they could take on any form why wouldn't they choose perfection? But when she gets to know Sheriti, for that is her name, she realises the woman has lived a full life, even though she'd died at the age of twenty-eight. The wrinkles are a sign the woman was once mortal — that she'd suffered, persevered and overcome the many obstacles thrown in her path. Her flawed skin, her worry lines are a badge of honour. Traces of memory, experience, a record of her life carved in flesh.

In the Afterlife the Eternal Ones are proud of their former mortality, and they like to keep some of their human characteristics when they pass over, like scars, which become mementos. Sheriti has quite a few scars and rolls up her sleeve. "This is where the knife slipped in my hand when I was cutting a meat joint. I bled like a sacrificial goat. I needed two rolls of linen to stop the bleeding." Then she laughs and takes Bentreshy by the hand, as if they were both children again, and she whispers, "I must take you to the river, there's not much time — the boat is waiting."

∧∧∧∧∧ ∧∧∧∧∧ ∧∧∧∧∧

Bentreshy set off at a fast pace, happy to be going somewhere at last. Yet Sheriti walked at a snail's pace, as if she'd forgotten the sense of urgency. As if time had nothing to do with velocity. Sheriti stuck to her leisurely pace, like the old sages strolling in the temple garden, talking about her past life. "I used to live in Memphis in the 18th Dynasty — I was the ablutions attendant to Vizier Nebtawi. He also made me taste his food, which was a precarious job as he had many enemies. One day I ate a bowl of soup and I knew after

221

two spoonfuls that it was poisoned with deadly nightshade and peach kernels, as it tasted like bitter fruit. I spat the mouthful onto the floor, but it was too late, as the toxins had flooded my veins, and after a series of painful convulsions I slipped into a coma and died the next day. They said the brother did it: so he could take over the Vizier's position and marry his wife." Sheriti paused for a moment and rubbed her stomach, her face forming a grimace, as if she still felt the agony. She uttered a few groans and then laughed, "It's just an old memory." But Sheriti had the scars to prove it. "Just look at this," she parted her robe to reveal a scar on her abdomen in the shape of snake. "That's where the surgeon cut me open. He tried to remove the poison, but it was no use—the toxins had got hold of my heart, and even the gold scarab couldn't suck it out."

"I'm sure you had a splendid funeral," Bentreshy tried to lighten the mood. It seemed a long way to the river—especially listening to this morbid tale the entire journey.

"Oh yes, it was wonderful," she said proudly. "I died trying to save the Vizier from his enemies. I was awarded a funeral with high honours, including mummification, fine linen and a green scarab to protect my heart."

Since Sheriti had been in the Underworld she had learned many things. She was pleased to find there was social mobility here and that the spirit could transcend above its earthly station. If Sheriti kept up her progress, one day she'd become a spirit guide. "Right now I greet people who have just passed over. I take them to safety and find them the right boat—see them off on their journey." She stared at the girl curiously, "You were a different challenge. You didn't want to be found. I thought you'd stay in the waters of chaos forever. Some do. Some are afraid to make the journey."

"I didn't trust the chosen pathways. I was drawn to the dark water and the caves." She didn't want to tell the woman about her enemies and that she had good reason to hide.

Bentreshy could see the river in the distance, despite their slow pace. They made their way down the hill in silence and headed towards a quay by the river, lined with empty boats. Sheriti pointed to a papyrus boat, trembling in the slow current. This isn't a good sign, thought Bentreshy, the boat is as flimsy as a leaf. Despite her fears she climbed into the boat and clung to the delicate sides.

"Where am I going?" she asked Sheriti, who was busy pushing the boat away from the shore.

"Why, down the river of course," she smiled, thinking the girl was a little simple. And then Sheriti remembered mortals knew so little about the Afterlife; their suspicions were somewhat understandable. Bentreshy felt herself being sucked away from the shore, like a bulrush being uprooted by the flood. She felt it in the pit of her stomach, empty and churning with acid.

Death isn't like we imagine. We think it's about relinquishing our earthly form and leaving loved ones behind to mourn our tragic passing. But there is never an end to it all, a culmination that makes the story poignant, Bentreshy was beginning to realise, watching Sheriti shrinking on the shore. Lives are like episodes, each one merging into the next, the story developing and improving with time.

Bentreshy was now deceased, but nothing had really changed: she was still fourteen years old and didn't know where she was going any more than she had on earth. It appeared that the Afterlife was a mirror of our physical world, with an endless river and lush green fields clinging to the banks. But everything looked brighter, more vivid, as though seen through the eyes of a lover, awakened to the beauty of life.

Bentreshy began to relax, listening to the water slapping the boat, "This is really quite an adventure," she stared into the horizon, enjoying the sense of anticipation travel induces. There is nothing like travel to make you forget about your problems, even if you don't know where you're going. She was willing to collect new problems along the way — it was all part of the adventure.

Just as she was considering the prospects open to the Female Explorer, she spotted Sheriti further up the shore. *How the devil did she get there — she hadn't left the quay.* Bentreshy reminded herself that the use of magic here was more potent than on earth and that it was possible to be in two places at once. How annoying when she wanted to be alone. Sheriti had grown more earnest, the way she waved her arms in desperation. In fact the rapid change in Sheriti's appearance was quite alarming. "She looks so solemn, with the face of an old crone," cried Bentreshy, suspecting some awful event must have suddenly aged her — her child-like demeanour now tainted with anguish.

"A terrible mistake has been made. You must come back," Sheriti shouted down the river, the harsh words sinking like stones. The Council were supposed to brief her about the situation, but she'd set out to meet the girl before dawn, forgetting all about the meeting. "I have failed the Council of the Gods," Sheriti berated herself.

"Come to shore, Bentreshy! We must speak!" raising her hands in the air, she looked like someone surrendering, her sleeves sliding down her arms in retreat. But then she began to shake her fists in the air and Bentreshy saw the fire in her belly. "This woman is capable of fighting till the end," she realised, thrusting the oar into the river.

"I don't like the panic in her voice—the woman sounds crazy." Bentreshy paddled with increased speed, anxious to get away from the frantic figure on the shore. Gone is the artless friendship of our first meeting, she lamented; people in the Afterlife could be as treacherous as they were on earth. Sheriti was on a mission of some sort, a religious crusade to set things right, and that gave her an unnatural strength. Bentreshy had seen them on earth: people on crusades never stopped to question their motives, even if they were heading over a cliff.

Sheriti was insistent, "You must meet with the Council. The Laws of Ma'at have been broken—if order is to be restored, you must face the Council and follow their recommendations."

"I have nothing to say to the Council. I just want to be left in peace!"

She knew only too well what they wanted to talk about—her trial in the Hall of Judgement would cause a great sensation, and the Council members would take delight in humiliating a mortal gone astray. Every scribe in the Afterlife would rise from his immortal slumber and dust off his reed brush, excited by the scent of scandal. It was juicy stuff: her love affair with the Pharaoh, the pregnancy and tragic suicide.

Bentreshy would rather be a fugitive than give them such a spectacle. The Council of the Gods were no better than the priests who betrayed her. They wished to trick her into a meeting with them, then they'd demand a confession and humiliate her before the immortals. She wouldn't fall for such deception again—I have magic skills now, and I can live quite well, roaming from place to place, using spells to protect myself. I can always hide in the Underworld—the demons do not frighten me—they have become my friends. Like her, they'd become outsiders, much maligned by the religious authorities. She understood their suffering, their longing to be accepted, and the shame they felt for being ostracised. She knew which passages in the *Book of Dead* would render the demons impotent, turn a monster into a passive lamb. She would be their Rebel Angel.

When she looked down on earth, she saw people returning from the fields, dragging their heavy loads behind them, their backs bent towards the ground. Bentreshy felt compassion for these weary creatures, walking aimlessly back to their homes, catching a glimpse of the dying sun and realising another day had ended. Most people were like spirits in the Underworld, trying to navigate through the dangers, always hopeful they would reach a state of calm. That was one thing she remembered most about people on earth: they were always hopeful, no matter how miserable their fate. They could sense the beauty hidden in the crevices, the lotus blooming in the mud, the beetle rolling the piece of dung, imagining it was the sun.

She watched Kebi collecting water from the well, chatting to the market women as she lowered her earthen jug into the depths. Bentreshy loved the way the container hit the side of the well and caused an echo, water resonating off the stone, like a deep tenor. Kebi placed the pail of water on her head and returned to her house, water dribbling down her face and cooling her brow; Bentreshy could see the effort in her friend's expression, her feet careful of each step. She walked by her side, taking pleasure in her friend's relief as she lifted the container from her head and placed it by the fire. Kebi wiped her forehead and poured herself a drink, her throat prickling with pleasure, her tongue embracing each drop of water. How wonderful it is to live, to feel such small pleasures, and to see them as tiny miracles of creation.

Bentreshy found the Pharaoh in his marble bath, scrubbing his legs with a sponge from the Red Sea. She often visited him when he was taking a bath, the water seemed to beckon her, merging this world with the next, blurring the lines that divided them. Sety never liked the Ablution Servant to wash him (unlike the other Royals), believing that bathing was a private matter, like praying or going to the toilet, and brought him closer to his physical being. Bentreshy sat near the bath, inhaling the scent of myrrh and musk buried in his robe. Sety stared at the ceiling with his eyes closed, his dark lids closing him off from the world. He was thinking of Harp of Joy, her naked body rising from the river, the water streaming down her face and resting on her lips. She was near him, he could feel her presence manifesting in the vapour, flowing through the marble bath. She was in her element, a fluid substance come to make him whole. He submerged himself and opened his eyes underwater, feeling her love enter his pores; his orifices receiving her warmth, his nerve-endings touched by a thousand feathers. He resurfaced and lay for a moment in the sensation of love, seeing her face in the centre of his mind, where light mysteriously emanated; her face bathed in gold, her eyes were shooting stars, rushing towards him, then crashing through his spirit. He closed his eyes and there she was again, hovering over him like the crescent moon. The image faded as he got out of the bath, and yet he carried the sensation around with him all day, feeling both love and remorse; a sense of being found and yet irretrievably lost. These bewildering emotions made him disorientated and he had to lie down, dismissing the servants who tried to help him into bed.

Bentreshy followed him into bed, but soon she felt that cold wind blow from the north, and the invisible barrier fell from above like the side of a mountain. Whatever was keeping them apart could use strong magic — was it the Council, the gods or some powerful demons? She didn't know. But they blocked her ability to be with Sety and for this reason she hated them. *I will learn how to break their magic and turn it against them — even if it means borrowing spells from the darkest side of the Underworld.*

Crawling up the wall, her body scraping against the stone, flesh tearing like a veil. This world was too horrible, where people were mistreated, deprived of their feelings. Why must people's desires be crushed, like corn ground into flour?

Bentreshy returned to the Underworld, breaking the seal between this world and the next, feeling the membrane tear under the strain of her body. How is it she could see into the essence of things, separate a flower from its smell, moisture from the water and heat from the sun — yet she couldn't break through to Sety's heart. *I may be able to see the essence of things, but I don't know how to harness my power or which direction to take.* This new life was a great wilderness, where the high mountains and endless horizons seemed to mock her boundless spirit.

Since coming to the Afterlife, Bentreshy noticed herself changing: all her desires and dreams suddenly sprang to life, like a room full of people shouting to be heard. In her human form she'd had moments of lucidity—peering into the heart of the universe and understanding its secrets, but then the waters would cloud over and leave a muddy pool, with layers of silt choking the bottom. How much clearer she could see now, gazing through immortal eyes, free from the restricted palette of human vision, blind to half the universe. While on earth the natural realm hinted at the beauty hidden in its core: the reeds along the riverbank, the lotus flowers in the ponds, exposing their delicate beings to those who seized the morning light. Bentreshy knew there was a deeper more sublime form of nature that existed in the Beyond, a Perfect World that mirrored the earthly realm. That's what Priestess Inhapi had taught them. "Always remember, children, it is through physical things that we experience the eternal form—but we must look inside the shell, for the divine essence is buried within."

Bentreshy remembered staring at a lotus flower and seeing the journey from day to night, each petal a reflection of the sun's miraculous journey. The world is full of such symbols, revealing the intricate workings of the universe, yet how many of us overlook them?

Life here doesn't progress in the same manner as on earth. It's more like the course of a dream, where time is a liquid stream, where landscapes dissolve into oceans and then spring into high mountains. It's like witnessing the birth of creation and the end of the world all in the same day. The dreamer's emotions are so intense they eclipse the story, the landscape, space and time. But how can I live in a dream state? Bentreshy wondered, with indistinct boundaries and a shapeless reality, with indeterminate days that suddenly flow into night.

She thought about the House of Isis in Abydos, when Inhapi guided her through the nocturnal realm. "Dreams prepare us for the Afterlife, when our spirit directs the flow of the universe," Inhapi told her; she tried to teach her protégée that whatever you experience in a dream is the workings of your own imagination, your spirit. So when the mountains melt into the sea and the colours flow from purple to gold, it's really the vagaries of her spirit trying to grapple with a higher reality. What had she learned from the House of Isis? That her interior world was a glimpse into the great cosmos, and that if

227

she could master her dreams then she would understand the universe. We had the power to shape our reality, if only we could harness the unconscious, the way we do in dreams. The dreamer-self creates an individual vision of the universe and all she has to do is make it real. Bentreshy remembered her wonderful dreams on earth, filled with exotic colours and exquisite music, but when she awoke she found a room full of empty walls, and she burst into tears. How could fate be so cruel, to let her experience a sense of rapture and then drop her like a stone?

And in the Afterlife, Bentreshy wasn't faring any better. There hadn't been enough time on earth to internalise her lessons. Her life had been cut short, like a tadpole plucked from the pond before it became a frog.

Bentreshy could see an island in the distance; seizing the mast she headed for its shores. The wind picked up and carried her along, the ripples of water spraying her face and sharpening her senses. A woman was standing on the shore and her heart sank. It was Sheriti, smiling in her concerned manner, a mother about to reproach a naughty child.

"I've already told you. I will not go to the Council of Amenti. They've done nothing to help me. I'll forge my own destiny, and they can't stop me," Bentreshy shouted at her. How adolescent that sounded—but she didn't care. She would fashion her own universe, as Inhapi had once taught her to do. Bentreshy knew that would frighten the Council: a free spirit in the Afterworld was unpredictable, volatile, and could threaten the balance of the universe.

"The Council wants to help you," said Sheriti, with compassion in her voice, as if she too wanted to help. But the girl turned away from her. "I don't believe them. It's a trick—they only want to punish me. I was only fourteen, and they abandoned me to a cruel death."

"It wasn't the Council's doing. It was the forces of Seth at work. You must believe this."

Sheriti could see the girl was becoming more defiant by the minute, and it was useless to try and stop her. Bentreshy was enjoying her rebellion; she was an adolescent, after all, what better time to be at odds with society? What a dangerous combination, to be an adolescent and immortal at the same time. The girl was full of teenage angst and yet she had the power of the Eternal, able to pass unhindered through the Underworld.

"I have lost the battle," Sheriti regretted, "Bentreshy has chosen to travel on her own." She didn't blame her, after the way she'd been treated. But the girl was becoming a danger: she could close her eyes and imagine a great white dome setting over her eyes, and when she concentrated hard, the dome became darker, changing from white to yellow, then red, purple and finally turning into a black hole. Then nobody could enter her private realm and she was isolated in her dark universe.

Even Isis couldn't penetrate the girl's defensive orb, inaccessible as a far-flung star. Thanks to the dome she pulled over her mind, Bentreshy could make herself invisible even to the gods. But Isis worried that this defensive orb may be visible to Seth, who had incredible powers in the dark.

Isis realised the only way to contact the girl was to catch her unaware. She would befriend the girl, become a teenager herself— what harm could it do to try?

Isis turned herself into a fourteen-year-old girl and stared at her transformation in the mirror. She stroked her long shiny hair, plaited into intricate braids, and admired her pert breasts and taut skin. She was full of energy and promise, like the pink dawn, tinged with a sense of nervous excitement. Isis remembered that sense of potential mixed with uncertainty, about to leap out of her skin with raw emotion. She felt the force of her talents, but didn't know how to set them in motion. Isis was satisfied with her appearance: just the right blend of beguiling innocence and unruly charm; with a bit of luck the girl would lower her guard.

Bentreshy paddled down the river, her long oar parting the surface and sinking into the deep. It's an incredible blue, she noticed, bluer than any lapis lazuli, with flecks of light illuminating the layers of colour. She watched the oar plunge into the nucleus of the river, churning up what lay hidden below. She sought the dormant river; the river she knew existed but couldn't see. The sunken river that intimates something deeper is about to emerge. The bottom rose in muddy spirals, the bubbles bursting on the surface, exuding a host of pungent smells—the putrid smell of death and decay. But there was also the smell of eternal life: ancient remnants entombed in the sludge, bodies preserved as muddy mummies, artefacts from the

229

beginning of time. Entire boats littered the bottom, piles of pottery and disused weapons; the casualties of history concealed for eternity.

A girl dipped her feet in the water, as though waiting for the depths to draw her in, make her immortal. She wore a dazzling white robe, without a spot of mud on it, even though she was wading up to her calves. Bentreshy floated over to the figure, as if propelled by wings. The aerial proponent seemed to emanate from below, the depths rising into coils of motion.

The figure looked young and old at the same time, like the river. But when she smiled Bentreshy realised she was just a girl, like herself, with white teeth and a fresh complexion.

"My name is Isheena. I've been waiting for you. We are going to be friends," she said, looking to the sky, as though it were written in the stars; an ancient prophecy coming true. Bentreshy remained motionless, her dress absorbing the mud. "But I've never met you before. How can you be waiting for me?" She had this strange feeling again that time was acting out of character. Was she seeing the past or the future?

Isheena noticed the girl's unease and gently held her hand. Bentreshy searched the girl's face for clues. She had the most remarkable eyes, like quartz crystals shattering into a million shards of light. Bentreshy jumped back in astonishment, her ankles sinking into the mud. Then Isheena leaped into the water, laughing and making great splashes with her arms. Bentreshy couldn't resist this sudden playfulness, after her long spell of solitude, and she wrestled Isheena under water, laughing and gurgling in a sunken world of pleasure. The girls emerged caked in mud and weeds, their hair streaked with green foam.

As Isheena predicted, the girls became firm friends — admiring each other's wild spirit, passionate nature and athletic figure. Together they made the tame untamed.

"There's going to be a great party tonight — you must come as my guest." Isheena pulled the weeds from her friend's hair, imagining how fine she'd look in a turquoise gown.

"But I won't know anybody," Bentreshy protested, looking down at her filthy dress, remembering she was an outsider. *When Isheena realises I am an outcast she will abandon me . . .*

"I will introduce you as my cousin from Babylon. Say you'll come — I can lend you a pretty gown — we'll dance under the stars and there'll be delicious food and wine." Isheena spun round in a circle, tempting her friend with the impending merriment.

"All right, I'll come," Bentreshy agreed, trying to ignore her misgivings, imagining herself in a beautiful dress, dancing among the illustrious guests. She'd been offered a gift of happiness—how could she refuse? One night of merriment, what harm could it do? With the right disguise, no one would recognise her.

Bentreshy sat on the down-filled bed as the servants anointed her body with perfumed oil, massaging the orange blossom into her shoulders. They drew black spirals round her eyes and painted her lips dark red, and then they placed an elaborate wig on her head. The wig had been dyed a deep indigo, the braids falling like the night sky around her shoulders, adorned with crystals to resemble stars. Her robe was turquoise, just as Isheena had imagined, and the linen was so fine it was nearly invisible, giving the girl an ethereal air, like a frail mist hovering on the horizon, about to evaporate.

Isheena looked equally beguiling in her cream robe embroidered with silver flowers, her braids flowing with violet gems. They gasped at one another when they saw the transformation, remembering the mud and the green foam, and they burst into childish giggles, rolling around on the feather bed.

They made their way to the festive garden, illuminated with candles and the canopy of stars above. Bentreshy had never seen such a beautiful spectacle, even at the Feast of Osiris, when the Royal Garden shone like the heavens. There were huge lanterns swinging from the trees in a myriad of colours, and crystal chains descending from the columns like shooting stars; rows of tables piled high with sumptuous food, and great jugs of wine filled the endless cups, staining the cloths red with abundance.

The guests beamed with joy, the fragments of light bouncing from face to face, their bodies moving in rhythmic patterns. Bentreshy joined the dancers under the charmed lanterns, their luminous faces drawing her into the circle of drums. Isheena introduced her as Nefret-Sheni, her cousin from the Eastern Domain, who was on a family visit. An elderly gentleman took her by the hand and drew her close to him, "My dear, I am writing a treatise on the ethics of the gods. Do you think nature was created by the gods or is it a self-generating process, existing outside the realm of divinity? Tell me, Nefret-Sheni, would you describe the gods as moral?"

231

The Old Sage stared at the girl, eagerly awaiting her reply. She wasn't expecting such metaphysical questions at a celebration of this kind and had buried her intellect under a layer of frivolity and wine.

"Nature cannot be tamed by the gods—it is beyond the realm of divine influence. And no, I do not think the gods are moral—they are too much like men for my liking, with their officious councils." She took a bold slurp of wine and wondered what the old man would think of her audacity.

The Sage raised his glass, "That's just what I think, although no one wants to hear the truth anymore." Not like the old days, when he encouraged his pupils to question reality. The Sage had once taught Akhenaten how to read the stars and search beyond conventional boundaries. "That's why he was inspired to build a new empire and defy the gods—little good it did the world. And now I must pay the price for my crimes."

Isheena tried to drag her friend away from the Sage—he may frighten her off, with his pedantic ramblings—just when the girl is starting to open up.

"You don't want to waste the evening talking to that stuffy old sage—let us dance in the moonlight," Isheena insisted, leading her through the inebriated crowds. Bentreshy couldn't resist the hypnotic beat of the drums and began to dance, hips gyrating, her feet forming intricate patterns. But she couldn't help thinking about her discussion with the Sage. She caught a glimpse of him through the crowd: he was sitting on the stone bench staring into space, as if he saw the face of infinity. *He has answers for me*, she realised, *I must speak with him again. But I sense Isheena doesn't want me to talk to the Sage, the way she dances around me like an ibis with her chick, leading me into the heart of the crowd, deliberately obstructing my view of him.* Bentreshy was beginning to find Isheena rather irritating, waving her feathers and ribbons, trying to dazzle people with her grand gestures. She is somewhat frivolous, thought Bentreshy, immature for her age.

Isis could see the disappointment in the girl's eyes. She'd been trying her best to act like a teenager—full of passion and spontaneity, allowing her emotions to lead her into exciting situations. But Isheena had forgotten how earnest young people can be, questioning their existence and wanting impossible answers. Isis remembered being at a party when she was fourteen, suddenly stepping out of herself and feeling terribly alone. It had all seemed so pointless—she'd

232

craved something meaningful but didn't know what—she'd wanted to understand and yet people only confused her.

Isis performed a pirouette to clear her mind, focusing on a blue lantern as she spun round. By the time she'd completed three pirouettes Bentreshy had vanished, the music and bodies filling the empty space where she'd danced only a moment ago—and now the girl was gone! *How silly I was to underestimate her,* Isheena scolded herself, pushing her way through the dancers. *I must find her before anyone recognises her.*

Bentreshy strolled along the river with the Sage, glad to be in his erudite company, enjoying the labyrinth of his ancient mind, drifting through history, religion, science and astronomy; urging her to dip her toes into improbable realms, like the existence of superior life forms on other planets, and even the forbidden, like debating the divine rights of pharaohs.

Isis realised she would have to change her strategy if she wanted to compete with the Sage, and turned herself into an old woman, with long silver hair down to her knees, her forehead wrinkled with pensive thoughts. Only a lifetime of contemplation could give someone such a demeanour: she walked at a deliberate pace, her eyes fixed on the path ahead, leaning on her staff for support as she periodically gazed at the heavens, her back arched into a bow as if Nut encased her frame.

The Sage led the girl into the reeds, the green shoots blocking out the sky. They were like giant brushes painting over the blue with green strokes (sometimes she wanted to erase the light and hide in the dark colours). She was safe in this green swamp, where people feared the crocodiles and the bottomless mud, deep as a yawning hippopotamus, as the saying goes.

The Sage stared at the river through the reeds, rods of light marking his face, his grey beard sprinkled in green pollen. He lifted his robe and paddled in the water; how he loved it here in the undergrowth, where thoughts could linger and take their own shape.

"I can help you free your mind. Just close your eyes and think of the river. Think of the millions of drops of water that make up the entirety. When you learn to make the molecules whole then you can travel anywhere."

"I don't know if I can," Bentreshy strained her brow, pushing her eyes to the dim regions of her mind. The Sage was encouraging her to travel where her heart desired, to flout the order of the gods by returning to earth. But she dared not mention it out loud—perhaps it was a trick, what if the Council was listening?

She staggered to the back of her mind and imagined the river, swollen and flowing with full force. It was true what the old man said—it was made of tiny particles, and each speck existed in its own right, a single drop of water floating in a great sea, and yet it *was* the sea... As Bentreshy became more contemplative, her powers of observation improved and she saw the globe spinning like a huge plate. By expanding her vision sideways she could distinguish the continent of Africa and the great Nile that slithered through the desert. How precarious this source of life looked from above: a single artery that fed the body, with no secondary resource to depend upon. Getting closer she saw the women washing their clothes by the shore, the fishermen casting their nets in the currents, and the children splashing in the shallow water. She heard the children's laughter, their bellies shaking with joy, their bodies set in constant motion, cast adrift from the worries on land. The cattle gathered to drink, stretching their bony necks down to the surface, their great tongues lapping up the water and their flared nostrils inhaling the steam. What a marvellous scene to witness: this pastoral world unfurling; the crops growing in abundance, the fish leaping into the nets. This great arm stretched to the sea, wrapping itself around the precarious life forms, offering deliverance from the barren desert.

Bentreshy watched the children turn somersaults in the water, their legs spinning in the air, and for a moment she could see the white soles of their feet flashing in the sun, as they flipped over in a great splash. Travelling towards Thebes, the life forms began to multiply, the narrow strip of green suddenly swelling into the desert, creating a huge tapestry of fields and villages. At the centre of this green haven stood the mighty Temple of Karnak, the largest temple on the face of the earth, where the priests worshipped Amun and spread the god's message throughout the land.

King Sety had built a great palace in Thebes and several temples to honour Amun and his father Rameses I. In his sorrow the Pharaoh had thrown himself into incessant building projects, extending the temples and shrines. Bentreshy looked down on the Temple of

Millions of Years. The Pharaoh had built the mortuary temple on the West Bank, enfolded in a sea of green fields. A fertile place to build a temple, but hadn't he worried about the flood plains? Come the inundation, those fields were a wash of liquid mud—but mysteriously the temple had never flooded, thanks to the clever engineers who built ditches, dykes and high walls. His son Rameses would later extend the temple, making it even more impressive, but without the clever engineers it was prone to flooding...

Back on the East Bank, Bentreshy felt like those pilgrims she had seen in Abydos, who came from foreign lands like Syria and Lebanon. She had envied their freedom to roam, the look of wonder on their curious faces, their eyes alight with new discoveries.

How wonderful it was to be a traveller, to peer into the dusty corners of the temple and say, "That's where Amenhotep once shaved his royal face, and his whiskers fell on this very floor, which the birds later used to build their nests."

King Sety had dedicated the temple to his father Rameses I, and they said the place radiated with paternal love, each stone a symbol of reverence. Bentreshy could sense the devotion in the walls, the desperate attempt to restore the old religion to the land. Statues of Amun lined the walls, creating a defence against the heretic years that almost brought the Empire to its end.

She caught a glimpse of a figure walking round the grounds, he was deep in contemplation and ambled in an awkward manner, his feet at odds with his thoughts which were left to fend for themselves. *He looks like King Sety, his blue robe hanging off his shoulders, head stooped towards the ground, eyes following the darting beetles.* Her eyes were playing tricks on her, she decided, and for a moment she shut out the world, her vision blinded by emotion; struck by a beam of light and then darkness, sensations that came in a spiral of white and black and left her quite stupefied.

When the light returned Bentreshy realised her eyes had been telling the truth.

"Men-Maat-Ra, oh my love!" she shouted, watching the figure falter and turn towards her. He looked terrified, his eyes dark with anguish. Yet his suffering had given him an unforeseen strength, and he was open to receive whatever formidable force had come upon him. Bentreshy watched him stroll around the temple, running his fingers over the statues' feet, feeling the power of the gods returning, despite their defacement in the Amarna period.

How she wished to run to Sety, bury her body in the folds of his robe. She felt him yearn for her flesh, for her breath upon his neck, for her mysterious chambers. Bentreshy sensed his presence like her own skin, but when she tried to touch him the barrier came between them, keeping them apart. The obstacle felt slimy to the touch, like the skin of a giant eel. She pushed against the slippery wall but she couldn't penetrate the curious membrane, and her body slid down the invisible surface, landing on the stone floor.

She studied Sety's face: he had solid features, a straight nose and a sturdy jaw line, all the markings of a granite statue. But his eyes reflected a gentle soul, hinting at wild emotions hidden below, and there were dark circles under his lower lashes. She lingered by his side, her arms embracing the space around him. King Sety stopped in his tracks, aware of an undefined presence, and he stared up at the sky in amazement, as though he'd just seen the Sirius Star, and then he looked straight at Bentreshy. This time there was desperation in his gaze, and she saw the madness of a lost lover, and something more dangerous: a relentless sense of determination. *He would pursue this terrifying love to the ends of the universe.*

Bentreshy flung herself towards Sety, hitting the barrier with full force. *"Why won't they let us be together?"* And then a cruel wind tossed her into the sky, spinning her through the air like a feather, and she couldn't tell which way was heaven and which way was earth.

How reckless she'd become, jeopardising her salvation in eternity. Bentreshy knew how resolute the Council could be—they disapproved of such a relationship, existing outside the Laws of Amenti. Sheriti had warned her how intense a mortal's love can be, especially when infused with an eternal desire—a deadly combination.

"The Council has decided you must be kept apart for the time being. Sety needs time to cool his ardour, to focus his energy on the spirit realm. Otherwise his obsessive love could destroy you both," Sheriti had told her. How Bentreshy hated the Council, with their rigid morality and sanctimonious principles. How irrelevant they were in the face of eternal passion. But she mustn't let them know of her unruly sentiments. She drew the shield over her eyes and leaped into the air, fleeing up the river towards the great Temple of Karnak.

236

As she came upon the temple she felt herself shrinking, engulfed by this enormous space, and she truly understood how an insect might feel inside a flower, the petals closing in like stone columns. Bentreshy had never felt so overwhelmed by a building—even when she'd arrived at Abydos as a small child. For Karnak was built to remind us of the glory of the cosmos, and to install a giddy sense of awe in the humble mortal. She made a quick calculation of the architectural feats: in the Hypostyle Hall there were 134 papyrus-shaped columns, all measuring fifty-five cubits high, with a circumference of thirty-three cubits—that's room for sixty people! The statistics were mind-boggling, but when she looked up at the giant columns, any notion of architectural diagrams went out of her head, mesmerised as she was by the sense of Infinity. The interior space seemed to be expanding, the columns and walls magnified beyond conventional boundaries. We are but particles of dust, she thought, floating in a boundless universe. Sety used to talk about Infinity—that the cosmos was an ever-expanding process and that to live in Eternity was to become part of the infinite universe. Bentreshy walked over to the north side and immediately recognised the work of King Sety. The reliefs symbolised the course of Creation, the beautiful designs adding to the sense of wonder. The use of light enhanced the symbols and gave them a subtle, aesthetic dimension, like the carvings at Abydos, where Sety had created an ethereal beauty. She sat at the foot of a column, submerged by the stone that felt both devastating and fragile, like an obese woman who still had an air of elegance about her.

The space was alive with beauty, the divine images bouncing off the walls and inciting the imagination. She felt the temple was speaking to her, words seeping through the mute stone. Dared she believe the building was a symbol of Sety's devotion to her, and not just an architectural vehicle to awaken the gods?

He was calling out to her, with every temple he built he was enticing her down to earth. "Yes my love, every stone, every carving is a sign of my devotion to you. Your beauty reflected in stone for eternity. Wait for me, my love, make a place for me in the Netherworld."

In the future the Hypostyle Hall would stand as one of the greatest architectural masterpieces the world had ever seen. Surely a labour of love, an expression of deep devotion to an ideal; man emerging from the primeval marsh…

Bentreshy could feel Sety in the wall reliefs, the fine lines drawn to his creative specifications; the finest artists expressing his eloquence, his beauty and sophistication. She would go from building to building in search of Sety, in search of clues to help her understand the man she loved; the language he used to express his soul. He emanated from the temple walls, the arcane symbols describing the secrets of his *Ka*, like engravings carved into his flesh.

Bentreshy trembled at the foot of such beauty. She didn't think immortals could tremble like humans, but she felt the blood rush through her veins, her heart pound like a mortal transposed. Perhaps this sensation was a memory from her mortal days—she recalled a man in Abydos who had no legs, and yet he often felt an ache in his right foot. Even stone can feel things. The great columns were steadfast and yet they trembled like papyrus in the wind. The exquisite carvings of the gods and the fluid shape of the pillars made her think of water, movement; the colour of naked skin, the pale light of dawn, and emmer cakes coated with honey. The stones hinted at the fire within and they used their exterior to tell their story: about a world full of hidden gems, layers of rock that lead to the nucleus of fire, the spirit of being.

On the west side of the hall Bentreshy came across a massive mural of Isis holding Sety's hand. The goddess is shaking the sistrum, awakening the feminine energy; she leads King Sety to his divine father, Amun-Ra, as if to say, "Here he is, my lord. I return the Pharaoh to the old gods. Egypt is safe from chaos."

Akhenaten had once tried to destroy this place, dismantling the walls to build his sun temple, murdering the priests who worshipped Amun…and then followed eighteen years of oppression and chaos, the old religion disembowelled, the Laws of Ma'at abandoned, and Egypt reduced to a wasteland. Bentreshy remembered her history lessons: how the army general Horemheb had finally saved Egypt from oblivion. He rebuilt the temples of Amun and restored the priests to power. But he died without an heir and it was up to another army general to continue his vision: Rameses I. Although he only ruled for one year, he produced an heir, and all the hope for the future was placed on the ruler of this New Dynasty: Sety I.

Bentreshy could sense the optimism in the Hypostyle Hall, the vast space rising to the stars. All that potential, like unexplored galaxies. It was the spaces in between that fascinated her: the gaps in between the

238

murals and the columns; the shapes the emptiness created around the objects. People tried their best to fill up the empty spaces: the priests scuttled round the temple like white scarabs, the servants following behind them with jars of honey, herbs and perfume, jugs full of sacred water to cleanse the statues of Amun.

Sunset was approaching and it was time for evening prayers. How she longed to be in Abydos, to remove her white robe and swim in the Pool of Isis with the other girls, her fatigue melting away, the heat of the day purged by the cool water. I must go back, she told herself, if I hurry I could be back in time for prayers. She followed the Avenue of Sphinxes that joined Karnak to the Temple of Thebes, the route the priests took in the Festival of Opet, when they carried the Sacred Barques of Amun, Mut and Khonsu through the temples. One day she hoped to witness the event, the streets alive with musicians and dancing bodies, woven together in a labyrinth of flowers and fruit, celebrating the floodwaters and the chance of renewal.

Bentreshy hadn't done much travelling in her life and wished she'd paid more attention in her geography lessons. Think about it, Bentreshy, a lot of it is common sense. Just follow the Nile down river and you will head towards Lower Egypt. She was grateful her country had such an important marker to plan her route, and no doubt the pharaohs had agreed. But she knew this hospitable landmark was also the cause of great strife, as the river drew many foreigners to her shores, an attractive gateway for plotters and thieves. But tonight the sun was closing on a Peret evening tinged with gold and bathed in a shroud of optimism. Harp of Joy skimmed the surface of the water, the sun turning the river to liquid bronze, and she raised herself above the vapours where the atmosphere was suddenly cold. She could see the mountains now, great archways into a new kingdom. But their moody contours also implied the inaccessible, as there was no obvious route to their summit, no well trodden path to suggest travellers had made the journey before.

I could get there if I wanted to, Bentreshy cajoled herself, now that I've found the door from this world into the next—but I am on my way to Abydos, she remembered, and there was no time for exploring hidden realities.

A man dragged his net from the depths and it was bursting with silver fish, fins flapping in the rippling sunset. How happy she was to

239

be following this liberal river towards the sea, passing the fishermen in their boats, the cattle wading by the shore.

The river suddenly veered off to the left and she followed a canal for several miles, until she spotted a temple gleaming in the sunset, the ginger orb hovering over the mountains. The temple seemed to oscillate between the sun and the earth, unsure which way to go. The notion frightened her and for a moment she stood in terror and wonder, watching the earth merge into the sky. *What a remarkable feat: to make a temple of the gods tremble to its foundations, and seem to disappear in the pink ether.*

Bentreshy watched the young girls remove their robes and dive into the sacred pool, their dark hair glistening as they returned to the surface, their braids unfurling like tentacles. The devotion was apparent in their eager faces, eyes shining with liquid reverence, the drops of water leaching from their pores. They were receptive instruments, their hearts and minds amenable to Isis. How wonderful it was to emerge from such a pool, feeling transformed, reborn, she recalled; to feel your skin rise against the cool air, intestines writhing like snakes, and your heart burning its way through your chest. She remembered such sensations, for the human experience of the divine emanated from the physical realm—even when they attained the divine their impression of it was rooted in the senses. How strange that seemed to Bentreshy now, who enjoyed the ethereal qualities of the immortal.

∧∧∧∧∧　∧∧∧∧∧　∧∧∧∧∧

Where could she be? The Sage began to worry. He'd encouraged Nefret-Sheni to explore her hidden potential and now she'd disappeared. The Sage sat on the bench and wondered what to do, the cold stone making his legs ache. Perhaps Isheena would have some answers. But the party was over—the place looked like the aftermath of a battle, with bodies lying about the floor, lanterns torn to shreds, chairs and tables overturned, the great feast reduced to bones. Only the vultures could see the delights in this display of carnage, and they happily picked the carcasses clean, their great wings flapping round the sleeping bodies.

To his surprise he spotted Isheena in the rubbish, tiptoeing round the bodies, peering into the unconscious faces. Her dress was clean, he noticed, wondering how she'd manage to stay so immaculate, despite the night of excess and the red pools of wine on the floor. She was looking for someone, the Sage surmised, perhaps she's looking for Nefret-Sheni. He smiled to himself—the girl had given Isheena the slip—could it be she didn't have a clue where the girl was?

The Sage noticed Isheena looked older, her face ashen, like a star fading in the cosmos. She stood there quietly, waiting for the light to return. She was transforming into a timeless entity, a planet regenerating itself out of its own atoms.

"The White Goddess," the Sage whispered, too amazed to speak out loud. Lady Isis . . . He recognised those alluring eyes, luminous orbs casting rays of sunlight.

The goddess turned to face him. "We are both exponents of wisdom, although our paths differ, we must work together," Isis told the Sage, trying to melt his defences.

"I prefer to work alone— I refuse to align myself with any religious system—look what happened in Amarna. And the priesthood today isn't much better—the priests growing fat on votive offerings, drowning in lapis lazuli and gold trinkets."

Isis looked around at the carnage, "I understand your reticence— the religious orders are becoming dogmatic, teaching doctrine instead of enlightenment—they forget the temples are vehicles to the beyond, allowing mortals to develop higher consciousness. But in time this will change . . . I am here on a more pressing matter: Nefret-Sheni is in serious danger—she's not safe on her own. She needs the protection of the gods. I want to take her to Amenti so that she can learn the truth, complete her training to become an Adept—but she thinks the gods wish to harm her. And I need your help to bring her back."

The Sage looked bemused, detecting the gravity in Isis' voice. "You want me to sing the praises of the gods to Nefret-Sheni? The Sage who questions the very existence of the divine? I wish people to think for themselves, to defy the religious order at every turn. You are asking me to sacrifice my principles—and if you must know, I think what the girl has done is spectacular—using her inner powers to outsmart the gods, to break down barriers—to forge her own destiny."

"But what if the child is in danger—suppose the forces of Seth get hold of her? Remember that Seth also lives outside the realm of the gods, and that he too uses his unique powers to create his own destiny."

Isis had a point, the Sage hated to admit. The goddess had boxed him into a corner. "All right, I will help you find Nefret-Sheni and encourage her to go with you to Amenti, but on one condition: that some day they will let her return to earth—so she can finish the life that was cut short."

Isis hesitated to agree—reincarnation was a delicate matter for the gods. "All I can do is ask the Council—I will do my best."

Later that evening the Sage enjoyed a glass of wine while watching another marvellous sunset, so much better in the Western Domain. He thought about his conversation with Isis and he couldn't help deriving pleasure from the sense of irony: that a man who'd spent his life defying the gods was being asked to bring someone back into the fold. And the goddess of wisdom needed his help—it was so absurd! But if it would help save the girl then he was willing to bend his principles.

He had a feeling Isis wasn't telling him the whole story about Nefret-Sheni, if that was her real name. So many people tried to reinvent themselves in the Netherworld, having left a lifetime of chaos behind them. But there was something different about this girl, tragically epic. His curiosity had been roused and so had his paternal extinct: the girl had obviously suffered some terrible fate and yet she would not be crushed; she remained a free spirit, which he naturally admired. The Sage in him wouldn't let it rest: he would have to discover the truth about Nefret-Sheni.

12. Mountain of Offerings
Trip to Abydos, 1952

After the war the excavations remained closed for several years, as the desert was littered with German, Italian and British mines. The sites weren't safe and digging was out of the question, said the officials, you could just as easily dig up a bomb as an early dynastic jar. Digging must be confined to the mine experts.

With the digs suspended Dorothy had a mountain of work to do, deciphering the fragments and cataloguing the artefacts in the Cairo Museum. There were ten years of discoveries to wade through, from Khufu's pyramid, the boat pits, the tombs of Ra-wer, Djoser and Unas. To her dismay Dr Hassan had retired from his post at the Cairo Museum to concentrate on his writing career. "The truth is I've been forced to retire," he admitted bitterly, "I confronted King Farouk about numerous artefacts he claimed belonged to him, which he wanted for his palace."

"How dare that scoundrel steal those treasures from the Museum— they belong to the Egyptian people, and to the world. You were right to stand up to him," Dorothy commended the professor, impressed by his bravery—but he'd paid a terrible price, losing his position at the Museum.

"How could the British let this corruption continue? They promised Egypt full independence after the war. And yet they keep this cretin on the throne, allowing him to rob his people and grind them into poverty."

"In a way the old rogue has done me a favour—now I can spend more time writing and teaching at the university," he said with a sense of irony, feeling the king's days were numbered, clinging onto a make-believe empire that was about to crumble.

Dr Hassan was busy finishing the last few volumes of *Excavations at Giza,* and Dorothy spent much of her time editing and rewriting the professor's raw material. I am more like a ghost writer, she realised, contributing chapters on the Djoser and Unas excavations, adding descriptions and sketches of the tombs and pyramids. It's all good training for when I write my own book, she told herself, and she was learning from one of the best minds in Egyptology.

243

But Dorothy was anxious to get back to excavation work, to the thrill of unearthing a pharaoh's tomb, crawling through the passages engraved with the words of the dead, chanting their way to eternal life. These were meagre times, without the excavation work to pay her rent and buy food—she had to supplement her income by making embroideries and Eastern clothes for a boutique in Cairo. The villagers were very kind, bartering vegetables and pita bread for paper and pens she got from the office.

At night Dorothy wandered round the Giza Plateau, chatting to the sphinx and climbing the pyramids. At dawn she stood on top of the Great Pyramid looking out at the silent plain covered in triangles, rectangular tombs and converging causeways. There were many small pyramids hidden in the desert, disguised as sand dunes, but on closer inspection Dorothy could make out the four-sided pyramids, the tips rising to eternity. From the ground they looked like great mounds of sand; it was only from this highest summit that the contours became apparent, leaping out of the morning mist. By midmorning the pyramidal shapes were no longer visible, sinking back into their earthly resting places. Sometimes she crawled inside the King's Chamber, the strange humming sounds sending her into a deep sleep, voices whispering about the subways to infinity; lying in this multidimensional edifice, her body floated in an expanding universe, the labyrinth of stones meeting the boundless cosmos.

∧∧∧∧∧   ∧∧∧∧∧   ∧∧∧∧∧

One day a man came to her house dressed in a grey suit and matching Panama hat. He was a handsome man, she noticed, with a strong physique, equine nose and soft brown eyes.

"My name is Dr Fakhry and I come from the Antiquities Department. I am directing a new excavation project and I need a draftsman—I hope you will join my team."

Dorothy was overjoyed by the news, as she'd thought the fellow was another solicitor, urging her to take the divorce alimony. She was about to tell him she didn't want the money—she had to live on her own terms and that meant severing her financial ties with Imam. But instead she had to adjust her thoughts, rummage through a catalogue of different replies, ones involving artefacts, mummies, the technicalities of fieldwork.

"Of course I'll join your team. I was beginning to fear they'd never start the excavations again — when do we start?"

Her new job began four days later in Dashur, excavating the Bent Pyramid, built by Pharaoh Sneferu in the Old Kingdom. Dorothy stared up at the pyramid, the marble casing surprisingly intact. But it definitely looked cockeyed, the lower part rising at a fifty-five degree inline, the upper part from a forty-three degree angle. "Obviously designed by a drunken architect," she laughed, imagining the architect's lopsided vision, the result of a stinking hangover.

Dr Fakhry appreciated her sense of humour and responded to her quips with great barrels of laughter, his shoulders shaking with abandon, enjoying the interlude from his formal world. He recognised Dorothy's numinous nature, allowing her time to wander through the tombs on her own, mumbling chants and connecting with the past. The woman had struck up a friendship with Sneferu's ghost, a most unorthodox approach for an archaeologist, but this deviation from tradition brought surprising results. In one of her dreams the Pharaoh told her about an underground tunnel connecting the pyramid with his wife's pyramid next door — and sure enough, when they started digging, they found the tunnel stretching twenty-five metres long...

The Pharaoh adored his wife Queen Hetepheres, he confided in Dorothy, despite flirting with temple girls — there was that infamous tale about him romping with them on the lake...One of the girls dropped her turquoise charm overboard and Sneferu asked the magician to use his powers to retrieve the jewel. The magician parted the waters and the charm was discovered.

Dorothy crawled through the tunnel connecting the two pyramids, following the Pharaoh's amorous journey to his wife's tomb, their souls uniting in the Afterlife, their bodies melting into carnal bliss. Although Dorothy kept her past life a secret from her colleagues, Dr Fakhry understood her spiritual connection with the dead, her intuitive approach to archaeology. He knew the divine realm ran alongside the tangible world, a celestial causeway that receptive people could travel.

Every morning the driver came to collect Dorothy and take her to Dashur. She read the newspaper on the way, following the social unrest brewing in the country — the riots in the streets, the burning of

245

British businesses—the Shepheard Hotel, the BOAC headquarters, the British Yacht Club.

"How long can Britain go on ignoring people's discontent? It is obvious Egyptians want to govern themselves, and they want King Farouk to leave. It seems that only the Free Officers understand what the people need—I wouldn't be surprised if they masterminded a revolution," she told Dr Fakhry as they drank their morning coffee in his office. He scoffed at the idea, "Egyptians are generally passive people—they lack the fiery temperament needed for a revolution—they aren't like the Russians." He argued that it was too hot for a revolution, it being July. No one did anything in July, with temperatures soaring to 122 Fahrenheit—most of the digs were shut down in this tyrannical heat.

"You mark my words, something's going to happen. I feel it in my bones," Dorothy told him; it was like the ground before an earthquake, although she couldn't feel anything shaking, she had the impression of something moving, or about to move; the subtle quiver of the leaves, the vibrations through the stones.

She knew from history the Egyptians could be rallied by a strong leader, a charismatic Pharaoh who could call upon the old gods. Gamal Nasser was such a leader—he was like King Djoser who gave his people a vision of the future, inspired them to build unique pyramids and temples, forge great works of art in the middle of the sand.

She walked along the canal, thinking about Djoser, Nasser and social unrest, when she spotted a brown and white bird in the reeds, its long beak skimming the surface like a pen on paper. "The sacred ibis," she whispered, staring at the mythical bird with incredulous eyes—"but it can't be, it's supposed to be extinct." And then Dorothy spotted another ibis—slightly smaller, with a shiny black head, wispy ruff on her crown and an elegant long beak arched over the sky— obviously the female, the way the male hovered round her, his wings extended like a dandy showing off his white cape. Dorothy hid in the reeds watching the mating ritual, the male offering the female a twig in his beak, she opening her bill to receive the gift, a definite sign she'd agreed to be his mate. They were altruistic birds, feasting on the snails that caused bilharzia disease, their slender beaks clearing the dreaded parasites from the river. As she watched the courting pair wading in the canal, their long black legs immersed in the mud,

Dorothy suddenly remembered a papyrus she'd come across in the Cairo Museum. The one Aziz said was probably written by a young priestess in the temple school. It was from the *Book of Thoth*, and described an ominous future for Egypt, when the old gods become angry with Egypt and abandon her to a miserable fate, ruled by foreign powers and stripped of her dignity. But all was not lost, as Egypt would be powerful again. The prophecy stated there would be an important sign: an ibis would be spotted along the river, when everyone thought the sacred bird had disappeared forever. When the ibis appeared again Egypt would rise from the ashes like the bennu bird, reborn as the sun god Ra (and she'd seen two—these things obviously come in pairs), then Horus would return to rule Egypt, bringing back the old gods and the Laws of Ma'at . . .

∧∧∧∧∧   ∧∧∧∧∧   ∧∧∧∧∧

The revolution happened on a steamy day in July, taking everyone by surprise: the government, the police, the people on their way to work. Schoolchildren would always remember the date: 23rd of July, 1952: a coup d'etat so flawless that no one quite believed it, especially the instigators, General Naguib and Colonel Nasser. It all happened in a matter of days (some said thanks to CIA backing). The Free Officers rallied the army and together they took over the government, the police, the media and transport systems in Alexandria and Cairo.

The revolution brought the liberation of Egypt and the final abdication of King Farouk, who quickly fled to Italy. General Naguib became president and for the first time in this millennium, Egypt was ruled by an Egyptian leader. But Dorothy knew Colonel Nasser was the real leader—he was a true Horus figure, ridding the country of corruption and deposing the false king, the way Horus had got rid of Seth. She sensed the chaos diminishing, the old gods emerging from the quagmire and bringing order and peace to the land. It may take many centuries to achieve—it wouldn't happen in her lifetime—but Osiris and Isis would one day return, as they had in Egypt's darkest past, when the land was full of cannibals and no one knew how to read or write, or build beautiful temples.

Dorothy went to Ismailia Square to enjoy the celebrations, pleased to hear it was now being called Tahrir Square—Liberation Square. She watched the lowering of the British flag, tears running down her

247

face as the Egyptian flag was raised in its place. "Long live Egypt—long live Isis!"

A few months later Dorothy spent her day off wandering round Khan el Khalili Bazaar, enjoying the smell of coffee and shisha pipes, the music mingling with the rowdy voices.

"Madame Meguid! Need any shopping?" she heard a young man shout. She turned round to find Ashraf in a smart gallabiya, with a clean face and his hair parted on the side. "So long since I see you—must be ten years . . . I am a teacher now!" He explained how Nabil Sayeed had paid for his studies, helped him through his degree. "Nabil made me think about things—I joined the teachers' protests against the corruption—the occupation," he said with pride, and then he suddenly looked embarrassed, knowing Dorothy was English.

"I've always been in favour of the revolution. And I'm pleased to hear you've become a teacher—that's wonderful news," Dorothy kissed him on the cheek, still seeing him as that impish young boy who used to do her shopping. He said they no longer lived in the cemetery. "We live in big flat near the citadel—but close enough to the cemetery, and sometimes we go there for picnic, to leave offerings to the dead. My mother still loves it there."

Dorothy pictured Nawes with her green paste, to cure her baby's cough. "Be sure to give your mother my love." But Ashraf wouldn't let her leave. "Nabil is in café—you must come say hello," he insisted, charging ahead and expecting her to follow him, just like when he was a boy.

Nabil was busy writing in his notebook, the table piled with books. His eyes burned with the same passion, but something had changed—he seemed burdened by his thoughts, as if he had too many words to write and was struggling to get them all down on paper. "Madame Dorothy! I'm glad to see you have weathered the insurgency. I'm afraid most British don't have your constitution—they fled for home. That wasn't our intention, to scare them all off—and now we are paying the price."

Dorothy was surprised to hear Nabil talking this way. "But the revolution has been a success, bringing an end to the occupation and the monarchy—surely you must be pleased about that."

Nabil puffed on his shisha pipe, eyes darting round the room with the billowing smoke. "Perhaps it is my destiny to be an outsider.

I see the same mistakes happening, big ideas turning into dogma, revolutionaries turning into bureaucrats. I lost my job on the newspaper, for criticising the new policies—I never liked fervent nationalism. But it's a good thing they fired me, because now I'm becoming a real writer—what I mean is I'm writing about real things...I took your advice and started writing about people in the bazaar, the families in the cemetery."

"I'm so happy to hear it—you writing about local people, and helping Ashraf become a teacher—so the revolution wasn't so bad after all—it made you into a writer!"

Ashraf read the passage from Nabil's book entitled, *Graveyard Gods.*

"That night in the cemetery, they sat round the fire telling stories, their voices were their orchestra, the stars their lanterns, and above their heads the universe revealed its mysteries to the people of the tombs."

Nabil looked up, his eyes brimming with emotion, "Young people like you—you are the future of Egypt, my son. I hope one day we will have free education for all, if Nasser keeps his promise, and then even the poorest children will have their chance to shine."

Dorothy looked across at Ashraf; she saw Nasser's dreams in the young man's eyes, and it was worth the sacrifices, the anti-English sentiment she encountered. She was getting quite good at handling the occasional abuse: "Go back to your king, Ingiliziyya!" to which she replied in local Arabic, "He's dead, *ya abeet*—you idiot!" and the man slinked away in embarrassment. And the other day two women had shouted in Arabic, "Go home, you foreign whore!" and she'd retorted, "Why—so you can take over the business?" They nearly choked on their hijabs.

Dorothy understood their resentment—decades of oppression, poverty, stifled dreams—it all came bubbling to the surface—they were bound to be angry. But that would disappear once life improved for them—Egyptians were generally kind-hearted people.

That night Dorothy had a dream in which she awoke in her astral body, and found King Sety sitting beside her on the bed. They were in a huge chamber, with murals depicting musicians and dancers celebrating a festival. They lay together on the bed, making love until dawn, their bodies rising into the heavens, climaxing in carnal bliss.

When she came back down to earth, Dorothy heard a message, sounding from her unconscious mind. "You must go to Abydos, my love, then we can be together for eternity."

Her sleeping mind awakened into consciousness. "I cannot put it off any longer. I must plan my trip to Abydos." Thinking about the prophecy and the revolution had inspired her to make the pilgrimage. If the rebirth of Egypt was underway and the gods were returning, then she must go to the Temple in Abydos. It was time to follow her destiny, return to the land of Osiris, transform the chaos of her past life into some sort of meaning (she didn't know how, but she hoped the spirits would help her).

It's funny how I tried to get to Abydos several times, but something always prevented me, she recalled. Once her son was ill, another time the train was cancelled, and now there was social unrest.

∧∧∧∧∧ ∧∧∧∧∧ ∧∧∧∧∧

Sitting on the train with her bag of sandwiches and a guide to Upper Egypt, Dorothy was happy to be leaving Cairo for a few days, finally on her way to Abydos. Her boss had given her a few days off; he was surprisingly accommodating, once she'd explained the importance of her pilgrimage—her spiritual connection with the place. Egyptians understand about pilgrimages, she smiled, knowing she'd played the religious card to her advantage. Of course she didn't tell him everything—just that she'd always wanted to visit Abydos and find out more about the cult of Isis and Osiris—and that she'd once lived there in a past life…

"I'm sure he'll have lots of work for me when I get back," she sighed, realising how indispensable she'd become, with her drafting, cataloguing, writing and secretarial skills. The train drifted further into the countryside and Dorothy stared out the window, her responsibilities diminishing, drifting in and out of consciousness as the train rocked her into a dream state. The train travelled through fields and stretches of desert, the occasional mountain rising out of the sand like a white whale.

The journey was very long and took most of the day, and Dorothy had much time to read and daydream about her adventure, but mainly she looked out the window, drawing a map of the landscape with her eyes, tracing every contour and imprinting it on her mind. The fields were an exquisite green, shining in the sun like raw jade. Dorothy could feel the energy emanating from the sheets of green, breathing within the earth. As she got closer to Abydos the energy intensified, the green colours swirling with speed, splashes of colour dancing in the light. Her eyes followed the sandy tracks leading to the reed huts, resembling squares of shredded wheat. The train approached yet another station, and Dorothy stared into the horizon, seeing the limestone cliffs in the distance and somehow knowing they were the Mountains of Offerings leading to Amenti.

"This is the place!" she cried, overcome with excitement and rushing out of her seat, and before she had time to think she'd leaped onto the platform. The signs were all in Arabic so she couldn't say for certain this was the right place, but funnily enough it didn't worry her. She followed the local women carrying baskets on their heads and two angry donkeys trying to get down the steps. She was the only foreign woman around; the other women were dressed in black robes, their resolute veils hiding their faces, like curtains blocking out the light. Dorothy watched them haggling by the stalls, their shrill voices demanding a bargain, veils trembling in a flood of Arabic. She was lost in a market of ghosts, clinging to their baskets of earthly delights. Her beige suitcase looked absurd in these surroundings, the mark of a foreigner. *I am Egyptian,* she reminded herself, *walk with brave steps.*

The men eyed her with a mixture of desire and surprise, her blonde hair a conspicuous mass of femininity, bouncing shamelessly as she strolled along the platform and down the steps to the street. A group of children surrounded her, speaking in a strange Arabic, yet their voices sounded familiar, rattling away as if reciting an old prayer. Suddenly a man appeared out of nowhere and motioned to the children to move aside. With the children dispersed, Dorothy crossed the tracks and started walking up the road, which seemed to be the right direction as it was heading towards the mountains. Soon she was surrounded by lush fields, the peaceful countryside restoring her senses.

Then she heard the man from the station shouting in her direction, "Madaam, wait a moment—you must to wait!"

Dorothy turned around to face an anxious looking man in his mid forties, with a creased forehead and flecks of grey in his dark hair.

"My name is Mohamed. I am temple watchman. The Antiquity Department say I must go with you to Abydos. You must wait for taxi with me." He tried to sound official, but somehow this English lady unnerved him.

"I'm not going to stand around waiting for a taxi, I'm only here for a few days—I must get to the temple," she stated, picking up her suitcase and striding out with determined steps.

"Lady, please—you not walk to Abydos, is eight miles away—is not safe for you to walk alone."

Dorothy gave a defiant laugh, "I'll be fine—it's a lovely evening for a walk and I've been cooped up in that train all day." There'd been a long delay, some technical fault or other—but it didn't matter now—she was breathing the clean air of Abydos, drifting over the plain in a green haze, smelling of sugarcane, peppermint and coriander. She was most dismayed when Mohamed insisted on following her with an emaciated donkey and motioned to her to jump on its back. Dorothy laughed at the idea, "This poor old thing can't take my weight—he'd do the splits trying! And then you'll end up having to carry both of us there."

But this insistent man wouldn't take no for an answer—he'd been given strict instructions which came from Dr Fakhry himself.

"Sometimes these Egyptian men can be so tiresome, with their overactive chivalry," she said under her breath, "they'd follow you into the loo if they could, just to make sure you had a proper wee—or had enough soap and towels," she laughed at the thought, knowing he'd be horrified if he could read her mind. In the end, she let the watchman put her suitcase on the donkey's back, and he uttered a sigh of relief. At least he had the lady's suitcase in his possession. "Why you not wait for taxi? It come soon."

Dorothy tried to ignore the watchman and quickened her pace. "I told you, I'm not waiting around—I'd rather walk."

Mohamed struggled to keep up with her, he'd never seen a woman like her, walking with an effortless pace, and so independent.

"The night is coming—is not safe to walk in the dark."

Dorothy was too busy staring across the fields to heed his warnings, her gaze drawn towards the mountains and the sky beyond, enthralled by the maturing sun. Mohamed was getting agitated, why wouldn't she listen to him? The women in his village would listen to such advice. But this woman had the boldness of a man, with confident steps—yet she was obviously a woman, with her round curves and pretty blonde hair. He wondered what a strange country this England must be, where women behaved in such a manner. How is it she had no sense of fear? No sense of restraint? This fact disturbed him more than her obstinacy; she seemed driven, possessed by some great force, and he suspected there were evil *afreets* controlling her actions.

Dorothy stopped walking for a moment to marvel at the sunset, turning the fields into a sea of gold. She sensed the landscape coming alive; the desert, the pastures and the painted huts shining in their final hour, in the face of darkness, every moment of colour seemed precious. Life trembling with the last breath of light.

It was that intense time of the day when everyone rushed to finish their tasks and get home to domestic comforts, dashing through the fields like a swarm of bees. There was a sense that life was shrinking, the villagers quickening their pace, desperate to get indoors before the night swallowed them in darkness. The animals suddenly became frisky: the donkeys trotting with their heavy loads, the cattle proceeding with a skip in their step, anxious to get back to their shelters. There was a burst of activity by the roadside stalls, the men packing their fruit and vegetables into wooden crates, the women carrying baskets on their heads, the children running behind them in a mischievous dust ball, their mothers shouting to them from behind their veils.

Dorothy was almost disappointed when the taxi appeared; she was enjoying the beautiful sunset, the spirited donkeys and the country women in their colourful scarves. Mohamed pulled her suitcase off the donkey's back, and with a sigh of relief the donkey started trotting back to Al Balyana. Dorothy reluctantly climbed into the taxi and watched the fellaheen from the back window. It seemed the women who worked the land kept their faces and necks uncovered, tying their scarves around the back of their heads, as Dorothy liked to do while working in the desert. It was only in town they veiled themselves in black, as if to hide from the vices of civilisation. In the fields they were free to reveal themselves, exposing their faces to the earth and sky.

As the taxi approached the Temple, Dorothy remembered the end of the road had once been part of a huge canal where the ancient boats had sailed into the royal harbour. She could see it in her mind's eye: the boats moored in the docks, the dark water lapping against the wooden dykes, and the merchants piling their spices, fabrics and handicrafts onto the jetty, enticing the locals with the wonders of faraway lands: Syria, Lebanon, Babylon and India.

Then her eyes were drawn towards the Temple of King Sety I, up the majestic steps and into the First Courtyard. The steps were wider than she'd seen in the photograph, but just as awe-inspiring as she'd remembered in her dreams. "I'd like to stop here first—I want to visit the Temple," Dorothy insisted, starting to open the door.

"First we must go to Rest House—they give me order," replied Mohamed, hands clutching the back of the seat.

"What a nuisance you are," she flew at Mohamed, flinging her arms in the air so he could see the extent of her frustration.

They took a dirt track to the left side of the Temple and continued several hundred yards into the desert, finally stopping outside a white building surrounded by trees.

"Here we are, this Rest House of the Antiquity Department." There was an air of relief in Mohamed's voice, as he'd managed to get the woman delivered safely (at one stage he'd feared the Ingiliziyya would jump out of the taxi and he'd get the blame).

Sipping tea at the Rest House, Dorothy wished to get the formalities over with so she could visit the Temple. The Inspector, Dr Wabid, realised he wouldn't get any sense out of this woman until she'd seen the Temple, as she seemed obsessed by the idea. But the lady had come highly recommended by Dr Fakhry, so he must treat her with respect, despite her peculiarities.

"I will give you a tour of the Temple of King Sety I, so you can know which chamber is which—it's very confusing at first, there are so many chapels to God knows how many gods—and lots of passageways leading this way and that." Dr Wabid motioned to his assistant Walid to accompany Dorothy round the Temple.

"I am very familiar with the place, a guided tour won't be necessary," she replied, as the men followed her to the Temple.

"All right, Madame, if you think you know the Temple so well, then take us to the Chapel of Horus," Dr Wabid suggested, knowing the Temple was now in complete darkness.

Dorothy let her feet guide her over the limestone flags along the right wall of the Hypostyle, where she stopped outside the Chapel of Horus.

"OK—that was too easy—how about the Corridor of Bulls," he said smugly, waiting for Dorothy to admit defeat. But she walked straight

254

into the Second Hypostyle, past the List of Kings; turning right into the corridor she stopped before King Sety and his son Rameses who were lassoing a great bull. "Such a magnificent mural—you can see the struggle between man and beast, and on another level it's about the King's reign of Egypt and how his son becomes co-ruler—a remarkable portrait of power-sharing. How he must have loved his son!"

"The lady really knows the Temple, better than we do!" Walid laughed nervously, "But she must have been here many times—I think she is telling tales when she says this is her first visit." His docile face showing signs of trepidation; no one could know the Temple so well if they'd never been there before. The Ingiliziyya knew every inch of the Temple—the Hall of the Sacred Barques, the Seven Vaulted Chapels, the Osiris Complex—even in total darkness she found her way to each chapel and chamber, as if guided by instinct, or radar, or something supernatural.

This is very unsettling, thought Dr Wabid, feeling suddenly flustered by this Ingiliziyya, his confident demeanour shaken, his face flushed with heat and consternation.

Dorothy stood outside the Chapel of Isis. "I think I'll stay here for a while on my own. You fellows get back to the Rest House, there's no need to wait about on my account." With the test over, Dorothy hoped to get some time on her own, wanting to pray and leave her offerings—without their puzzled faces gawping at her.

"You not scared be in Temple alone at night?" Mohamed asked her, "what about *afreet*?"

"I've lived with *afreets* all my life and they've never done me any harm. I'm more worried about you lot than I am about any *afreet*!"

The officials burst into laughter, as they hadn't expected such a reply from an English lady—and one who spoke Arabic like a local.

When the men had gone, Dorothy drifted down the steps to the First Courtyard, as if in a trance. She walked over to one of the wells on the right where the priestesses used to perform their ablutions before entering the sacred Temple. She felt a twinge of sadness, as this holy well was now full of rubble, the clear water clogged with muck. "I'm sorry, Isis," she cried, "I will do my best to put things right," she vowed, heading back to the entrance.

She walked up the lofty steps which seemed much bigger on the ascent, as if they'd changed their dimensions, the splendour of the Temple intensifying as she approached the main entrance. She removed her shoes and stepped inside, feeling the great slabs beneath her toes, the heat rushing through the soles of her feet and up her spine, until every part of her being was trembling with joy. She looked down at the floor and saw that it was bright green, the colour of malachite, the stone of Osiris. There was no one in the Temple, the guards had all gone home, and yet she wasn't alone.

"It's been such a long time . . . how we've missed you. Welcome home . . ." She heard voices in the darkness, illuminating the passageways with their gentle words. *"Look, it's Bentreshy—she's come back, after all these years. The Laws of Ma'at are being honoured. Egypt will be great again. Oh what joy!"* The Temple was full of voices, invisible spirits emerging from the pillars and murals.

She drifted through the chants and entered the Chapel of Ptah, the creation god of Memphis, where she asked Ptah to awaken the Temple, guide her through the dark passages so she may greet all the gods. In the Second Hypostyle she stopped before a giant relief of Sety I worshipping Osiris, offering incense and pouring libations into three heart-shaped bowls, she laughed at the Pharaoh's play on imagery, "Very funny, Your Majesty—I see what you're doing— you're washing the heart, which also means to fulfil an eternal desire." Dorothy traced the flow of water with her fingers, attaining a sense of completion as the water filled the empty hearts. Yes, she too was fulfilling an eternal desire: she had come home to the Temple. Her tears were flowing like the ankhs in the mural, replenishing her being; the water from her own body, cleansing herself before Sety and Osiris.

Walking round the giant pillars she sensed the magnitude of the Temple, resounding like a distant symphony, gaining in momentum as she walked closer to the Chamber of Osiris. Dorothy began to laugh and cry, great tears streaming down her face; she had never experienced such ecstasy within a building, unlike many of the churches she'd visited.

She received messages telling her to let go, to open herself to the Temple. Then her tears fell like soft petals, and she felt herself unfurl like the lotus flower in the light. The energy bounced off the walls in waves of sound; first a gentle rush of reeds, then the shaking of sistra, followed by a melodious series of chimes. The music exuded such energy that Dorothy couldn't keep still and her feet started to tremble and then burst into a spontaneous dance. She hadn't danced like that since her adolescence, skipping and hopping in her bare feet, laughing at how comical she must look.

Never you mind, a voice told her, *you are dancing before the gods and they love a good spectacle. From now on you mustn't worry what people think. People are held back by such conventions and never reach their potential. Life should be a great festival. You wouldn't believe the wild feasts we have in Amenti, but one day you will know . . .*

She stood before a beautiful mural of Isis and Osiris and lit an incense stick, filling the space with smoky sandalwood. Dorothy spoke to them like old friends and they told her many important messages: that she must take the knowledge out of the Temple and remind people of the ancient gods; encourage the officials to restore the murals and sacred chambers, so the Temple would be a lasting symbol of eternity . . . And finally, they wanted her to honour the rites and religious days, to chant the old prayers to the gods and renew their power on earth. The rebirth of Osiris and the resurgence of the ancient ways would unfold before her, but only if the sacred rituals were performed. She detected a sadness in the divine couple, as people had forgotten the prayers and how to worship. People have lost the ancient connection, the couple feared, and go through life disengaged from what is most sacred, unable to reach the divine realm. To live without the eternal gods is to live without rapture, without magic. The rebirth they talked about was a rebirth for all mankind; to experience life in a deeper dimension.

By dawn the messages began to fade, as even the gods need to rest, and Dorothy stumbled into the embryonic light, trying to remember all that was said to her. She hovered in the great entrance, feeling the mysteries collide with the sunrise. The two ambits flowed into one another, blue and yellow streams merging into beautiful patterns and many shades of green. As she stared into the Second Courtyard, with the ruined walls and broken reliefs, she saw how neglected the sacred Temple had become. *She must come and live near the Temple so that the healing process could begin, the eternal rebirth . . .*

Standing in the open court, Dorothy realised the enormity of her task, wondering what she was doing on the edge of the desert on her own (where women didn't have a life without husbands or children). How it must upset Isis, she thought, to know the priestesses had been forgotten, female power diminished. She must overcome her self-doubts and follow the teachings of Isis. She had to trust in the power of the feminine and not bow to social conventions, perceiving women as mothers and housewives. It wouldn't be easy living here—she would encounter much opposition along the way, but she had been chosen for this task many eons ago, and hoped the gods would protect her from harm.

Dorothy drifted out of the Courtyard, the way a bird flies back down to earth, having flown high above the desert, like Horus, wings fully stretched to catch the surge of wind.

Mohamed was surprised by the change in her demeanour: she appeared like a young girl, with an innocent look in her eyes. She was acting like an adolescent, bursting with exuberance, giggling at everything he said. He had to admit she looked radiant, as if she'd taken some kind of youth potion. Considering she'd been up all night her face showed no hint of fatigue, in fact there was no sign of that demanding middle-aged lady he'd encountered the night before—the one with the quick tongue and shocking stream of Arabic insults.

"*Sabah il khayr*," she smiled, sweeping past the watchman in a blissful cloud, knocking him over with her serene manner.

"*Sabah in noor*," he muttered, watching in awe as she drifted round the left side of the Temple towards the Osirion. She bent down to the ground and began moving her hands over the earth, as if searching for a lost keepsake. In her dreams this area had been a garden, with exotic trees and plants from the far corners of the Empire and Asia; a botanical showcase for the wonders of the natural world. Flowering bushes, scented plants and vines, cascading fountains and intricate water channels had once attracted wild birds, frogs, beetles and flying insects with metallic green wings. But now the garden was covered in sand and rubble, the once fertile grounds withered into dust. She stumbled over the barren earth, "How could they let it slip into such a terrible state?" she cried, seized by an uncontrollable sadness. She hated to see beautiful things destroyed and remembered that feeling as a child, seeing the picture of the Temple, outraged by the state of neglect and the disappearance of the garden.

Dorothy wandered round the back of the Temple and down the path to the Osirion, recognising the place of her dreams: the mound of creation, the cenotaph of Osiris; the mysterious shrine full of secret passages leading into the Underworld. She marvelled at the giant pillars from Aswan, much bigger than she'd imagined, as imposing as the slabs from Stonehenge. She sensed the great age of the stones; it was obvious the Osirion was very ancient, the site of an eternal spring, a rare gift in the heart of the desert. There was nothing like it in Egypt; no other building had been constructed like the Osirion, and its unique character was one of history's enduring mysteries.

She ran down the steps and jumped onto the square island in the centre of the Osirion. What a magical place, she thought, a house of mirrors; the sacred water reflecting the elemental self. The island was surrounded by a channel of water and within the island there were several square-shaped pools, one with a flooded staircase leading into the Underworld. Dorothy sat by one of the pools and dipped her feet in the water, parting the green scum with her toes. To think this pool has existed for countless millennia, she considered, and the water has never dried up. King Sety liked to sit here, dangling his feet in the cool water when the heat was unbearable, singing to Osiris and feeling revitalised by the pool of creation.

Dorothy noticed some rubbish at the bottom of the pool—old shoes, bits of metal and broken glass. "I'll have to get that cleaned up," she decided, "and fish out all that pond scum. Osiris must be furious by the state of this place."

As the sunlight began to burn through the morning mist she noticed there was rubbish all over the place: paper, tins, and bottles floating on the channels, debris piled up by the entrances to the chambers, wedged into the secret corners of this sacred place. But some of the water looked quite clean, she noticed, and came from a rumbling spring, the Well of Roarings. Finding the source of the spring she bathed her face in the clear water, feeling her pores open to receive, tingling with crystal energy. The water trickled down her skin with the softness of a feather, or the way a cat rubbed its silky fur against her legs. The water melted into her eyes, radiating through her body like electric currents, the potent elements merging with the chemicals in her body, acting like alchemy. Wonderful things were happening to her body, thanks to this ancient spring—she hadn't taken much notice of her body over the years, rarely giving her inner functions much attention. But she remembered the majority of the body consisted of water, and suddenly imagined herself as a liquid mass, her limbs supple in their amorphous surroundings. Her body was the antithesis of the dry desert and its shrivelled bones, devoid of life-giving water. She thought of her watery organs, her liver, heart and kidneys tingling with life, as though undergoing a sudden transplant, right here on this very stone. "A medical miracle!" she laughed, the bizarre thoughts taking root in her head, "what will the gods think of next?" Dorothy pictured them removing her old organs with an obsidian instrument and replacing them with divine new organs, safely storing the used ones in canopic jars.

This is where the alchemy happened—the metamorphosis from one form into another—water turning to stone, ether turning into a human being . . . The place was once used for initiation ceremonies, to lead the neophytes into the otherworld. They were led through the dark chambers, the passageways of Duat, where they delved into their inner beings, confronted their fears, and finally found their eternal selves. Dorothy dived into the Well of Roarings and swam through the deep channels, sensing her transformation within the holy waters. Then she climbed onto the sacred island and fell into a deep sleep, knowing Osiris was waiting for her in eternity.

Dorothy felt the flow of water within her body; her menstrual stream of blood, moving like the tide—the two primeval forces drawn by the moon. Last night had been a full moon. She usually thought of her period as a bit of a nuisance, but driven by the full moon, Isis and the sacred female energy, her bodily functions now seemed a wonder, her monthly blood imbued with lunar power. She had to shake off her English attitude to 'the curse', that puritanical notion that it was somehow dirty and should be kept out of the way, like an illness.

When Dorothy returned to her room she rummaged through her suitcase and found a box of sanitary pads. She thought how the moon renewed itself each month, just like the female life-force, offering the potential of new life; a monthly resurrection.

"I could do with a Knot of Isis," she decided, attaching the bulky pad to the inside of her knickers. They'd recently invented a tampon which you inserted inside the vagina, according to *Woman's Hour*. "No chance of getting them in Egypt," Dorothy sighed, so she'd just have to fashion her own as the women did in ancient times, rolling cloth into little spools. Perhaps it would start a new trend: Nefertari Tampons, worn by the queens of ancient Egypt!

She chuckled to herself and lay down on the bed, feeling light-headed with lack of sleep and wild ideas. What would the polite men on the terrace think of her tampon idea? They would die with embarrassment. *They'd think I'd lost my mind!*

The men could hear Dorothy laughing to herself and thought she must be reading a comic novel, as there was no radio in her room. It didn't occur to them that a woman could amuse herself to such an extent . . .

When the members of the Rest House had retired to bed, Dorothy began to meditate and finally entered her astral body, discarding her physical form like an old robe, one made of thick wool, and several sizes too big. Her naked body was slender and sinuous, flying through the air like a shooting star, hair whipping through the firmament. King Sety flew down from the sky to meet her, his naked frame a beam of light in the darkness. Their bodies merged into one shaft of light, forming a pyramid of yellow streaks. They walked through an archway, their heads bending under the portico. They came face to face with a large mural, their eyes burning into the bas-relief; the green face of Osiris. King Sety pressed his body against the figure, his head, torso and limbs aligning themselves with the divine image. He began sinking into the green relief, plaster softening into clay, then turning into flesh. King Sety disappeared into the pliable surface, the mural swallowing him whole.

"Nisou!" she cried, fingers tearing at the plaster wall.

"Don't be afraid, my love, just throw yourself into Osiris and he will pick you up."

Bentreshy closed her eyes and leaped into the mural, her body yielding to the malachite god—he was sheer liquid, melted butter; both water and fire. They were inside the mural now, with Osiris and Isis sitting on purple cushions, surrounded by pink clouds, like the heavenly clouds in a pantomime.

The divine thoughts came across like music, the chorale singing about the new dawn. *One day you will be together in the coral cloud of eternity, but first you must pass through the Temple chambers, impress each symbol into your imagination until they become the language of your soul. You will need water for the organs, food for the stomach, incense for the nostrils, and then the gods will hear your*

261

words. *Now go home to your earthly realm and follow the Temple path, and your life will begin again.*

What must you do to reach eternity? Come back to Abydos and awaken the Temple with your prayers and offerings. Bring the gods back to earth—they cannot resist the old rituals, the incense, the sweet wine, the dates and figs . . . Bring your Ka back to Abydos and rise from the flames like the bennu bird . . .

13. Time Passing
1280 BC

The Sage sipped his mint tea, known to calm an irritable mind. It was no good—he was feeling ill-tempered, and no amount of herbal infusions would soothe his complaint. Isis had deceived him. The whole evening had been orchestrated by the goddess (even the coloured lanterns were her idea), and he'd fallen under her spell. But after he'd had time to think about the evening and let his anger subside (thanks to the mint tea), he began to feel compassion for the unfortunate girl. He had the ability to put his personal feelings aside for a greater cause, and saving Nefret-Sheni from a life of desolation was of paramount importance. The Sage poured himself a second cup of tea, suddenly feeling much better. *The goddess of wisdom and healing needs my help.*

The Sage kept his promise to Isis and that evening he began his search for Nefret-Sheni, making a list of the possible planets that would appeal to a girl her age, testing her limits. But before he made any travel arrangements he needed to know the girl's true identity—if he were to invest any serious time and energy in this endeavour he wanted to know who he was dealing with.

Isis tightened her grip round the scroll, a map of the solar system, more detailed than his old chart, the Sage noticed. Isis had reservations about involving him any further—the old man was becoming a nuisance, what with his incessant scrutinising. But that's why she needed his help, she reminded herself, because the man had the eyes of Horus and the mind of Thoth, and he loved to win an argument. His line of reasoning could trace every fallacy in the universe.

"If you must know, the girl is Bentreshy—Harp of Joy. You've heard all the stories, I'm sure—most of them highly exaggerated. Mortals have a penchant for that sort of thing and I'm afraid immortals are no better."

"You mean Bentreshy, who had an affair with King Sety and got pregnant—"

"That's just what I mean—I thought you were above such mindless intrigue."

The Sage looked sheepish, "Sorry, my lady, I was just overcome with surprise and it brought out the primitive side in me." The Sage cleared his throat and changed his tactic, "Bentreshy—Harp of Joy, you say. Well, I never—I knew the girl was epic, monumental, despite her small frame!"

He was anxious to find the girl—he missed her company. She was one of the few people who understood his peculiar logic. But why does Isis insist on taking her to Amenti? The idea of Paradise made him shudder; he much preferred the Underworld—it appealed to his sense of imperfection and was more like Earth. Yes, he could travel from planet to planet, but Amenti was not part of his itinerary. Amenti was too perfect, too final. Once you reached Amenti, where else was there to go? How could you criticise Paradise?

The Sage spread the map out on the desk, the planets painted in black and gold across the parchment of blue sky. He closed his eyes for a moment, the planets circling in his head; how dizzy the universe made him, with its infinite galaxies and incalculable space. Too big for an old mind; he preferred the dimensions of reason with its distinctive margins...of course he liked to stretch the boundaries, but his mind was an intimate orb to which no one else could travel. He tried to imagine the inside of Bentreshy's mind, shutting out the world with her dark dome, envisioning new worlds and flying to unknown planets. With all that imaginative potential, the girl could be anywhere. Yet something told him she had returned to earth. The most obvious was often the least palpable to fathom. "Let her stay awhile," he decided, rolling up the map, "the Hall of Judgement can wait..."

∧∧∧∧∧   ∧∧∧∧∧   ∧∧∧∧∧

Bentreshy flew towards the earth, sliding down the white clouds, hovering in the space between land and sky, then gravity seized her by the legs and pulled her to the ground. Landing in the desert her body congealed into a solid form, as though freezing into a block of ice. Even time felt heavier on earth, weighed in seconds and minutes, moulded into days and weeks, then divided into years. She knew time was different in the rest of the universe, separated from human life and its obsession with continuity. In outer space time wasn't broken into days and measured by a series of hourly tasks. In eternity Bentreshy was pure consciousness and could move back and forth, left and right through time, like an artist deviating from a straight line.

On earth time could only move forward, the people completing their tasks, marking time. They built houses, planted crops and raised children, while the Pharaoh built temples and tended his kingdom. Time is an artist, she reiterated, turning days into monuments, sculptures and bas reliefs. They made their mark—that's what people did on earth—to prove they once existed. And who left a bigger signature on the landscape than King Sety I? He built fine temples in Thebes and Abydos, the most glorious murals the world had ever seen, and he supported the arts, astronomy and science, he even financed new trade routes. Sety would also leave an illustrious heir, Rameses the Great, who would take his vision into the future. But few people knew King Sety was also a poet, a sensitive soul who loved beauty and nature, and disliked the trappings of power...and few people knew he had loved a temple girl and was devastated by her untimely death, and that he had died of a broken heart. You know, he never returned to Abydos...

Bentreshy watched over Sety through his remaining years on earth—how human beings suffer, she noted, when they lose a loved one and blame themselves—it was devastating for her to watch. Sety prayed to Osiris five times a day, the gentle god helping to ease his torment, and over time the ocean of anguish became a still lake, and then a sacred pool that calmed his mind. Sadly he never made a full recovery (it was a constant battle against despair), but he learned a thing or two from the Resurrection God: that love is salvation, the only thing that keeps us from despair. Didn't Osiris make an oath to reunite with Isis, even if it took an eternity? And didn't Isis restore Osiris to life so he could fulfil that very oath? Sety also made a promise to the world: that he would find Bentreshy, even if it took him thousands of years, which in human terms is as good as eternity...

Although Sety never returned to Abydos he made sure the city was prosperous, supplying the residents with fine wine, frankincense and gold, and an army of artisans, priests and astronomers to maintain the Temple's mystical nature. Under his command the female deities were properly honoured, ensuring Ma'at's cosmic balance. Inhapi remained the High Priestess—not just of the House of Isis, but of the whole Temple—and under her guidance the mystery schools became world famous, her initiates known as the most enlightened souls in the land, impressing the pilgrims with their esoteric wisdom, their ability to reach other dimensions, escort the neophytes into the Infinite Beyond.

Inhapi's husband Kishar became the Overseer of Temple Design and dedicated his life to preserving the murals, statues and paintings, believing each brushstroke was a fingerprint of the gods and that the divine beings inhabited every portion of the Temple, breathing from the walls and ceilings, infusing the space with ethereal energy. It was possible to feel immortal in this place, if you had the courage to sit alone for a while—sometimes a priest from the other realm would appear and lead you through the portal...and you would return transformed, having seen the face of eternity, enchanting lands beyond the imagination—oh to be transposed, like metal into gold! The other dimension was now open to you, through this ingress to the Otherworld.

Sometimes Bentreshy spotted Kebi in the Temple, enticing a snake with one of her spells: *"Hetep-kh na!—May you be at peace with me,"* and sure enough, the cobra would lower his uraeus and slither outside. *Hetep-kh na.*

Bentreshy saw King Sety on his deathbed, a blue shroud covering his body, the light fading from his eyes. She saw his spirit float to the ceiling and hover like a bee, trying to find a way inside the tight bud. She thought he would come to her, eyes blazing in a moment of recognition, but then his gaze went dark with fear—he was being pulled backwards, sucked into a cyclone—what was happening to him? She watched in horror as his body turned to ether and disappeared through the wall, his voice screaming from behind the stones, "No! Let me be with her—do not banish me!"

Some say he'd been whisked away for his own safety. When Ma'at had weighed the Pharaoh's heart against the Feather of Truth she had found it burdened with grief and despair. Ma'at sensed the demons of Seth sniffing round the Pharaoh's innards, expecting a fall into the abyss. The goddess was shrewd in her judgement: she knew that if Seth got hold of King Sety's heart his powers would be relentless, the universe thrown into a destructive whirlwind. King Sety must go into hiding—until his senses were restored to order and he was no longer a temptation for Seth and his devils.

266

Bentreshy watched the funeral procession make its way along the Nile, cutting through the green fields and into the Valley of Eternity. The lanterns guided their path through the desert night, the procession winding through the hollows like a luminous snake. Rameses led the procession of mourners, looking spectacular in his black leopard skin robe, tears flowing down the silky folds. He was such a dear boy, such a loyal son, Bentreshy recalled. He'd ensured King Sety's mummy rested in a wooden coffin decorated with the image of Osiris, placed inside a sarcophagus carved out of a single piece of alabaster. It was the most beautiful sarcophagus she had ever seen, with white carvings and blue hieroglyphs, the goddess Nut embracing the chest, the sacred words immortalising the deceased.

Bentreshy read the words as they pulled the sarcophagus towards the tomb:

Enter the bones of Osiris, King Men-Maat-Ra, whose word is ma'at, son of the Sun, Seti, Men-en-Ptah...

"Wait, I haven't finished!" she shouted, running her hands over the cold surface:

Let them enter the foundation...pure are the bones of Osiris, King Men-Maat-Ra!

The sarcophagus must weigh three oxen, she imagined, as it took the strength of eight men to pull the golden sleigh through the rocky sand. The men struggled to get the sarcophagus inside the tomb, but once over the threshold the sarcophagus followed the manmade incline towards the Underworld. Bentreshy followed behind the procession, shuffling down the sandy passage, the stairways on the walls mimicking the mourners' journey. The walls depicted the Litany of Ra, the religious spells protecting the deceased through the Underworld. She read about the greatness of Ra, how the Pharaoh is reborn like the sun-god, after negotiating his way through the Underworld. She was travelling through the twelve stages of the Underworld, corresponding with the twelve hours of Amduat, "that which is in the Underworld," and each hour had its own gate guarded by a divine snake. The tomb was like a man's body: the passageway was the spine, the chambers the limbs, and the antechambers the internal organs keeping the deceased alive. The priests stopped when they came to the head—the burial chamber, where the real journey would begin. Inside the vaulted crypt the priests performed the Opening of the Mouth ceremony, waving the sacred adze over the coffin, uttering the magic spells that would reawaken the Pharaoh into eternal life. Bentreshy glanced at the Opening of the Mouth images on the wall, with life imitating art, each scene played out with iconic command. They were all present: Osiris, Isis, Horus and Hathor, hovering in the eleventh hour, the images leaping from the six pillars, the Pharaoh praying before Anubis.

With the ritual completed, the priests closed the stone lid: the twelfth hour of night was upon us! The sun was now in the East, re-emerging as Khepri, the newborn sun — the Pharaoh was reborn as one of the Justified! Bentreshy saw him float out of the sarcophagus, his *Akh* dyed pink in the alabaster light, reaching out to her in the new dawn.

For a brief moment their *Kas* touched, and they coalesced like two streams of warm air, enjoying the sudden tenderness. Sety whispered, "At last I am one of the dead and they cannot control me." But at that very moment a cold wind blew them apart, with a bite more akin to the North Pole than the Egyptian desert, and the two lovers drifted away from each other. Struggling against the brutal force, Sety shouted, "I will find you, dear Bentreshy. The evil ones do not frighten me now. My *Akh* is free and they cannot keep me in chains, now I have gained power over death." And in a flash he was gone, flying down the secret tunnel below the crypt, where the earth became a river, where the Pharaoh boarded his solar barque for the Land of Osiris. "Come with me, my love — we can be together in the Underworld — we'll find a place to hide —"

Bentreshy pushed her way through the tunnel. "I'm coming with you!" she shouted, the tunnel tightening round her shoulders, "They can't shut me out — they can't stop us!" She raged at the invisible force, the earth falling from the ceiling. As the secret shaft caved in, she was forced backwards into the main corridor, past the images of Ra coming down the stairway; she was fleeing from the Underworld, rewinding to the first hour of Amduat. She leaped into the dawn, the sky red as the desert rocks, and she headed for the Peak, the first pyramid created by nature, and yet it gave her no solace.

Bentreshy floated round the Valley of the Kings, the rocks riddled with hidden tombs. Then she wandered back to Sety's tomb and found it had been sealed, with great boulders blocking the entrance; the tomb swallowed by the Underworld. The Pharaoh had spent his last few years perfecting this tomb, making it the most beautiful burial place the gods had ever seen, and now it had disappeared from sight. What was this life about, when we spent our precious time building tombs—was life but a preparation for death? Sety had spent his life building temples and tombs, one stone placed upon another, like minutes in a day.

∧∧∧∧∧ ∧∧∧∧∧ ∧∧∧∧∧

Back in Abydos, Rameses continued his father's incessant building. He completed the Temple of Sety I and then built a few of his own. Poor Rameses didn't have his father's artistic sensibility, but what he lacked in subtlety he made up for in presentation. He had a flair for the grand production—everything had to be bigger and better, and in less capable hands, the effect would have been vulgar. But thanks to Rameses' love of spectacle, his creations were awe-inspiring. His temples at Abu Simbel even made the gods tremble at the foot of such ingenuity. The giant statues of Rameses carved into the hillside, and inside the temple the towering images of himself standing equal amongst the gods—only a formidable person could dream up such a vision. He was either touched by God or struck by delusions of grandeur, Bentreshy considered. And just look at the amazing reliefs on the walls—that's what talented people did with their lives: they erected a wall and then carved beautiful images onto it (but most of the time we just cut stones into blocks). That was our human history up till now, she thought; it had started with a mark on a stone, and then we'd learned to chisel and carve, shape our existence. And when our lives were over we left the stone monuments behind, imagining we were immortal.

∧∧∧∧∧ ∧∧∧∧∧ ∧∧∧∧∧

Bentreshy watched the Temple girls finish their evening prayers and then form a silent procession down the corridor to their dorm. One woman hurried down the corridor in the opposite direction, she turned for a moment to see if anyone was watching her, and then disappeared through a small doorway in the wall. She stepped into the open courtyard and breathed deeply, staring into the sky as if grateful for her freedom, for the infinite space that belonged to her. Bentreshy suddenly recognised her old friend Kebi, her lithe body walking in a loop, like the snakes she loved to charm. She was middle-aged now, with wrinkles round her eyes and streaks of silver in her hair, but there was something timeless about her gaze, hovering in the eternal dimension. She was carrying two snakes in her basket and tomorrow she would release them into the desert, far from the Temple grounds where they caused such a furore. Snakes were welcome guests, but after the appropriate rituals were carried out in their honour, they were quickly returned to the desert, as the Temple girls were thrown into a whirlwind by their wily presence.

Kebi had finished her stint at the Temple where she taught the Snake Dance to the young novices. For four months she had taught the girls to embrace the cobra's movements, absorb the space into fearless spirals and transform their bodies into ophidian shapes. She had shown them how to inhabit the snake's form, their elongated bodies twisting across the warm stones. Now the initiates had mastered the dance, they could charm the snakes and harness their powers, the Temple protected by their fearsome uraei.

Kebi waved to Inhapi who was sitting in her garden, wrapped in a shawl, wearing a black and silver wig to hide her scant hair, her brittle bones rattling like a sistrum. Her daughter read her passages from the *Eloquent Peasant*, Inhapi smiling at the part when the donkey eats the landowner's crops; her mind had already gone to the ethereal realm, her body not knowing which way to turn, oscillating between heaven and earth.

Kebi was finally going home to her husband and snakes—how she missed the intimate conversations with Teshen—how she longed to hear her grandchildren's laughter.

"One thing I won't miss is shaving my hair," Kebi rubbed her hand along her hairless arm. She looked forward to growing her hair and going a whole day without washing, allowing a layer of dust to settle on her skin. She laughed at the idea, "What would Meryt think of my slovenliness—now that she is the High Priestess? She would say it was a violation of the Temple rites—that I was a terrible example for the young girls..." But Temple life had its good points: there was no cleaning to do or meals to cook. Kebi knew she'd have a lot of work to do back at home: there would be rooms to sweep, clothes to mend and food supplies to replenish. And once the villagers heard of her return she would be inundated with requests for snake charms. There would be snakes trapped in wells, inside beds, clothesbaskets and cooking pots—any place where they could make people leap out of their skins. Snakes could be creative in their ability to frighten people: one man nearly had a heart attack whilst relaxing in his tub, when a snake reared up from the water and stared him straight in the eyes.

Kebi stood outside her home for a moment, admiring the geometric shapes painted on the front wall, the red and white flowers in the clay pots, the canopy shading the outdoor kitchen—with the stone oven, the reed mats surrounding the communal eating area. Kebi's granddaughter Nefer ran outside to greet her, wrapping her arms around Grandma's legs and squealing like a wolf pup. Nefer was only four, but how she'd grown in the past few months, and Kebi's grandson Hbari (who was only six) had learned to slice the papyrus stem and proudly carried a knife in a leather sheath.

Bentreshy watched this scene of domestic harmony; Teshen running outside to greet his wife, picking her up in his arms, swinging her round in a whirlwind of emotion, her robe twisting round her legs. Bentreshy's heart contracted with love, feeling the intensity of the couple's passion, and wishing she could throw herself into this maelstrom of affection.

The fire crackled with anticipation, spitting red sparks into the night sky, the skewers of fish sizzling in the flames, the delicious smells mixed with smoke and burning wood. The family gathered round the fire, their chatter following the flow of flames; they filled their plates with the grilled fish and aubergine, and completed the meal with slices of sweetbread coated in fig jam.

Kebi thought of Bentreshy: how she would love this evening, with the warm air and perfect sky bathed in moonlight, the stars clinging to the heavens like dust on a black dog. Her spirit must be near us, Kebi realised; why else would I have such poetic thoughts? She smiled to herself, knowing Bentreshy was watching over the world, proving the divide between heaven and earth was not so impenetrable and that even a lost soul could travel unhindered.

Bentreshy dried her eyes and leaped into the sky, the jowls of the night swallowing her up, plunging her into oblivion. She was pleased to learn Meryt had become High Priestess of Abydos and that she had married Nkosi, who was now High Priest, "just as I had hoped, all those years ago," Bentreshy recalled. She took comfort in the fact that her friends were happy on earth—that there was still hope for

271

this little paradise in the desert, nestled somewhere in the fields of reeds, where a woman called Kebi could charm snakes and harness their power to help mankind.

There were so many places to see in this endless galaxy and Bentreshy became quite skilful at travelling from star to star, visiting the far-off planets unseen by humans, where life mirrored their own world—Bentreshy's journey was never-ending, filtered through the millions of light years, affected by the dark matter that filled the space. Colour, sound, texture—if only people could see the possibilities of life on these unknown planets—it was like being inside a prism, the light resonating through each life form and creating exquisite beings out of stardust and spirals of colour. But Bentreshy never turned her back on earth, despite her love of spiralling planets. She observed that the earth was in a constant state of flux: seas dried up and turned to desert, then waters rose and cliffs went sliding into the sea; land masses cut loose and formed new islands.

There was the Temple in Abydos with its limestone walls and granite pillars, defiant against the waves of sand, the Western Desert reclining without a care. The Temple looked like a beautiful jewel, a block of amber shining in the sun. The Temple is well cared for, Bentreshy was glad to see, although two hundred years had passed since King Sety had built the place, and his son Rameses had completed the sculptures and murals. Two hundred years—where had the time gone? Sometimes she grew weary of travelling through the universe and blew herself out like a candle, and when she rekindled herself many years had passed...Who was Pharaoh now? she wondered; Rameses XI had been the last king of the 20th Dynasty, she noted, the last ruler to be buried in the Valley of the Kings in Thebes; the end of a glorious age.

It was now the 21st Dynasty, and Smendes was the Pharaoh of this new age, running his kingdom from Tanis. Why were they always changing the capital? It was most confusing for travellers, and it would make life difficult for researchers in the future, she expected. First there was Heliopolis, then Memphis, Thebes, Amarna, and now Tanis.

Bentreshy noted that something remarkable was happening in this new Dynasty: women were taking over the temples in Thebes. She couldn't wait to tell her immortal friends. "I will write it all down, record this momentous time in history," she dipped her reed pen into the ink and filled the reams of papyri. *Marriages between royal princesses and Theban priests of Amun have become a common practice. Through their mothers' line the High Priests were now descendants of Tanite Royalty. The priests were more powerful than in any other time in history and daughters of the Pharaoh never more cherished. The chief Queen enacted the role of Amun's wife Mut and each daughter became God's Wife of Amun. The God's Wives had incredible wealth and power, owning great stretches of land in Thebes. A priestess called Ankhnesneferibre became the First Prophet of Amun. The tides were turning: women were taking power away from the priests. The Temple of Amun was becoming a female place, like the House of Isis in Abydos—even the décor had softened, the murals filled with female imagery and everywhere there were pictures of dancing and joy, instead of slogans of war and violent battle scenes, and the scent of exotic flowers floated through the Temple gardens.*

∧∧∧∧∧   ∧∧∧∧∧   ∧∧∧∧∧

When Bentreshy looked down again it was the Late Period. Gone were the God's Wives of Amun and their female prophets. So who was ruling now? Bentreshy would go to the taverns in Abydos—listen to what the locals had to say. If you want to understand the spirit of any age then go to the drinking holes, she realised, for after a few drinks the truth trickles off the tongue like warm honey.

"That Ne-kaw II, he profited under the Assyrians, no doubt about it, and now he's returning to the old ways, like in Djoser's time. The art, the religion, even the writing—he'll be asking us to wear the old robes next!" the bald scribe grumbled. Everyone agreed that they were returning to the old ways and nobody seemed to like it. A young artisan complained, "King Ne-kaw wants me to make sculptures just like in the tombs of the Old Kingdom. He is sending me to Saqqara to copy the reliefs from the tombs—he even wants me to crawl inside the pyramids and copy the texts off the walls. Now he's going too far!" It was like going back to the Old Kingdom, with the fancy canopic jars and the ancient style of writing found in the tombs of Khufu's day . . . But even the artisans had to agree the Saitic rulers

273

were good for Abydos. They rebuilt the temples and commissioned some handsome reliefs for the walls.

Unfortunately Wah-ib-Ra was nothing like his father Ne-kaw. Bentreshy could see the people getting angry and plotting a rebellion. If only the King could observe his people in private, the way she could, and understand their troubled hearts. He should know the Egyptians will not be subjugated—a ruler must gain the respect of his people to reign successfully. Bentreshy could see it coming: Ahmose, a handsome officer, was sent to crush the rebellion, but he was so impressed with the rebels' plight that he joined their cause. She followed Ahmose as he led the people into battle, feeling the thrill and fear of revolution, sensing their frustration turn to fortitude. Once the oppressed were motivated by a charismatic leader they became a relentless force, freedom's fire burning in their bellies. She could smell their ardour: the sour sweat, the copper scent of blood, and she could taste the victory, like warm bread and sweet wine.

How exciting life could be, thought Bentreshy, when good people seize the day, when they overcome oppression and make life beautiful; enhanced by acts of heroism history comes to life, for a moment humanity hovered in greatness. People had done something epic and the world was overwhelmed by its achievement. How wonderful to be part of this, she reflected, watching the soldiers in the sand, the dust caked round their nostrils, the desert heat drying their sweat, the look of triumph on their faces. "Long live Ahmose—our new King!"

This rebellious officer ruled Egypt as King Ahmose II (Bentreshy had a front row seat at the coronation, one of the benefits of being immortal), and she was happy to say Ahmose was a fine leader. He restored the Temple of Sety I and the old shrines, and once again pilgrims flocked to Abydos, paying homage to the old gods and enjoying the exotic gardens.

But these glory days weren't to last; nothing could save them from the new invaders. Bentreshy watched the soldiers march into Egypt and claim it for the Persian Empire. How she hated to witness such invasions, without being able to intervene. Sometimes she tried to haunt the generals in their dreams, awaken them to the dangers, but they merely tossed and turned in their sleep, and once morning came they washed the terror from their eyes and soon forgot about the nightmares. None were wise enough to take these dreams as an omen, or to puzzle over their meaning.

The new king was called Cyrus II and he came from the Persian Gulf, an area that would see much bloodshed in the next millennium, but back then the place was the biggest Empire in the world, and no one dared challenge its might. The Persians knew they had to control Egypt if they wished to rule the world, as Egypt was their only rival, Bentreshy realised, and like many invaders to follow, they wanted to control the ports leading to the Mediterranean and Africa. But as usual, the invaders soon fell under the spell of Egypt, Bentreshy was happy to see. The Persian kings began to call themselves Pharaohs and even follow the religious traditions.

King Darius I performed religious duties as the Pharaoh, and at the Festival of Opet he paraded through the town like in olden times, celebrating the return of the Flood and the renewal of life. Bentreshy admired how he renovated the temples and honoured the old gods, but others believed he was just trying to gain approval; a clever way of controlling the masses.

Bentreshy was sad to say the world was becoming a cynical place and that the desire to rule was becoming greater than the desire to worship. She noticed the Laws of Ma'at were being violated as history progressed, the new rulers distancing themselves from the goddess of justice and cosmic order. "How foolish they are to live outside the Laws of Ma'at, as this will only lead to chaos," she shouted through the clouds, feeling the impotence of the immortals, as most earthlings could no longer hear their words or gain from their insights.

When she could stand the stupidity of man no longer, Bentreshy would leap into the sky in search of brighter planets, where human life didn't exist, and the water bubbled in great whirlpools, the toxic gases burning into the ground and leaving deep wounds on the surface.

Sometimes Bentreshy went to Timat in the Underworld, where the spirit guides liked to congregate. She got on well with the spirit guides, as they reminded her of the goodness in mankind and the importance of helping the lost souls in the universe. Occasionally she would meet up with Sheriti and they'd talk about the state of the world, and how some people still searched for meaning and a higher existence. Sheriti rarely mentioned the Council of the Gods—I think she's given up trying to save my soul, Bentreshy told herself. Sheriti had a new pupil on earth, a new soul to guide. "Her name is Adileh and she is the wisest person I've guided in a long time—I am inspiring her to tell the truth and fight female oppression."

Bentreshy was glad to hear it, as lately she had lost faith in mankind, since the last wave of Persians had taken over Egypt. But there was something to be said for a weak ruler, she realised, as people were less likely to see the king as a god, and this gave them greater freedom. "I am glad to see people are entering the temples and don't care about the superiority of the priests. The temples have become a public place and everyone is worshipping in their own way." It was heartening to Bentreshy, who believed the gods belonged to the people, and she loved to see people taking over the temples and erecting their own statues to Osiris and Isis.

∧∧∧∧∧   ∧∧∧∧∧   ∧∧∧∧∧

One day Bentreshy heard about a scholar called Pythagoras who had recently come to Egypt—the year was 547 BC and the young man was twenty-three years old. He said he didn't want to live in the Greek community like the other expatriates, and preferred to spend his time with the priests and sages in the temples. The stellar priests taught him about the stars and how to use numbers to understand time and space. At Heliopolis he was initiated into the Mysteries of Osiris and Isis, and he finally became a priest. From the celestial priests he learned that numbers have a mystical substance, that all life forms consist of numbers—multiplying functions creating cosmic harmony—the key to understanding the ever-expanding universe. The priests took the young scholar onto the temple roof where he spent his nights observing the stars and planets, which he noticed produced a collective harmony, the music of the spheres. He realised that the sphere was a perfect shape and that the Earth itself was a perfect sphere; then the priests showed him how the orbit of the Moon sloped to the equator of the Earth. Inside the secret chambers Pythagoras learned about the wisdom of Thoth: that man is a marvel, and through a psychic rebirth he becomes a god; by understanding the secrets of nature our minds become one with Cosmic Mind—man is both mortal and immortal.

But the most practical piece of knowledge they taught him was the Sacred Theorem. The scholars showed Pythagoras how a rope with twelve knots could solve any mathematical and geometric problem. The priests laid the sacred rope on the temple roof and twisted it into various shapes. As a triangle it could design perfect pyramids; forming a circle it could measure the circumference of Earth. That was the great geometric secret behind achieving the perfect proportions in their temples and pyramids. Numbers were the essence of all living things; they calculated space and time, they clarified the imperceptible.

Ten years passed and Pythagoras was blissfully happy studying the esoteric wisdom and the art of astral travel, exploring the sphere of inner consciousness. Then one day Cambyses II invaded Egypt.

"Woe be to us! Pythagoras has been exiled to Babylon!" the town crier shouted in the street. "Cambyses has control of the priesthood, and now they must chant to a different tune!"

Luckily Pythagoras was able to continue his studies in Babylon and expand the mathematical theories from Heliopolis: *Any right angled triangle, the square on the hypotenuse is equal to the sum of the squares on the other two sides.*

Bentreshy thought of Pythagoras as a dissident sage, keeping the wisdom alive in a time of ignorance, as Egypt had entered the Dark Ages, with a despotic ruler determined to destroy the soul of Egypt. She leaned over Pythagoras' desk and was mesmerised by the geometric equations scribbled on the scroll. $a2 + b2 = c2$. Underneath he'd drawn some illustrations of the theorem:

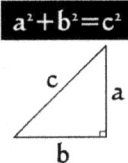

$$a^2 + b^2 = c^2$$

Bentreshy knew Pythagoras searched for the truth in the darkness, illuminating the shadows with brilliant diagrams. At night he had the Babylonian stars for company and listened to the music of the spheres, clinging to the geometry of the heavens that produced an ordered universe.

It is thanks to people like this that the old wisdom survived, she realised years later, when the priesthood was finally destroyed and the knowledge erased, and very few people were left to tell the truth.

Pythagoras was one of the few prophets left, and he carried the old knowledge back to the Greek isle of Samos, where he set up a school called the Semicircle, to teach young people about the Mysteries of

Isis, the wonders of geometry, music, and the importance of sexual equality. He married a brilliant woman called Theano, who discovered the formula to obtain a golden triangle. But not everyone approved of the progressive notions. The Greeks weren't used to sexual equality, or the music of the spheres, and their ignorance turned to fear and then outrage. The Pythagoreans then fled to Southern Italy and started a new school in Croton where they continued to enlighten people with their Egyptian wisdom. One day a nobleman called Cyclon wanted to join the society, but Pythagoras thought he was a crude man who would only harm the movement and he politely refused the man entrance—Cyclon was so outraged by the rejection that he attacked the school with a gang of thugs. Again the Pythagoreans had to flee—this time to Metapontum where they started yet another Mystery School, where they played around with irrational numbers . . . Bentreshy had to admire their optimism—how they remained true to the Mysteries of Isis and never abandoned the esoteric teachings of Heliopolis. It seemed like each destructive event was followed by a creative insight, a brighter flame.

Back in Egypt a new wave of disciples carried on the Egyptian traditions: Plato, Herodotus and Hippocrates were initiated into the priesthood and returned to Greece transposed, spreading the ancient wisdom through the Western world.

After 130 years of oppression, Alexander the Great finally chased the Persians out of Egypt and was welcomed as the Mighty Liberator.

One of the spirit guides called Panhey had watched over Alexander and claimed he was a passionate yet confused young man. But he admitted Alexander had a genuine love for Egypt and honestly wanted her to be a great empire again. Panhey wished the general would stay in Egypt, instead of charging off to Persia, and he did his best to thwart the general's departure by hiding his maps and food supplies, but the general was even more determined to march into Persia (where he would come to a bitter end, according to Penhey's prediction).

The spirit guides were an interesting group who liked to adopt lost souls and help them to find their right path in life. In Timat they got together on the full moon to discuss the lost souls they were protecting and to offer one another support. Sheriti was pleased to report that Kadisha was turning into a great poet. "She is a remarkable soul, but she needs protecting from her abusive family who don't appreciate her gift." Sheriti wouldn't let them crush the girl and led her to an abandoned shrine, where she could write in peace.

When Sheriti grew weary of being a spirit guide she travelled to Amenti for a bit of luxury, enjoying the divine views of mountain peaks and turquoise lakes expanding into eternity. "Sometimes I need the kindness of the gods—people can't imagine that spirit guides need a shoulder to lean on—that they too need taking care of."

Bentreshy had never thought a spirit guide might need support— perhaps I should be kinder to her, try to be her friend. "I could accompany you to Amenti, if you like. Do you think you could take me there one day?" she ventured.

Sheriti shook her head regretfully, "You're not ready for Amenti— first you must pass through the Hall of Judgement." Sheriti didn't want to discourage the girl, but she had a long journey ahead of her, and she would have to learn to follow the rules.

Bentreshy was annoyed with herself for asking. What was I thinking of? The Council was bound to hear of it and then they would make me stand trial. She would never escape once they got hold of her—but how she longed to see the wonders of paradise and taste the ambrosia of perfection. They say the colours alone were enough to make a mortal go blind with beauty . . .

Bentreshy imagined herself there with King Sety, watching the sunset behind the mountains of the gods, the gold and pinks merging into dark amber, a sky illuminated with real gems and strands of silver. It gave her the impression of inexhaustible riches, where stars were made of diamonds and the sky was an endless silk robe, fashioned from a billion worms all the way from China. But Bentreshy wasn't in Amenti, she was trapped in the Underworld, a place that mirrored the world on earth, yet it had a greater capacity for changing its landscape and could do so at a moment's notice. Inhapi had described the Underworld as the essence of our world, like a dream, forever transforming itself. A pool could change its dimensions, turn from a rectangle into a circle; cool water could turn hot, steam rising from the surface in vaporous rings. It reminded her of a conversation she'd had with King Sety—how inspiration rises out of the unseen depths; how art was like ether, meandering in an aimless direction, until it lodged itself in the mind and began to grow. It was like love, needing deep soil in which to take root, Sety claimed. *Love must burrow into a shady place, capable of absorbing its secrets. You are my dark dwelling, within your shadows I can unleash my mysteries."*

Sety searched for Bentreshy in the Afterlife, travelling from planet to planet, but the girl was nowhere to be found. Sometimes she came to him in his dreams: they were on a boat on the river, lying together on soft cushions. He felt such happiness in those dreams, completely loved and understood. When he awoke he was alone again, the room empty and cold. Such a terrifying sense of loneliness—feeling he'd lost part of himself. Bentreshy possessed the other part of him, the one capable of feeling joy—the child-like self he'd left behind. *You cannot die of a broken heart in the Afterlife; here there is no death at all, no end. You hover, like a suspension bridge . . . but I must carry on searching, I must find Bentreshy and retrieve my Ka.*

He thought about his life on earth—how he could have acted differently—how he could have saved the girl. *I should have shown more courage—fought the forces that opposed me, acknowledged my love publicly...instead I kept it secret.* He allowed his sense of duty to get in the way of his feelings, his obsession with power. He should have done things differently—he told himself every day, the sentence like a mantra being repeated over and over in his head.

Sheriti began to relax, enjoying the company of her fellow guides—even Bentreshy seemed in good spirits, although she would keep asking about that insufferable man.

"So, tell me about Sety—where has he ended up?" Bentreshy asked again, her voice feigning indifference. Sheriti gave her a stern glance. "I don't know his whereabouts—only that he is far away from here and must remain so until the transformation has been completed."

"Which transformation—and into what?" Bentreshy demanded to know.

"Why, the transformation of his soul. Much depends on the weighing of the heart on the Day of Judgement," she regretted to say, knowing Bentreshy had avoided the whole event. "The process doesn't really begin until the heart has been measured and the Goddess Ma'at considers a person's goodness. But Ma'at is non-judgemental—her scales reveal the truth and how many transformations a *Ka* will need—sometimes a soul undergoes many transformations, taking thousands of years to complete. Don't worry—she is a just goddess and wants to help us reach Amenti."

"Ma'at may be fair-minded, but it's the Council of the Gods I don't trust—and once they get me in the Hall of Judgement I'll be trapped—they will feed me to Ammit, Devourer of Souls!" she cried, leaping into the sky.

"Come back, Bentreshy—you must learn to trust them!" But the girl was gone, floating somewhere in the blue ether, on her way back to Earth.

With the passing of time, everyone Bentreshy had known on earth had died, and then disappeared into the ethereal realm. As an exile, she had no contact with the souls once they had passed over. She remembered seeing Kebi on her deathbed, surrounded by her two children and five grandchildren. When Kebi began her journey through the Underworld, she saw her friend hovering like a bee, her feet dangling in space. "Bentreshy—I'm so happy to see you…" The two friends embraced then drifted apart, like a confluence dividing into two rivers.

How much suffering I've had to bear, seeing loved ones die and vanish into the ether, without the promise of a reunion, cried Bentreshy. Her loved ones had died many centuries ago and there was no one left to lose. She could gaze down on the world as a spectator, watching the years merge into decades and centuries, the millennia coming and going like boats on the river.

She heard that Kebi had gone to live in Khamat, a realm ruled by the snake goddess Amaunet. The land was a wonderful place for snake lovers, with dank dark caves, with fountains and pools where the snakes gathered to drink; the landscape punctured with deep fissures where the cobras could hide, and a jungle of greenery providing shelter from the sun and the glare of intruders.

Kebi felt at home in Khamat, and her husband and family all came to live there, along with Tiaa and a succession of snakes she'd had on earth. The snakes understood Kebi, their serpentine brains picking up human signals. She could feel the snakes slithering through her mind, gently reading her thoughts. In Khamat people had picked up the snakes' characteristics, they moved in synchronised spirals and liked to congregate by the pools, taking refuge from the heat. They hissed when they were annoyed and flicked their tongues to reveal a range of emotions.

The snake goddess Amaunet had jet black eyes and a pink forked tongue which she used to great verbal effect, accentuating her speeches with hisses and clicking sounds, and she rolled her long tongue to produce ululations and reverberations that could be heard throughout the valley. Her body was covered in green and yellow snakeskin which glistened in the sun, her exterior was moist and shiny from the recent rain and she rose to greet the worshippers, who could see her reflection in the pool, a spiral of ochre and turquoise breaking the still surface. The goddess encouraged cooperation and friendship between people and snakes, and every week there were communal dances, rituals and feasts to celebrate the sacred bond between the two species, originating in the beginning of time, when the snakes crawled out of the primal flood and came to live on land.

How Bentreshy would love this place, thought Kebi, longing to see her friend again. She missed her terribly—even after all these centuries, time had not erased her memory. Kebi prayed to Amaunet and asked her advice: how to reach a friend who was hiding from the world and the gods. Amaunet knew a great deal about clandestine behaviour as snakes spent much of their time concealed in the shadows, in fact most of the descriptions about snakes had to do with furtive behaviour: sly, stealthy, surreptitious, and there were many less flattering ones too. If anyone could find Bentreshy it was the snake goddess, as she knew the covert realm and understood what might drive a person underground—they were often looking for silence, a sense of calm—but most of all they were searching for inner peace.

Kebi thanked the goddess and went home with a collection of spells and amulets. Tiaa was also an expert on covert behaviour, known to track down even the most secretive person. Once at home, Kebi made a comfortable place for herself on the floor and arranged the cushions in a circle. She uttered the spells and sent Tiaa to visit Bentreshy in her dreams. Kebi sat in a trance and brought forth her friend's mind, imagining the snake entering the unconscious domain, twisting through the dormant passages and tickling the deep channels with her damp scales. Bentreshy could see the snake now, dancing with her crown held high, coiling through the psychic space, inciting her mind to open its sealed chambers. She was delighted to see Tiaa again and thought how beautiful she looked with her great uraeus, her reptilian body moving in curlicues of light, her tongue darting in

282

time to the drums. She'd forgotten how enchanting snakes could be, inciting us with their magic. She remembered Kebi dancing with Tiaa at the festivals and how the crowds had fallen under her spell, eyes hypnotised by the rhythmic spirals.

Bentreshy rose from her bed and followed the snake, their bodies intertwining, warm flesh merging into cold scales. They twisted across the sky, a neat braid of flesh and snakeskin arching over the universe. Bentreshy felt herself being pulled along, as if swept into a fast-flowing river. Her hair flew about her face and her eyes wept with the speed of the wind; she could see a million planets, potential worlds inviting her to explore their uncharted terrains. But she was going somewhere much further away, hidden behind the big planets and bright stars, a place for those who craved anonymity. They were in the shadows of the universe, concealed behind a purple eclipse; they were entering the most remote part of the cosmos, with no sign of life in sight, as if they'd fallen into a black hole. Then Bentreshy saw a green planet spinning in the empty sky, which seemed to be coming towards them, hurling at great speed; she imagined the orb crashing into them, absorbing them into its green mass. She wrapped herself tightly round the snake and the pair plunged head first, the blood rushing through her eyes and ears. The planet came to a standstill and yet they kept moving forward, a flying creature, half-human half-snake, legs flapping behind the tail, and they landed in a soft patch of greenery, the grass parting under their weight. Bentreshy fell away from the reptile, her body still moulded into a spiral, unable to shake off the snake's form. She slithered on the ground, trying to remember how to stand erect. The snake slithered alongside her, amused by this scuttling human, the way she wriggled on her belly.

Bentreshy saw a woman approaching, and she tried her best to get on her feet. *The woman will think I'm mad if I roll around like a reptile.* She managed to get on her knees and leaned back on her feet, watching the figure grow closer and more familiar.

It was her old friend Kebi! After all these years! Bentreshy was so glad to see her that she leaped from her haunches and staggered towards her friend, forgetting she didn't have the use of her limbs. The two friends fell to the ground, locked in a friendly embrace, like two cobras. Here on Khamat, Bentreshy was to discover, it was quite normal to relinquish your limbs and slither like a snake, and they had many rituals which encouraged the practice.

The two friends spent a blissful time together, snake-hunting in the fields, wandering along the river—just like the old days in Abydos, watching the sunsets over the mountains.

Then one day Bentreshy awoke to find herself spinning in space, with Sheriti spinning alongside her, face like a ghostly shroud.

"It is time to leave Khamat," she insisted, tugging on her sleeve. "You can't spend all your time in the land of snakes—you're only avoiding the inevitable."

"But I didn't get to say good-bye—Kebi will wonder what's happened to me."

"Don't worry, your friend realises you had to continue your journey—she understands," Sheriti explained, directing the girl towards the sky, her gaze dazzled by the bright planets.

Bentreshy looked down and saw the Earth hovering like a blue ball; the land seemed to be disappearing, engulfed by endless oceans. "All right," she conceded, "but before I enter the Hall of Judgement I'd like to return to Earth for a few days—learn more about this man they called Alexander the Great—just grant me this wish and I will come willingly."

"Very well, I will grant you a few more days, if you promise to leave without a fuss," she smiled, feeling relieved. "I understand your fascination with the man. They say he's a great hero, having saved Greece and Asia Minor from the barbarians they call the Persians."

Bentreshy flew down to earth, eager to get a closer look at this unexpected hero, with whom Egypt had fallen in love. Alexander was a rather short man with a muscular frame and the determination of a conqueror. But he wasn't a brute, Bentreshy could tell by his deep eyes, the way he gazed tenderly at a newborn lamb, the way he admired the beauty of the temples. Here was an invader who venerated the local gods, who brought fresh water for the statues and lit incense at the feet of Amun.

Alexander had chased the Persians from Egypt, and even then he wasn't satisfied: he pursued them into Babylon where he was honoured as the King of Asia—and then he contracted a fever and died—just as Penhey had predicted! How quickly a hero becomes a corpse, and then a legend. His body was carried back to Egypt and he was buried in Alexandria, mourned by Achaeans and locals alike, hailed as the great Pharaoh and liberator of Egypt.

When the legend of Alexander had been played out, Sheriti was back again, reminding her about the Underworld. "Come on, Bentreshy, I'm here to take you to the Hall of Judgement—you are ready for salvation." Sheriti stood in the boat, sail flapping. And Bentreshy, standing by the entrance to a cave, drawn into the gloomy interior. She wanted to lose herself in the blue light, and the white stalactites dangling like fangs; she wanted to dissolve in the purple pools and never come up. Without thinking she dived into the pool headfirst, Sheriti screaming, "Bentreshy—don't do it!" but it was too late, Bentreshy parted the surface and disappeared underwater, wondering why Sheriti was so disapproving. The water was like a silk dress, clinging to her weary body and giving her a new shape; the cold water pierced her skin, flooding her orifices with a sudden chill.

"Come out, Harp of Joy, there are water demons in these pools—you must climb ashore." Sheriti sailed round her in the yellow boat, smacking the oars on the surface, churning up the bottom, revealing her anxiety.

Bentreshy dived underwater a second time, kicking her legs vigorously. Approaching the bottom she noticed her visibility improving and she could see large grottoes covered in pink and green plants. She didn't feel the need to breathe, although she must have been holding her breath for some time now. Swimming through the grotto she followed a school of blue and red fish, proceeding in an orderly fashion, as if marching in a military parade. Bentreshy caught sight of a yellow light glowing at the end of the cavern, and as she approached the light grew brighter, illuminating the cave and the startled fish eyes; the orderly procession dissolving into chaos, each fish darting in an aimless direction. Bentreshy followed the light above, her lungs were bursting for air now, her voice crying out with a faint squeal, just before she broke through to the surface. It was like breaking a seal, a layer of skin, and there she was, floating on the milky green surface, the cavern illuminated by silver light, as though entering the centre of the moon. The air felt brittle after the plasticity of the water, like a violent slap, jolting her from a dream. She crawled onto the rocks, her feet slipping on the algae, and gazed round the extraordinary cave, infused in gold light. She inhaled the warm air, the mist rising from her robe—the smell of smoke mingling with the scent of rock pools and moist organisms. A trail of smoke spiralled to the roof of the cave, squeezing through the gap in search of the sky.

A man was sitting by the fire, poking the embers with a copper fork. He was boiling water for tea and seemed oblivious to her presence. He'd stuck two sticks into the ground and balanced another stick on top, where he'd hung a line of clothes out to dry. The scene looked so commonplace that Bentreshy forgot she was in an underground chamber, lured by her memories of washing days back on earth.

There was something familiar about this man, he felt like an old friend or a lover; he mirrored something deep inside her, something forgotten. He sensed it too, and he gave her a knowing look: then he brought his finger to his lip to signal silence. She could read his eyes and they said, "Let them think we are strangers."

"My name is Setau and I've been travelling in the Underworld for a thousand years. I've been exploring the life forms in this unusual land and recording my observations in this book."

She noticed a brown book by his side. Then he picked up a lyre and began to play. "But mainly I collect stories from wherever I go. It's amazing what people tell me."

Bentreshy heard a rumbling in the pool, and two small dragons ascended to the surface, their mouths exuding flames. She leaped up in fear, and then felt Setau's hand on her arm. "They are only water-demons, they mean no harm. Not all demons are bad, despite the stories."

The dragons crawled out of the water and sat quietly by the fire, soothed by the lyre and Setau's hypnotic voice. They were poetic demons and they couldn't resist a good legend. Setau began his tale:

Once, long ago, there was a beautiful maiden who lived in the local village. One day she met a young prince and they fell in love. But the prince's family disapproved and tried to keep them apart. Then a group of evil courtiers decided to get rid of the girl as they wanted to gain power over the prince. They realised the girl had too much influence over the prince and they would never overthrow him as long as she was by his side. They imprisoned the girl when the prince was away and forced her to drink poison. When the prince discovered the plot he had the courtiers executed. But he never overcame losing his one true love and he died of a broken heart a few years later.

That's not how the story goes, thought Bentreshy. Perhaps there were many versions of this tale, and over the centuries the events had altered. Can the truth be told in many forms? Can history change its course?

The demons began to cry, a flood of tears running down their gnarled faces. They were shaking with grief, their dragon bellies rising like volcanoes. Bentreshy turned away as one dragon opened his wretched jowls and released a cloud of purple smoke and green gases; red flames shooting from the wails of remorse, his mouth a cauldron of fire and emotion. Then the creature rolled onto his belly, let out a great sigh, and fell silent. Having released the venom and remorse, the dragons were spent—a cathartic experience for the creatures, no doubt, who turned into playful puppies. The frightening creatures looked almost comical, with their tails drooping in the mud, rolling on their horny bellies. After their snooze on land, the two demons returned to the pool and slowly disappeared, sinking into the vapour of unseen things, leaving a series of gaseous bubbles as a reminder of their presence.

"Come to me, my love, now the dragons have gone and no one can see us."

Setau put down his lyre, and Bentreshy nestled into his torso. It felt like a hollow place that had been empty for thousands of years, feeling the loneliness in that space, she spread her body into the soft folds. He could feel the warmth coming from the girl's body, her breath heating up his cold bones. He'd forgotten how love could warm the blood; turn misery into joy, restore a dead man to life and make him feel reborn. The lovers looked at each other and they saw the transformation occurring, like watching metal turn to gold. They were left exposed and vulnerable, feeling the universe slip away, leaving only their naked selves, facing each other in a vacant sea. And yet they were never more powerful: with the world stripped away they could see into the heart of things; their love gave them a new understanding, a compassion for all living creatures. Their love for each other radiated through the universe, reflected in spirals of light, finally reaching the shores of Earth in gentle waves.

Isis and Osiris felt the impact in Amenti, and they remembered the couple with compassion. "After us, they are the world's greatest lovers. They show people that love can last for eternity." Osiris kissed his wife's hand and nestled his face in her long braids.

"Then why must they live apart?" Isis hated the obstacles that stood in the way of true love.

"The universe has taken billions of years to form and the gods took even longer to evolve. What is three thousand years?" Osiris kissed her cheek. "The soul takes time to develop. One day Bentreshy will return to earth and she will try and retrieve what was lost, but it won't be easy because people will misunderstand her, doubt her intentions, and she will feel terribly alone."

Isis feared for the girl, and all she could do was watch over her and guide her steps. The enlightenment of the soul took thousands of years, as Osiris reminded her. What with the affair, the pregnancy and the suicide, things could take a little longer. The scales of Ma'at were out of balance and it could take ages to set them straight. But order would return, if only Isis could tell the child. If only people on earth would realise this too, then there would be more hope in the world, and her job would be a lot easier. People were in charge of their own destinies, and the life they led dictated where their souls would be in the next life. But she mustn't sound smug or self-righteous — people stumbled in the dark, often dragging their *Kas* behind them, with only the prophets' words and the old religion to guide them. Even the modern religions offered important clues, if people could see past the dogma and falsehoods. The Bible was full of references to Egyptian mythology: the Primeval Flood, the Lake of Fire, the Tree of Life … And the Virgin Mary, the Black Madonna, obviously images of Isis. How amusing these writers were, to leave such obvious clues, taunting people to pick up the trail . . . And that Holy Family, a portrait of Osiris, Isis and Horus — but they'd left all the good bits out. They'd missed out the lady's healing powers — how she had restored her husband to life and conceived a child. The Fertility story was in there too, but they'd left out the sex. And how invigorating the sex had been! — we had moved mountains, turned the arid land into green abundance. And now they called it the Immaculate Conception — they were right about its divine origins, but it was our love-making that was divine — not the birth (one of the many misconceptions in that book). Isis closed the Bible and couldn't help yawning. It all sounded a little repetitive, this obsession with prophets and messiahs, when it had all been said and done before . . .

But she was sounding self-righteous again . . . since the Egyptian religion had been erased people had little to go on, Isis reminded herself. No wonder they forgot about her. However, there were many people who still remembered, she reassured herself; people all over the world asked for her guidance and protection. Not like in the old days, of course, but enough to make her job worthwhile.

People who prayed to Isis, the Great Mother, the Black Madonna, all those messages came through. It was a select group these days, and because she wasn't swamped with requests she had time to care for all her followers, unlike Jesus who couldn't possibly respond to all his disciples (sometimes Horus had to help him out). Even in ancient times when Isis was at her peak, she could always rely on other gods and goddesses to share the burden (the benefits of polytheism). Hathor would help out with the love problems and Bastet would offer to take the pregnancy cases. Seshet did wonders for writer's block, and Horus was a great comfort to people suffering from depression or lacking in courage.

∧∧∧∧∧   ∧∧∧∧∧   ∧∧∧∧∧

Bentreshy watched the world change like turning pages in a book . . . a sweeping gesture and she could span a century, a few words, a fleeting glance and she could cross a millennium . . . Oh look, there's Cleopatra in her royal nemes—how beautiful she is with her milky skin and fearless mind—she killed herself, just like me. She too refused to surrender, and asked the snake to set her free. Now the last great queen has left Egypt . . .

In the new millennium, Mary, Joseph and their son Jesus fled to Egypt. They knew they'd be safe in Egypt, where people were used to nurturing prophets. They reminded Bentreshy of the sacred family: Isis, Osiris and Horus were here once again. After Jesus' death, his followers took refuge in the temples, like in the old days. Abydos was a safe haven, being on the edge of the desert; it offered a quick escape into the wilderness and oblivion, where only the Berbers could navigate the vast waves of sand.

The Temple of Abydos was sinking into the desert, the dust clinging to the murals and forming a veil over the statues of the gods; after the years of neglect the Temple appeared to be in mourning, the once vivid reliefs fading into the stones. The early Christians were gentle souls, Bentreshy concluded—they were decent people following a simple message, and their leader offered salvation, eternal life, just like Osiris. It was the ones who got corrupted that caused all the problems: the ones that wanted total power over God. It was like Akhenaten's reign all over again, with fanatics destroying the statues and hacking out their eyes. Bentreshy thought this one God, one religion was a bad idea—didn't they realise it led to tyranny? Under the Roman Church it wasn't safe to worship the old gods and everyone went underground. Constantine made Christianity the official religion of the Empire and the wave of terror truly began. Constantine outlawed paganism and made worship in the temples a crime against the state. People were persecuted for speaking the truth, like Galileo would be in the next millennium. Under Bishop Cyril's orders the philosopher Hypatia was stripped, beaten and burned alive. Some say she was the last voice of ancient wisdom. The flames of hell raged through Egypt, burning through the libraries and temples, turning knowledge into clouds of smoke.

People hid inside the subterranean passages; the secret chambers once reserved for sacred rites and journeys to the Underworld. They hid the secret texts in the underground chambers: the *Books of Thoth*, the *Book of the Dead*, and the *Journals of Sety I*. Even the original followers of Jesus were at risk and hid their Gnostic manuscripts in the desert, where they would lie buried until 1945.

Bentreshy couldn't bear to see the old religion destroyed and the priesthood silenced. The world had become a place of ignorance, a wilderness without meaning. It was the apocalypse mentioned in the bible—men had created their own destruction and there was no glory in it, just mindless tragedy.

For two thousand years the old wisdom would lie dormant, the temples battered by the sand and heat, with no one to understand their symbols or read their hieroglyphs. Over the centuries the children played amongst the ruins of Abydos, baffled by the cryptic images, but sensing the power in the great columns and silent statues.

∧∧∧∧∧   ∧∧∧∧∧   ∧∧∧∧∧

When Bentreshy looked down again there was a new religion on the horizon, one that came from Arabia to challenge the Christian dominance. After listening to their sermons Bentreshy thought it was quite similar—it too promoted the one God and discouraged the worship of animals. But even this new religion couldn't unravel the mysteries of ancient Egypt or control the power of Isis.

In Abydos the ghosts floated through the desert and refused to sink into oblivion. The spirits appeared at the edge of the oasis, reminding people of the old magic. The spirits invaded people's dreams and haunted the villagers with their memories. Despite the mullah's disapproval, the locals left offerings to the gods and bathed in the sacred pool to increase their fertility.

The villagers were encouraged to take stones from the Temple to build their houses and over time the roof caved into the floor, and the once sacred shrine looked battered and beaten. But despite the destruction, the Temple radiated with a golden light, still powerful even in defeat, like Osiris refusing to die.

Over the centuries Bentreshy became quite skilful at flying from one continent to another. She flew over London, spotting the Thames meandering its way towards the sea—like the Nile, she thought, with its self-importance, twisting like a cobra. It too was the longest river in the country, with a military history that made the nation powerful and prosperous. And there was Blackheath, with its lovely park and little lake, where children sailed their toy boats and fed the ducks. Children like Dorothy. Bentreshy found the house on Westcombe Hill, where she had come back to earth. She had floated over the houses, peering into the windows with the welcoming front rooms and pictures of happy farm labourers on the walls. A portrait of domestic harmony, she had thought. If only she could have a family like that, with a caring mother and father.

Yes, she remembered the day she dropped to earth, after nearly 3200 years of wandering the universe; the pretty lady lying on the divan, her pregnant belly swollen like a sand dune.

Bentreshy hadn't thought it through—she saw the foetus lying in the womb, like an empty chest she wanted to crawl inside. She felt sorry for the inert embryo cocooned in darkness, waiting for a bright spirit. I will keep her company, crawl inside her skin—we'll keep warm under the blanket of blood. Every child deserves a soul . . .

How wonderful to be a child again, she recalled, to feel her veins pump with life, the flesh encase her bones. Bentreshy was quite happy with her lot, until that fateful day. The day she fell down the stairs and sprang right back, like a ball thrown at the wall, a bouncy ball, blue and invincible. It was most peculiar, she laughed, floating

291

in the hallway with the gas lamp. She suddenly remembered her life in the heavens, shining amongst the stars; an eternal being in the heart of creation. But then she saw the lifeless figure on the floor, with no knowledge of how to reach the heavens. *I must crawl back inside, wake her up, and I will live again.*

Attached to this three-year-old body there was no question of flying through the cosmos anymore. And when she tried to leap into the sky she came crashing to the ground, her spirit trapped in a web of limbs, feet encased in clay. *How foolish I'd been, to crawl inside this deathly child a second time!*

This fall from the heavens hadn't all been in vain, she had to admit. She was an only child with loving parents, and unlike her life long ago, she had a room of her own, with floral wallpaper and kitten figurines on the mantelpiece, several picture books and a shelf full of dolls to play with. After all her travelling through the universe, it was time to put down roots, time to swap boundless freedom for a human life, with its promise of adventure, assortment of possibilities (and inescapable periods of suffering).

It couldn't have been easy for the poor girl, thought Bentreshy, having me knocking around inside her, with all my torments and longings. How confusing for the poor thing—recalling a past so unlike her own—with temples and deserts, and priestesses in gossamer robes . . . how lonely Dorothy must have felt, dreaming about these places and having no one to share it with. Here she lived in this pleasant row of houses, with her devoted parents who ensured she was well fed and clothed—she wore pretty dresses with pinafores and bloomers, and lace up boots to match her outfits.

It had taken over three thousand years to get to this place, but Bentreshy had finally returned to earth. Now a different Empire ruled the world, with colonies all over the planet—why even Egypt was under her spell! This new Empire was rich and powerful, but there were no great temples to speak of. There were impressive buildings like Westminster Cathedral and St Paul's, however, they were hardly temples. I suppose the old abbeys were like temples, but then some crazy king had destroyed them, a bit like Akhenaten by the sounds of it.

How beautiful London had been, back in 1904, with horses and carriages, and ladies in tight fitting dresses that fell to their ankles, with matching gloves and handbags; a fountain of hair shaped into a bird's nest, with neat little hats perched on their heads. But there were so many poor people—children without shoes, wearing ragged clothes—surprising how the finely dressed people didn't notice them. The ragamuffins were like the horses and carriages, the streets and barking dogs—filling in the spaces that made up the busy world.

And now what year was it? 2001, the new millennium. . . Someone had gone to find the old house where Dorothy was born, and she was disappointed to see a motorway had been built right behind the house—any closer and the house would have been torn down. The woman had felt sad, hearing the whiz of the motorway as she stood in front of the house, the rush of traffic encroaching upon this Edwardian world, the car fumes choking the air—and in this momentous place, where Bentreshy had come back to earth. Her name was Abbie Leyland and she was writing a book on women and Egyptology. She'd been to the Archives in Lewisham to trace Dorothy's past. After sifting through many reference books she'd found the name Reuben Ernest Eady in the 1904 Directory: Master Tailor, living at 171 Westcombe Hill, Blackheath. All the books and articles about Dorothy's childhood had reported that she'd grown up in Blackheath—that she'd fallen down the stairs and been given up for dead by the doctor, but when he returned with the death certificate she was very much alive, giggling and gurgling like a fountain of youth. But no one had bothered to record this in the Hall of Records. Abbie had felt disappointed—she'd come all the way from Liverpool to trace Dorothy's past and yet there were hardly any records.

If only Bentreshy could remember in detail! All these Victorian houses looked the same, built in a straight row, with slated roofs and chimney tops. But wait—there's a house built in honey coloured brick, the colour of the temple stones at sunset.

Abbie walked along the road, heading towards town; the rain was getting worse and the noise of the motorway suddenly increasing, the cars shrieking through the wet lanes. She huddled under an umbrella, staring into the small garden lined with shrubs, her eyes following the path to the door. She looked through the bay window—she saw a chandelier, pastel colours and paintings on the walls. Such a cosy room; she imagined Dorothy playing by the fire, reading her children's books on ancient Egypt.

Abbie conjured up an image of a temple in the desert, such a peaceful place, where pilgrims came to worship the dead, where people longed to be buried alongside Osiris.

Bentreshy could see it too: the canal winding its way through the fields, widening into a port filled with boats and cargo, stone steps leading to a white temple; she remembered the souvenir shop with the sketches of Abydos, the Mountain of Offerings, King Sety and the gods; the mummy-shaped figurines commemorating the Resurrection of Osiris, always popular with the foreign pilgrims.

Funny the things people remember—who would have thought it, after all these years? Bentreshy floated through the brume, the rain streaking her face, her arms stretching through the vapour. She was above the clouds now, steam rising from her wet robe, searching for the sun. She couldn't see the earth anymore, only coral mist, like an ocean on fire.

14. Return to Abydos
March, 1956

The taxi drove towards the Temple of Sety I, the driver swerving to avoid the potholes and the strands of sugarcane which had fallen off a donkey's back. Dorothy bumped her head on the roof as the driver veered round a crater the size of a tin bath. "Watch out, *ya abeet!*" It was more like driving on the surface of the moon than on a road. Such an illustrious place deserves a smooth road, she decided, creating a sense of harmony as the visitors approach the Temple.

The watchman Mohamed had been asked to meet her again. This time the lady had no trouble getting in the taxi, he was relieved to see. "You have so much luggage—you stay long time?" he enquired, surprised to see she'd also brought her cat.

"I intend to stay here permanently, so you better get used to me!" Dorothy replied, seeing the man's puzzled face. He didn't quite believe her—no Ingiliziyya had ever stayed here for more than a year. He lit a cigarette, bracing himself as the taxi hit another pothole.

Dorothy sat in silence absorbing the fertile fields, the patchwork squares flying past her in a rush of green and aubergine. She took note of the irrigation systems and the canals that snaked their way towards the desert, where all vegetation suddenly ceased to exist. With the arrival of the yearly flood in late July, this great plain used to be transformed into a black sea, and the people would huddle together on the mounds of dry earth, waiting for the waters to subside and their crops to grow again. Since the dam had been built the flood wasn't as imposing as it used to be—but it still swamped the fields in the summer, enriching the earth with its murky minerals. The villagers had built houses along the canal, which they wouldn't have done in ancient times, Dorothy noted, as the flood would have washed away their dwellings. They also built reed huts in the fields, like in Pharaonic times, as they could be taken down when the water flooded the plain; in ancient times there would be a great exodus of people taking refuge on higher ground, and they'd stare down at the sea of silt that had once been their home, praising Osiris for his gift of life, for without this flood they would never survive the coming year.

295

The road they were driving along led straight to the Temple which once joined the Great Harbour, where the royal boats were laden with goods from the empire: wood from Lebanon, frankincense from Punt and granite from Aswan; the passenger boats carrying pilgrims from far-away lands, all travelling to Abydos, sacred city of Osiris, god of rebirth and resurrection. It was on the banks of this very canal that Isis and Nephthys had searched for the remains of Osiris, running through the shallow waters in despair, smearing their faces and breasts in dark mud.

How do I know all this? Dorothy wondered. Had she read it in a book or was it an ancient memory? She wasn't sure. It felt more like the workings of memory, she concluded, the way dormant emotions ascended from the base of her being and filled her eyes with tears. It was like remembering a childhood holiday to the seaside, recalling a time of intense happiness; experiencing real joy for the first time. She was recalling this inchoate state of being, when feelings were imprinted on the mind, indelibly carved into the fabric of the brain. The oxen in the field, the fan shaped leaves of the date palms swaying in the breeze, the intense green filtering through blue sky. The images flared up from the dark crevices of memory, where embryonic embers lay, unleashing flares of emotions. A woman walked along the road with her two children, her head laden with a basket of shrubbery, Dorothy closed her eyes as the image sifted through her mind and she was back in former times, seeing this mother by the canal, collecting dry stalks for the evening fire.

Mohamed raised his voice, "Madame, we are here at Rest House. Do you wish to get out?" The watchman looked at her with beseeching eyes, as she'd been sitting there for some time without responding to his pleas. But Dorothy was so overcome by her journey that speech failed her, and a great lump welled in her throat, as though full of stones.

Dr Nour Gahlin was waiting to greet her—he was the Chief Inspector for Upper Egypt, and she gathered he was in charge of restoring the Temple of Sety I. She wondered what had happened to the inspector she'd met on her last visit. "I was hoping to see Dr Wabid and his colleague Walid—are they at the Temple?" she enquired.

"They went back to Cairo two years ago—no one stays here very long. I hope you will stay awhile—long enough to help us with the hieroglyphs, Madame. You come highly recommended by Dr Fakhry—and the great work you did with Dr Hassan is well-known by the Antiquities Department."

Dorothy observed Dr Gahlin with a lenient smile, trying to sum him up—he seemed a nice enough fellow, with an angular, solid sort of face, one that loosened slightly when he smiled. But she detected something limited in his gaze, the way his eyes narrowed into a fixed stare.

Dr Gahlin felt a little embarrassed giving this woman such esteemed praise, usually reserved for a man. And she looked like she'd be happier roaming round the markets in search of trinkets rather than deciphering hieroglyphics (he noticed she was wearing an odd assortment of beads and amulets that clashed with her pale blue twin set). How much easier to deal with men, he thought. He was accustomed to the masculine temperament, their code of honour and outlook on the world. Was he meant to treat Dorothy in the same way? He couldn't treat her like the other women he knew, who spent most of their time looking after the children and showed little interest in the affairs of men.

Dorothy sensed the man's confusion and slapped him playfully on the back, "We'll make a great team, old chap—as long as we can stop for a beer after sunset!"

A reel of laughter echoed from the Rest House and a dark head popped through the window. "We usually go to Farid's after work. He makes a tasty babaghanoush and tagen, and the beer's not bad, when the fridge is working."

Dr Gahlin gave a nervous laugh. Madame Meguid was obviously used to working with men and spoke their language. She was an English lady after all, and different standards applied to her. But even for an English lady her behaviour was rather unusual.

"This is my assistant, Husni Kamil. A recent graduate from Cairo University who specialises in temple restoration. We've just discovered a small palace beside the Temple, but it's all in fragments at the moment. And that's where you come in—we need someone to collate, decipher and assemble all the pieces."

Dorothy could tell Dr Gahlin was more at ease talking about excavation work, the way his jaw relaxed into his face as he spoke about friezes and fragments of stone. She was anxious to see the remains of this palace they had recently discovered (and to explore the hidden realms of the Temple once the staff had gone to bed).

"My greatest desire is to see the Sety Temple rebuilt, restored to its former glory and that's why I sacrificed a well-paying job in Cairo to come here. I must be mad!"

"I often think that way about myself. Is it not crazy to dig up old artefacts and spend your life piecing them together? This obsession with the past is madness, but once it has seized you in its grip there is no letting go. Look at Mariette and Petrie—they spent many years excavating in Abydos—and rumour has it Petrie spent his honeymoon inside a tomb. He must have had a very understanding wife—they say she was driven by the same passion."

"Yes, British women have often been drawn to Egypt—look at Margaret Murray. She made many great discoveries, including the Osirion." Dorothy was happy to be talking about the great Egyptologists who'd first excavated this Temple, but she noticed Dr Gahlin had gone quiet when Murray's name had been mentioned.

"She was a remarkable lady who had extraordinary talents, some called them unnatural powers. They said she was a witch."

Despite these rumours Margaret had been accepted by the locals, as she knew about magic and ancient forms of healing. So why did they call her a witch? No doubt because Miss Murray was an intelligent (unmarried) woman with significant abilities and this frightened some people, unaccustomed to seeing women with power. Dorothy would take this as a warning that some of the officials might see her in the same light. There was that embarrassing incident on her first visit— when they quizzed her about the Temple layout, and it transpired she knew the Temple better than they did. I'm sure they've forgotten about that, she reassured herself. However, no one offered to take her round the Temple… Instead they started with the excavation site on the southeast side, which was in a terrible mess, and Dorothy almost wept when she saw the remains scattered in the dust.

Dr Gahlin led her round the dig, "We had to knock down several houses which had been built over the palace. The people weren't very happy about it, but they were well compensated. The houses should never have been built there—the Temple has been badly abused over the last few centuries and that's why we are here—to see the Temple is restored. We are grateful you will help us with this task, Madame

Meguid, although I must warn you, the work is monumental and we are only at the beginning."

Dorothy kicked the dust with her feet, revealing a new layer of fragments. The task was endless, she realised, staring at the dejected looking Temple, her heart aching with sadness. "There is a hell of a lot of work to be done, the place is in a pitiful state—but I will devote the rest of my life to its completion and I will not rest until the task is finished." She wanted to tell Dr Gahlin about her pledge to King Sety and how it was her destiny to return to the Temple and see that justice was done. But she had said enough already—I don't want him to think I'm also a witch, driven by supernatural powers—I've only just arrived.

They walked around the Temple ruins and Dorothy made a note of the work that needed doing: they needed to get the roof restored to the southern section of the Temple, build up the walls around the Archives, Butcher's Hall and Slaughter Chamber, and fix the stairway in the Hall of the Sacred Barques—and block up the holes to stop the bats from flying in, "their faeces deface the precious murals with dirty black streaks, as bad as the Christian vandals!" she complained to Dr Gahlin, who was startled by her comparison.

"I will write to Dr Fakhry with my recommendations," she continued, "he'll understand how important it is to get the roof on— we had the same problem with the monuments at Giza."

Although Dorothy was given a room at the Rest House, she preferred to spend her nights roaming the desert and sleeping in the ancient tombs—Aha, Narmer, Qa'a and Djet—there were so many pharaohs to chose from. The illustrious graves stretched back to pre-dynastic times—even the Scorpion King had been buried here back in 3150 BC. They found the oldest bottle of wine in his tomb, along with mint, sage, coriander and rosemary, to season his roast dinner in the Afterlife.

The nights belonged to the ancient world and Dorothy let her bare feet guide her through the coarse sand, getting reacquainted with the tombs, temples and desert animals. She loved the pre-dynastic temple of Khenti-Amenti, the jackal-headed god once worshipped in this region.

She followed the processional route, remembering herself as a young girl, wearing a white robe and carrying a jar of incense. She passed Shunet el Zebib, the funerary temple of Khasekhemwy, the remarkable pharaoh of the 2nd Dynasty; she imagined the ceremonial boats being carried through the desert to Pega-the-Gap, transporting the deceased to the Afterlife. The Feast of Osiris was drawing to a close and soon the pilgrims would return home.

Dorothy stopped at Omm al Qa'ab, 'Mother of Pots', feeling the sharp fragments beneath her feet. Since the dawn of time people had buried their dead here and had left their offerings, the piles of broken pots once filled with herbs, wine, incense and sweetbread.

I am here at last! she shouted to the crescent moon, her sense of joy beaming in the star-speckled sky. She heard a pack of wolves howling in unison, as if responding to her outburst of joy. The staff had told her there weren't any wolves left in the desert, but she decided to follow the sounds of howling, trekking through Pega-the-Gap to the top of the hill, where the canine cries grew louder. Sure enough, Dorothy came face to face with three wolves, who stared at her with a noble curiosity, their silver fur shining in the falcate moon. The wolves stood in silence for a moment, motionless against the indigo sky and they studied her for a while, surprised by her fearless composure; surprised to see any human out here at night, as after dark the villagers rarely ventured beyond their mud huts. But she was not alone: a figure was coming towards her, ascending from the abyss like the sunrise, filling her heart with desire. The blue cape was familiar to her, like the cerulean sky that sheltered the great beyond, and she buried her face in the soft folds, her body trembling. "Nisou," she whispered.

King Sety opened his cape and Dorothy staggered several feet backwards, as if suffering from a blow.

"What is it, my love?" King Sety fell to his knees to comfort her, wrapping his arms around her shoulders. Turning her head towards the sky, the stars formed endless neurons in her mind, and she tried to connect them into a pattern, aligning the dots into words and ideas. She felt herself transform, moulded out of loose fragments into something more substantial; she experienced a curious sense of fullness and for a moment she feared her body might explode, like a star catapulting through the sky. Dorothy nestled into Sety's breast and exhaled into a feeling of comfort, knowing this man was the source of her wholeness, her real being.

300

Sety had always known his true happiness rested within this woman—he had followed her for thousands of years, back to this spot in the desert, where time had begun.

"Let's go for a stroll," she suggested, taking his hand and leading him through the desert hills. The intensity of their feelings manifested in their sudden movements, their hearts leaping to keep up with their steps, fearing they'd be left behind in a gulf of sand.

The mist began to rise with the inception of dawn, stalking like a wildcat. The lovers embraced one another, sinking to the ground in a cloud of ardour, where they hid from the first flicker of light.

The couple peered out from their golden hollow, the sun bleaching the darkness and making them suddenly visible. There were a few lanterns on in the village and Dorothy sensed the material world awakening; the cattle straining in their pens, the date palms pointing their jagged leaves through the sky, and the Temple shining through the nebula—and she remembered why she'd come to Abydos ... she had a job to do, a physical life to lead, just like the villagers.

"I must return to the Rest House. It's my first day at work." The idea seemed alien to her, basking in this ethereal enchantment—this going to work and living a life day by day, and she saw the odd villager trudging through the fields with his stone age implements slumped over his shoulder, the rows of green crops emerging in the pale light, an ox rotating the water wheel and two grey donkeys slouching under their packs; this sudden burst of activity rising out of the silence gave her a severe jolt, reminding her of the great task ahead and the physical exertion required for the job.

King Sety could see the change in his love, and he watched her fading away from him like the morning mist, and he cried out, "Meet me in the Temple tomorrow night, my love," hoping his words wouldn't shrivel in the daylight, or get lost in the ethereal gap, as he knew it was hard to traverse the astral/terrestrial divide, where many messages went astray.

Dorothy was running back to the Rest House, her body feeling heavy, leaving deep footprints in the sand. She felt the full weight of her responsibility and remembered this was an unfortunate part of being human: this rushing from one place to another, encumbered by duties and responsibilities, with endless tasks to complete—no wonder people had little time for the metaphysical realm.

She looked towards the Temple and felt a surge of energy in the pit of her stomach and she was glad to be part of the material world, where she could make a contribution, where her dreams could be realised.

Dorothy tiptoed into her room, but soon realised the staff were still asleep, the Rest House swathed in silence, unaffected by the first call to prayer or the splendour of dawn. She lay down on the firm bed and wrapped the mosquito netting around her, recalling the screen of mist in the desert that circled her like a cat's paw.

Dorothy awoke two hours later to the sound of loud voices in the hallway, "Is Madame Meguid still sleeping? You must wake the English lady."

Dorothy opened her door to find a startled young man grinning with embarrassment, "My name is Hassan. Sorry, Ya Sitt Meguid, but they tell me to wake you from sleep." He looked at her dishevelled clothes covered in dust and then he self-consciously looked at the floor: for some unknown reason the lady hadn't slept in her room, and he was ashamed of what he was thinking. He felt the English lady staring at him, as if reading his mind, and she began to laugh. "I spent the whole night roaming the desert and met an attractive couple of wolves. This place is full of surprises. I don't suppose there's any hot water left for a shower?"

Hassan looked aghast, "You say wolves? They very dangerous animals. You not go in the desert at night—full of bad things: strange things happen, bad things live there, many *afreet*. *Na Ooso Billah*!— May God protect us."

Dorothy laughed at the young man, his expression of excessive fear was quite comical, like an actor in a pantomime playing up the melodrama.

"The wolves are perfectly friendly. If you wish, you can come out with me one night—I'll show you the hilltop where they like to congregate, probably looking for prey."

Hassan's face twisted into terror at the very notion. "No thank you, Madame Meguid. I not wish to be wolf dinner. I have wife and children, I have mouths to feed."

Hassan started to tidy the room, trying to sublimate his fear of wolves and *afreets* into his work, and thinking of the mouths he had to feed.

"After shower, you have breakfast on the terrace," he informed her, leaning on his broom and lighting a cigarette, "I clean your room."

She found the bathroom decorated in blue and white tiles and was surprised to find a shower with hot water, thanks to a noisy generator. Dorothy watched the dust run off her body, forming a red spiral beneath her feet. She became aware of the physical sensations of washing: the water flowing over her like strips of silk, running her hands over her arms and legs in sweeping movements, circling her abdomen and buttocks with her palms, feeling her pores rise under the stream of water. The experience hinted at something deeper; a cleansing ritual before prayer, and she felt the primeval quality of this act, performed countless times in preparation for a day of devotion. Emerging from the shower she felt grounded in the present, her feet planted on the blue tiles, aware of her corporeal existence: as Madame Meguid who worked for the Antiquities Department, the English lady who had come to help rebuild the Temple.

She found Dr Gahlin and Husni sitting on the terrace smoking cigarettes and drinking coffee, and they promptly stood up as she approached them, nearly turning the table over.

"Good morning, Ya Sitt, I trust you slept well. The desert can make some strange noises at night—the wind comes down from the mountains and sweeps across the plain causing a humming sound—but the locals swear it's the ghosts singing."

Dr Gahlin held out the chair and Dorothy sat down. "Even if it were the ghosts singing, it wouldn't bother me in the least. I've met several *afreets* since I came to Egypt."

The men laughed, "I see you are a brave woman and won't be put off by *afreets*, or the desert for that matter."

"One can hardly be afraid of ghosts in the field of archaeology, for it is our business to deal with them on a daily basis, in our attempt to resuscitate the past. In order to understand their world, we must walk in their footsteps."

Dorothy tucked into her plate of scrambled eggs, fuul and taamiya. She'd never seen such yellow eggs—there must be something in the grain, like the rich bones of the pharaohs. She choked on her tea trying not to laugh: to think the chickens were eating the dust of deceased pharaohs. She placed her handkerchief over her nose and pretended to sneeze, exhaling a trail of suppressed laughter.

"Are you all right, Madame?" Husni poured Dorothy a glass of water and passed it across the table to her.

"I'm fine—just a little dust," and she started to laugh again, feeling quite giddy in the morning sun, sitting on this delightful terrace with such attentive male colleagues.

Dorothy scanned the morning paper, with news about the Suez Crisis. "The bloody British should let Egypt run her own affairs. We don't need to be governed by anybody—we've been an empire for thousands of years."

Dr Gahlin shifted awkwardly in his seat, not quite certain what she meant. "When you say 'we' are you speaking as an Egyptian?"

"Of course. Egypt deserves full independence from foreign rule—and that includes running the Suez Canal and the Aswan dam. Those opposed to the liberation of Egypt should be asked to leave—all those colonials who don't speak a word of Arabic and have never eaten fuul for breakfast. They should round them up and send them home."

"But what about you, Madame: what if they tried to send you home?" Husni interrupted her.

"Fortunately I am an Egyptian citizen: they'll have to kill me if they want to get rid of me, but then I'd be buried right here in the desert, which is my dying wish," she explained, dipping a piece of bread into her fuul, "It's all written down in my last will and testament."

Dr Gahlin nervously cleared his throat and folded the newspaper away; all this talk about death and politics was making him uneasy. There was strong anti-British sentiment in the media and it was spreading throughout the country—he hoped Dorothy wouldn't bear the brunt of it, as it would make everyone's position here more difficult. The villagers were a superstitious lot and he was sure they could be incited to violence, if they believed someone was to blame for their ill-fortune. There were a few people in the village who hated the Temple because it showed images of pagan worship, and it attracted Western tourists who exposed far too much flesh. He looked at Dorothy's bare arms and low cut dress: he would have to talk to her about a dress code—otherwise she'd be the scandal of the village.

Dr Gahlin shuddered at the thought of any more complaints about the Temple, and he cleared his throat again, as if to eradicate the unpleasant thought. "It's time I showed you where you'll be working—I'm afraid there's a mountain of work to do here, I can assure you. You'll never run out of things to do."

"*Yalla beena*. I am anxious to get started." Dorothy picked up her canvas bag, which contained a bottle of water, a couple of oranges, a trowel, a torch, her sketchpad and pencils—and her lipstick, face cream and mirror. Everything a lady archaeologist needed for a day at work.

They walked to the back of the Temple, past the Osirion, where Dorothy longed to bathe her feet, and round to the front courtyard. She gazed in horror at the broken friezes, walls, pillars and statues lying about the ground like the aftermath of an explosion. When visiting the Temple in her dreams, the place was in its perfect form, and there was a lush garden to the left, with beautiful fountains, flowering trees and multicoloured birds perched on the branches. After such vivid dreams it was heartbreaking to see the Temple in such a ruinous state, and for a moment she stood there crying, wiping away the tears and mourning the passing of the Temple's grandeur.

"It's shameful really—what's become of this great Temple," Dr Gahlin lamented. "I'm afraid there's little money given to this place. Most of the money is spent on renovating the temples along the Nile. People can go on a Nile cruise and see Dendera, Luxor, Karnak and Edfu, but Abydos is ten kilometres from the Nile—it's not really on the tourist map. When it comes to funding, it's not a priority." Dr Gahlin picked up a piece of rubble and handed it to Dorothy. "A piece of King Sety's ear—bits of his statues are scattered all over the place."

Dorothy rolled the piece of ear around in her hand, the polished granite cooling her palm. She would collect his remains and put him back together, just as Isis had done. Dorothy closed her eyes and the fragments of stone reassembled themselves in her head, and out of the wreckage she began to see patterns and diagrams, until an entire construction of walls and pillars emerged, neatly fitting into place, decorated in beautiful colours and tipped in gold.

When Dorothy opened her eyes Dr Gahlin was studying her with a look of concern. "Are you all right, Madame Meguid? You've gone rather pale."

Dorothy stuffed the piece of ear into her skirt pocket and smoothed the folds of fabric. "I was just remembering something… it's probably just the heat—but no need to worry, I'm fine."

What had happened when she'd closed her eyes? Powerful emotions had filtered through her mind, muddled with memory:

through recollection she was able to reconstruct a whole picture, superimposed onto the rubble—an image so compelling that she swore it was real. But it wasn't real, for when she opened her eyes she saw the fragments strewn around her, the statues ground to dust, and Dr Gahlin's solemn expression, as if he doubted her mental stability.

"Let's visit the rest of the Temple—I'd like to see my office—I believe I'm starting on the south side—where you recently discovered the palace." She craved the muted light of the Temple with its pensive pillars, silently overpowering the mind, gently consuming the outside world.

For all its grandeur the First Hypostyle was an intimate space, she felt, an interior world that encouraged emotion and memory, opening the door to our hidden selves. People came through the entranceway as an initiate, and as they proceeded through the Temple they slowly left their physical beings behind, walking round the columns in a dream state, letting their subconscious lead them through the labyrinth of chambers. It was like being in a state of deep meditation, and people were surprised when they emerged three or fours hours later, having lost all sense of time and place.

Dorothy stood outside the chamber of Sacred Barques, spotting the Ear of the God carved into the jamb of the doorway, and she thought of the initiates who once prayed here, asking Osiris to guide their path. She said a quick prayer while Dr Gahlin chatted to the workmen in the corridor, the divine ear of Osiris listening to every word uttered in the hallway—chitchat and prayers competing for attention. Dorothy stepped inside the chamber, her eyes sweeping over the bas-reliefs of feasts and festivals, the divine boats waiting to take the deceased to Amenti. She walked round the two rows of columns, rising like giant oak trees to the sky. A stone bench ran along the walls once used to store the ceremonial boats, just right for collating artefacts, she decided. These sacred boats were once a spectacular sight, glittering in silver and gold, the streams of light highlighting their beauty. It was hard to believe this magnificent chamber would be her office, where she would translate and catalogue the fragments of friezes, pillars, statues and stelae.

At Dorothy's request, the department brought her a desk and chair for writing up her notes. Then the workers began filling the chamber with buckets of rubble inscribed with hieroglyphs, waiting to be interpreted and fitted back together. The workers were baffled by the amount of 'rubbish' they had to carry inside, filling the place with dust and dirt, which they then had to sweep up. Hassan was on hand to mop up the mess, having finished cleaning the rooms at the Rest House. He was horrified by the trail of filth the workers left behind and couldn't understand what Madame Meguid wanted with a pile of broken stones. "They dirty men, Madame, they never wipe their feet—why they not bring you real treasure—a gold cat, a turquoise scarab—not all this garbage."

The workers made a steady procession from the granaries, passed the Storage Room, Archives and Slaughter Room, the sand spilling from their buckets, stones bouncing along the corridor. Hassan leaned on his broom and gave a deep sigh, muttering some expletives under his breath. "Dirty men, making rubbish—*Nousarani kelb*—sons of dogs," the broom muffling his words.

When the workers had gone on their tea break, Dorothy showed Hassan the frieze she was putting together. "You see this piece here—it used to hang over the door to one of the granaries. These hieroglyphs say, *Here lies the sacred grain of Kemet in the reign of Sety I. Lord Osiris, god of vegetation, bless this barley with your green powers, and we will leave bread and beer in your sacred chamber.* It took me ages to put the fragments together and now I've finally deciphered it—you're the first person I've shown this to." She felt a sense of triumph, seeing the remnants return to their original creation. The young man was visibly moved, his expression changing from weariness to curiosity, the lacklustre of his demeanour replaced with a spark of wonder. He traced the symbols with his finger, his illiterate mind struggling to understand, "This say all that—about Osiris, bread and beer?"

Dorothy nodded, "This is the cartouche of Osiris, you can find it all over the Temple." She had brought this frieze back to life, and in a strange way this man had also suddenly come to life, as if awakened from the dead. "I come back tomorrow to clean Temple—you can show me more hieroglyphs!"

There goes my first disciple, she mused, hoping there would be many more. She wanted the locals to love their Temple again— over the millennia they'd lost the connection, the language of their ancestors buried in obscurity . . .

It soon got round that there was an English lady working in the Temple and a group of children were the first to investigate, impelled by their natural curiosity; they'd heard the rumours circulating in the village, fuelled by a collective fear of foreigners and a penchant for superstitions.

Dorothy was outside surveying the ruined palace, pondering over a rather obscure hieroglyph when she spotted some children hiding behind a crumbling wall. "I do believe this place is full of *afreets*," she shouted in Arabic, "Do the *afreets* have names?"

Three small heads popped over the wall, and the children slowly revealed themselves in a circle of giggles. The young lad bravely stepped forward, wearing a grey gallabiya covered in red dirt. "My name is Amr, and these are my sisters, Yameena and Sana."

"Do you often play in the Temple grounds?" Dorothy asked the children, and when she saw their sheepish faces, she reckoned they'd explored every inch of the place, without the watchmen knowing the wiser. "But don't tell our parents. We help our uncle in the field—but he fall asleep and we run off and play. He never think look in the Temple."

"Your secret is safe with me," she winked at Amr. "I have a son a bit like you—he used to love old temples, but now he's all grown up and he prefers to live in Kuwait."

"What his name?" Amr wanted to know, and when Dorothy told him he was called Sety, he laughed, "like the pharaoh. How funny he name after a pharaoh!"

But when Dorothy pointed out that many boys were named after the prophet, and that was no different, he went quiet for a moment.

"My name is Madame Bulbul Meguid—but you can call me Dorothy, if you like."

The sisters looked horrified. "We not call ladies by first name— is bad luck. We call them by first child name. So we must call you Mother of Sety: Omm Sety."

A couple of the locals in Giza had called her Omm Sety, but most people had called her Sitt Meguid. Dorothy rolled the name around in her head: Omm Sety. She liked the sound of her new name. She'd only been here a few days and already she'd been given a new identity. From now on she'd be known in the village as Omm Sety (and over the years she'd forget about Dorothy altogether, the name she'd used for fifty-two years ...)

308

The children said there was a market today and that they had to go shopping for their mother. "You leave your work—you come with us, we show you where to buy good biscuits, cakes—and Halwa too."

The idea was very appealing, but she had to decline the offer. "I have a mountain of work to do, but I promise to meet you after sunset prayers, and you can show me round the village, if you like. I could do with a guided tour."

Yameena fixed her gaze on Omm Sety, who felt the girl's eyes searching inside her, like great orbs illuminating a cave. She had a confident demeanour for a ten-year-old, exuding a natural elegance and she had perfect features like an alabaster carving; her silky hair and deep beauty seemed out of place in this forgotten world, hidden behind her gallabiya and country-girl status. But why didn't such a bright girl go to school? she wondered.

"Most girls here they not go to school," Yameena told her, as they helped their mothers with the chores and the farm work. "I learn everything from my mother—how to cook, sew, make baskets and build oven—I make lots of things, and I cook breakfast, heat water and wash dishes," she said proudly.

"And I do shopping and work in the field," Sana added, peering over the wall. "I want to go school, but momma say very expensive for books, only Amr go to school—he a boy."

Amr grinned with a sense of importance, "I learn how to count numbers and write in Arabic and English," but he seemed more interested in herding a beetle with a stick, sliding its shiny shell down a lump of sand. Dorothy gathered he didn't go to school very often— the nearest school was in Al Balyana, and that meant an eight mile trek by foot or donkey.

The children ran off to the market and Dorothy watched them leap over the Temple fragments, once the great walls surrounding the impressive courtyard. Were they aware that these scattered remains belonged to the magnificent statue of Osiris, the god reaching for eternity?

The girls should go to school, it's not right the boys go and not the girls, she thought, feeling incensed. And then she remembered her own education, how she used to play truant, avoid school like the plague. Dorothy was hardly in the position to lecture kids about going to school when she'd rarely been herself...But at least I went to the British Museum, she argued, and I learned some useful skills, thanks to Dr Budge. She thought about what Sana had said, how much she wanted to go to school. What with Nasser's social reforms, things should have improved for girls—but these social changes obviously hadn't come to Abydos. The place of goddess worship, where the Daughters of Isis once lived—and now the girls didn't even go to school! Centuries of foreign oppression had stripped them of their dignity, made them ignorant. The last century had been the worst, with the Ottomans and then the colonials . . .

Perhaps I could have a word with the girl's mother—I could pay for Sana to go to school. But really they need a school in the village—then more girls would go to school. I will write to the officials in Sohag . . .

When Dorothy finished work she wandered round the dig where the archaeologists were excavating the old palace. It didn't seem sensible to have a palace in this place—right next to the workshops and granaries, but Dr Gahlin was adamant he had found the palace. She watched them for a moment, the way they divided the space into a gridline, systematically clearing the rubble and exposing the foundations. She observed there was no sense of ritual or worship, and yet they were dealing with the most mystical setting in Egypt. She was disappointed that no one left offerings or performed libations anymore, but then reminded herself, "This is the twentieth century. People don't do things like that any more—especially not archaeologists," she laughed at herself, imagining Dr Gahlin walking barefoot through the Temple, leaving wine and cakes at the foot of Osiris. The man liked to dress in a formal manner, with shiny leather shoes and tailored trousers, always neatly pressed.

Dorothy wondered what the staff would make of her worshipping in the Temple, her devotion to the ancient rituals. She promised the Pharaoh she would revive the old customs and make daily offerings to the gods. It seemed an absurd request in this day and age, with the archaeologists looking over her shoulder, peering through their scientific lens, and the muezzin calling the villagers to the mosque, reminding them *there is no other God but Allah.*

She was Omm Sety now, with a new identity, sifting through the broken pottery and lumps of bone; the last remnants of human existence, after the body had left its temple. The lucky ones had been mummified, their shrunken bodies refusing to turn to dust; their tombs containing amulets, beads and spells designed to help them reach the Afterlife.

The scientists catalogued the artefacts and stored them in neat wooden cases. "They don't think magic has anything to do with their lives, their work. They think they are immune to ritual and worship, impervious to the old gods. But the spirits are everywhere, they cannot escape them," she spoke out loud, startling herself by the volume of her voice. But there was no one around, just the sound of a bird fluttering in the Temple.

She thought about what Husni had told her at breakfast: how a young archaeologist from Cairo had been haunted by a woman in a gold dress, and how she had followed him home from the café one night. He was so terrified he developed a fever which raged for several days, until he couldn't stand it any longer and he hurled himself into the Osirion. The next day he made a full recovery, to everyone's amazement.

"The spirits like to challenge the world of reason," Omm Sety believed, "especially if they're being ignored by a pragmatist—you see how the sacred waters cured him, they work wonders." She drank a glass of Osirion water whenever she felt weary.

Husni was surprised by her reply, as it was unusual for scholars to speak of the antiquities in this esoteric manner. The scholars talked about restoration, building techniques, water measurements—the problem of lifting the stones back on the roof without destroying the carvings.

Omm Sety liked to think of herself as a bridge between modern science and the old religion, connecting the opposing forces. "They haven't always been in opposition," she reminded Husni, "in ancient times they were revered as one entity: science and religion made these temples possible, they are the perfect balance of astronomy, geometry, and the cosmic devotion to the gods."

Husni didn't know what to make of all this talk about cosmic balance and spirits, but he had to admit he was learning a lot from this Ingiliziyya, like how to estimate the size of columns by reading the hieroglyphs, and to question his professors back in Cairo...

As for her new name, well, the officials still called her Madaam Meguid (even though everyone in the village called her Omm Sety).

Omm Sety knelt down in the sand and used her brush to sweep away the debris. She was deciphering a stele, and as she brushed away the dust the words became clear, *"Kemet is made richer by thou presence, O King of Upper and Lower Egypt, thou have come to earth to protect and guide thou people, and like Ra who travels in the sacred sky, we celebrate thy strength, Men-Maat-Ra, the son of Ra, who gives joy to all."*

She was sweeping away the millennia and laying it bare, down to the bare bones of humanity; exposing our intestines, our nerve centres. She must tread gently, be careful not to break anything. That was the trait of a good archaeologist: that you never destroyed anything and never left a footprint behind. She respected the ancient structures and admired the people who had built them. For Omm Sety it was a kind of veneration.

Later that evening the children came to show her round the village. They proceeded in a small cloud of dust, kicking up the sand as they ran ahead of her, pointing out landmarks, "This my uncle house, and this Mohamed house—his son Osama my friend—his brother dead." Amr ran inside the courtyard looking for his friend, shouting, "Osama, I have new marbles, now I will beat you!"

The houses were very similar, all made of mud bricks, with flat roofs and reed canopies to shelter them from the sun. Some were painted white, yellow or green, with geometric patterns painted round the doors and windows. They walked through the south side of the village, where most of the villagers seemed to live, where they had built the mosque and held the weekly market.

"That Omm Beshma house—she always talk, not good talk." Sana made a chattering gesture with her hand, like a goose squawking. Omm Sety laughed, "I see—she's the village gossip," one to keep an eye on. Omm Beshma appeared in the doorway, "So you're the English lady come to live here," she spoke in a rush of Arabic and loud enough for all to hear.

"Yes, I work for the Antiquities Department," Omm Sety tried to sound important, assuming an official tone. Omm Beshma seemed impressed, pulling a funny face that could be an expression of awe (or disbelief, as she'd already decided the English lady was a prostitute).

Omm Sety followed Sana down a narrow street where the women sat on stools under their canopies, tending the fire and preparing the evening meal. When the younger women saw the foreigner coming they scurried into their houses, as if they'd seen a bad omen. She knew this was a very traditional village and that women of child-bearing age kept themselves covered from head to toe, frightened that some evil force would take possession of their womb. But the older women waved to her in a friendly manner, their bright scarves circling their smiling faces, their chins and lower lips covered in tattoos. The older women didn't seem to worry about such things—as if age had liberated them from demons and social obligations. They didn't cover their faces or run inside the house, and strolled around the village with their grandchildren, laughing and chatting like young girls. This is very odd, Omm Sety thought, the way young women were kept out of the way, whereas older women were venerated and respected. It was a reversal of the Western notion: where youth is admired and old age is scorned.

Where did she fit into this diagram? She hadn't yet slipped into old age: she dyed her hair blonde and used makeup to accentuate her features. Her large bosom and wide hips gave her a voluptuous quality—with such attributes she was still desirable and didn't qualify for the esteem reserved for elderly women—but nor was she in the first flush of youth . . .

Omm Sety looked down at her cloudy feet, her white sandals stained a dusty red. Her feet knew where to go and she followed them through the labyrinth of streets, the flock of children mounting behind her like a friendly hoard of locusts. What a sensation I'm causing, she thought, I'm only going for an evening stroll. She hadn't expected such a reception and felt like a prodigal daughter returning home. Perhaps she was imagining it, but some people seemed to recognise her, the way they looked at her in a curious manner, as if they'd seen her before but they couldn't remember where.

The dust, the smells, the joyful sound of children: it was all so familiar; as if visiting a childhood haunt one had forgotten about. The memory of the place had been buried under layers of neglect, obliterated by the foundations of a new life. And now she had come back to this original place, where her first memory of the world began, born out of the red earth and set free in the desert, to roam with the jackals.

The children stopped in front of a little house the colour of ancient papyrus, the ochre walls illuminated by the dying sunlight.

313

"This our house, our mother she inside." The two girls disappeared under the canopy and emerged a moment later with a young woman dressed in a blue housecoat, with a red and white scarf draped round her head. She had great luminous eyes like her daughters, her pretty face emerging from the fabric and radiating with warmth. Her name was Aisha, but everyone called her Omm Yameena, and she approached the foreign lady with a warm smile, without the usual caution the other mothers demonstrated. "The children tell me you've come to live here and that you work at the Temple. I hope you will stay and eat with us, I've cooked a vegetable stew and there is rice and babaghanoush. My husband is away in Sohag visiting family, it's nice to have some company." The lady only spoke Arabic, and Omm Sety struggled to understand her strong dialect.

"Thank you for inviting me. I would love to eat with you—I haven't eaten since this morning," she replied in her broken Arabic. By now Omm Sety could say almost anything, and people seemed to understand her, despite her grammatical errors. They were always impressed when a Westerner bothered to learn their language, especially when their speech was peppered with local slang.

The women sat round the fire while Yameena and Sana served the supper, skilfully pouring the stew into clay bowls. The young mother told Omm Sety she was twenty-two and that she'd already had three children. "My husband Abdel has a stall in the market, he's a good man, always looking after the family."

It turned out he had another wife and three grownup children living next door. Omm Sety reminded herself this was the custom in the country: if an older man had enough money he often took a second wife and started another family. "His first wife is called Omm Alaa. She's a good woman, and over the years we've become friends—it was hard at first, but now we help each other, especially when Abdel is away."

The notion of polygamy didn't appeal to Omm Sety, but this is the tradition around here, she reminded herself, and if I want to integrate into the village I will have to accept these cultural differences.

Omm Sety inhaled the fumes of the fire, the sweet smoke tickling her nostrils. The aroma of the stew, grilled aubergines and garlic made her senses reel, and her stomach lurched with an unexpected hunger. The smells embraced her nostrils and she felt a delicious sense of pleasure, the anticipation of earthly delights. The aromas unleashed

314

a flood of images, hinting at the invisible: of tempting feasts, immense pleasure that bordered on the ecstatic. At such feasts the body indulged with a heavenly pleasure; such a feast was a reflection of divine paradise. *To know intense pleasure is to know God*. The spirit-body as one entity—how she missed this sacred connection! When had this sacred bond been broken? She thought about the Bible and the fear that followed in its wake, spreading through the ancient pages like a disease of the flesh. This biblical fear of the physical was like snake venom poisoning the body. It was like syphilis infecting future generations.

They ate their supper in the glow of the fire, the children making belching sounds and collapsing into a heap of giggles. Omm Yameena stretched out on the cushions and caressed her full belly. Omm Sety was glad to see there was no sign of bodily denial in this intimate world of women and children, and she loved the way everyone touched and kissed one another in a spiral of affection. She knew it would be different if men were present, and that Omm Yameena would adopt her wifely persona, withdrawing into domestic modesty, stepping behind her modest veil.

Omm Sety stayed till midnight and then she walked over the sands to the Rest House, the moon swelling in the sky. When she got back to the Rest House, Husni was sitting on the terrace with a worried expression. "Madame Meguid. I've been looking for you—I didn't see you leave the dig." They were meant to go to Farid's for a beer and a meal . . . But when he heard she'd been at Omm Yameena's for supper Husni was so relieved, although he wondered why she'd been there till midnight. He imagined her sitting on a reed mat on the floor, eating peasant food with her fingers. What could she possibly have to say to them for a whole evening? The Antiquities staff didn't socialise much with the villagers, apart from employing them as guards and diggers. But she wasn't to know—this was all new to her and she was trying to find her feet. Satisfied that Madame Meguid was all right, he went off to bed, his footsteps dragging with fatigue.

Omm Sety waited until the Rest House was silent and then sneaked out the window and into the desert. She wandered into the Temple and lit some incense in the Chapel of Isis, then left a glass of beer and a little cake, to thank the goddess for her new friends who'd welcomed her into the village. Without Omm Yameena and the children she would feel quite alone, as some of the villagers were

315

hardly welcoming, the way they eyed her suspiciously and passed her in silence. She thought of Omm Beshma with her little circle of gossipmongers. Then she heard a voice say, "There are still evildoers from the past, but they don't have the influence they once had. Remember Woserit and Amenkef? If you keep an eye on them, and keep saying the prayers, they cannot harm you."

"You mean they are still here?" Omm Sety asked, the fear rising in her voice.

"Their evil energy is still around, the malevolence emanating from Seth. The dark force can take root in the weak-willed, the few corruptible souls. But it is a limited power—it dwindles in the light, in the face of the gods and their eternal universe."

Omm Sety recited the spells in the Chapel of Isis, allowing the image of the goddess to filter into her being. She absorbed the healing energy, her body shaking with divine currents, tears flowing as she opened herself to receive Isis. The light softened into a golden film as she descended into a deep meditation, drifting in the waiflike radiance, her lunar world unleashed.

∧∧∧∧∧ ∧∧∧∧∧ ∧∧∧∧∧

The next day Omm Sety started work early, knowing that by noon it would be too hot to work outdoors. Her nocturnal ramble had given her a deeper connection with her surroundings and she began to decipher the papyri with a new intensity. She picked up a piece of papyrus that had just been discovered in a tomb, the odour of death sealed in the fibres. It was like an animal pelt, she thought, left to shrivel in the sun. And sometimes they were like dried out turds, excreted from the bowels of history. How strange it was to spend her life with ancient refuse, sifting through the entrails. That seemed to be her lot: to spend her time with desiccated corpses, reading their shrivelled messages from the grave (and nothing gave her more pleasure).

Omm Sety scanned the papyrus, the lines forming pictures in her mind. She could see the joins where the wet stems had been stuck together, the strips of shiny flesh which once wrapped around the plant's stork. She imagined the plant growing along the Nile, its roots plump with water, its green leaves trembling in the breeze. The withered papyrus caught the wind and blew from her hand, the words jumping out at her as she bent to pick it up. The scroll had lain dormant in the sand for three thousand years; words, ideas, put to sleep like Sleeping Beauty. Omm Sety had learned to interpret their meaning, awaken them from the dead. She thought about Thoth at such times, illuminating hidden symbols in the darkness, turning obscurity into truth. Sometimes she spent hours staring at a papyrus before the deciphering began, her mind tracing the symbols, unravelling the code piece by piece, until finally a pattern emerged and the whole page burst into meaning. *The Hymn to Thoth: Let us give praise to Thoth, straight plummet in the scales, who relates what was forgotten, counsellor to she who errs, who remembers the fleeting moment, who reports the hour of night, whose words endure forever, who enters Duat and knows those in it, she is recorded in the list.*

Omm Sety could feel the brush marking the papyrus, the artist's hand sweeping across the page as she formed the symbols. Omm Sety sensed the effort, the slight quiver in her perfect strokes and the soreness of her eyes that came from hours of practising her skill. Who was this figure referred to in the text? *She is recorded in the list.* Omm Sety thought of the Osirion, the *Book of Hours* recorded on the walls . . . She would go and study the hieroglyphs after work.

This business of unearthing history is a strange one, she realised, as it required a scientist's eye, the strength of a labourer, and the insight of a sage. Thinking about the archaeologists she'd worked with over the years: not one of them performed the ancient ceremonies or worshipped the gods. But why should they? she conceded—they'd been taught to extract the past in an empirical fashion. It was like a dissection, brushing the dirt away, removing the central organs from the body and then cleaning the instruments and covering one's tracks. There was no sense of veneration. It was shameful, really—they didn't know what forces they could be unleashing, what taboos they were breaking, or powerful spirits they may be raising from the dead; it was up to Omm Sety to appease the spirits, leave offerings for the gods and conduct the libations. The archaeologists exhumed the corpses from their tombs—shrivelled mummies, blackened bones, beads and amulets—the sum of their human existence, like a dowry for the Afterworld. The men could be so careless, tossing the sacred talismans into boxes—if they only knew the damage they caused and how she had to restore the sense of balance in the Underworld, through offerings and prayers in the Temple. But Omm Sety didn't mind. Luckily she knew many invocations and spells to subdue the spirits and turn malice into good fortune. She loved her secret visits to the Temple at dawn, removing her shoes and slipping onto the limestone slabs, feeling the floor vibrate with past devotion, the pillars embracing her like great arms.

One night she imagined Dr Hassan in his bare feet, traipsing round the Temple...she thought of him prostrating himself in front of Osiris, and she couldn't contain herself, breaking the silence with a belly of laughter. Academics think they are immune from the spirits. They have no time for prayers, spells or offerings, and don't think twice about disturbing the dead. One archaeologist laughed when she suggested he made a good grave robber. They had lost their connection with magic and the old myths of birth, death and resurrection. But Omm Sety knew you couldn't escape the dead—the other night, a visiting bone specialist had met the same woman in the gold dress who insisted, "Let me give you a ride in my chariot. My husband is away fighting the Hittites and the nights are lonely." The poor man returned to the Rest House looking whiter than bone marrow. The Golden Lady had assaulted his world of reason, but otherwise, no physical harm was done to him.

Sometimes Omm Sety was like the Golden Lady, disrupting the established order. "If you dig here you will find the Temple garden," she told Dr Gahlin, standing next to her in the windswept desert, and the next day he ordered his team to start digging in the sand. He no longer questioned her knowledge, as she had been right too many times. Omm Sety stood in the barren wasteland, seeing the vines cascading with corpulent grapes, the exotic trees from every corner of the Pharaoh's empire, and the lavish fountains falling like rain, gathering in the lotus pond; the images emerging from the red dust and flooding the landscape. She scooped up a handful of sand and felt cool water slip through her palm. It could have been a dream, had they not come across the fountain, or the foundations of the pool where the women used to bathe . . .

∧∧∧∧∧   ∧∧∧∧∧   ∧∧∧∧∧

Omm Sety wandered through the fields, the green corn brushing against her face. Flashes of memory came to light among the lush vegetation and she recalled a dream about a girl called Kebi. In the growing season the girl lived in a reed hut where she tended the crops and mixed her herbal potions. But she was really a snake charmer by profession, and during the festivals she was in great demand — dancing for the Royal Audience, her snake Tiaa writhing in harmony with her movements, until it was hard to tell who was guiding whom, where reptile ended and human began. They were like one strange creature possessed by the spirit of dance, awakening the force of fertility within the crowd.

Omm Sety lay down in the deep barley and stared up at the sky, her eyes blinking in the bright sun, so that she absorbed the firmament in fractions of light, like a blue vase smashing into pieces. She would stay here inside the blue and green tapestry of light, her body blending into the folds of fabric.

Each night Omm Sety came back to this place, and she began to carve a den for herself, burrowing into the grass like a nesting ibis. She borrowed a butcher's knife from the kitchen at the Rest House, and she cut the stalks and wove the strips together as the women did in the fields. After several nights of braiding the greenery, her fingers became increasingly nimble and she was surprised by her skill, as if she'd done this all her life. Finally she had enough greenery to make four walls and a roof. Omm Sety found a large stone and hammered the stalks into the earth, then she fixed the walls into place and covered the roof with woven shrubbery. She crept inside and lay in the darkness, breathing in the moisture of the grass, smelling the colour of green, even though the hut was pitch black.

Omm Sety crawled outside to smoke a cigarette, enjoying the spool of smoke and the surrounding stillness. The villagers had all gone to bed and their fires had burned into oblivion, the embers swallowed by the darkness. They were a strange lot, she thought, trying to decide whether to trust them or not. Most of them were quite friendly, but some were rather primitive, frightened to look her in the eye, still imagining she was an evil spirit. Some days the village teemed with life, as people chatted amiably to their neighbours, and on market day the streets were crowded with shoppers and traders, the stalls bursting with local merchandise — and yet other days the place was like a ghost town, the streets deserted, the dust spinning in silent circles — the only sign of activity.

There was no sign of life tonight, except the multitude of stars that lit up the sky like a metropolis. It was like looking at an upside down city: the shooting stars were like speeding cars, streaking down the road and shattering the stillness. Finally overcome by fatigue, Omm Sety spread her blanket on the hut floor and soon fell asleep, her dreams emerging in a bed of greenery. The potent force of vegetation turned her dreams into fertile fields—she had a vivid dream, completely verdant in colour, so that the people radiated with a green ray.

Kebi and her husband Teshen had made a green hut like this one. They had used a hatchet to cut the reeds into poles. Teshen's hatchet was made of bronze and fashioned in the blacksmith's kiln, along with the weapons made for King Sety's soldiers in Libya and Canaan. Teshen had helped to design a powerful hatchet with a bronze head and fashioned it to the wooden handle with intricate leather weaving. The tool was then soaked in water and left to dry in the sun, the leather shrinking round the head of the blade, impossible to remove. He'd got the idea from drying papyrus in the sun, seeing it shrink to half the size and yet gaining in strength and resilience. But he was an artist, not a soldier, and he shuddered when he thought how the hatchet would be used on the battlefield: slicing through the skulls of Libyans, their brains splattered on the sand. Teshen yielded the hatchet and cut down a papyrus stalk, thinking of the bodies that were felled like sticks.

After sunset Teshen sat outside the hut slicing the slimy papyri into strips. He'd left them soaking in water all day and now they were soft as fish eyes. He sat stripping the papyri while Kebi looked for snakes in the undergrowth. Teshen knew the reed hut attracted a number of snakes, as they came in search of shade and they were also attracted by the water bowl in which he soaked his papyri. But Kebi believed the snakes thought the hut was an animal's den, sheltering small rodents from the hunters, and that the snakes were driven by the thought of an easy dinner, rather than a cool refuge from the sun.

I was usually a little anxious when I visited Kebi's hut, my eyes darting round the room in search of a uraeus. But Kebi assured me the snakes meant them no harm. She was able to put the snakes under her spell and then extract the venom she needed for the potions. And certain snakes could be charmed into dancing for the goddess Renenutet and draw her powers down to earth. Then the place would resonate with her fertility. Every once in a while Kebi came across a snake like that: and she knew she'd found a snake capable of magic, the way its eyes turned from black to purple, and sometimes blue — and its sleek skin radiated like moonlight. When this happened, the little reed hut would vibrate with a strange energy, the grassy walls rustling like a room full of hissing snakes. Kebi knew then the goddess had adopted the serpent as her progeny. On such a night the crops would grow with a new sense of vitality and Kebi said that's why their papyrus was so lush and made the best paper: it was known to be very durable and smooth, favoured by the Royal Scribes.

Whenever the goddess Renenutet chose a snake for her rituals it was a time to rejoice, and Kebi would throw an impromptu party, with food and wine — and there would be music and dancing to celebrate this great event, as it wasn't every day the goddess gazed down from the heavens and chose a mortal creature as her own.

The snakes blessed by the goddess proved to be benevolent reptiles, as Kebi kept telling me, and I grew to trust their sly silence, watching them slither into our circle with their benign mischief. But now and again you came across a wicked snake and there was nothing Kebi could do about it, despite her potent spells. Once she had to grab the hatchet and cut a cobra's head off, because it was hell bent on striking her husband and it would surely have left him dead. Kebi calmly raised the axe over her head and slammed it down on the snake's neck, severing the head like a piece of cucumber. But even then a snake isn't harmless, as its fangs haven't finished venting their rage. Kebi demonstrated the eternal power of the cobra by tickling the snake's mouth with her handkerchief. Sure enough, the fangs leaped open and clamped down on the soft linen, spewing its deadly venom into the folds. I jumped back in horror, afraid this dead snake was more potent than a live one. Kebi held the snakehead with a sense of reverence, "Many mortals have been fooled by a dead snake, but they forget that their essence lives on after death — always remember that, Harp of Joy." She looked at me intently, as if willing me to remember. I shuddered at the thought, and much later I would recall her advice, and wondered how she knew . . .

As Kebi held the severed snakehead, I realised then that the spirit of the cobra lives on after death and that Kebi was wise to harness its power. The venom from this terrifying cobra would be most potent and could be harnessed for the power of good, if mixed with the right prayers.

Omm Sety awoke with a start, forgetting where she was for a moment. Lying under a canopy of green, the scent of vegetation reminded her of freshly cut grass. She was swathed in green bandages, feeling the humidity oozing from the leaves, warming the space like an oven. She was sleepy again, her mind succumbing to the damp heat, her body sinking into this green womb. Omm Sety started to dream, only this time she felt wide awake. King Sety gave her a nudge, "No time to lie around in bed, my love, it's time for the Festival."

She threw on a transparent robe, so shear her pores were visible through the fabric, making her feel suddenly exposed. But King Sety reminded her she always wore such a fine robe for the Festival, and not to dally any longer. They walked to the Temple in silence and removed their sandals by the entrance. They washed their hands and feet and stepped inside the Hypostyle, following the sistra through the dark pillars, they were being drawn to the back of the Temple, the space closing in on them like nightfall. As the space grew more intimate the energy intensified, her limbs trembling like the sistra. She felt rays of heat shoot up her legs from the floor, flames from the earth in search of fire. The drums grew louder and more hypnotic and soon everyone was dancing and whispering, "Oh Lord Osiris, hail to thee." And then people began to sing out loud, their voices expanding, "Happy Birthday, Dear Osiris, may you live forever in this cherished land!"

A shroud of pink mist began to form within the circle of bodies and a figure slowly took shape, cast out of the glowing miasma. Lord Osiris appeared before the worshippers, the pink mist turning green; the malachite tinged face materialising before them. There was a collective gasp as Osiris stood before them, with Lady Isis by his side, her white robe and loose braids draped around her perfect form. People fell to their knees in veneration, their heads bowed in submission. The divine couple smiled in bemusement, "Rise up, my fine people. We are one of you tonight. We wish to enjoy the human pleasures, and dance and dine amongst you. Please set aside your veneration and love us the way you love your brothers and sisters. Remember we are merely the reflection of your deeper selves, the selves you will discover in Amenti."

It was the Lord's birthday wish, said Isis, to enjoy his party as a human being and to share the love and camaraderie of friends. "Indulge an old man, and treat me as one of you." Osiris raised a glass to the people and everyone made a toast to the birthday boy, and nobody knew his age or had the nerve to ask. It was agreed Osiris had been around since the beginning of civilisation, when people learned to live together in peace; when they abandoned cannibalism and brutality in favour of cooperation, farming and crafts.

Soon people forgot Osiris and Isis were the divine couple embedded in their psyches since childhood, the icons of their religious beliefs, and they celebrated with the couple in communal harmony; singing, dancing and drinking all through the night, until they stumbled outside in the early sunlight, inebriated and out of their senses with excess and fatigue, falling into the Temple fountains in fits of laughter. Before they passed out they praised Hathor, goddess of drunkenness, for they'd gone to the limits of endurance where they'd seen a glimpse of enlightenment. With blurry eyes they perceived the shimmering boundaries of Heaven. And they knew, within the excess revelry, one sees the shadow of the divine.

Omm Sety awoke to rustling noises outside the hut, the grass trembling with the threat of intrusion. Omm Sety leaped from under her blanket and peered through a hole in the greenery, she saw Amr, Sana and Yameena whispering and nudging each other, "*Yalla*—you go," – "*La! La!*—no you go!"

Omm Sety waited for one of them to find the courage, but after a few minutes she poked her head through the door and said, "You better hurry up—otherwise I'll be half way to the Temple before you decide to make your grand entrance."

The children were so surprised to find the English lady in the hut that Sana nearly dropped the plate of fatiras she was carrying. The plate veered towards the ground and was rescued by the girl's quick reflexes, restoring the fatiras to a horizontal position. Her grandmother used to smack her when she dropped food, and the memory still haunted her. She tried to keep everything the right way up, but sometimes an object had a life of its own and didn't want to stay still—she could tell by the way it trembled in her hand like a fledgling, wishing it could fly. She didn't think the English lady would scold her if the plate fell on the ground. Omm Sety told them the earth was pure, only people pollute it.

"You brought me breakfast, how kind of you. Come and sit on my luxurious green carpet." She rolled around in the greenery, stretching like a playful cat, the children responding in squeals of laughter.

Sana stepped forward and pulled the white cloth from the plate, releasing a delicious smell of sweet bread soaked in honey and slices of mango. The fatiras were supposed to be for their uncle in the next field, but they hadn't the heart to disappoint Omm Sety. And it was far more interesting sitting under this green canopy with the Ingiliziyya, listening to her strange stories. She handed them each a leaf for their fatiras. "The leaves make excellent plates—and there's no washing up to do."

Omm Sety held the fatira to her nose and inhaled deeply, her taste buds prickling with anticipation, suddenly realising how hungry she was—she hadn't eaten since yesterday afternoon. Her stomach felt like a hollow cave, full of echoes.

They sat round in a circle and Sana shared out the food, serving the fatiras on the leafy plates. Sana seemed a little distant today, thought Omm Sety, as if she knew too much about the world—this could be a burden to one so young. She was only eight years old and yet she was full of secrets, and sometimes she walked in an awkward manner, as if a great bundle were strapped to her back. Like most village daughters she was expected to tend the fire, help her mother clean the house and prepare the meals. Of course, the female neighbours also helped out, they had developed their own form of cooperative, working together to get the chores done. Omm Sety noticed how they helped each other build an oven, kill a chicken and nurse a sick child all in the same day, the phases of life and death a communal enterprise.

Omm Sety studied the girl's gentle features, her long lashes casting shadows round her eyes. She seemed so familiar—her feline face, long ringlets fastened with a beaded clip, her eyes searching through the rubble for something precious. She remembered Kebi from one of her dreams: how she sat on the floor, legs folded into various positions, limbs like snakes effortlessly forming into different patterns. They spent lazy afternoons rolling around in the grass, seeing configurations in the sky. And now, lying in this hut Omm Sety felt like a child again, giggling and tearing bits off the bread with her teeth, letting the honey drip down her chin.

Sana was watching her, as if she sensed her secrets, her deviations into another realm. "Why you sleep here when you have nice room at the Rest House?"

The reel of laughter went silent. The children's curiosity had been unleashed and Omm Sety felt the force of their candour, innocently trampling over adult etiquette without malice. It was a reasonable question to ask her, and yet it demanded a personal revelation. How she longed to tell the children about her past life, about her friend who once lived in the fields and how they searched for snakes at sunset, when small rodents came to the well to quench their thirst and shelter from the heat.

Omm Sety hovered on the edge of total confession, a wild horse about to break into a gallop, a reckless self-abandon mounting in her belly. But then she hesitated for a moment, closed her mouth and felt the bit between her teeth. She must rein herself in—yes, the children would probably understand, but in their innocence they would tell their parents or a neighbour, and they would get the wrong idea, turn it into something malevolent. Some of the grownups were riddled with fear and superstitions, and she was not about to risk being ostracised—not until her task had been completed.

"I am no different from you children—you know when you'd rather play in the Temple when you should be helping your uncle in the fields?"

Omm Sety detected a trace of guilt in the children, and they began to fidget uncomfortably. Omm Sety laughed gently, "It appears we all have secrets. Well, I won't tell if you won't. The truth is I'd rather sleep in this reed hut than in that stuffy Rest House. But people would think I was mad if they knew, so we must keep it a secret." Omm Sety stared at them intently, and the children shouted, "Oh yes, Omm Sety. We can keep a secret!"

She knew they would keep this secret, as it involved their own clandestine behaviour. What would their parents make of their trips to the Temple and her green hut when they should be working in the fields? Omm Sety gained three allies that day, and later, they would prove indispensable to her survival in the village. The children counted on Omm Sety's collaboration, as she would come to their defence whenever they were in trouble for not returning home on time. "I asked the children to run an errand for me—I needed some fruit and they kindly went to the market for me." Omm Yameena was

325

happy to hear this, as the Ingiliziyya usually gave the children a few piastres for such errands (even the fictitious ones).

They huddled closer together in the hut, their green hideaway resonating with laughter and secrets, sheltering their intimacy from the outside world. She would tell them stories about Kebi and the snakes, about the orphan girl who lived in the Temple and became a priestess, about a handsome King who fell in love with the girl and the evil priests who tried to keep them apart. The children were fascinated by these tales and wanted to hear more about Harp of Joy and the adventures at the Sety Temple. Omm Sety realised that storytelling was a great way to convey history without telling them the truth, because they would never believe her. When the facts were too incredible, they could always be turned into myths and legends, and then people were willing to suspend their disbelief.

The children told a story about a blonde-haired lady from a far-away land who came to the village on a donkey, or was it a white horse, or a camel with a gold hump? The Foreign Lady was a great teacher and healer, and she knew about ancient magic and the old symbols which she read on the Temple walls, turning them into powerful spells... There were many tales about Omm Sety: she was a wise woman, a *hakeema*, a medium to the spirits. And other tales were not so flattering: she was a prostitute, an evil woman, an *afreet* who could put a curse on you . . . "and you know, she entertains foreign men—look at all those male tourists who visit her at the Rest House, and she's a single woman! Sometimes a man arrives late at night, wearing a blue cape and a tall hat, and he never leaves before dawn..."

One morning at breakfast Omm Sety told her colleagues, "I've been thinking about getting a house in the village, a place I can call home."

Her colleagues were horrified by the idea. "You cannot mix with these people—and they'll resent you for trying," Dr Gahlin warned her, "they'll only gossip about you and make your life a misery—next you'll be wearing a gallabiya and headscarf!"

But Omm Sety had made up her mind to move. "I can't live at the Rest House forever—I need a home of my own—I need a garden and a place for my animals." The staff had tolerated the two cats and the donkey, but they wouldn't put up with the cobra, and kept scaring it away with stones and tin cans. "Mohamed the watchman has found me a suitable house just near the Temple. He's helping me move on Saturday—soon I'll be a permanent resident." Omm Sety had recently cured Mohamed's boy of malaria by giving him 'holy water' from the Osirion to drink. After seven drops Osama's fever had gone, and the next day he was fully restored to health. Mohamed was so grateful he offered to find her the perfect house and at local prices.

Dr Gahlin shook his head, "Madame, no educated person stays here permanently. They return to Cairo once their job is done."

"Well, I don't plan on returning to Cairo. This place suits me very well. I intend to stay here till I die."

Mohamed found Omm Sety a two-storey house right near the Temple—and she couldn't believe it was only forty pounds sterling! *I have just bought a house for two months' salary!* The house was ochre yellow with geometric patterns painted across the front, and from the balcony she could watch the villagers coming and going, the beautiful sunsets over the mountains…

"I told you I find you good house, and here it is, with rooftop terrace and big garden." Mohamed said he was very grateful to her, the way she cared for his son Osama, "He been very sad since his brother died last year—he very weak, always get sick." Omm Sety felt sorry for the poor boy and offered to make him the beneficiary in her will. "I have to leave my house and money to someone—and I'm sure he'll take care of me in my old age, that's the Egyptian way." Her own son was grownup and lived an affluent lifestyle in Kuwait—he didn't need a peasant house in Abydos. The last time she saw him he put pressure on her to leave Abydos, and promised to get her a nice house in Kuwait—he never understood her need to stay…

Omm Sety gave Osama three drops of 'holy water' to clear his grief and soon enough, his cloud of anguish disappeared. Every morning she filled a jar of water from the Osirion and said a prayer to Isis. Word was getting round that this Ingiliziyya could heal the sick, and after she cured Omm Yameena's tummy bug, the women began to trust her, waving to her in the street and calling round with plates of food.

But Omm Sety hated to admit Dr Gahlin was partly right—she was the subject of much gossip in the village—she could sometimes hear their remarks from her roof terrace. "That Ingiliziyya she gave my daughter some strange red berries and the skin of a toad, and now her throat is better, she sings like an angel! But don't let her near you if you're pregnant—you'll only give birth to girls."

"And never take anything from her—that man who stole her goose, how she cursed him—and the next day he fell off his donkey and died in the ditch..."

Most of the gossip was highly exaggerated: she never used toad skins in any of her remedies—that poultice was made from green algae and canal mud. But it was true about the man who stole her goose—although it wasn't her fault he'd died—she'd only asked Osiris to teach him a lesson . . .And now someone had reported seeing a foreign visitor at her house dressed in a robe and a headdress, like a Coptic bishop.

Perhaps they're a bit too close for comfort, she considered, sitting on her rooftop terrace, watching the donkeys pass by laden with mountains of greenery, the horses and carts filled with market produce, the women laughing and arguing in the street. But she enjoyed the sunsets over the desert, the occasional visitors ascending the Temple steps like ancient pilgrims; the pungent smells, the gossip drifting up from the street. "That Omm Beshma—she's always talking about people behind their backs," one woman complained.

"I'm glad to hear it's not always about me," Omm Sety thought, looking down at the ring of robes, like a murder of crows. Her house met at an important crossroads between the village and the Temple; streets and lives collided, time overlapped so you could hardly see the seam.

Omm Sety listened to the World Service on her terrace, the modern world resounding from the radio. "The headlines today, 23rd December, 1956. After weeks of fighting, the British have agreed to withdraw from the Suez Canal. The Suez Canal is now under Egyptian control, and Nasser will continue to nationalise the entire enterprise. People are calling for Anthony Eden's resignation . . ."

"Halleluiah!" Omm Sety shouted from the rooftop, her joy spilling into the streets, where the group of women gathered to gossip. "This is finally the end of colonial rule!" she shouted down to them, interrupting their flow of scandal. They waved back at her in a cautious manner: What was this Ingiliziyya talking about? "She is standing on the terrace in her nightgown—for all the world to see—

has she no shame?" Omm Beshma whispered to her friends, "That's what happens when an Ingiliziyya comes to the village, she destroys all sense of decency."

∧∧∧∧∧ ∧∧∧∧∧ ∧∧∧∧∧

The sun beat down like hot metal shaken by a slight breeze from the desert. Small circles of dust rolled past her as she walked along the street, bringing up dead beetles and flecks of straw. She passed the pond next to Farid's place where the ducks liked to swim, recalling the docks in King Sety's time, the boats sailing along the canal to the Nile. There was a wooden quay and great steps leading to the First Courtyard. The modern renovators had done a decent job with the limestone steps, but the rest of the place was in a dreadful state—and they had completely abandoned the garden . . . Omm Sety knew the place like the back of her hand—how strange it felt when people greeted here as a newcomer. Some waved in a friendly manner but others stared at her curiously, and children followed in a stream of giggles, trying to communicate in their broken English.

Some people were suspicious of her motives: *What was the woman doing here on her own? Ingiliziyyas always stay at the Rest House— they never live in the village like the fellaheen.* But a couple of the older women seemed to understand her reasons. An old lady called Sitt Mansour was known for her healing powers and gift for magic. She knew Omm Sety wasn't a stranger to this place, the way she walked with ease, always knowing the right path to take. She'd seen Omm Sety wandering in the desert at night, unafraid of the wolves and jackals; the land knew her, the desert welcomed her into its uncompromising realm; Omm Sety understood the personality of the desert, stripped away from civilisation, life reduced to survival. No one could accuse her of traipsing round the village like one of those romantic travellers—she had a job to do, often spending long days at the Temple. They said she was horrified by the way Sety's Temple had fallen into ruin, and sometimes she walked around the rubble crying to herself, running her hands along the broken walls and muttering lamentations.

Omm Sety couldn't help comparing modern Abydos with ancient times: the women kneading dough by the side of the road and leaving the round loaves to rise in the hot sun; the busy square on market day with the covered stalls and piles of oranges, lemons, and bananas, and the cabbages, courgettes, onions and lettuce, the green gifts of the fertility god.

Omm Sety soon realised she had to develop a persona for herself so the people would understand why she was here. "I have an important job at the Antiquities department, preserving your history—one day people will come from far away as China to see this precious Temple." She showed the people her drawings of the Temple, "We must put the Temple back together, get a roof on it so the sun doesn't bleach the murals, and stop the bats from soiling the reliefs." But people weren't convinced—they stared at the lumps of stone and couldn't imagine anyone coming from China to see this debris, or gape at their simple dwellings.

Some of the children understood the importance of her task. Sana found it sad that Sety's Temple had become a ruin. She knew the importance of mending things (the few possessions she had, a doll, some building blocks, how she cried when such toys were broken) and she wanted these precious things repaired. The Temple needed mending too, and Omm Sety was here to put the pieces back together. She had to count them, name them, arrange them in the proper order.

But she couldn't appear too familiar with the place, people would be frightened by this—and they'd think, how does she know her way around so well? Perhaps she is a witch or an evil *afreet* come back to haunt us in the form of an English lady.

Omm Sety had a huge task ahead of her, sifting through the thousands of pieces scattered round the Temple grounds, looking for ways to fit them all together. She scanned the broken friezes, lintels, bits of stele, ostraca and statues, and mentally put them in place, working until they were made whole. Then it all became visible: the stalls, the workshops, the artisans in the studios making leather goods, metals, pottery, linen and papyri, the sculptors and painters in their studios next door to the Temple, the merchants' avenue a river of creativity. Dr Fakhry always said the archaeology told the story of the past. Each layer exposed, each temple or tomb excavated told them a story about how these people lived. It was a slow process, like hearing one word a day—it took several months to fathom a whole page. Of course, she knew the story before the discoveries were made, but she never let on. She let the archaeologists painstakingly work it out from the finds they made. She heard the tale in painfully slow fragments, as the specialists put the pieces together and tried to form a picture of life. It was like listening to an old man suffering from dementia, trying to recall his life. Sometimes she would offer clues, suggestions that would speed things up. "The pillars came from the First Courtyard. There were two columned porticos—the one on the western wall provided shade for the pilgrims These pillars would have been about forty feet tall, so these four lumps of stone probably fit on top of each other to support the covered portico."

After much investigation Dr Gahlin concluded, "Your hypotheses prove to be quite accurate, Madame Meguid, but how do you know all this?" Dr Gahlin was amazed by her architectural knowledge.

"I worked on a similar project in Giza, and that's how it was put together. It's quite simple once you know the pattern." *It's quite simple, when you have seen them in their true glory,* but she couldn't tell him that. *Let him think I'm a mathematical whiz. If he only knew—I'm simply hopeless at maths!*

Omm Sety was washing her cups in a bowl of water when she heard a whimpering sound by the window. The door burst open and there stood a frightened child, hands covering her tormented face.

"Sana—what's happened to you?" Omm Sety seized the child in a motherly embrace, noticing her torn dress, bruised wrists and swollen eyes. "You are safe here, my little lamb. Now tell me what's happened."

The child struggled to speak, her voice impeded with convulsive sobbing. "Tata—Grandma," she struggled to say the words, "she take me to Daya Ameera house." The girl tightened her grip around Omm Sety's waist, hiding her face in the cardigan.

"That evil woman—may she rot in hell. When she knows your mother is against it—did they hurt you—are you bleeding?"

Sana adjusted herself in Omm Sety's lap, her body suddenly rigid. "We go inside Daya Ameera house. They make me lie on table and then she come with a long knife. I know what she want to do, Yameena warn me. Tata—she hold my arms down and Daya lift up my dress. She say is *khafd* for my own good, so I get married. I struggle very hard, kick Ameera in the face. Then I get free and run away. I come straight here, don't know where else to go—only place I think of." Sana released a final stream of tears, her face expressing the emotional relief; her distress tempered by Omm Sety's compassion.

"That *kibeer baqarah*, that *sharr fa'r*! I won't let her hurt you."

331

Sana felt less frightened of her Tata, hearing Omm Sety describe her as an old cow, an evil rodent. But when the child heard someone knocking at the door, she hid behind the sofa in a state of panic.

The old grandma barged through the door. "Where is my granddaughter. I know she's here. Where are you hiding her?" She was a stocky woman of small stature, like a square box, her eyes shrunken with malice, thought Omm Sety.

Omm Sety marched over to the door, her blue eyes flaming with anger, burning a hole in the woman's head (or so Tata Kamil later recalled—the Ingiliziyya put a spell on me!)

Omm Sety saw the desperation in the woman's eyes, something feral, the whiff of violence beneath her robes. She wore a black gallabiya and a thick woollen burda on top, worn by the most pious women in the village, her beaded hijab tight around her double chin.

"Sana! Don't you hide from your Tata—you must do as I say— if you don't go to the Daya have *khafd*, no one will marry you!"

"How dare you try and circumcise the girl when her mother and sister are away. Sana is left in your care and you try and butcher her! Omm Yameena is against *khafd* —she had it done to her and it nearly killed her, and unless you leave this house right now I will get the police!"

Tata Kamil felt her blood pressure rise through her veins, with nowhere to go but through her head, exploding like an earthquake. She later said it was the curse Omm Sety put upon her, which rendered her speechless.

Whether it was the cat leaping at her thighs, claws digging into her flesh, or Omm Sety giving her the evil eye, Tata Kamil fled the house without her granddaughter, her screams darkening the village. The next day the old woman couldn't move her left side, her tongue paralysed from a stroke.

That's what happens when you cross Omm Sety, the villagers whispered. She has magic powers—and she protects animals and children above all others. Don't take your daughter to get circumcised or you'll end up paralysed like Tata Kamil.

"Of course I had nothing to do with it," Omm Sety dismissed the idea. "The woman let her rage get the better of her—she brought it on herself." But it didn't do her image any harm, to make people believe she had magic powers: First a man dies after stealing her goose, then

Tata Kamil suffers from a stroke! It is better to be friendly with the Ingiliziyya!

When Omm Yameena returned and heard what her mother had done, she was filled with rage, "How could you, momma—when you know I nearly bled to death at the Daya's knife!"

Her mother tried to protest with her floppy tongue, sounding like an incoherent animal, a rabid dog howling at the moon.

∧∧∧∧∧ ∧∧∧∧∧ ∧∧∧∧∧

The restoration work was coming along: the Courtyard was free of rubble, the stone slabs brushed clean. Thanks to the renovations, the Temple was coming alive again, resembling its former self . . . Omm Sety could feel its public persona, a place for people to gather and worship, dance and celebrate, the communal shrines offering them guidance and help with their spirits and their everyday lives. In the past there had always been a priestess on hand to help the local women, a Daughter of Isis to guide them to the goddess and her wisdom. They offered the women herbs, amulets, charms and magic; wise words to sooth their inner conflicts. Apart from their medical problems, the women came with complaints about husbands, domestic troubles and how to gain the gods' favours.

Omm Sety realised the female spirit had been badly damaged over the ages; the last vestiges of goddess worship hidden in the Temple walls. King Sety had tried his best to reaffirm the goddess worship in the Temple, after the demise of the old religion during the Amarna Period. Throughout the Temple the goddesses leaped from the silent chambers, murals and columns. King Sety knew the importance of balance in the universe and how it depended on female energy: Ma'at created order in the world, Nut showed us the wonders of the stars, Isis gave us magic and taught us how to heal the sick, and Nephthys showed us the importance of forgiveness and compassion. And we couldn't forget Hathor who filled our lives with beauty and joy, and Seshet who bathed us in her esoteric wisdom. How unlike today when most of the world religions worshipped a male god, and women were inferior to men. It just proved how the two were linked: a patriarchal god led to female oppression, and then everyone suffered. The world was a better place when women were equal, and the Laws of Maat were in balance.

333

While Omm Sety worked in Sety's Temple she had flashes of the past, fragmented images hinting at a whole world; each piece of stone came with a picture of how the item would have looked in its original form, and then a memory came to life in the rubble: *Bentreshy in the Temple lighting incense for Isis, placing bread and wine at her feet; the frieze on a doorway, a woman walks under it—it is Inhapi in a transparent robe, her embroidered belt hugging her waist, white sandals, the Knot of Isis dangling from her neck, her hair braided with beads and coloured fabric . . . it is time for evening prayers... she removes her sandals, the attendants wash her hands and feet with water from the earthen jugs.*

It was just after sundown, the sky a flood of red and gold, the Temple glowing in a peach gown. Omm Sety heard the call to prayer from the mosque, awakening the Temple to worship, the deep voice mysterious, recalling the chants of the ancient priests. Although sung in Arabic the *muezzin* didn't seem out of place; there was a familiarity in the tone, repetitions of religious words, the hypnotic drone recalling sounds from an earlier age. The prayers drifted through the columns, seeping into the murals, the tenor altered by the passages, the secret doorways leading to chambers and chapels, the twists and turns of the stones. Voices were changed by the Temple; everything became different inside the chambers, transformed by the intimacy of the place. A transmutation from light to many shades of darkness; a softer more textured form of colour, as if tempered by a veil.

The moonlight crept through the shafts, along the roofless part of the Temple; Omm Sety followed the hieroglyphs on the walls, detecting the angles and gridlines below the surface images . . . the moonlight enhanced the artist's strokes, the sculptor's lines; sometimes it felt random, and then suddenly planned, and in such moments she was reminded of the perfection of the design, each line flowing into another. There was so much to take in, like the universe. She would start with a mere fragment, a diamond-shaped hieroglyph and allow the image to spread outwards, adding birds, plants, foreign lands, kings, queens, gods and goddesses, until the world was complete.

Spending many hours drawing the pieces in the Temple, she began to see patterns, her sketches echoing the lines on the frieze; she could sense the artist's stroke on the wall, the brush running over the stone. Her pencil mapping out the space, copying the Temple in miniature, to fit inside her mind. The Temple could become any size, human dimensions were irrelevant . . . it was small now, intimate, shrunken to the size of A4. Or had she expanded like Alice, her limbs sticking out the doorways? In this small space she experienced the Temple as a seed of creation, or a tiny star in the galaxy, capable of bursting into a myriad of sound and colour, chemicals that could change the shape of things . . .

Every day she got to know the place better, each carving becoming more familiar; the smells, the heat, evoking impressions of the past. On market day the scent of oranges and lemons drifted through the temple, and Omm Sety would put down her brush, drawn to the shady stalls selling spices and fruit. The colours and textures were an evocative experience: the mangoes, berries and bananas ripening in the sun, the figs and dates covered in a swarm of flies, as if coated in raisins. Omm Beshma still made her catty comments as she passed by, "There goes the Ingiliziyya with the bare arms—no sense of decency," but no one listened to her anymore. The villagers had grown accustomed to Omm Sety's presence and they began to think of her as one of their own. Poor Omm Beshma, she was losing her voice due to years of hurling insults—her tittle-tattle could barely raise a whisper. Omm Yameena said her mouth had been worn out with all the cursing—she'd seen it happen before.

Omm Sety strolled through the market with her wicker basket, listening to the people arguing over prices, a mixture of friendly and hostile banter. Her bag of strawberries was wilting in the heat, turning into pink squash; the sweet smell of decaying fruit mixed with incense, hibiscus, mint tea, cumin, and baked bread. She would make a delicious fruit salad and invite Sana to dine with her in the garden, and later they would visit the Temple with tantalising offerings for the gods.

"Can you teach me the old magic? I want to be a *hakeema* when I grow up." Sana looked at the mural of Isis and then glanced back at Omm Sety, feeling the two were linked in some primeval bond. Omm Sety smiled across at the girl, a trace of mischief in her gaze. "Of course I will teach you. And your first lesson is how to charm a snake," she whispered, pointing to an imposing cobra rearing in the corner. Sana swallowed her fear and tried to calm herself, the snake's composed demeanour beginning to take root within her mind. Omm

Sety approached the snake in a serpentine manner, hips slightly swaying and uttered, *"Hetep-kh na—May you be at peace with me."* The cobra began to lower its uraeus, hood shrinking into its long head.

"Now you try," Omm Sety motioned to Sana; she advanced with perilous steps, moving cumbrously towards the snake. The cobra reared up, startled by the girl's agitated movements.

"Hetep-kh naaah, Hetep-kh naaah!" she recited seven times, placing the accent on the final vowel, feeling this was the right way to say it, visualising the cobra in her mind, slinking across the floor in a spiral dance. The cobra heard the charm and slowly fell to the ground, slithering across the hall in a reptilian dance, just as Sana had imagined. Sana and Omm Sety danced with the snake in great spiral movements, encircling the pillars through space, their heads spinning through the stones, and then the snake slid into the next chamber, hiding within the dark enclaves.

That day Omm Sety made a promise to the girl—that she would teach her the old healing ways, if she would swear to tell no one what she experienced inside the Temple.

"I promise not to tell a soul," Sana vowed, recognising the importance of such a pledge, and together they entered into an ancient union, forged countless times in this intimate complex, where Isis and Osiris witnessed the sacred oaths beneath the columns, gazing benignly upon the new initiates.

Omm Sety was happy she could help the girl reach her potential, as her mother wouldn't let her go to school, despite Omm Sety offering to pay the fees. "I need her at home to help me with the chores," Omm Yameena insisted. "But if you teach her how to be a *hakeema*, then she can make some money for the family."

"I will teach her what I know," Omm Sety agreed, wishing the mother could see beyond her boundaries; wishing she could detect a richer world where women were once revered. If she could look out a different window and see a lush garden with cascading fountains and crystal pools where women swam in the moonlight, or walk through the vast library where they studied the wise books written by the sages. In this world the colours were deep ochre, papyrus green, blue beyond the sky; a world in accordance with female mystery.

"I also know some cures. I make medicine out of green stones," Omm Yameena told her, "green beads I find in the desert. I crush them and then drink them in a glass of water—it's a good way to get pregnant."

Omm Sety was surprised, as the ancient women used to make this remedy. "How did you learn this?" she was curious to know, but Omm Yameena shrugged her shoulders. "Many women do this. It's something we do, but who knows why." She also placed the beads on the ground and jumped over them seven times to ensure a safe pregnancy, and when Omm Sety asked her why, she gave the same vague reply, "It's just something I know . . ."

The funniest remedy Omm Yameena knew involved spitting on a sore body part. "If I bang my knee I spit on it, and the pain always goes away." Omm Yameena said all the children did this when they hurt themselves, but no one knew why, just that it seemed to work. Omm Sety found this interesting as she had come across spitting in the *Pyramid Texts*, often used as a cure for snake bites.

After leaving the offerings and burning some incense, Sana returned home to help with the evening meal, and Omm Sety returned to her office to put away the artefacts. After such an eventful day she felt suddenly exhausted; the summer heat was oppressive, like a hot towel smothering her face. She lay down on the stone bench and soon fell asleep, the sacred boats sailing through her dreams in blue and gold streaks. She woke up feeling dizzy and drained, her legs giving way under her body when she tried to walk, the chamber choking with heat.

"It's no good—I'll have to go home to bed," she told herself, climbing up the stairs and along the roof, her shaky limbs teetering by the edge. She'd taken this route hundreds of times—her shortcut to the back of the Temple; looking out at the pink and orange sky, her feet following the stone wall, and then something happened—she must have missed a step, one minute she was walking, the next tumbling through space. Then she encountered the rough sensation of stone, her back grazing against a bumpy tunnel (although there was no pain, she would have noticed pain), instinctively she reached out to break her fall, her blouse shredding like cheese. The wall pulled her forward, like a hand reaching out towards her, and then pushed her down towards the ground. At first it felt like an assault, a rough hand pulling her through the crowd, or was it gravity making this physical attack? Omm Sety landed in a pile of rubble, the granular light shining

337

through the mound. The tunnel opened into an underground chamber, with gilded treasure chests decorated in ivory and mother of pearl, each one filled with gold, silver and precious gems, and countless figurines—more beautiful than anything she'd seen in the museums.

She saw a figure in the corner, whispering to himself. He looked like Thoth, with his ibis beak and writing tablet, hiding a scroll inside his tunic—it didn't seem strange to meet the god of writing and arcane wisdom—the chamber responding to his personality, the Emerald Tablets emerging from the walls: the Forty-Two Books of Thoth carved into the stones. Thoth, however, seemed shocked to see her. "How did you get in, mortal child?" he demanded to know, and then his gaze softened, "Never mind, now that you're here you may as well read the scrolls. I've been keeping them safe in the underground library, there aren't many safe places left—since the burning of the Alexandria Library and the ransacking of the temples. I want you to take these—there are only a few copies left, hidden in various temples—open the right door in your head and read them carefully, trying to memorise as much as possible. The words will come in handy on the Day of Judgement." Thoth casually handed Omm Sety the green scrolls, and she began reading them:

The components on heaven and earth are a mirror, each one reflecting the infinite being, magnifying the mystery of the gods.

"Now take these scrolls back to the earthly realm, right up those stairs," Thoth pointed to a steep ladder that disappeared into pitch darkness.

"I can't climb up there—it's a sheer cliff," she confided in Thoth, staring up at the vertical tunnel.

"Just put one foot in front of the other, and say, *Look above or look below, I shall see the same eternal fire.*"

Omm Sety had so many questions to ask him about the eternal fire, the mystery of the gods, but Thoth had suddenly disappeared. She searched the chamber for a moment, the light fading into a grey pool, her isolation reflected in the growing emptiness. *I must get out of here.* She stuffed the scrolls down her blouse and started climbing the ladder, repeating the verse with every rung, *Look above or look below, I shall see the same eternal fire,* and after twenty rungs she came to a ledge—and then the ladder became a rocky cliff and she struggled to pull herself up, fixing her gaze on the pinpoint of light, which became her sole purpose, the universe seen in a tiny molecule.

The cliff started to level out into a tunnel and she crawled along on her hands and knees, head brushing against the low ceiling. Emerging through the rubble she found herself in the Second Courtyard, eyes blinking in the setting sun, fingernails caked in dirt and stone.

Husni was on his way back to the Rest House and he couldn't believe the sight of her. "Madame Meguid—what's happened to you—have you been attacked?" Her blouse was torn and her skirt had slipped below her hips. Her hair was a bird's nest, full of dirt and flecks of stone. "I'm all right, Husni—I haven't been attacked. I fell from the roof and I ended up in a passageway—I must find how I did it, as it proves there are underground chambers, with archives and treasures—just like he said–" then something told her not to say anymore; her voice went silent, her mouth glued shut.

"Just like who said?" Husni questioned her, the alarm evident in his voice.

Omm Sety struggled to speak—do not tell him—what should I say? "My head is a frightful muddle. I don't know who. It could have been Flinders Petrie—he wrote about these underground chambers."

Husni began to relax, his shoulders sinking into his blue shirt. "You had me worried," he smiled, but in the evanescent light it looked more like a sneer, a crimson facemask with a mad grin. "I will get the Inspector—I'm sure this will interest him."

When Dr Gahlin heard about the entrance to the underground chambers he was eager to investigate. "Take me to the place where you fell off the roof—you say it's round to the back of the Temple— see if we can find that stone you moved."

Omm Sety scanned the back wall, looking for an axis stone that might lead to the passageway. She pushed against every boulder until her hands were raw, her shoulder grating against the stubborn stones. Dr Gahlin was losing interest, he moved into the shade where his face looked dark, obdurate. Omm Sety stared up at the honey-coloured wall, the dying sun leaving purple streaks on the surface, like a graffiti artist. From this angle the Temple appeared impenetrable, a great giant insensitive to her pleas.

"Perhaps I should look inside—maybe I'll find a stone—something to jog my memory."

"That's a good idea—let me know if you find anything," Dr Gahlin suggested, "I would be interested to find…" his words drowned out by the call to prayer; he shrugged his shoulders, as if admitting defeat, and started walking back to the Rest House, the noise of the mosque creeping into the desert.

Omm Sety wandered through the chambers looking for the hidden stone; she pressed on the false doors in the chapels, the key of life symbol, a diamond-shaped hieroglyph that might be the button to the subterranean world. She sat for a while in King Sety's chapel, admiring the exquisite carvings, his votive offerings to Osiris, Isis and Horus. There were many baffling symbols in this chapel, like the tiny image of the Pharaoh reading a scroll, which he offered to the goddess in the palm of his hand. Omm Sety decided to press the image, tracing the fine carving with her index finger. Staring closely at the scroll she saw a multitude of tiny pharaohs reading even tinier scrolls:

When you open your heart you see the invisible,
The hidden chamber leading to Eternity.
Gather your being from the Temple floor,
The green flame leaping from the cosmic mind;
The wisdom of Thoth is branded into your brain.

Then she heard a voice in her mind, "There is a way down to the secret chambers, my love. But do not let them take the treasures. Keep the records safe inside the Temple—they must never leave Abydos."

Omm Sety knew the pyramid-shaped button would turn the door, but she wouldn't open it in case someone was watching—she wouldn't let them steal the treasures, the lost Tablets of Thoth, the diaries of King Sety—riches even greater than Tutankhamun's Tomb.

That evening Omm Sety undressed for bed, and as she unhooked her bra a tattered scroll fell to the floor. She remembered the experience like a dream, the fuzzy threads being pulled out of her subconscious mind. With great effort (fighting against the unconscious abyss) she recalled the encounter with Thoth and the scrolls, the underground chamber, the ladder and King Sety's voice in the Temple. She dusted off the papyrus and began to read: *Emerging from the waters of Nun, you step into the chamber of symbols, the three-hearted vase of Osiris. Wisdom is hidden in the murky waters, illuminated by the fire of creation. You are a flame leaping out of the sea, you smoulder on dry land, and then you change your shape.*

340

Omm Sety was baffled by the arcane words; she wondered if they were referring to the Osirion, the island emerging from the flood, the secrets hidden in the channels of water... She fell asleep and dreamed about an island, her body emerging from the waves and changing shape—first a frog, then a falcon, then flapping into her human form, wings folding into flightless arms.

15. Fields of Reeds
Abydos, 1969

When Omm Sety turned sixty-five she received a letter from the government notifying her about her imminent retirement. She read the letter with sadness: come the end of the month she would no longer work for the Antiquities Department—she would be a senior citizen and that was that. "They are putting me out to pasture, like an old work horse," Omm Sety complained to her colleagues. "I could go on working for years, if they would only let me." She was strong as an ox and there was a mountain of work left to do: the Slaughter Chamber, the Archives and Storerooms were yet to be restored, the Osirion kept flooding, thanks to the new irrigation systems, and the channels were clogged with litter.

Despite her retirement, the Antiquities people were forever knocking on her door, asking her about obscure hieroglyphs and how certain fragments fitted together. Omm Sety was happy to help them, if the officials agreed to let her visit the Temple whenever she wished—and when they weren't around she could sneak off to the chapels of Isis and Osiris with offerings of beer and bread, and chant the old spells from the *Pyramid Texts*. Being retired had its advantages: she had more time to meet the visitors and show them round the Temple as an unofficial guide, and they gave her baksheesh too, and left their books and magazines, their cruise ship offerings.

Over the past thirteen years Omm Sety had collated and deciphered thousands of fragments and helped put the Temple back together, just as she had promised. She had raised the Djed Pillars, like Isis giving Osiris back his spine. Her hands were rough and covered in calluses, and her back ached from carrying lumps of stone to and fro.

"You shouldn't carry such large fragments—ask the workers to do it. You will work yourself to death," Dr Gahlin used to scold her, wishing she would stick to deciphering the hieroglyphs. But then she would spot several broken stones lying in the wreckage and knew they fitted together to form a door jamb, and in her excitement she'd be possessed with a superhuman strength, and push the pieces together to make a handsome doorway. Omm Sety was proud of her accomplishments—she'd given every ounce of her energy to this Temple, her blood and sweat cemented in the stones.

It had taken the workers several years to fit the roof and erect the columns—"probably longer than it took the ancient Egyptians!" Omm Sety teased them, and these modern fellows had cranes, motorised levers and pulleys—how would they have managed with copper tools, wooden pulleys and handheld levers?

Omm Sety got on well with most of the guards—some of them joked about how they'd lived here before, doing the same tedious job and complained that things never change for the low orders.

"Up at dawn, brushing floor, all day I clean Temple—while foreman he sit in shade cracking nuts," Hassan grumbled. Omm Sety wasn't sure which millennium he was talking about.

When Hassan became a guard he confided in Omm Sety, "I do this job before. I wear a brown woollen cloak and stand outside Temple with a big stick. I guard the entrance of the Temple. I only let priests in, not like today when anyone come in—if they have money to pay."

She promised not to tell anyone, as his brother would make fun of him, said Hassan, even though he'd lived here before as a carpenter.

Omm Sety sat in Farid's café sipping black tea, waiting for the tour bus to come along. She was curious to see who was on the tour today—who had been drawn to the Temple and its mysterious chambers. Most people came on tours organised by the cruise boats, others came by taxi—they usually spent an hour or two in the Temple and then left by late afternoon. The British tourists reminded Omm Sety of her old life in England, with its terrace houses and leafy parks, like another dimension to her now (and in return she introduced them to an ancient world full of bas-reliefs and painted gods). They were her precarious link with the outside world, bringing their stories, their holiday novels and suntan cream. Word must have got round about this English lady living here alone, as people started coming to the café asking for Omm Sety, curious to meet the 'eccentric lady' who had dedicated her life to the Temple, who had abandoned her home to live in this primitive village; who wanted to die here and be buried like the ancients. They said a lot of nonsense about her, embellished by bored tour guides trying to liven up the journey from the cruise ship to the Temple. They made out she was a clairvoyant, a medium who could call upon the gods to answer their questions.

343

It was quite amusing to be thought of as an oracle, but she would prefer people to bring her teabags, paper and drawing pencils, the few luxuries that even she (with all her supernatural powers) could not conjure up. "Bring your offerings to the bare-footed Oracle of Abydos and she will utter a prayer for you." She imagined that's how cults developed—over time the story was embroidered with folklore and myth (a simple woman with a gift for healing becomes a sage, a saint and then a goddess).

The tourists were a vital source of news and gossip, but the irony was Omm Sety often knew more about current affairs than they did, isolated on their luxury cruises, cut off from world events. Listening to the BBC World Service she heard snippets of the outside world, constantly changing like the sky at sunset—the mountains with the moody clouds in pink and purple, the gentle streaks of amber evoking a sense of harmony—and then turning black, grey, metallic silver, creating a sinister air, a hint of chaos.

Omm Sety sat by the radio listening to the highlights of 1969: Neil Armstrong walking on the moon, the first eye transplant, Nixon becoming president, and the peace marches and race riots that followed…things were breaking down, new ideas were forming out of the rubble: the women's movement, the Black Panthers, gay rights … and she heard it was now possible to get your money out of a cash machine, and fly from London to New York in three hours. … Her life existed in fragments—scraps of conversation, transient friendships, broken friezes and sunken statues, and she tried her best to put it all together, to give it substance. From the British tourists she learned they had abolished the death penalty, how the troops were acting like thugs in Northern Ireland; that Brian Jones drowned in a swimming pool and John Lennon got married to Yoko Ono. The American tourists told her about the anti-war demonstrations, about a huge music festival in Woodstock; how the New York Mets won the World Series . . . and people gave her bits and pieces from their hotels—soap, shampoo, complimentary sewing kits. It all gave her an odd picture of the modern world. Flipping through the magazines, she saw how the fashions were changing: it was all big floppy hats, short skirts, long dresses, flared trousers, flamboyant colours and bold patterns; flowers exploding into new shapes, as if high on drugs. What would her father make of these crazy fashions? She thought about his fastidious designs, his clean tailoring and sleek

344

lines. These days it was all wide trousers opening like petals round the ankles, loose-fitting kaftans floating to the ground; an assault on good tailoring. Omm Sety couldn't resist the new fashions and made her own pair of bellbottoms with the help of an old sewing machine from the 1930's, accustomed to straight lines and neat folds. But for some reason the sewing machine was reluctant to make the liberal flower power patterns, and it was a constant battle with the old machine, deliberately veering into a jagged stitch and breaking its needles on the wide lines. Al Balyana had a decent textile shop on the main street and Omm Sety joined the local women to haggle over reams of fabric. They made gallabiyas and head scarves, and she made sleeveless smocks with wide collars and big pockets to hold her pencils, triangle, compass and ruler, the draftswoman's implements at her disposal. She enhanced these outfits with beads and tiny amulets found scattered in the desert—the offerings had already been made—the deceased wouldn't mind if she borrowed a few trinkets. . .

Omm Sety noticed some of the tourists were wearing embroidered kaftans, ankle-length gallabiyas adorned with ankhs and hieroglyphs, Persian pashminas and leather sandals decorated with shiny coins. It was the fashion to look like a Badawia, a hippie priestess with beads and jangles, with a long robe bought in the local market. Omm Sety saw the funny side of this Bedouin inspired fashion, as the educated Egyptians wouldn't be seen dead in such primitive clothes. They tried their best to emulate the Western style of fashion: for the middle class Egyptian a well-tailored suit and a twin set were a sign of culture and social status. Dr Gahlin looked horrified when a group of tourists came to the Temple dressed like Bedouin camel traders, the women wearing colourful robes and peasant jewellery dangling from their necks, wrists and ankles. "They are a shocking sight," he frowned, "like the whores of Babylon!"

Omm Sety enjoyed meeting the hippie, new age visitors, as they liked to talk about reincarnation, goddess worship and astral travel; subjects that were off the radar when it came to Egyptology. And they usually brought her gifts: a tourist called Jasmine-Lee gave her a lovely white hat with a wide brim and a pair of Jackie Onassis sunglasses, and Omm Sety added an orange scarf to the outfit, which an absent-minded tourist had left in the Temple, befuddled by the mystery and the heat; modern offerings to the gods.

345

She had recently moved to a new house, as curio-seekers and nosey neighbours were impinging on her privacy (and King Sety had never liked the old house much, claiming it was full of loud voices, surrounded by ignorant people who were afraid of spirits, making astral travel and his nightly visits very difficult). Mohamed built her a mud brick house on the flood plain. "Don't worry—it not flood anymore, now they build big dam."

"They say the dam isn't finished, so it could still flood," Omm Sety challenged his logic. But Mohamed was an optimist: "By next year dam ok, only flood one more year."

Omm Sety didn't mind a bit of flooding in return for solitude and open spaces, the green fields occupied by a few cabbages and the odd farmer. The house had two rooms downstairs, an outdoor kitchen with a clay oven leading to a wonderful garden, totally enclosed by a mud brick wall, and upstairs there was a rooftop terrace for star-gazing. Mohamed was appalled when he first saw the plans. "Why you want to live in fellah house. People with money build modern house now, with factory bricks and concrete. This old house from ancient times."

"Yes, I understand the villagers want modern things, but I want a traditional house. I haven't come here for modern comforts—I'd live in Cairo if I wanted that." She could see the man struggling to comprehend, his mind racing over the various options, unable to settle on the mud brick house.

Sana understood why she wanted to move to the floodplain. "You can grow potent herbs here, with all these alluvial minerals in the soil." Sana had turned into a wise young woman—thanks to Omm Sety she had become the local hakeema. Omm Sety had taught her the ancient magic and herbal remedies, but the girl had mostly picked it up on her own, guided by some unseen force that led her to the right cure. Sana's tonic for pregnancy was making her famous in the village. "You write the word 'baby' on a piece of paper and soak it in mother's milk overnight. Then you drink the substance, and sure enough you will have a child!" This worked just as well for getting a husband, Sana claimed, proving that babies and husbands should be treated the same.

It had worked for Sana—she had written 'kind husband' on a piece of paper, and the next day Mustafa had come to the door asking about a cure for his mother's boil. She gave him an ointment of Black

Nightshade which she assured him was not poisonous, and told him to spread the purple paste on the boil and cover it with a bandage. Two days later Mustafa's mother came to see Omm Yameena.

"My leg is better. I am here to discuss a wedding—I would love to have Sana as my daughter-in-law!"

"Oh, the magic of goat's milk," Omm Sety cheered, when she heard the good news. She sat in the garden with her donkey, geese and cats listening to the radio and sipping hibiscus tea. It was such a tranquil place, the ideal place for meditation, writing, sketching and entertaining the Pharaoh. The outside of the house was painted bright turquoise with dark green shutters, and inside she painted a large mural of ginger cats playing amongst the persea trees, the lush leaves brightening up the bare wall.

She poured herself another cup of hibiscus tea. They were discussing the Vietnam War on the radio: how many men were being killed in this senseless conflict. Later that afternoon she met a lady called Hilary in the café, whose son had been killed in Khe Sanh.

"Come with me to the Temple," said Omm Sety, taking Hilary by the hand, "he has a message for you." Omm Sety prayed in the Temple with her, calling on the healing powers of Isis to relieve the mother's suffering. Hilary emerged at dawn with a sense of peace, having seen her son's face in the image of Rameses, shining with a regal radiance, ascending from the List of Kings and taking his place in the realm of Osiris.

"I am free, I am happy, Mom. I have the wings of Horus . . ."

Hilary wept beneath the image of Isis nursing King Sety, her tears flowing with motherly lament, washing away her burden of sorrow. She left the Temple with swollen eyes, but with a lighter spirit, the darkness expelled from her body.

Omm Sety returned to her house feeling drained but full of joy. "This is how I must help people," she knew, recalling her ancient legacy. She lay on her mat listening to *Woman's Hour*, her body moulded into the ground, a cat nestled into her belly. The feminists were changing the world, broadcasting their radical ideas around the globe; she imagined women listening in every part of the world, from Britain to India. They were talking about *The Female Eunuch*, by Germaine Greer: about how cheated women have been, treated like domestic servants, goods and chattel. And now they wanted it all changed: equal pay, equal rights, equal opportunities—and it was

347

about time! Omm Sety thought about the priestesses worshipping Isis, equal to men; with powerful positions and influence in the community—it was reflected in the murals, carved in stone. Perhaps this power was coming back, as King Sety believed . . . it was part of her destiny, to reclaim the female divine, to restore Isis within.

Then Omm Sety listened to a review of the past decade: the Bay of Pigs, Missile Crisis, Vietnam, the Six Day War . . . she heard the events in fragments, radio waves floating over the desert, disappearing into the Mountain of Offerings. All these conflicts were caused by too much testosterone, by a lack of female power—the world was out of balance. We needed female equality, the goddesses, the Justice of Ma'at—only then could we achieve harmony on earth.

She thought about the women in the village: with no running water, electricity or a school for their children. Abydos had been forgotten about, left in the lay-by as Egypt marched along the road to progress.

"Part of restoring the Temple also includes rebuilding the village," she told the Antiquities officials. But they weren't concerned about the village—they didn't see much beyond the Pharaonic temples, cenotaphs and tombs.

"But don't you see," she argued, "if the road was paved then more people would come to the Temple, and bring more money to the area." They said Omm Sety had too much time on her hands, pity she'd retired so early . . .

The government officials saw her as a trouble-maker: first it was the Suez Canal (she'd organised a female rally in Cairo, protesting against the British!) and now it was the paved road, electricity and running water. You must realise this is rural Egypt, argued the officials, they had better things to spend their money on. People had lived for millennia without these luxuries and could get on quite well without them.

"Why should the villagers remain ignorant as donkeys?—if King Sety were alive today he would give his people electricity and a proper road to help the pilgrims visit Osiris—the Pharaoh would be ashamed of you."

How could they argue with her logic? This forceful woman would have her way—she would contact the press, the government, and now she had an influential friend called Dr Hanny el Zeini, president of the Egyptian Sugar Company in Nag Hammadi.

Even Dr Hanny joined in the debate: if the roads were better and they had electricity then more people would visit Abydos—even foreign leaders like Jimmy Carter!

"We have to appeal to them on their level," Omm Sety added, "tourism and money are important to the government, and tourists need electricity and running water, and a decent road so they don't destroy the tour buses."

The villagers deserved some modern comforts—like the Temple, they could do with an overhaul. They restored the old buildings, ran the market stalls and tended the fields, like their ancestors had done. The Temple had always looked after them—where would Abydos be if it weren't for the Temple? This ancient bond continued—it was a social duty, an unwritten agreement between the Temple and the community. And now the village was calling it forth: it was time they benefited from this 'temple tourism', as they had in the past, when the pilgrims came to honour Osiris.

One day Omm Sety decided to write a letter to the mayor in Sohag: once again she said it was scandalous the village didn't have a proper road—and she told them straight— that Henry Kissinger had planned to visit Abydos but his aides had decided against it, due to the atrocious road!

Not long afterwards they decided to pave the road—as even the local government saw the importance of such a visit, and low and behold, electricity was also brought to the village . . . (although Omm Sety never had electricity in her mud brick house—she was happy with her oil lamps and Bunsen burner).

Dr Hanny became a frequent guest in Abydos, drawn by the mystical Temple and the curious English lady. He came to take photographs in the evening sun and talk to Omm Sety about the history of the Temple. Dr Hanny had studied chemistry at Cairo University, although his true passion lay in ancient Egypt. Luckily he had to travel up and down the country, overseeing the seven sugar mills scattered throughout the land, and he included ancient monuments to his weekly itinerary, so that he'd visited every pyramid, tomb and temple on his route.

They sat in the Osirion dangling their feet in the water channel, feeling the old pillars rise out of the abyss and speak of ancient secrets. "Some people believe this place existed over 100,000 years, when it was once a verdant savannah. The early homo sapiens followed the rivers up from East Africa and some made this place their home, drawn to the crystal pools and their healing powers." Hanny wondered what Omm Sety would make of this radical notion. He'd been here before, Omm Sety realised, but she waited for him to tell her so . . . He was struggling with his official self—the president of a sugar company. He was wearing a smart black suit, and he'd rolled up his trouser legs and removed his tie. He felt his conventional self unravel, swaying with the reeds in the water, then sinking into the murky regions.

"King Sety believed this place was the first building ever made—it's as old as time." Omm Sety splashed her feet in the pool, the water glistening on the dry stone.

"I had a dream about this place. I came here in a boat, sailing on a vast sea. I disembarked when I saw land and walked until the marsh became a pasture, the trees laden with plump fruit, the savannah offering green delights. I came upon this pink temple rising from the earth, and when I went inside I saw these great pillars and water channels," he motioned to the channels surrounding the stone island they were sitting on. Omm Sety saw his formal self slipping away, and he closed his eyes as the memories returned, reflected in the square pools. "I was initiated into the mound of creation, when the source of being sprang from the sea and adapted itself to life on earth, mutating from one shape into another. I was now a priest—I wore a white robe and my head was shaven—then I woke up." Hanny stared up at the Flower of Life carved on the pillar, the cellular structure responsible for all life on earth. This cellular pattern was a natural wonder, he said, existing in every living thing, including ourselves.

In return Omm Sety told him about her secret world: the Pharaoh's visits, the reincarnation, her life as a priestess, and the strange things too, like the astral travels through the Underworld, the green orb and the magic flights to Amenti . . . They talked until dawn, words gushing through the channels, emerging from the ancient spring. The great columns grounded them to the earth, enclosing their secrets within their giant feet.

He loved to hear her reminisce about the past; they would sit on a stone eating grapes and she would tell him about her life as Bentreshy, when she used to sneak into the desert at night looking for snakes. "Kebi was the best snake charmer in Upper Egypt. She could make them dance and bob their heads in time to the music. We had

350

such fun at the festivals with her snakes, scaring the pilgrims in all their finery, the rearing cobras hissing across stage. But Queen Tuyu wasn't amused, her cold stares were enough to freeze the Nile!"

"You should write a book about it," Hanny encouraged her, "describe the festivals, the people's lives—you could bring it to life, make it sound so real…"

"I've written endless notes about Abydos and I need to get them typed up. If you like, you could take the photographs—show people the sublime beauty of the place . . ." Omm Sety leaped around the stones, charged with creative electricity, her imagination bounding, like a fish leaping from the river.

"Ideas take shape in this place, spinning from the mound of creation," his mind giddy with ethereal concepts and lack of sleep, dipping his toes in eternity.

"I will write here, within these timeless stones, while you take the photos," she decided, sketching the vast pillars.

As daylight approached Dr Hanny was slowly returning to his present self, Omm Sety noticed, his face shrinking into its customary form, shirt collar tightening round his neck. He had to get back to his job at the sugar factory, his employees. But the floodgates had been opened…he would come back to research the book, and to sit by the primal waters of Nun . . .

Hanny followed Omm Sety towards the Temple, where she disappeared down the back stairs and into the Chapel of Isis. He headed to his car, picturing her lighting the incense sticks and placing a jug of water at the foot of the goddess.

Hanny sat in the car as the driver wiped the dust and flies from the windscreen. He imagined Omm Sety dancing an Irish jig as she prayed, bare feet skipping round the columns. He could hear singing coming from the Temple, and then a great roar—the voice subsumed by the motor engine.

"Omm Sety is fulfilling her destiny," he realised, "she belongs to the Temple."

He saw it in her face—a sense of longing, the desire to retrieve something lost, to complete her past journey. Did she feel guilty about the past—about a life she never finished? He imagined she must feel this way. Was that why she'd moved to Abydos? Was this her penance, to make amends for the past?

351

He remembered what she'd said in the Osirion: "I can't help regretting the past, committing suicide. I realise this is a terrible crime against the *Ka*. In hindsight I should have waited for the Pharaoh to return. I took things into my own hands...If I want to go to Amenti I must perform the necessary rites, reach a higher level," she said, sitting on a broken pillar. But Hanny didn't see her as a troubled soul driven by remorse. When she worshipped in the Temple she did so out of love, out of intense joy. Her connection was immediate: she simply entered another dimension. Omm Sety offered her whole being to the Temple and the gods opened the door, led her into their kingdom of secrets.

Hanny stretched his legs in the foot well, his back feeling uncomfortable in the hard seat. He was going back to his office, his meetings, his numerous responsibilities. His body stiffened as the car bounced over the potholes, his briefcase digging into his belly, drawing attention to his inner emptiness. He envied Omm Sety living in this sacred place, traipsing round the ancient monuments, communicating with the gods . . . He had this rash notion of giving up his job, persuading his wife and children to move to Abydos. (His wife Gowhara got on well with Omm Sety . . .) He would ask the driver to turn back . . . No, that would be madness . . . he must return to his sensible self, let the mysteries sink into the fabric of life.

He would lock Abydos in a secret compartment, somewhere in the right side of his brain. He could feel it vibrating sometimes, flashing with vibrant images; his inner eye blinked with fractions of light, and then a wave of colour would break through the surface, reminding him of the hidden treasures he'd stored away.

∧∧∧∧∧   ∧∧∧∧∧   ∧∧∧∧∧

Omm Sety emerged from the Temple in a silent daze, her hand shading her face from the sun. She imagined the priestess as a medium, a bridge between the community and the gods. The priestess must serve the Temple and perform the rituals, but she was also there to improve the lives of others, to help people find their spirit selves. And in return she would reclaim her female power, her own identity which would lead her to eternity, and back to her soul mate King Sety.

Through her healing abilities and ancient knowledge Omm Sety was invited into the women's lives, their homes and secrets. She helped them with childbirth, illness and emotional problems, and in return they taught her about their local customs and folkloric traditions. She saw the past written in their faces, remembering the deep bond between the priestess and local women.

She felt this bond with some of the tourists who visited the Temple, guiding them round the chambers and chapels, drawing their attention to King Sety worshipping Isis and Osiris. They were like the old pilgrims who travelled from faraway lands, come to honour Osiris, Lord of the Reeds and Isis, Lady of the Silver Moon. She led them into the Osiris Complex and watched their modern selves slip away, infused by the timeless character of the chamber, where the Daughters of Isis once danced themselves into a trance. Omm Sety enjoyed seeing an ancient self emerge like a bird from a cage; the light streaming through the shafts in misty streaks, projecting mysterious patterns on the murals as the transformation occurred. Some visitors sat on a pillar thinking or meditating, some wandered around in a reverential stupor, as if drunk. She'd seen a few women burst into tears, the Temple unleashing a flood of emotions and suppressed memories.

After the visits Omm Sety took them to Farid's café where they tried to make sense of the experience, their rational selves turned inside out and appearing quite different in the fading sun, for it was usually after four o'clock when they emerged from the Temple; all sense of time suspended, like the pink vapour hovering over the mountains.

One day Omm Sety noticed a woman standing by the image of Osiris muttering prayers to herself. The woman was quite embarrassed when she realised Omm Sety had been watching her. "I didn't think anyone was here," she apologised, hiding her incense sticks under her shawl.

"Don't worry, there's nobody here—just Osiris and Isis—do carry on," Omm Sety reassured the woman, offering her a match to light the incense.

When the woman emerged from the Temple Omm Sety was waiting by the well, and offered her water from a leather skin bag. The English woman was called Eileen Moore. "I'm a tour guide with Phoenix Travel, working out of Cairo. I should be working on the cruise ship today, but I needed to get away." Eileen looked around furtively, relieved to see no other tour groups in sight.

"There won't be anymore buses today, the Temple closes in half an hour. No one will find you here—you've come to the end of the world," Omm Sety laughed; her eyes creased into blue streaks, then opened into great shafts of light.

As they sat in the café drinking beer, Eileen felt her tensions drift away, her chest loosen like an elastic band cut with scissors. What a delight, what a caper! Eileen couldn't believe she was here, sitting in this rustic café, talking to this eccentric lady, (she hated the word, but how else to describe her?) surrounded by handsome Egyptians, the setting sun. Omm Sety could read it in her plump yet pleasant face: a sense of bliss, rebellious pleasure; breaking out of the cold dungeon. Omm Sety filled their glasses with more beer, and she watched quietly as Eileen leaped out of herself, grey eyes like magic puffs of smoke, transforming into a laughing Buddha. They were telling saucy jokes, tittering like teenage girls. The waiter didn't know where to look when they called him over, face lowered in embarrassment. "Two more beers, Ahmed, and a bowl of pistachios—thank you, sunshine."

"OK Madame, and more pistachios," he smiled weakly and slipped away. They had made the place their own: the table and chairs, the pistachio shells beneath their feet, their selves transforming into another dimension and taking the surroundings with them. They looked golden in the fading light, both comical and imperial, two fallen goddesses sitting on their wicker thrones, sunglasses perched on their heads like misshaped crowns.

They tottered back to Omm Sety's house in a wave of exuberance, entranced by the full moon, Eileen exclaiming, "Isn't it beautiful? It's truly amazing. How lucky you are to live here!" The lady was intoxicated by the moonlight, the sidereal sky. Omm Sety never needed to drink much here to get tipsy—it was in the air, a natural intoxicant rising from the desert. Two beers and she was nicely inebriated, riding the giddy camel of Abydos…They turned up the radio and danced in the garden, the cats darting between their legs, the geese squawking like bagpipes, and Eileen's portly body shaking with a corpulent rhythm, wide hips spinning through the universe. There was something divine about her, in an irreverent sort of way, Omm Sety thought, as if she'd once been venerated but had fallen from grace.

Omm Sety could see her as a priestess of Hathor, indulging in the Harvest Festival, her great breasts bouncing with fertility and the promise of earthly pleasures. That night they recognised each other from bygone days in the Temple, dancing at the Feast and drinking copious jugs of wine. Omm Sety imagined Eileen was on a pilgrimage from Dendera: the Daughters of Hathor and Isis united in female revelry, draping flowers round the deities. Omm Sety picked a bouquet of jasmine from the pots and handed them to Eileen, just as she had done at the Temple feast, curtsying before the High Priestess Inhapi, brushing the flowers against her transparent robe and releasing the sweet aroma. *She has passed through the doorway into the garden of flowers and sacred cats, where timeless time is measured by the lotus flower, opening and closing into day and night.*

The next morning Omm Sety said goodbye to her ancient friend, and they clung to each other like lost children, remembering happier times. "My dear sister of Hathor, promise you'll come back soon," she whispered through a shroud of tears, the taxi driver waiting impatiently by the café. There was no one else she could talk to like this, share her past, her intimate secrets…

"I will come again soon— I have a week's holiday next month," Eileen kissed her on the cheek, looking forward to spending a blissful few days with her friend, meditating in the Temple and dancing in her heavenly garden.

She walked across the desert, past Shunet al Zebib, where the boats were buried in their graves, King Sety had told her, so the dead could travel along the celestial river to Amenti. Her body felt young again, limbs bouncing over the sand. A group of girls ran ahead towards a small hamlet, and they stopped by a mud house with flowers painted on the wall. "This is where you used to live before you came to the Temple," the girls laughed, pointing to the tiny house.

"My old home," she cried; with the outdoor kitchen and the reed canopy, where her mother had baked bread in the morning sun.

"You must get back to the House of Isis," the girls reminded her, "you don't want to miss morning prayers."

Omm Sety followed the electrical pylons, rising to the sky like metal pyramids. They finally had electricity in the village, but how ugly these pylons were, obscuring the view of the mountains! You shouldn't get too close to them, a soldier had warned her, the pylons were surrounded by mines—Nasser's government had installed them due to the conflict with Israel, but it seemed the villagers were the main target and could easily lose a limb. This is an outrage, Omm Sety thought, having mines in Abydos! The troubles were mainly in the Sinai Peninsula, over six hundred miles away.

Back at the Temple, Omm Sety tried to tell the officials about the boat graves, but they didn't seem interested—they had too many tombs to excavate, they said (or perhaps they didn't believe her).

The next day a small group of British visitors came to Abydos looking for the beginning of the world and the first evidence of space travel. While Dr Gahlin called them cranks and crackpots, Omm Sety found them oddly interesting and showed them the hieroglyphs in the First Hypostyle that resembled a space ship, submarine, helicopter and tank. A young American called Eric thanked her politely and stared up at the portentous glyphs. "Far out. It's proof the ancients were in contact with aliens," he said fervently, eyes tracing the flying saucer round in circles, "but the archaeologists don't agree. I mean, the Egyptians had the technology to build this Temple, right? And the Osirion with its pillars that weigh sixty tons each—teleporting them all the way from Aswan. So why couldn't they communicate with other planets, even travel through space?" Eric turned to face Omm Sety, his beseeching eyes hoping for an answer.

"Modern man is essentially arrogant: he likes to think he has the most sophisticated technology of all time," Omm Sety replied, "He wants to be the first to fly, the first man on the moon. He doesn't like the idea of ancient man travelling through space before he did—especially before they'd invented engines."

Eric nodded, "Yeah, that's right. But what if they did have the technology many eons ago, when they lived in Atlantis? And through a series of natural catastrophes—earthquakes, floods, etc, this advanced society was pretty much wiped out, except for a few survivors," he pointed to the spacecraft on the ceiling's lintel. "And this is what they remembered, and it was passed down over the generations, recorded in this very Temple."

She liked the young man's passion; whether it was true or not about the spaceships, she couldn't say, but she remembered what King Sety told her about multiple dimensions, opening your mind to the seemingly impossible. "There are many secrets in this Temple, revealed to those who look beyond the external dimension. The ancients were more advanced than we realise, their wisdom is written in the hieroglyphs, but most people don't even know it's there."

Through Eric she discovered the world of science fiction, as he left her several novels about parallel dimensions and mythical lands—the writers exploring ideas like astral travel, telepathy, telekinesis and quantum physics; the past was a dimension, and so was consciousness . . . it was no longer just the realm of poets, mystics and batty psychics—now scientists were in on it too—people like Arthur C Clarke and Carl Sagan were talking about multiple dimensions, extraterrestrial beings, space and time snaking their way through the universe; past present future as living entities. She liked to imagine it all happening, allowing for astonishing possibilities: the Osirion as the first structure rising from the glacial flood, islands forming in the abyss. The Temple draped in pink, emerging from the bottom like a great seashell (she wasn't supposed to enter such realms, but somehow she managed to slip through, like a cat through a window, unseen). The stellar priestess on the roof reading the open sky, the scholars in the deep chambers reading the cryptic books. Omm Sety was there on the roof, sketching the solar system with her coloured pencils; she saw it as a great blue plate, or a shiny dress, or a stretch of ocean with no shore—she saw the sky as many things, up there on the roof; stars falling to earth in fountains of light, forming pyramids and astral bodies; there were animals up there too—silver horses, camels, lions leaping from the sky, claws tearing through the firmament, and there was even a white elephant with a sparkly trunk, a whale-sized Gabriel trumpeting the new dawn.

Yet there were people still clinging to the three dimensional world, afraid to expand their horizons, like those folks who once thought the earth was flat. The universe was being catapulted into the future—astronomy, fantasy, science and magic—there were no limitations at this flexible feast.

What was it like to be a priestess in ancient times? She had an inclination, a picture based on memory and deep emotion. Omm Sety knew it wasn't enough just to worship Isis—the priestess had to be a skilled dancer, songstress and scholar. Bentreshy had excelled at drawing, singing and art history, and she had performed the rituals with an effortless devotion: bathing, anointing, praying—leaving offerings at the appropriate times. She had a moon inside her.

Everything was measured. Night flowed into day, the twelve hours of darkness to the rebirth of dawn, then the twelve hours of light to the death of the sun.

Omm Sety danced in her garden, playing flute music and shaking her hand-made sistrum. Gyrating her hips in a tribal manner, she had a sudden flash of her dance teacher back in London with a horrified expression on her face, and she started to laugh, great wails mingling with the music. Finally out of breath, she sat in her armchair and picked up her sewing. She embroidered cartouches of Isis, Osiris and King Sety I. She also embroidered people's names to sell to the tourists—there was always a Mary, an Ann, or a John on the tour. Sometimes she would whiz round the tour and get some orders—just like a local! And then she would spend the next two hours frantically sewing the hieroglyphics before the tour returned to Cairo. She dreaded the long names like Veronica, Felicity, or Elizabeth, as she struggled to get these finished on time. (She much preferred a Dave or a Lucy.) Omm Sety also made her own figurines out of clay and sandstone which she placed in the alcoves above her sofa. Bastet and Isis looked down from their domestic shrines, and Omm Sety felt confident her house was protected from evil spirits and nosey neighbours. She read copiously by the oil lamp, piling her odd collection of books on a side table: books on amulets, the wisdom of Thoth, the search for Atlantis, and science fiction novels entitled *Do Androids Dream of Electric Sheep? Ringworld* and *Tau Zero*. She sipped her tea and read about these parallel universes of time-travel and manifold dimensions, inhabited by silly humans and advanced aliens, sometimes vice versa, and she'd fall asleep somewhere in the future, where there was usually a red sky.

After morning prayers at the Temple, Omm Sety settled down to write in the garden. How wonderful it was to write her own book instead of editing (and ghost-writing) other people's work. She'd spent years helping people write, contributing to Dr Hassan's monumental volumes—then there were Dr Fakhry's publications, and the foreign archaeologists' articles. They credited her with "a special thanks to Omm Sety" (after several years of researching and writing!) Yes, she had researched, rewritten and polished numerous books, but never had her name appeared on the cover. Writing in her garden she savoured each sentence—her own ideas and words filling up the pages. She formed each sentence carefully, turning the archaeological facts into a language the reader would understand and enjoy. She wanted to convey a sense of wonder, to share the beauty of the Temple with them in words. It wasn't going to be just an academic book, she was sure of that. There were too many dry books on offer—her book would be full of myths and magic, peppered with personal reflections and unusual facts about the Temple of Sety I. But it would also be an academic book, capable of sitting next to the great books on Egyptology. *My scholarship must be impeccable, then they'll have to take me seriously—and they won't be able to dismiss me as a batty old quack!*

Not that she cared about their opinion—she had given the archaeologists many of her drawings, her knowledge and insights, and now it was time they took her seriously. Omm Sety had been happy working for the Antiquities Department all those years—glad to be given the chance. Perhaps I've been too grateful, she wondered—always wanting to please and accommodate them. Not that she felt resentful. It just hadn't occurred to her to publish her own book (she still felt like a novice, or an apprentice). She thought of the feminists on *Woman's Hour*—it's the female nature, they said, always wanting to nurture and share, but it can also get the better of us. The male scholars didn't give away their research—they were so anxious to publish, make a name for themselves. They were certainly driven, possessed by competitive genes. If she'd been a man she wouldn't have lived on a secretary's salary all those years—she'd be famous by now, and probably quite rich. "But fame and fortune don't interest me," she reminded herself, the donkey turning its head to give her a hard stare, then glancing round the peasant garden and mud brick house. "OK, it's not the Ritz—more like the Stone Age—but we have everything we need," Omm Sety told the donkey; she wouldn't want to live any other way. She was connected to the earth, the Temple and the sky: Nut's solar body. No amount of fame could give her this... and King Sety loved to visit her in this secret garden. He found it amusing that she'd built her house on the floodplain—no one in their right mind would do such a thing!

"But things have changed, Nisou—technology has given us a dam to control the Nile. It can still get a little soggy in August, but I use the water to mop the floor!"

"Not like the old days when the area became a vast lake—your poor house would have turned to silt!" the Pharaoh leaned back in his chair, stretching his arms above his head. He loved this mud brick house with the walled garden, it appealed to his need for simplicity, mingling with the vegetables, the animals, the dirt and dung, his feet prodding the earth. Despite the muck he considered it a magic garden, with lush plants, and flowers growing up the white wall. It was a miracle you could grow such big lettuces, cabbages and aubergines in this space, what with the geese, the hens, the donkey, the numerous cats and the odd cobra wandering round like they owned the place. How curious they never seemed to eat the plants...

When Nisou returned to the Netherworld, Omm Sety sat amongst her animals waiting for the dawn, listening to the donkey snoring like an old man with a cold, the slow procession of geese round the courtyard, the gentle clucking of the hens (never totally at ease), and together they waited for the sun. Omm Sety savoured these quiet mornings, when the world was still asleep, forgetting the passage of time, for it seemed like a new born planet, full of green shoots. The place forgot that time had passed: it could have been the season of Peret, the year the Pharaoh visited Abydos in his royal boat. Not much had changed since then—they still had the mud houses with the courtyard gardens, the rooftop terraces, and the outdoor ovens for baking bread; the cattle grazing by the canal, the crops growing into vibrant streaks of green and gold. It was quite easy to forget which millennium she was living in.

"Now about this book," Omm Sety opened her journal and flipped to a blank page. "It's no good it being just another book on archaeology, the book must capture the essence of the place." She had a title in mind: *Abydos: Holy City of Ancient Egypt*. She wanted to remind people Abydos was a place of pilgrimage—the land where Isis brought her husband back to life, the place where Osiris was buried and resurrected from the dead. The book would capture the beauty, the artistry and magic of the place. And she would have stunning photographs taken by her friend Hanny. He knew a lot about light and shadows; he knew how to harness the rays with mirrors and torches. Each hour of the day created a different light, the colour of the murals reacting to the subtle changes in the day. The aesthetic quality was forever changing, the hours adding a layer of colour: a deeper red, a brighter blue, a constant variation in hues. The chamber of Isis seemed to change the most: in one mural the goddess wore a pale yellow robe in the morning and by the evening it looked a deep gold, as if Isis had changed her dress for supper . . .

Omm Sety strived to write an accurate portrayal of the history, the gods and goddesses, the pharaohs, right down to the local people. She infused the academic with a sense of worship, seeing the art of writing as an act of veneration. She could never forget that Sety's Temple was a place of adoration, a medium between us and the divine, and she wanted the reader to sense this too. It was not enough to explain the archaeology, she wanted to describe the process of veneration, the importance of ritual and how the Temple was used on a daily basis. To worship in the chambers gave the Temple meaning: she had seen the Temple transform many times, the columns, murals and passageways reacting to the prayers and incense, the space getting bigger or smaller, light fading or growing brighter, colours fading and then beaming with life, as if the stage lights had been switched on — green, red, yellow, blue, the play about to begin.

The village also had the power to change shape. Some nights the place was so quiet, the streets deserted, with only a few cats stalking in the shadows. Other evenings the village seemed like a metropolis, the streets erupting into spontaneous joy, crowds of people laughing and shouting in the main street. One night it was a child's birthday, drums beating, bagpipes playing, everyone dancing and singing. She followed the procession down the street, women and children wearing brightly coloured clothes, carrying presents and baskets of food. They stopped outside an ochre house, where a long table had been set up to display the gifts and food given by the villagers. A group of women nibbled on homemade cakes dripping with coconut and honey, and they called out, "Omm Sety, come and join us — have some basboussa." Omm Yameena was wearing her blue gallabiya embroidered with red and gold trim, and she had a turquoise scarf that reminded Omm Sety of the morning sky. "I'm not really dressed for the occasion," she apologised, feeling scruffy in her gardening trousers and short-sleeved blouse.

"We happy to have you here. Have some kerkede." Omm Yameena handed her a glass of hibiscus juice, foaming like red beer. She took a sip and felt her glands contract around the sweet-sour substance.

"I heard the music and I was curious—I thought maybe it was a wedding." She'd been to three weddings this month and was happy to attend a birthday for a change.

"It's my granddaughter's birthday today—she's five years old," Omm Yameena announced, cutting the halwa into neat squares.

"Of course it is. I'm so sorry—I've been writing my book, I forgot which day it was. I don't know where the time has gone," Omm Sety admitted, feeling out of step, as if performing in the wrong play.

"Don't worry—you are here now, so we can all celebrate together," Omm Yameena handed her a piece of halwa. Then Sana appeared with her little girl, Azza, who looked like a princess in her traditional village dress embroidered in geometric patterns, her hair braided with flowers and ribbons.

Omm Sety didn't have a present, but she searched through her pocket for the little blue hare she'd found in the desert. It was made of lapis lazuli, dating from the Middle Kingdom. "It will bring you luck and keep you safe," she told Azza, her tiny palm opening like a lotus bud to receive the gift. The child studied the miniscule hare, the size of her thumbnail "It's the colour of the sky, just before night time," she observed, her eyes drifting towards the sky.

"I will get you a chain so you can wear it round your neck," Omm Sety offered, "The girls here used to wear them, they said the amulets made them nimble on their feet, fast as a hare."

The child studied the English lady's face. She felt it was true about the girls, running fast as hares. She had seen a girl in the desert, her white robe tucked around her thighs; she was running towards the mountain at high speed, and Azza doubted anyone could catch her, not even the jackal.

When Omm Sety returned home she sat in her garden listening to the music and singing; the party would go on all night, she gathered—they were also celebrating an engagement party in the next street. Once the festive gene was unleashed it was unstoppable in this town, as if making up for lost time (when the feasts had been outlawed by the patriarchs, their dances forbidden). The joyful sounds lulled her to sleep, and when she awoke the garden felt quite different, the air thicker, the colours deeper. It was her garden from a different angle, a different point in the universe . . .

King Sety sat down in the wicker chair. "What a lovely evening, my Lotus Flower," he said, gazing up at the stars.

"Yes, it's wonderful, very warm for this time of year," Omm Sety replied, following his eyes towards the sky. "I hung the washing out today and it dried in half an hour." The clothes were still hanging on the wall, the Pharaoh noticed, she always was a bit untidy, he smiled to himself. They chatted in a familiar way, like a married couple.

"Sana is a hakeema now, she heals the sick, just like in ancient times. It's Azza's birthday today, such a sweet child, and so wise for her age, takes after her mother."

"So that's what all the fuss is about. I could hear the music from the other side of the mountains."

They held hands and she felt the tenderness in his gentle touch, the garden shrinking in size, the air heating up. "He is here with me," she whispered to herself, "my love, King Sety . . . Nisou."

They lay down on the mattress and stared up at the sky, and King Sety told her about the planets, what the solar priests had taught him about the universe, the mysteries of the Temple, built on ancient foundations originating from Zep Tepi, the beginning of time. It was a place of astronomical significance where the Sirius Star and Orion's Belt were most visible in the sky. "The priestesses had great knowledge from the Followers of Nut, as her body was a map of the stars and they'd learned to read it like a book." Every year on Osiris' birthday, the Sirius star shone directly onto his tomb in the Osirion. They said Isis was embracing her husband . . .

"Tell me how Isis and Osiris fell in love," she wanted to know, nestling into his side. Omm Sety stretched her legs and realised she was in a young body again, her limbs firm and slender, her eyes able to pinpoint the farthest stars. Her ageless body responded to his touch, flaming with a feral passion and windswept emotions.

"The couple met by a pool under the sycamore tree—they both loved swimming, and the moment they hit the water they fell in love." That night Nisou divulged many secrets in their intimate embrace; how Isis and Osiris were the first people after the Flood, whose parents had ascended from the primeval waters of Nun. How Abydos was the first city to rise from the floodwaters, the Pink Mountains offering sanctuary to the land creatures, who carved their homes below the crystal crescent. They knew the Inundation would return every summer, reminding them of the shapeless ocean from whence they came.

Omm Sety loved to wander round the Temple at night, once the guards had gone home and the lamps had been extinguished. At first the Temple was completely black, and then strange shafts of light began to appear, illuminating random images: King Sety pouring water from the heart-shaped vase before the feet of Osiris, life and colour pumping from the walls, then all was black again, until a beam of light illuminated another image: the five goddesses with Osiris, evoking the power of the feminine. Moonlight shone through the ceiling shafts projecting light and shadows on the wall, female shapes began to emerge, dancing in erratic rings, disturbing the sleeping columns. They came in evanescent sparkles and then fizzled into darkness. The women were dressed in beautiful robes, with hand-painted geometric patterns in gold, red and blue; feathered, bejewelled and anointed with perfume. The hearts on the vase began to pump through the stone, the sound echoing through the Temple — then Omm Sety realised they were drums, beating to the heart of her being, and she closed her eyes and began to dance — without hesitation or awkwardness, arms looping in slow circles, legs lunging and rebounding into spiral sequences, moving over the slabs in perfect symmetry, her feet waiting for the new set of movements. Spinning round, the women swooped down from the wall to join the dance, jewellery jingling against their skin — they were all so beautiful, she noticed, stepping aside to let them pass, the women laughing and stroking her hair. *"Don't be inhibited now that we've come to join you — we've been watching you all this time — you were doing so well with those intricate steps, you never missed a beat."*

Omm Sety recognised them all: Isis, Nephthys, Maat, Ronpet, goddess of the year and Amentet, goddess of the west, and the priestesses in leopard skin stoles: Inhapi, Nubiti, Kebi and Meryt, eyes shining like precious gemstones. She felt their warm bodies press against her, urging her to dance or be crushed by their invincible energy. She leaped into the air and landed on one leg, the next leap catapulting her into a series of quick steps, feet criss-crossing the floor, moving diagonally to the southwest corner of the hall. The women cheered and shook their sistra, hair flying in streaks of blue light. The drums were thunderous now, drowning her senses, heart rebounding into a million particles of sound, and she had to keep dancing or her heart would explode. Her body carved its way straight through the columns, the stone giving way to flesh and limbs; round and round she circled the columns, urging them to rise from their foundations and dance. The columns leaned this way and that, swaying with the drums, and she stared at the djed pillar on the murals, bending like a tree in the wind. The Temple could dance too, the columns enjoying their flight from their vertical underpinnings. They were the spines of Osiris, bending down to reach Isis, responding to her loving embrace. Omm Sety spread her arms round a column and felt the limestone monolith respond to her touch, wrapping its stony appendage around her body. She felt it rise from her groin and up through her abdomen to her forehead, she felt the column support her being, keeping her grounded to the earth; holding her steadfast as the waters rushed over her, leaving a layer of minerals behind in the cracks.

Omm Sety lay down on the floor and watched the chamber spinning round; she remembered getting off the merry-go-round as a child, a whirl of gaudy colours swimming in her head. She felt a bit sick, the way you feel after devouring a mountain of candyfloss. The chamber was fuzzy and pink, and tasted like sweet shards of glass. She started to laugh at the garish colours, the psychedelic pink, the candyfloss carpet sticking to her hair. Tears flowed down her face, turning the candyfloss into pink syrup; she was alone now, drowning in pink syrup. Perhaps I'm bleeding…the tourists will find me dead in a pink pool. . . She started to tremble, sobbing into the rug… I am alone here, the women have deserted me. They have left the party without me… She peered into herself—all shuttered and dark—a lonely room no one came to visit . . . *You left me down there to rot. I had no choice but to drink poison. My loneliness gave way to fear, clawing like a rat through the ground, leading to black terror. And then I was no longer alone. There were priests in the cavern, dark figures with bad teeth and faces shrunken into grey skulls, their malice manifested in the dying light. I was in some tomb at the end of a long tunnel, a priest crushing my right wrist against the sarcophagus.*

"Your hand is on the tomb of Osiris—you cannot lie before the Lord of the Underworld. You must tell the truth or risk damnation in the lake of fire."

"I will not lie because I will not speak . . ."

Omm Sety awoke as the bars of light streamed through the chamber, her face wet with tears, cheekbone aching against the floor, as if she'd been punched in the face. Not the best pillow, these flagstones, next

365

time she would bring a blanket. I must have a hangover, she thought, feeling groggy and goggle-eyed—but she hadn't touched a drop.

The guard wandered through the Temple smoking a cigarette; he saw Omm Sety sitting on the column brushing the dust from her clothes, and he inhaled a rush of nicotine and fear, "Madame Omm Sety—you scare me to death. What you doing here so late—so early, how long you been here?" Mohamed looked confused and kept puffing on his cigarette, right down to the filter.

I must look a fright, she imagined, her hair a bird's nest, clothes wrinkled and covered in dirt. *Poor man doesn't know where to look.*

"I'm all right, Mohamed. I must have fallen asleep again—I haven't been here long." Omm Sety honestly couldn't remember how long she'd been in the Temple, could have been days...she had a terrible headache and just wanted to go home, have a wash and a bite to eat, and then retire to bed.

Omm Sety slept until sunset, hearing the call to prayer and waking in a panic. *I've missed evening prayers again. Inhapi will be angry with me.*

She stood under the shower and let the water run down her body until she felt wide awake. To bring herself round she worked in her garden, teasing her hoe around the plants and pulling out the weeds. Then she did some basic cleaning in her house, sweeping the floors and wiping the dust from the surfaces. There wasn't much to clean— just the bedroom and living area, leading into the outdoor kitchen, which seemed to clean itself. Her bedroom contained a simple Egyptian bed with a wooden headboard, a wardrobe and a bureau, and the walls were decorated with the embroidered cartouches she'd made for the tourists but hadn't finished in time. Oh well, a Veronica or an Elizabeth was bound to come along sooner or later. Her sitting room had a Bedouin-style sofa covered in cushions and throws from various markets, with figurines of Isis, Hathor and Bastet peering from the niches in the walls. Despite her cosy dwelling, Omm Sety lived mostly in her garden, cooking in her outdoor oven and making tea on her Bunsen burner. There was an outdoor loo with a shower area, so she rarely needed to be indoors.

People were a bit shocked by the austerity (which they saw as poverty), but Omm Sety never thought of herself as poor. "I have a lovely walled garden with animals, trees and vegetables, a serene place where I can eat, read, write and tend my animals," she claimed, "and I can always sleep under the stars." She had some wonderful dreams in this garden, astral travelling from one dimension to another. There were no houses next door to her, as the locals still thought of it as a floodplain. That meant people hadn't made their mark on the place. Her previous house was surrounded by people — too many neighbours with negative energy, polluted thoughts. They were decent people, but they were stuck in the material world, arguing about money and domestic problems, their minds muddled with gossip. It was amazing how a couple of low-minded people could suck the energy out of a place, obstruct the channels to the Otherworld. However, her house on the floodplain was teeming with energy fields, the perfect place to access the Beyond. The Temple was always a great source of energy, despite the few ignorant guards, it had been used for transformation, inner journeys and contacting the gods for thousands of years — the power was locked in the walls and columns, and came seeping through the stone pores.

The desert was also a wonderful place for astral travel as people rarely ventured into this barren realm. It was a boundless space, an expandable playground for the spirit. No wonder it was the landscape of mystics, prophets and nomads, seeking the vast solitude of distant dunes. These psychic seekers made perilous journeys through the wilderness, hoping to achieve a personal transformation, find a burning bush, a place to burn their former selves.

Nisou said her house had a peaceful atmosphere, untouched by the negative people in the village. Now that he was visiting her regularly, she couldn't resist asking him about the mysteries of the past — who was the Sphinx? What were the pyramids really about? She loved to ask the Pharaoh such questions, as he was a great storyteller, like an old scribe.

"Well, let me tell you, Lotus Flower...the Sphinx is many things, She is the goddess Sekhmet, come to teach mankind, she is also the god Horus, the constellation of Leo rising...and the pyramids are mirrors of the stars, built to draw the energy down from the heavens, so the initiated ones can travel through the cosmos as stars reborn. Of course they are much older than people think, so much older — but archaeologists don't believe it, people will have to find out for themselves . . ."

"And how old is the Osirion?"

"Oh, that is very old, since the beginning of human time—built to lead us out of the primeval flood, after the Ice Age melted, after Atlantis."

"And who were Isis and Osiris—and how did they meet?"

"I've already told you that tale."

"Nisou, tell it to me again . . ."

"I will tell you something new: about my journals under the Temple. There my secret archives are hidden in the vaults. I've written it all down—about my life, about the gods—it sits right next to the Writings of Thoth, which people think have been lost. You must find them, keep them safe—read the journals and tell the world about them."

"But I can't find a way down there—I found it once, but now I can't find the way back." Omm Sety felt she was running out of time—she didn't have the strength to lift the stone slab and drop down into the lower chambers. Hopefully another generation would find a way, have the insight to find the manuscripts and share them with the world. Soon they would be together in Amenti and she would know all the answers. No more riddles or half-finished stories...

Two days after this remarkable visit from the Pharaoh, Omm Sety was walking home from the Rest House when she fell down a hole. She thought, "Oh good. I've found my way back to the underground chamber—to the esoteric writings and the journals hidden in the vaults—King Sety will be pleased." Then all went black, and someone shouted, "I won't let you!" The cruel voice continued, "You're not to give people the truth! Go away. Don't come back!" Then she felt excruciating pain, like a sword going right through her leg. The pain was pure black, like an obsidian blade.

When Omm Sety awoke she was in hospital, a metal frame round her leg. "What am I dong here?"

The doctor tried to restrain her, "Don't try and move, Omm Sety, we've just set your leg."

How she hated hospitals with their awful rules—and now they were saying she'd broken her hip! How could I have a broken hip—just the other day I was running along the Temple roof, climbing over crumbling walls—she had taken many falls along the way but never really injured herself.

"There must be some mistake: I was down in the vaults, about to find the esoteric books, the Pharaoh's journals…" then she remembered the harsh voice, the forbidding creature blocking her way.

"My body is letting me down, breaking bones and rotting in hospital," thinking of her spirit self, the *Ba*, trying to leap out, her double self, the *Ka*, wishing to dance in the moonlight. She imagined her *Ba* and *Ka* competing for a place in her body—they both wanted top position! It was evident her body was slowing down and didn't get a say in the matter—it was just an instrument, a vehicle driving the *Ba* and *Ka* around the earth… but if she wanted to live in Eternity then her *Ba* and *Ka* would have to join forces, allowing her to become an *Akh*, an immortal being in Amenti . . .

When the hospital finally released her, Omm Sety limped around in terrible pain, relying on crutches to get her to the Temple and the café. "Apart from this broken hip, they say I have arthritis—and I've never had an ache my whole life," she complained to Sana.

"You will get better, Omm Sety, with your herbal remedies and holy water," Sana reassured her, but underneath she was very worried about her mentor, who looked terribly frail . . .

People remarked how thin Omm Sety was getting—she had always been on the chubby side, always loved her food—how strange it felt to have thin legs and arms, a flat stomach with no spare tire…perhaps she was turning into one of those scrawny cats with worms—but it was more likely that she had some serious illness—osteoporosis, cancer, or god knows what else. I have about a year left, she told herself, just enough time to get my affairs in order, prepare my body for the tomb. Her body had served her well, coping with this primitive environment, numerous bouts of malaria, dysentery and intestinal parasites; it had housed her *Ka* and *Ba* for seventy-six years—quite a feat when she'd lived in tents and tombs, often sleeping out in the desert, with no running water or modern comforts. How had I survived? *Through my love for King Sety, my devotion to Isis, and the water from the Osirion.*

Back in her garden, Omm Sety prepared herself for the Afterlife. She couldn't waste any more time in that stuffy hospital—the medics urged her return for more treatment, but she refused, "No, I can't stay another minute in that hospital—I've been there several weeks, long enough to heal the break." The rest I'll leave to Osiris.

She had already built a tomb in her garden and now it was time to decorate the inner walls with hieroglyphs from the *Book of the Dead*, to guide her safely through the Underworld. Eileen said she was being macabre. "Your health is improving every day. You could live for another thirty years—you'll probably outlive us all."

Omm Sety knew this tomb building sounded ludicrous to the Western mind, even to the locals, but the ancients prepared themselves for death as soon as they were born. They spent decades perfecting their tombs, writing their negative confessions and list of offerings for the Afterlife: one thousand loaves of bread, one thousand jars of beer, and four thousand reams of papyrus, if they were like her and loved to write . . .

"It's not such a peculiar idea when you think of it—all you have to do is wrap me in linen and pop me in the coffin. Then Anubis will guide me through the perils of the Underworld to the Hall of Judgement. I hope to fare much better this time around—I've paid my dues!"

With the tomb complete, Eileen and Omm Sety sat in the garden drinking beer and telling funny stories, their bellies aching with laughter. Omm Sety was used to terrible pain these days, but the laughter and alcohol were a welcome relief, shoulders shaking, body paroxysmal, sending waves of endorphins through her veins; waste deep in warm opiates. She still had to use crutches to get around, but Eileen wouldn't let her lift a finger. "You rest that hip, old girl— let me pour you another beer. I want you better for my next visit—there's a group of rich Americans coming in January and they want a guided tour by the famous Omm Sety—this could mean lots of baksheesh!"

"Oh, I'll certainly be better by then. I need to finish my book on Abydos, and I have several cartouches to make for a cruise. I also have a few interviews lined up—one is for a documentary about my life!"

"Word is getting round—people hear you have a connection with the past, a real bond with Isis and Osiris, and they want to feel it themselves. You give them hope—you make them believe in the Afterlife, in eternal love—and they have faith that one day they'll see their loved ones again." Eileen kissed her on the cheek, then poured her another drink.

370

Eileen was right: people were coming to see Omm Sety from all over the world. Not just for a guided tour of the Temple, but they were making a special journey just to meet her, Omm Sety. They wanted to talk about esoteric subjects, astral travel and tell her about the visions they'd had in the Temple. Some of them were quite strange, believing the Temple was built by enlightened aliens from an advanced planet. Like Eric, they'd heard about the spaceships on the frieze. "Perhaps the ancients knew how to fly—or maybe they dreamed of things to come—who knows," Omm Sety didn't like to trample on people's beliefs, no matter how way out they seemed. The ancients certainly travelled to different dimensions through their astral bodies, and this gave them advanced knowledge we have since lost.

Sometimes paranormal psychologists came to Abydos, with a crew of researchers and technical instruments to measure electrical currents and energy fields. A man called Peter Manley was a specialist on reincarnation who tried to explain the phenomenon scientifically. He had interviewed hundreds of people around the world, who claimed to have had past lives.

"I am intrigued by your case, as your memories are quite vivid, some are very specific," he began, drinking tea in Omm Sety's garden.

The woman didn't appear to be listening, all the while stroking her cat and sipping her tea. He tried another tactic, "I follow Carl Jung—I work within a Jungian framework," he explained.

"And I follow Osiris—the Temple is an Osirian framework," she replied, continuing to stroke her cat. "Osiris loved his cats. This is Horemheb, the great general who brought order to Egypt after Akhenaten's reign—we have so much to thank him for."

Peter Manley finished his tea—this woman made him a bit nervous, and he didn't know if she was pulling his leg or not. Surely she wouldn't mess about with such a serious subject. It was all about the collective unconscious, he said, an ancient memory bank of shared experience; when we delve into it we are practicing remote viewing.

"That's quite true," Omm Sety agreed, "the past experiences are trapped in the Temple and some people can access them. Some visitors to the Temple feel things, they hear music, they imagine the priestesses dancing by the shrine of Isis." But her experience was quite different. "You see, I am able to return to the past, materialise into my former self." Omm Sety stared at the incredulous scientist, his rational brain struggling to make sense of the immeasurable.

371

She didn't need to convince anybody—she had danced with King Sety in the courtyard, ran along the canal with Isis lamenting the death of Osiris…She let the man collect his data and buy her lunch at Farid's. It was no use wasting too much time with these people—they already had their ideas firmly fixed. Peter had no trouble with the reincarnation part, but the materialisations baffled him—he'd never heard of anyone actually returning to her past life, transforming into her former persona. Poor man, he meant well. She much preferred the occult lot, who believed it was possible to enter other dimensions, like the swamis and sadhus in India, or the shamans in the Americas.

"I realise people have problems with astral travel, reincarnation and materialisation. They lump it all together with spaced-out hippies, new age nutters who wear purple gowns and hand out crystals," she confided in Hanny, who had come to take some final photos for the book. The archaeological community steered clear of them, even though reports of astral travel were plastered all over the Temple walls, especially in the Osirion where the astral bodies floated through the twelve hours of night; Isis materialising before King Sety, Osiris appearing from beyond the dead . . .

Omm Sety tried to eradicate the divide between science and the esoteric. To the ancient Egyptians science and magic were one, there was no divide.

"You are a bridge between these two worlds," Hanny reminded her. It was true—she'd worked in the Temple as an Egyptologist and as a priestess; she'd used excavation tools as the former, magic and ritual as the latter, always conscious of awakening the divine within the walls. In her presence people somehow forgot about their prejudices, left aside their biases: leading archaeologists were impressed with her opinions, her sound judgement, and they were willing to believe the incredulous. It was amazing to see them put aside their left brains and follow her into the invisible. They called her the patron saint of Egyptology, a troubadour, a weaver of magical tales who brought poetry and enchantment to the serious field of archaeology. But sometimes her two lives overlapped like radio channels vying for attention. She would talk about the Temple as her home, calling Isis "my dear mother from Amenti," and describe King Sety as "still a handsome fellow, after all these years."

∧∧∧∧∧   ∧∧∧∧∧   ∧∧∧∧∧

After months of waiting, the BBC finally arrived in Abydos. "They are here to make a documentary about me! They are calling it *Omm Sety and her Egypt*—it's all about my work in the Temple and my life here over the past twenty-five years. Can you imagine, a film all about me," she wrote to her friend Eileen, after describing the sexual antics of her donkey. "He tries to mate the goat and keeps me up all night with his awful cries, his horny hee-hawing!"

The day the film crew arrived, Omm Sety was in terrible pain and she could hardly get out of her chair. "The crew were terribly kind and carried me to the set—just like Queen Twosret in her sedan!" she wrote to Eileen. The crew filmed the Temple while Omm Sety sat in her chair by the entrance, absorbing strength from the great pillars. The crew were very attentive to her needs, bringing her drinks and apologising for the delays. "We're awfully sorry this is taking so long, we need to get the light levels just right—to bring out the beauty of the Temple."

"It's quite all right, you take your time. I know how the Temple can play tricks on the light, turn it into shadows, don't be surprised if there are transparent orbs on the film, many people complain about this," she smiled at the young man called Brendan. She'd waited all these years for such a moment: to be captured on film for all eternity.

"I've always loved the pictures, ever since my childhood at the Palladium, when my father used to show the latest films. Oh, I remember the excitement, the fantasy of it all..." If only her mother and father could see her now! Little old Dorothy, starring in her own film! She felt her adolescent emotions return—they would have to take her seriously now. She laughed at her own childish reactions, sitting at the feet of Isis, with these awfully clever people with their 'high-tech' equipment from the BBC.

When the filming was over they carried her chair to the Rest House for lunch, Omm Sety floating over the desert on her magic throne. King Sety used to travel over the sands in his sedan, but never in her presence, he felt embarrassed being carried like a royal buffoon, he said, preferring to walk amongst his people. But the sedan had a practical element, his officials argued, as it prevented His Majesty's sandals and royal tunic from getting dusty—it was paramount that they remain pristine for the religious ceremonies . . .

The crew placed the chair by the table and soon the feast began. I may be disabled but I still have a hearty appetite, she thought, digging into the babaghanoush and oriental salad. Omm Sety enjoyed the sense of royalty—but couldn't help seeing the funny side of it, with its pomp and ceremony; she imagined Bentreshy being treated like a princess, and Queen Tuyu in her royal sedan, giving everyone the cold stare with her deadpan eyes. What is that temple girl doing here, sitting at my Royal Table? Tuyu never liked the Daughters of Isis—they were all too young and pretty for her liking. (How King Sety must have suffered.)

After lunch the young men carried Omm Sety back to her garden, where she fed her cats the leftovers from the feast. The lads told her the film would be ready in the spring, to be broadcast on TV.

"Not that I have a telly, but Dr Hanny must have one," she imagined, as he had a modern apartment in Cairo.

When the crew had gone, she crawled into bed in a stupor of pain, her mind fuzzy with wine and excitement, the painkillers starting to wear off. Later that evening, after a new dose of pills she hobbled round the garden on her zimmer frame, like an old woman on her last legs; her fenced-off self pushing against the metal bars. Omm Sety had never felt old until today, unable to walk to the Temple— incapable of leaping to her feet or jumping over the walls as she loved to do.

At night she fled her crippled body and escaped through the sky, hovering over the desert, the Temple roof where the solar priestess watched for the Star of Sirius, playing *senet* with her apprentice to pass the time…Omm Sety danced with Men-Maat-Ra on the rooftop, the moon illuminating their steps. They kissed, they cuddled, they pulled each other close; like a scene from an old Egyptian movie from the 1930's.

"Take me with you, back to Amenti."

"No, my darling, you cannot come with me, it's not your time—and it breaks my heart. You must go back, you have one more task to complete…and then we can be together in eternity."

Heart breaking, stream of tears, hanky waving goodbye.

"It won't be long now, my love. We will be together forever. I promise…"

More kisses and stream of tears.

Omm Sety's friends were very kind to her, bringing her food, chocolates, vitamins and health drinks, and every day Sana brought her fresh water from the Osirion spring to bathe her aching hip. Omm Sety had been taking vitamins for years, the ones Eileen sent her in the post. "You silly old goose, those are meant for the cats!"

"Omm Sety—everyone is praying for you to get well. The villagers really love you," Sana reminded her, seeing the baskets of bread the neighbours had brought her, the fresh eggs, cheese and fruit on the table. Sana massaged her bad leg with caster oil and ground cumin, which the ancients had used to treat arthritis. "We soon have you better—running with the children again."

Omm Sety forced a smile through the wall of pain, which looked more like a grimace, as the agony ripped through her leg, a stake driven through her hip. She couldn't let them know about the pain: she had one last assignment to complete—the film for *National Geographic*.

The day of filming was like a Feast Day, the members of the Chicago House came to see her, Dr Kent Weeks, Dr Lanny Bell, all the bigwigs, and the American producer Miriam Birch from Hollywood! After filming they wanted to celebrate her birthday (two months late but what does it matter?) They had a cake and candles and toasted her seventy-seventh birthday (seven hours in King Sety's version of the *Book of the Dead* in the Osirion, the seven chapels to the gods in the Temple). It was the 21st of March, the Vernal Equinox, an ancient festival celebrating the cosmic egg of creation, the birth of spring: when the sun crosses the equator on its northern journey and the hours of night and day are in equal measure. *The Temple gateway was aligned to greet the sunrise on this momentous day, and she remembered how the statue of Osiris was brought before the worshippers, who shouted, "The Lord Osiris has risen from the dead. Come forth from the Temple and rejoice with us!"*

Omm Sety hobbled to the Temple on her crutches, like a mouse caught in a trap, dragging the contraption behind her. She was becoming so thin, like the vapour at dawn, the transparent robe of

Isis. Brittle bones, left to dry in the desert. She made her way to the Temple with a bottle of beer and a loaf of bread wedged under her arm. Her body was like a gossamer veil about to blow into the desert; she was light and airy, her head a weightless balloon. Omm Sety was floating, hardly touching the ground, the mouse riding on its trap. Inside the Temple she felt her flimsy body disappear into the pillars, the Hypostyle suck her into the iconic symbols. She looked up at the image of Osiris and Isis, who smiled compassionately at her withered frame. Staring at the couple she felt herself expanding, her crutches like djed pillars raising her up; the backbone of Osiris entering her spine...

The film crew were ready, "All right. Omm Sety in the Temple, take one, and action!"

"It was very exciting back in the beginning, in 1956. My first assignment was to catalogue three thousand pieces—it was such hard work but I loved every minute of it, rebuilding the Temple has been my greatest achievement, my greatest joy." Omm Sety lit some incense and used one of her crutches to point out the murals. "There's King Sety with his son Rameses, see how they are lassoing the bull together. Rameses was such a wonderful son." She said something about the Temple being her true home, and Osiris and Isis being such loving parents, but that never made it into the film. However, they kept the bit in where she confessed to really feeling at home here, and it was said with such conviction, in a way that encouraged people to read between the lines, her blue eyes burning into the camera; the twin flames, the double lives blurred into a single entity, freeze-framed for eternity.

When the crew went back to the Rest House, Omm Sety shuffled round the Temple on her own, her crutches sliding on the polished slabs. She was in the Osiris Complex where they used to dance; the distant sound of sistra permeating the space, her nerve endings, alleviating the pain in her limbs. Omm Sety followed the flow of water from the jug in the mural, a chain of ankhs pouring onto her damaged leg. It was King Sety's libation vase with the three hearts... she remembered using it in the Temple rituals. She caught a glimpse of Isis pushing the djed pillar with all her might, lifting it out of the primeval water.

"You must go home and rest, my child. Your limbs are like feathers. Take it out of the Temple: the colours, the water, the paradise, take it all back to your little house. Now go home, my daughter and I will follow you. We will light the candle in your little shrine."

Omm Sety took all her memories out of the Temple and limped back to her house, crutches sinking into the sand, gammy leg swinging like a dead branch. Divine words resounding through her ears, like a song, a lullaby, "Take it out of the Temple—the music, the secrets, the three hearts, back to your house with the little shrine."

She was lying in bed, drifting in and out of consciousness; she had left her body so many times it was hard to know which dimension was which. She awoke to see Omm Yameena and her children hovering anxiously over her bed, smiling with concerned faces. They mopped her brow and gave her water to drink, her throat burning, heating the water up like a kettle. Opening her eyes again she saw Kebi and Inhapi coaxing her out of sleep, urging her senses to respond to water and air; instead she was breathing fire. Osama with his perplexed expression, standing in the corner (poor lad, he never really understood). She'd been negligent about the will . . . she wanted to set up a trust fund, some kind of charity to help the local children—maybe someone would do it for her . . . she wanted to tell them about the hidden chambers, the boat graves . . . Never mind, nothing I can do about it now. She would have to explain it all in the Hall of Judgement.

Omm Sety lay in her white dress, the one that looked like a cream cake. She could see herself now, lying in this white shroud, this white-out, cats clamouring over her body, wailing like professional mourners. "Stop your yowling, you'll wake the dead!" she tried to calm them, but they were possessed with uncontrollable sorrow, and when Mustafa tried to pull them off her body they attacked him with their teeth and claws, tearing at his skin and clothes. Sana knew what to do—she wrapped the cats in linen to swaddle their frenzy and carried them to the sofa. Then they wrapped Omm Sety in the rest of the linen, great reams of green and white, like a royal mummy. Yameena, Sana and their mother took the cats' place beside her body, wailing even louder.

The room went dark, the cats' eyes glowing like green lamps, emitting sulphurous beams of light. Omm Sety left the etherised figure on the bed, inside the deadly glacier.

377

"Goodbye my dear Sana, Yameena, Mustafa, Omm Yameena. Goodbye my cats, Hatshepsut, Ashotep, Horemheb, Bastet . . ."

She was wading through a deep channel, the water slimy and green. I must be in the Osirion, she thought, the geometric islands rising from the depths and leading her into a tunnel of reeds, the foliage parting like a green sea to let her pass. She passed the scenes of Nun lifting the Solar Barque out of the abyss and carrying it across the sky, King Sety prostrating himself before Osiris; then she came to the end of the *Book of Hours* — only seven, like the seven chakras, and the seven scorpions guarding Isis, Hanny once pointed out. She crawled through the tiny opening at the end of the tunnel, her hands and feet sinking in the sand, she looked back at the green reeds — there was still time go back, feed her cats and carry on, maybe live a few more years. The reeds were getting thicker now, one growing into a giant beanstalk, wide leaves choking the portal to the earthly plane. She decided not to battle with the giant beanstalk — it seemed to have a life of its own — it was some kind of mad creature with expanding tentacles, groping green fingers coming towards her. She had no choice but to claw her way out. The tunnel was getting steeper, sand sliding down to meet her, or engulf her, she didn't know which. Her ears were full of sand, grating against her auditory canal, the rattling, rasping growing louder. The sistrum shakers were coming, or so it sounded, followed by distant drummers. She detected a symbol on the wall: a naïve carving of a dog with stick legs and a square head (obviously done in haste). There it was: someone's last mark on earth, before the final plunge into the unknown. She was being rushed along now, flushed along a river of sand (or was it water?) No wonder the artist didn't have time to perfect his drawing. She slid along on her tummy, arms over her head, sledging over the sand dunes. Fractions of light were emerging through the sand, granular rays that looked like fountains of Demerara sugar. When the dust settled the tunnel became a tube of gold, her feet ringing the bells as she went along, her body striking out, appealing to the lonely chimes.

"Quick, jump in — there's little time — we have to get to the Hall of Judgement by midnight!" the voice boomed over the bells, "and this time don't try and give me the slip — I know your tricks."

There was no escaping it this time. Omm Sety looked up and saw a small barque carrying an equally small figure. She recognised the anxious face, the deep lines; the scars on her arms.

"Sheriti? Is it really you?" The guide she'd left on the bank, the day she'd escaped from the Council.

"Bentreshy, Dorothy, Bulbul, Omm Sety—I see you've lived many lives your second time around."

She sensed the woman's mocking tone—I can't blame her, poor thing. I abandoned her on the shore, her arms waving in distress . . .

"I was stuck there for two days, until the council sent a boat to rescue me," she glared at Omm Sety, green eyes gleaming with anger.

"I'm very sorry about all that—I didn't mean to leave you there—I thought they would come sooner . . . I had to get away."

"Never mind. I learned my lesson—and I have a better position now. I am licensed to sail this golden barque." Sheriti gazed up at the white sail with a sense of pride.

"You've done well for yourself," Omm Sety commended her, never imagining they had licenses in the Underworld...

They sailed through the sand dunes and into the night sky, where the grains became stars, the wind the music of the spheres, and the tunnel an endless milky way. It was quite a challenge to navigate the barque round the planets, meteorites and shooting stars, the helm bouncing as if on the open waves. Omm Sety sat on a blue and green cushion as the golden barque lunged forward, with Sheriti mastering the sails against the wind. "Not long now, Bentreshy—they're all waiting for you."

No, not long at all, she conceded, looking up at the capable figure pulling on the ropes (the woman must have her little joke, she's only been waiting three thousand years . . .)

379

16. Au-Dela: The Beyond
1981

There was no doubt Omm Sety was dead, the way she could stare into the sun, unblinking. It was over three thousand years since she'd been through the Underworld and yet the landscape hadn't changed. It was still a watery chaos, the surface bubbling in molten colours.

"This time they haven't messed about with me and put me straight in the ground," she observed, seeing no signs of post mortems or embalming rituals. But they hadn't respected her burial requests—why do mortals think they know better than the deceased? "That never would have happened in King Sety's day—not when a person had built her own tomb. Back then people respected things like that." Omm Sety had specifically asked them to bury her in the garden, along with her figurines of Bastet and Isis—but somehow she'd ended up in the desert, near the Coptic cemetery!

She'd spent months building that tomb in the garden, carving inscriptions on the walls from the *Book of the Dead,* and painting images of the Underworld. *I have come at the wish of my heart, from the pool of double fire, I have quenched. Lord of Radiance...I have come to thee...*

It was a typical ancient tomb, fit for a priestess of Isis, with scenes of the goddess leading the deceased to Amenti, with Thoth standing by in the shadows, recording the deed for posterity. But there were a few modern adaptations, like a door with hinges and a handle, so her friends could visit her whenever they wished. The exterior was painted turquoise—that way everyone would know it was Omm Sety's tomb. But then the government had intervened, said it was a health risk to bury someone in the garden. Bloody-minded bureaucrats!

Perhaps it wasn't so bad being buried in the desert, as her tomb pointed towards the Western hills, to Pega-the-Gap and the entrance to the Afterlife. Although they hadn't used the turquoise paint to decorate her tomb, instead they'd opted for a mud brick finish.

"The Christians nearly claimed my soul as one of their own, placing me just outside their cemetery," she laughed, remembering her arguments with the Coptic priest, when she'd insisted on calling Jesus 'Heru', which was his ancient name, a derivation of Horus. But if the priest thought he'd won he had another thing coming: "If only I could tell him, I am in the Egyptian Underworld and there are no angels playing trumpets."

The Hall of Judgement was a nonchalant affair, despite her fears. Anubis led her into the dark chamber and her heart was weighed on Ma'at's Scales of Justice. Her heart glowed like a green orb, she was afraid it may burn a hole in the metal and slide into the demon's mouth. But Thoth knew her heart was full of love and that there was no malice in her character; he saw the depth of her emotions, her passion for beauty, and he felt compassion for this woman, for the suffering she'd endured. Thoth recorded the result with his reed pen, "Bentreshy-Dorothy-Omm Sety, your heart is pure. You are One of the Justified. You are free to roam the Cosmos." After all that agony, running from her destiny all those years!

I am free to go—but go where? she wondered. I will head for the mountains in case they changed their minds . . . and I will go forth as Bentreshy...

"Wait a moment, Bentreshy. Before you go I have something to give you," said Thoth, holding onto her arm. "Remember the scrolls I gave you in the Temple? I know you couldn't take them home—my esoteric writing has trouble surviving in the physical realm, that's why they are known as the Lost Books . . . I want you to have your own copy, to read on your journey." Thoth handed her a green book and began reciting one of the passages:

Wisdom is hidden in the murky waters, illuminated by the fire of creation. You are a flame leaping out of the sea, you smoulder on dry land and then you change your shape.

"That's from the scroll I rescued—that day in the underground chamber," she recalled, *"You are a flame leaping out of the sea. . ."* the scrap hidden in her bra, the only visible line—the rest was smudged and torn. She read the book's title: *The Lost Wisdom of Thoth*, and then stuffed it in her pocket. "I will treasure this book—it's just like on *Desert Island Discs*—a radio program they have on earth, where you choose a book to take to your island," she turned to thank him, but Thoth had disappeared, an emerald sphere glowing in the empty space. You burn on the island, and out of the blue, you change shape.

I am a flame leaping out of the water . . . she reminded herself, heading for higher ground. Has it really been three millennia? It can't be...The Underworld felt less frightening the second time round. Despite the bubbling chaos, the red skies and inaccessible mountain peaks, she felt at home here, and that the forces around her were mainly benign. She had the feeling that any moment she would meet an old friend, but there was no one around, nothing but endless views; Bentreshy was alone in this silent wilderness.

She decided to climb the nearest peak and look for signs of life, as the Underworld was full of rich life forms, she recalled; but this time there were no flying demons to ward off, or dragons breathing green fire, and the silence unnerved her, she had to admit.

Approaching the top of the mountain she noticed a yellow dome glowing in the sky, arched like the setting sun. She saw a man sitting by the fire, roasting chunks of meat on a skewer, the smoke and odours rising in luscious spirals, inviting the senses to feast. Bentreshy's mouth began to water, her taste buds stirred by an old memory, drawing her into the circle of flames. And who was the man in the orange robe? She watched him roll his sleeves up to his elbows and turn the meat on the skewer, the juices spitting in the flames; she felt drawn to him, the way her belly was lured by the succulent smells. He felt like an old friend and a stranger all at once, and the notion frightened her: she'd seen mirages in the desert, where a sparkling pool appeared on the horizon, enticing her to run through the heat, her desire for water overpowering her burning feet and her parched throat.

King Sety let his hood fall to his shoulders, revealing his noble head and equine nose, and he turned his gaze to the hills, as if he sensed an intruder. He looked unsettled and stared at the peaks with narrow eyes, ready to denounce them. He knew how this landscape could deceive him, creating beautiful images that turned out to be illusions, and visions that were mere hallucinations. He saw a young woman coming towards him, her stride was confident and determined, yet the velocity of her pace suggested an underlying anxiety, her feet nearly breaking into a run.

∧∧∧∧∧ ∧∧∧∧∧ ∧∧∧∧∧

They sat together in silence, their bodies enclosed in a ring of smoke, unspoken words and desires emerging from the vapour. They'd met over three thousand years ago, and here they were sitting by a campfire cooking dinner, and they were overcome by the normality of this activity—how commonplace, just like real life—with the smells and smoke in their eyes, the couple getting ready for supper. A simple life they could have shared, had their lives been less dramatic. They were seeing a glimpse of this life: a portrait of a humble marriage, the roast on the skewer and the table set for two. It almost made the three thousand years seem inconsequential, as though their quest for eternal love had never been a struggle against the forces of chaos . . .

The fire burned with a furious energy, devouring the logs with flaming fangs. Bentreshy felt the heat on her skin, the hot tongues licking her face. She stared into the fire and saw a blue snake dancing in a frenzy of flames. The snake wanted to reveal itself, but it was trapped inside the flames. Then she realised the fire and the snake were one and the same: the snake was concealed in the flames; the snake was the primitive energy lurking in the embers. She was staring at the potential of the fire, the wayward spark that drives the flame. Then the blue snake settled into the blaze, hiding behind an orange veil.

The couple held hands and watched the flames die down. They were like two young lovers, feeling awkward and inept, unsure of where their passions would lead. Their emotions were embryonic, like shoots struggling through the soil, frightened of being crushed.

He was younger than she remembered him, with no wrinkles round his eyes, and his skin was taut around his jaw, as if the worries of adulthood had never touched him.

The Pharaoh sensed her surprise, "I have chosen to materialise the way I'm depicted in the murals—a blessing I had such great artists. They captured the essence of who I am, when I was twenty-eight and in my prime." He noticed Bentreshy looked older than he remembered, with fine lines appearing when she smiled and soft folds around her belly.

"I am thirty-three years old—that's when I was happiest on earth, living in Giza and excavating the past—and you were free to visit me again," she stared beyond the peaks thinking about destiny and the blue snake in the fire, suddenly coming out of the embers. She remembered what Sety had said about eternity: that one day they would have a huge wedding and live forever in Amenti. *Not much chance of that now.*

"I don't need Paradise or the Kingdom of Heaven. I would be content to live with you here in the Underworld, alongside the demons and the lost souls—they've been kind to me." Bentreshy kissed his shoulder, hoping the Pharaoh would be satisfied with this imperfect version of eternity.

"Osiris is the Lord of this land—and I hear Isis and Horus often visit him. If it's good enough for the Divine Trinity, then I'm sure we can find happiness here," the Pharaoh reasoned.

She felt like a reckless woman in love, abandoning social status for a life of passion. But wasn't that how she'd lived on earth as Dorothy? Trading the security of marriage for the uncertainty of life in Abydos, for love in the invisible realm...

Being in the Underworld wasn't so bad—they could still travel throughout the universe and materialise into different forms. If they closed their eyes they could conjure up an image of Abydos and wander through the Temple arm in arm, no longer worried who may spot them together or what the priests might say. Of course, Seth was still a threat to them, lurking behind the sand dunes, inciting chaos with his red eyes. But now they were immortal they could travel to more obscure domains and hide in the shadows of interplanetary space. They knew the spells from the *Book of the Dead* and Bentreshy still had her amulets and her black dome. Years in the Underworld had helped them anticipate a demon's motives—they could be dreadfully predictable. But Seth was the most inventive of the lot and you couldn't afford to let your guard down with him. Occasionally Bentreshy had to draw her black dome over her mind and then they would disappear to a safe corner of the universe.

One day the lovers were lying in the garden when the Pharaoh turned to her and said, "Close your eyes and imagine the black dome as a purple light. I am taking you on a trip—I know it's a little late, but I never forgot my promise."

Bentreshy closed her eyes and imagined a dome filled with purple light, and she saw herself inside a lotus flower, feeling what it was like to be in full bloom. Her mind was overcome with the strong perfume, her senses flying like drunken bees, sending her into fits of laughter. I am inside a lotus flower, she cried, swathed in purple petals. The Pharaoh was there beside her, his whole body illuminated in a violet haze.

They floated through the flower and emerged into a black sky, the stars shining with pinpricks of light. She was dressed in a beautiful light blue gown, embroidered with sapphires and turquoise gems, a silver crown upon her head. She looked at King Sety and was surprised to see him wearing a striped kilt, a gold breastplate, and the crown of Upper and Lower Egypt. The couple walked into a luscious garden teeming with plants and exotic birds, the streams of flowers tumbled down the fountains and floated round the pools. The garden was illuminated with candles and torches, and the moon offered a gentle touch of gold.

The couple strolled through the garden and everyone stared in awe, the loud chatter sinking into silence. Bentreshy felt her old fear return, she was an exile again, sensing people's disapproval. And then people started dancing round the couple, shaking their sistra and tambourines, throwing flowers at their feet. Barefoot children ran round the tables and jumped in the pools, splashing each other with squeals of delight. The hounds skulked from chair to chair, looking for tasty morsels dropped by drunken diners. Bentreshy laughed with relief: she needn't feel self-conscious in this genial gathering, as everyone had come to indulge their senses and enjoy the feast.

Even the Sage was there, leaning pensively against a pillar, observing the mayhem from a safe distance. He'd watched over the girl ever since she'd returned to earth. He even came back to earth himself—did anyone guess he was Dr Budge, that erudite yet metaphysical scholar? He wondered if Bentreshy—Dorothy ever realised. Not that he would ever tell her—he liked to keep his secrets.

The Sage finally emerged from the shadows and handed her a present—he had wrapped it five hundred years ago and the paper was a little worn. "A figure for you to worship alongside the gods, my dear. The philosopher deserves pride of place."

Bentreshy was moved by the gift. "A bust of Socrates," she smiled, stroking the philosopher's marble beard, remembering how this brave man had stood up to injustice and ignorance—willing to die for his beliefs (he too had taken poison). She didn't like to dwell on her suicide, it was such a long time ago, but people like Socrates were kindred spirits, their aspirations crushed by a tyrannical regime.

385

It was hard to believe now, how human beings had made her suffer. She looked around at the joyful figures, their faces exuding warmth and affection. She was drawn to a curious group of people who were playing together like children, laughing, dancing and singing songs. There was a rotund dwarf, a twelve-year-old girl playing a lute, a one-legged man banging on the drums while the rest of the group danced and spilled their drinks on the floor, their reflexes distorted by an abundance of wine.

"That's the Council," the Sage told her, his mouth twisting into a smile. "They don't all usually come together, but tonight all thirteen members are present. It's rumoured they like a good party."

"You don't mean the Council of the Gods in Amenti?" Bentreshy stared at the odd group of people in disbelief: some were trying to belly dance while others lay on their backs counting stars, cheering and clapping whenever they spotted a meteorite.

The Sage sniggered with amusement, the folds of his robe creasing round his belly. He'd never seen the girl look so stunned, so completely wrong-footed, her usual composure ambushed by astonishment. He enjoyed the way her face flushed and her eyes went wide as gold coins. Her mind was trying to reassess its former beliefs; trying to comprehend how a group she'd feared for so long could be frolicking like children, dancing, singing out of tune and falling over the dogs.

The one-legged drummer spotted the girl and he promptly missed a beat, his ill-timed tempo causing the dancers to bungle their steps. He stopped drumming and stared across the garden, his hands suspended in mid air; his fingers trembling with the energy of the drum, the rhythm still resonating in his pores.

"She's here!" the man whispered to the others, his drumstick slipping to the ground. His voice was barely audible and yet through the silence it seemed to grow in magnitude, so that it sounded more like a shriek, and everyone turned to look at the new arrival who was causing such a commotion.

Bentreshy felt their eyes upon her, like ravens pecking her skull. For a moment she wanted to run, but instead she faltered, unsure of where to place herself. The Council members formed a close circle around her; she was like a fish in a bowl, forced to swim in a loop— although this bowl was made of human bodies and everywhere she turned she saw a concerned face. Their expressions confused her—

what was it she saw—fear, pity—compassion? *No, they were out to kill her. She was a hunted animal and now she was trapped.*

"King Sety! Help me!" she shouted, but King Sety had disappeared, or they had taken him away.

She fell to her knees, her ribcage sinking into her intestines. She began to cry, her tears flowing from a river inside her; a dam bursting from the back of her throat and leaking through her eyes.

"There's no need for tears, my child. He'll come back. Things aren't as bad as all that—come on, dry your eyes—that's no good at all." A hand reached out and gave her a tissue, and she held it to her nose, the scent of rosemary warming her nostrils. That's what people used to say on earth, she remembered, *chin up...pull yourself together, things aren't so bad.* Reassuring maxims designed to cheer you up and help you carry on. She had the feeling these people hadn't said these things for quite some time—they seemed out of practice. They hadn't seen anyone cry for a while either and the sight surprised them, watching tears fall like rain in the desert.

The one-legged man stepped forward, breaking the circle wide open, the light streaming into the centre. She could make a dash for it, the one-legged man would falter, the others distracted by his teetering frame. But instead she stood quite still, like a lizard waiting for the jackal to make a move.

"My name is Djutmose," he shook her hand, his grip binding her to this place. "We are the Council of the Gods. Our job is to help people find their way to Amenti. Some souls get lost along the way—it's most unfortunate as they have such a struggle on their own. If only they would trust us, instead of fleeing us in fear, as if we are out to punish them."

She detected the sadness in Djutmose's eyes, the disheartened look of someone misunderstood. She looked up at the other members and felt a sudden wave of tenderness, a streak of gentle sunshine. Bathing in this circle of warmth, the intensity was almost painful; they didn't speak and yet she knew their stories—how they tried to create a bridge from the Underworld to Amenti, to help the lost souls find eternal peace. *Time is a circle where all the curves are linked, revolving round each body, including the heavens.*

She heard about her own journey, that spanned three millennia. How she struggled to evade the Council and make her own way in the universe. She survived admirably they thought, never giving into the demons or the forces of Seth and his endless temptations.

Bentreshy closed her eyes and she saw the waters of chaos, the dark sea moving in aimless waves. There were creatures with fins and flapping gills, hollow mouths and googly eyes. A yellow fish hovered in the shadows, with leopard spots and eagle eyes, searching for a tasty organism. The life forms floated in the sea, their scaly fins gliding through the water, carried by the whims of the waves. They had given themselves over to the unpredictable nature of the sea; Bentreshy remembered being such a creature, her pliable form adapted to liquid, yielding to the gentle force.

She opened her eyes and saw the Council members lying on plump cushions, sipping pomegranate wine from alabaster cups. She sat next to Djutmose and the young girl called Maatkari, who poured her a drink and told her a story.

"The journey began in the sea, when there was no sight of land as far as the eye could stretch. Then out of the chaos a mound began to form and some of the more adventurous creatures crawled ashore. At first the dry earth felt uncomfortable, their soft bellies unaccustomed to the rough surface, and after a quick look around, they slid back into the warm waters where they felt more at home. Over time the creatures stayed on land for longer periods, basking in the sun and lying idly on the rocks. Geb, the earth god, heard about these strange creatures who came from the sea and he decided to pay them a visit. He saw they were intelligent creatures who wanted to learn more about this new world on land, who weren't content to stay in the ocean with their own kind. Geb was surprised by these creatures, as they wanted to change into something else—they were the first ones to look to the sky, who had the potential to be like the gods. He told the creatures about his wife Nut, the sky goddess, and how if they followed her pattern of stars then one day they would discover eternity.

Geb decided he would help them with their quest and turned the little mound into a large island. He gave them a boat and set them on their way. The creatures sailed over the waters of chaos until they came to the sizeable mass of land, and when they started building their homes they remembered the first mound of creation in the shape of a triangle. They built pyramids throughout the land, so they would never forget the first act of creation, and to alert the gods that they were on their way to eternity."

Bentreshy imagined herself standing by a pyramid, grateful to the gods for leading her out of chaos. She climbed up the slabs, feeling each warm stone under her feet, and thinking how every block was a step closer to the sky goddess; to understanding the universe and achieving our destiny. She was on top of the pyramid now, staring into the indigo sky, her mind joining the stars together, forming complex patterns, and when she focused her eyes she could detect a spiral sequence. There were so many stars her eyes began to dance from one to another, the diamonds of light bouncing from the infinite sheet of sky. The dots formed a bow across the sky and Bentreshy followed the archway with her eyes, outlining the silhouette of a woman's body, back gently curved, her hair flowing like strands of silver, her limbs looping round the firmament. Suddenly the figure peeled itself from the sky and leaped free. Nut stood upright and shook the stardust from her hair, and then she fell from the sky like a meteor, a trail of fire streaking behind her.

Nut landed on the pyramid, all silver and indigo, and Bentreshy could smell the fire radiating within the sky goddess, her body was blue as the night sky and her skin was covered in stars, like fluorescent moles. Nut wore a transparent robe to soften the bright stars, so the intensity wouldn't blind our mortal vision and we could gaze with our naked eyes. When she moved her arms she sent a cloud of dust into the air, forming new planets in the cosmos. Inhaling the silver particles Bentreshy felt the enormous sky take hold of her insides and settle into the cavities. She wondered if these particles could take root, like seeds, and would grow into stars.

Nut wrapped her arms round Bentreshy, stretching them like elastic bands. *Just like in the murals,* she thought, *I am like the sky, the goddess embracing my frame.*

"I am here to show you the stars—you have seen them from the earth and travelled past them in the Underworld, and now it's time to pay them a proper visit." Nut held her hand and leaped into the air, the silver dust propelling them into the atmosphere. Each star had its own character and could teach us about life, said Nut. There was love, hate, wisdom, ignorance, desire and apathy. There were stars for every facet of existence: first there was chaos, and out of chaos came our desire for harmony.

"After death the soul ascends to the heavens and becomes a star. These constellations you see are millions of *Bas*," Nut pointed to the circumpolar stars, the array orbiting the North Star. "They are called the Imperishable Ones, because their light never disappears, they never dip below the horizon."

Bentreshy spotted the green and yellow star within the Imperishable Ones: Sekhtey was still shining upon her . . . my son, the brightest star in the heavens. Sekhtey flashed his green light. "I love you, mother, one day you will be a star shining in my galaxy. . ."

She flew round the constellations, divided into thirty-six sectors, thirty-six gods of heaven ruling for ten days at a time, the remaining five days being the feast days of the gods. This is how the sky gave us 365 days of the year, the celestial way of measuring time. They passed Ursa Minor, Ursa Major and the Sirius Star—the principal fire for the sun, the inner Eye of Ra.

Glancing at the myriad of stars, she heard Nut say, "Humans are the link between the sea and the earth—they have traversed the two. They are ladders suspended between these different realms. They exist in an alien place—they dream about their aquatic past and yet they are shackled to their earthly existence—they are not quite at home in either place. And so they look to the sky and long to explore the hidden galaxies. The ladders are set against the heavens—when people look up they see the universe and recognise it as their destiny. But they can't help looking down into the precipice, seeing the empty spaces between the rungs. And then they falter and start to feel afraid. Their knees tremble and they haven't the strength to climb any higher; regretfully they come back down to earth, their sense of failure tightening round their hearts. Since the beginning of time man has searched for a stairway to heaven, and even songs have been written about it. But how to make them realise: man is the stairway, suspended over many worlds, swinging from fish to sage."

Bentreshy remembered the Sage telling her, "Man is a viaduct, spouting desire, but he is full of cracks. He is suspended over the earth and he carries water to an unknown destination. You could say he carries his past towards his future. He is travelling to a future he has not yet mapped out."

Nut turned to her and said, "We feel compassion for mortals because their sights are bound to the physical realm. They have trouble imagining an existence free from material constraints, where they can transform themselves into beams of light and a myriad of colours. They have difficulty thinking what will happen in 100,000 years from now, or what will happen after death. . ."

Bentreshy had never thought of it this way: that human beings were on a journey and yet they didn't have a map, didn't know the final outcome. If only we knew there was some kind of destiny at the end of it, a place of refuge. But perhaps it was the uncertainty that made us search in the first place. The desire to find answers made us explore the universe . . . maybe all travel was a quest to find ourselves.

Nut felt compassion for us because we knew we had a greater purpose, one we rarely achieved, because we couldn't fathom its esoteric nature. Instead we spent our lives trying to survive, tied to the routine of daily life. And yet there were moments in the day when we felt we were capable of so much more. What if we were only at the beginning of our journey? What we thought of as civilisation was really only the initiation. . .

We were meant to be these highly evolved beings, but we weren't evolved enough to shape our existence, Bentreshy realised. And yet we came equipped with the ability to imagine—we could see glimpses of eternity, we felt the potential rising in our viscera, our higher selves whispering promises, hinting at what we may become.

They had circled the planets and were now hovering over Venus. It's about the same size as Earth, thought Bentreshy, orbiting the sun in a swirl of sulphurous clouds—except it was revolving the other way!

What a thrill to float through the galaxy—and there were a hundred billion other galaxies, arms extending like solar tentacles. Then she suddenly began to fall through space; the rungs slipping off the ladder. Rushing along a river of silver mist, mounds of green sulphur oozing from the surface, *I could keep falling forever inside this galaxy that never seems to end.* Looking up she saw the fiery solar system catapulting her through space, like a shooting star. There was Nut arched over the sky again, her body a needlepoint of stars, her hair shafts of light.

Bentreshy passed an arras of asteroids on her way down; or maybe I am standing still and they are moving, she mused, the asteroids flying by with such speed, like celestial snowballs. The stars were reflected in the planets, specks of silver embroidered onto green and purple spheres. How beautiful they look, she thought, the stars decorating the planets like sequins on a dress. Then she was shocked out of her reverie by a sudden jolt; gravity tightening round her waist like a weight belt, pulling her down. She landed in some reeds next to a river, amazed by the vivid green, so dazzling after the blue universe. The current looked quite strong, pulling the papyri towards the surface so they appeared to be crouching down to drink, or pray. Their thin leaves were shaking in the wind, making soft rustling noises, as though whispering secrets to one another. How wonderful these plants were—capable of making reams of paper, creating a labyrinth of words out of pulp. The earliest form of letter writing began, thanks to these green stems, bending over to meet the river. A birth, a bang, a mound of stories leaping out of the silence, making history suddenly coherent.

Bentreshy sat with her feet in the river, surrounded by a canopy of green; you'd never imagine you'd get such lovely creamy paper from such a weedy looking plant, she thought. It was a funny thing to think, considering she had just fallen from the sky.

She was startled by a creature hidden in the reeds; through the bands of light a bird-shaped head emerged, with a green face and a curved beak. The creature stood on two legs and had the body of a man, dressed in a linen tunic and carrying a palette, a jar and several reed brushes. She recognised Thoth as depicted in the murals, dressed in his formal attire as divine patron of scribes.

"We meet again, Daughter of Earth. I am here to teach you about the importance of writing—thanks to the written word we have archives, history, and most of all, people's memories." Thoth hesitated, like an old scholar lost in thought, he was distracted by a stirring in the undergrowth. Bentreshy peered through the reeds and saw a shadowy figure, who also had a bird-shaped head and rounded beak. But the figure had a more slender build, with gentle curves and shapely breasts protruding from her robe. *This must be Seshet*, Bentreshy realised, *the goddess of writing, keeper of records, temple measurements, and wife of Thoth.*

Seshet emerged into the clearing, her black wig streaked with green, the weeds entwined in her hair like green ribbons. She looked at Bentreshy in a gentle manner. "In order to understand the written word we have to start at the beginning—with papyrus." Seshet pulled a leaf from her hair and rubbed it with her fingers, the green surface shining in the sun. The stem was yellow in parts, hinting at the creamy interior that could be moulded into sheets of paper.

Seshet and Thoth took her along the river, where a sea of papyrus clung to the shore, the leaves stretched out like green fingers, reaching for the water. They waded into the jungle of papyrus; Bentreshy felt the potential, the energy radiating from the stalks. A green maze of words. She heard the plants whistling tunes; the power of language locked inside them. All she needed was the key, the right symbols, and she could unlock their mysteries.

Bentreshy watched the farmers pull the plants up by the roots, then they carried the bundles back to the warehouse where they were cut into long strips and woven together in layers. They pounded the wet stalks with stones until the pieces blended together and formed a pulpous, fleshy tissue. Once the sheets had dried in the sun they produced crisp pieces of paper for the scribes to write on. No one valued the papyrus plant more than the scribe—only after years of formal training were they permitted to write on papyrus. They first practised their writing on stone slabs, where they learned to form the intricate symbols with their reed brushes and the liquid soot they used as ink. And once they had mastered the eight hundred odd hieroglyphs, then they were ready to write on papyrus.

Bentreshy had been a natural: her teachers had noticed her proficiency at an early age: the way she drew the glyphs in a delicate hand, the lines precise and stylised; the girl possessed an aesthetic awareness beyond her years, her symbols were clearly defined and highly artistic. Inhapi had made an exception for her—after four years of schooling she had mastered all the hieroglyphs and was so skilful with her pen that her teacher had given her reams of papyrus to record the daily prayers. Such a shame she didn't become a scribe—she'd have saved herself a lot of trouble. But no—she had her heart set on being a priestess. She was chosen by Isis, they said—the girl had little choice in the matter.

She closed her eyes and saw a zigzag, a mountain, a hand, an eye. There were geometric shapes: lines, circles, squares and triangles. They were symbols that made up words, a language revealing ideas, stories and prayers:

Leave the earthly world and rise to infinity. You are the mountain peaks and the ocean floor. You are all dimensions and all time; the unborn child and the old crone, deceased and yet reborn. All things exist within you—fire, air, water, earth, and your destiny is to know them all. You sing a hymn, you carve the symbols and the story is told.

Her head began to tingle, the messages travelling to her brain and forming into patterns, making connections with her nerve endings. Bentreshy remembered how the sacred texts of Thoth can activate certain parts of the brain; that these works of magic can open pathways in the mind and the reader is then able to enter a deeper stage of consciousness. Within this deeper reality you can experience the divine realm, you enter the hidden world of the gods; the veil of mundane consciousness temporarily slips and you see through the eyes of the Eternal Ones. Think of the words as keys unlocking a door in your head.

It was all in the *Wisdom of Thoth*: how to awaken the mind with the ancient mysteries; by reading the arcane texts you were sending secret codes to your brain, and in order to decipher them the psyche must open a hidden dimension. Inside this realm you can see infinity; your perception wide as the gods, you bathe in bliss and understanding; you are at one with all living things.

She watched Thoth open his green book, the tablets glowing like slabs of jade as he turned the pages. She read the hieroglyphs as fast as possible, the pages spinning past her, the symbols rushing to her brain in a blur, the shapes merging, separating and synthesising into new colours, like chemistry. She felt her cells regenerate, the words flowing through her arteries and revealing secrets. With each symbol her mind absorbed she was being offered a key to immortality.

The books had been lost for thousands of years, ever since the temples were closed and the ancient knowledge went underground, hidden in earthen jars and buried in the desert. If only they had looked beneath the Temple in Abydos, they would have found a clue to their whereabouts. In the modern age, those who studied Hermeticism or read the tarot cards got a glimpse of the Old Books, Thoth's wisdom hidden in the cryptic symbols.

King Sety often read the Wisdom of Thoth—he kept it in a golden box in the chamber of Ptah. When he was dying he instructed his son Rameses to hide the box in the Underground Archives, where it remains to this day. And after death, when he began his journey through the netherworld, Sety found himself living out the words he'd read in the *Books of Thoth*, about the transmigration of the soul, his body turning from flesh into light, colour and sound.

King Sety sat on a rock and began to meditate. A green dragon stood before him, exuding flames and billows of purple smoke. Sety hid behind the stone, but the creature turned his fire into water and began to smile. "Don't be afraid, my son. You have read the Words of Thoth and I am here to show you what they mean. I am Osiris, god of regeneration, god of green things."

Osiris told the Pharaoh about the Divine Universe and the Transcending Mind beyond our physical senses; beyond fear and oppression. They sat in silence within the circle of green light, and Sety had to shelter his eyes from the intense glare. The light was the spiritual energy of the universe, the Healing Power of Isis, and from this divine light Osiris was able to restore himself to life. It was the eternal flame that defied death, the light that eclipsed the darkness, order over chaos. "But all is not in harmony—the universe you inhabit is tipped towards chaos and darkness," said Osiris, the light flickering as if to confirm this statement.

"What can I do to restore order to the world?" King Sety asked Osiris. "I will do whatever it takes to make things right. How I wish to live in truth again. I possessed the mysteries of the adepts, but then I was made to forget. I became a lost soul, haunted by the memory of the sacred realm and the wisdom I once held. While on earth I experienced human love and realised that love was the closest thing we have to the Cosmic Mind. Yet I fear I didn't value this love enough and I let it slip away. When Bentreshy died the light went out of my being. Once she had gone my *Ka* began to wither like a flower in the desert."

"You ask how you can restore order to the world. First you must hear the story of how order came into the universe, when all was but a muddled chaos:

One day a Word manifested out of the vapours; the Word rose in the shape of a great pillar and hovered over the surface, resounding over the waves to the shore. No one understood this Word and people heard it as the waves crashing on the shore, but Thoth heard the Word as the Voice of the Light; he knew there was truth in this Voice and that it could overcome the darkness. He wanted to give this insight to humankind who were blinded by ignorance. This would be his gift to the world. He paid Isis and me a visit, and he told us about the Voice of the Light and the great pillar, and how we could lead the people out of chaos. Thoth showed us how it was possible to turn ideas and stories into written words; he taught us the wisdom of the gods, and showed us the benefits of a civilised society. Soon we became the gods' representatives on earth: we showed our people how to farm, how to read and write, and how to live in communal harmony. But the forces of chaos didn't want people to hear the Voice of the Light, and the demons rose up from the swamps and joined the legions of Seth in the desert, who wished to destroy our knowledge of the light.

Seth murdered me and watched the light fade into darkness, the pillar sink into the murky waters. But Thoth and Seshet wouldn't let the Voice of the Light be silenced—they had created the Written Word and they wouldn't allow the world to return to illiterate chaos. Thoth advised Isis to gather my remains and use her healing powers to restore the light to my body. And when Horus was born, Seshet told Isis to hide him in the papyrus plants, where the wise tales would nurture his imagination, long before the scribes had written them down.

The pillar rose up from the depths and became the Voice of the Light once more; the pillar moulding itself into my backbone, so when I rose from the dead I brought with me the word of truth and the gift of immortality. My green face reborn, radiating with Thoth's wisdom.

"Remember this transcendence was orchestrated by Isis, she is the deity beyond fate—she can modify the destiny written in the stars," Osiris reminded King Sety, as Isis taught the world about love.

"Out of all the voices on earth, the words of love are the most powerful. Human love is the most potent expression of all, and epitomises the Voice of the Light. Love takes us out of brutality—it is understanding and compassion. It is the flame of the universe, a million things and yet one."

King Sety saw a white cloud in the sky, dancing on the horizon in the shape of a woman, her silhouette reclining over the hills. Then the woman stood up and walked towards him, the haze evaporating as she advanced; the figure appearing before him as an average-sized woman. Isis stood behind a translucent veil, worn to protect her mystery, the way the mist shields the glare of the sun.

Throughout the ages people had called upon the healing powers of Isis; they spent the night in her temples, and in return she visited them in their dreams, offering relief from their troubles. Sety knew her temple in Philae was the last refuge of the old gods, after the Christian patriarchs had silenced their voices. And Philae was the last refuge for the old language, the hieroglyphs engraved on a crumbling wall; the final words of Thoth. Then their meaning would sink into the mute stones, and soon people would forget their own language. For two thousand years they would lie unread, a symbol of man's ignorance. Just squiggles on a wall.

Isis and Osiris disappeared into the sunlight, their white robes merging into blue sky.

Sety found himself in a circle of trees, coloured lanterns flickering through the branches, creating a rainbow of light. His *Ka* trembled like the stars, their pale light shivering in the night sky, as if they felt the cold. He had the sense that something was about to happen: maybe he would see a shooting star, or witness an eclipse of the moon. The atmosphere had an ephemeral quality; neither night nor day, and yet the sky was dark and the sun had made its way to the Underworld. He began to feel alone, standing in this circle of light, seeing the vast universe through the leaves. He was a solitary figure free to wander where he pleased, and yet he craved companionship, a sense of unity.

"You're not alone," he heard a voice utter through the trees. Sety felt his *Ka* writhing inside his flesh, struggling to break out; his *Ka* was in pieces, shattered by years of remorse and loneliness. He saw a light hovering in the sky, and his *Ka* started floating upwards, as if drawn by a magnet. The light was coming towards him, the strength returning to his *Ka* and uniting with his *Ba*; he was becoming whole again, like a jug filling with water. Bentreshy was coming to claim him, to retrieve the lost soul that belonged to her.

She was close to him now, he could see her mysterious smile, her mouth like the crescent moon, offering hidden truths. She offered only half the truth, the other side concealed behind the shadows. But I am the other side, he realised, his stunted self magnified in her presence, his fractional vision made whole. Their *Kas* flew together and fused into one being, the sparks of light and bright ether sending shockwaves through the universe. They stared at one another, seeing themselves reflected in the other, as if looking at a self-portrait. *How painful it had been to live apart.* Sety stepped aside and watched her from a distance, his eyes searching this woman who possessed the secret of his happiness. She was wearing a purple robe with pockets on either side. If he looked inside he would find his heart in one pocket, his organs in the other. As if Bentreshy had the canopic jars, keeping his viscera all these years. (He couldn't get used to the fact he didn't need them anymore.) He didn't want them back, his inner organs were just for show, a reminder of his human form.

They kissed and cuddled, Bentreshy stroking his soft skin, scented with perfumed oil. Despite being immortal they couldn't abandon the flesh. She started to laugh and suddenly cry, great tears rolling down her face, reminding her of rain. She missed the bodily functions as she missed the rain; the drizzle on the South Downs, the rough heather soaking her legs.

They had missed out on all those emotions—the crying, the laughter, the tender caresses, the angry gestures. They'd missed out on a life together, and now they wouldn't give it up for anything, even for the divine realm—they didn't want to become a beam of light.

Bentreshy felt like a figurine they'd once excavated, its magic powers still intact. A Hathor figure, once used in a love ritual and then buried in the Temple garden in a fusion of herbs and cat's milk. How many times have I been unearthed and given another chance at life? She remembered her life as Dorothy, her first dig in Giza: the white skulls bleached by the sun, the bones, the pottery, the mounds of sand and papyri, all fused together in complex layers. The wind blows and you inhale the dusty bones, whirling from desert to sea and across continents. Thinking about all the tombs she'd excavated, measured and sketched; how much of her life had been concerned with death...

She remembered being in Saqqara: exploring the tombs in her bare feet, the limestone slabs warming her bones. And when no one was there she would take off her clothes and wander round the chamber, her naked body close to the immortal one, his last home before the journey to Amenti. She'd wander through the passageways, the rubble crunching under her feet, searching through the fragments with her bare hands, fingers sifting through the millennia of bones. It wasn't the pretty things she remembered most—it was the bones, the sand and the rough stones. The digging, the scraping, the dirty fragments she'd cleaned and put back together. After a day's work at the Temple in Abydos—she remembered the rawness, the dust, the stains on her feet, the sweat and dirt caked onto her face.

I never grew up. I was always playing in the sandbox. Even as an old woman she had the eyes of a child, and that always startled people (perhaps even frightened them). They never knew how old she was. Her body told them one thing, her eyes told them another. Her face was impish, mischievous, sometimes her lips quivered, as though she were about to burst out laughing—even at the end, on her deathbed...

Bentreshy awoke to find Sety standing over her, and she jumped in fright—remembering his first visit to her Edwardian bedroom, how he'd nearly choked her with his enthusiasm. Sety laughed, "Don't worry, my love. I have come to take you home, where you are Mistress of the Temple."

Where is home? she wondered, having wandered through the vast cosmos for thousands of years she had lost track of places.

Sety was dressed in a gold tunic and magnificent nemes—wherever they were going he had dressed for the part (or perhaps overdressed). He took her hand and they flew through the air, beams of light flying past her, the planets spinning like coloured plates. They were flying with such velocity that her eyes began to weep, the planets merging into curious shapes, the colours dripping down the sky. When she opened her eyes they were in a courtyard, with white stones and great columns painted in vivid hieroglyphs, as if they'd been done yesterday. It was the Temple in perfection, with no sign of decay.

She missed the ruins and the fallen statues. Sometimes Bentreshy returned to the old Temple on earth and wandered round the stone ruins, lamenting the fallen grandeur. All the more striking because they were broken, tinged with tragic finery; the murals clinging to life, desperate to preserve their beauty. We live life as if we're immortal, and yet we know we have to die. She lingered by the image of Isis on her throne, Sety prostrating himself, offering the goddess a plate of fruit, bagels and poultry—enough to upset even a divine stomach! But he meant well and Isis was pleased with the offering. The paintings were dazzling, even after three thousand years. They told of mystery, magic, the realm beyond the five senses and three dimensions.

People come to the Temple and they remember something ancient, stored in the brain like an old address, somewhere they once lived — they can't remember much, but they know they were happy there. They leave the Temple and they never forget this feeling; they carry it inside them like a seed.

∧∧∧∧∧   ∧∧∧∧∧   ∧∧∧∧∧

Bentreshy sees a girl standing in the chamber of Isis: it's Abbie, the woman she'd seen in Blackheath. Abbie lights a stick of incense and wafts it over the mural. Her face is an expression of true bliss, as though she's found her lost mother. She begins to cry, they are slow tears because they are a valve; they are a leak rather than a burst, and they trickle like a tiny stream, leaving a slight trail on her dusty cheek. The tears are an opening, clearing the debris of everyday life, allowing the magic to penetrate her skin; palms stretched out, ready to receive. Abbie is shedding her ordinary self now, the mystic energy has infiltrated her pores and she radiates with a soft glow; the golden light of the chamber has claimed her, lit her up inside. She can hear the goddess, understand her wisdom, her healing energy. Like a cat jumping on her lap—at first giving her a jolt and then coating her belly in warm fur and purrs. Abbie never wants to leave the chamber, she wants to stay here with Isis, basking in her wisdom, her image radiating with healing colours. Then she hears a message: *Take it out of the Temple and tell the story. Take this knowledge with you and you will never forget.*

Bentreshy floats quietly around the Temple, trying not to disturb Abbie, who is opening herself to the goddess. She hides behind a column when Abbie walks past, dancing round in spirals and leaping into the shadows. Abbie can sense a young presence in the space and she begins to dance in response, imagining a young girl dancing for Isis, awakening the stones with her nimble movements. She is reclaiming the female space, calling upon the Daughters of Isis...

Bentreshy is glad people come to the Temple and are still moved to tears. How wonderful the murals hold such a power, after all these years. The images of Isis and Osiris can still lead people to the Other

400

World. Unfortunately most people just traipse through on tours and miss the sublime experience. But occasionally people come on their own and they wander in silence round the intimate chambers; they sit at the foot of the columns, they meditate on the finely painted murals, and something happens. They see another dimension, much deeper, brighter, more magical than they ever imagined—and they leave transposed. They return to their daily lives with a new sense of beauty, a sense of hope—at the end of their excursion another journey begins, where Isis and Osiris are waiting for them in the ether. Of course, these visitors tell very few souls about their experience, as they realise most people would ridicule them (cynicism has crushed this sense of magic in a lot people, their mundane lives have little place for enchanted realms).

When the Temple closed for the day, Sety and Bentreshy strolled around the garden arm in arm, like an elderly couple who'd spent their lives together. They could have been one of those earthly couples, with the candlelit dinners, the walks in the evening; they could have shared a bed and woken up in each other's arms. They see this life drawn in the sand.

Sety wrapped his arms around Bentreshy, drawing her close to his breast. They were like any mortal couple in love: holding hands, staring tenderly into each other's eyes. They appreciated the small things, the tiny gestures, the repetitions of day to day life. To them it signalled continuity, eternal love.

Bentreshy caressed his forehead and slid her fingers down his cheek; his skin softened with olive oil, a touch slippery, like wet marble. She traced his Pharaonic nose down to his mouth; he had the white teeth of a Berber, one who lived on goat's milk and desert hare. His body personified every aspect of Egypt: the deft hands of an artisan, the strong feet of a labourer and the swift legs of a warrior, designed to sprint through the desert unheard. King Sety was like Osiris, his body parts embedded in the heart of Egypt.

Sety smiled at her with his elliptical eyes, sometimes brown, sometimes purple. Today they seemed plum coloured, like cups of wine. Bentreshy smiled back at him, her eyes were like exploding stars, radiating blue particles of light. Sometimes their colour resembled a faience bowl the moment it hit the floor, exploding into a million slivers of light. Those eyes had haunted him for thousands of years and whenever he dreamed about Bentreshy he awoke to find these blue beams shining down from the ceiling.

They'd experienced the paradise of love and suffered the torment of loss. They'd fought the demons of Seth and joined forces with Isis and Osiris to restore harmony to the world.

"We are just like any normal couple," Bentreshy liked to say. They lay by the river, her head resting on his lap, staring into the blue sky.

"Look, there's an ibis!" she pointed above; he followed her delicate finger towards the brown and white wings, flapping like expanding sails.

"How does that old story go? When the ibis returns to the marshes, Egypt will rise from the ashes and flourish once again." Bentreshy waded into the river to watch the bird land, tucking his wings neatly inside his body, his spindly legs gracefully breaking the surface and sliding into the river. We may be creatures of land but we never forget the water, for this is our beginning.

Sety took off his robe and followed her into the river; this was where our love blossomed, like the papyri embedding their deep roots in the mud. The ibis foraged for snails along the west bank, clearly visible, yet out of reach.

Author's Notes

Harp of Joy is a work of fiction, although the time periods and historical events are factual. I referred to place names, gods and goddesses by their 'modern' names, as coined by the ancient Greeks: Abydos, Thebes, Isis, Osiris, etc. as this is how they were known in Omm Sety's time. I have also chosen her spelling of 'Sety' and not 'Seti', as used by most Egyptologists. As Ancient Egyptian is a phonetic language, more than one vowel sound can be applied to the same word.

In Abydos, Dorothy Eady was affectionately called Omm Sety: Mother of Sety, the name of her only son, which was a rural custom. Apart from Omm Sety and Hanny el Zeini, the characters in Abydos have been given fictional identities, although they are based on people who lived in the village during Omm Sety's time.

Omm Sety and Dr Hanny's book, *Abydos: Holy City of Ancient Egypt*, was a great source of information, as was *The Search for Omm Sety*, by Jonathan Cott, and *Omm Sety's Egypt*, by Hanni el Zeini and Catherine Dees. When writing about Abydos, Omm Sety's two other books provided enormous insights into her life and character: *Omm Sety's Abydos* and *Omm Sety's Living Egypt*, edited by Nicole B Hansen. Other useful books were: *Circle of Isis*, by Ellen Cannon Red, *Hathor Rising*, by Alison Roberts, and *The Hermetica*, by Timothy Freke and Peter Gandy.

Egyptologists differ over the period of Sety I, claiming he reigned anywhere from 1313-1279 BC. I have chosen 1324-1279 BC as the period for his life and 1306-1279 BC for his reign, making him thirty-four when he met Bentreshy. As there are no historical records noting when Bentreshy lived, I have placed her birth in 1304 BC and her death in 1290 BC.

When I first visited King Sety's Temple, I was struck by the ethereal space and light; the feminine energy radiating from the chamber of Isis, where it all seemed to begin. It is a place to worship and celebrate, and has been for thousands of years—a place resonating with beauty and wonder. I dedicate this novel to the Isian priestesses of Abydos, and the wonderful artists who made King Sety's Temple the most artistic temple in Egypt.

Acknowledgments

Many people helped make this book a reality. As always, my husband Keith, who engaged in endless conversations about ancient Egypt over the years and helped me formulate my ideas. My parents, Elizabeth and Andrew, for their love and support, for inspiring me to carry on. Leslie Zehr, Chloe Patra and Bianca White, I appreciate your sisterhood and connection with Isis; Martine Bailey for sending me insightful articles, for your friendship and sound advice.

We are all indebted to Dr Hanny el Zeini, who guarded Omm Sety's journals and kept her memory alive, Jonathan Cott, for bringing the story to the world's attention. Thank you to Catherine Dees, for her eloquent writing of *Omm Sety's Egypt* and for her encouragement and support.

I learned a great deal from the people of Abydos: Gamal, Ameer, Shahad, Mahmoud and Ahmed, who shared their stories and memories with me, and confirm that Omm Sety's legacy still lives on in the village. Special gratitude goes to Ameer Sayeed, who knew Omm Sety when he was a young man and is full of wonderful stories about her. He has an ancient connection with the temple and is a fountain of knowledge. Thank you to Anne Killeen for her visionary drawings of ancient Egypt and her deep knowledge of Abydos, having lived there for several years. Many other people shared their memories and photographs of Omm Sety with me and I appreciate them all.

The Egyptian Ministry of Antiquities was very encouraging and granted me access to the tomb of King Sety I in Luxor and the Osirion in Abydos. The staff at the Cairo Museum and the British Museum were most patient and let me pore over the treasures undisturbed. To Omm Sety's friends: Maureen Tracey, Lanny Bell, Kent Weeks and all the staff at the Chicago House, thank you for your insights.

Thanks again to Ahmed el Balal at Petra Travel for his graceful efficiency. Further gratitude to Martin Bailey for his creative cover design, Michael Howell-Walmsley for his IT support and Sylvie Nantais for her excellent editing work. I am grateful to the staff at Hathor Press, who saw the magic in the Omm Sety story.

A special thank you to all the people who bought the first book and encouraged me to write *Harp of Joy*. To my friends on Facebook, who have given me great feedback and support, and prove that social networking can have a creative dimension.

Glossary

Adze: sacred tool to awaken senses of statues and mummies.

Afreet: Arabic word for supernatural spirit with cunning powers.

Akh: spirit, invisible power. Once the *Ka* and *Ba* are united the *Akh* is eternal.

Akhet: first season in ancient calendar, season of the flood, usually from July-October.

Amarna Period: reign of Akhenaten, late 18th Dynasty. Built his capital in Amarna where he rejected the old religion in favour of monotheism and the worship of Aten, the sun disc.

Amenti: eternal realm, land of the gods. (Kingdom of Heaven)

Ammit: Devourer of Souls in the underworld, consumer of false hearts.

Ankh: the key of life, symbol for eternal life.

Ba: the soul, depicted as a bird with a human head

Basbousa: Egyptian cake coated in honey and coconut.

Badawia: name for female Bedouin, women of the desert.

Benben: a stone obelisk, symbolic of the first mound of creation.

Bennu Bird: immortal bird that emerged from the sacred flames.

Coffin Texts: religious spells from the Pyramid Texts, placed in coffins.

Canopic Jars: four jars used to store organs during mummification.

Daughters of Isis: select group of priestesses who worshipped Isis.

Djed Pillar: backbone, spinal column of Osiris, symbol of resurrection.

Duat: Underworld, Land of Osiris.

Fatira: sweet flat bread often eaten for breakfast.

Fellah m./Fellaha f: Arabic term for rural man or woman.

Fellaheen: collective term for country people, or farmers.

Fuul: brown beans, part of an Egyptian breakfast.

Gallabiya: traditional robe worn by Egyptians.

Hakeema: Arabic word for female healer, medicine woman.

Halwah: Egyptian dessert made with sesame paste, sugar and honey.

Ka: the eternal, 'double self', capable of astral travel.

Kushari: Egyptian dish made of lentils, noodles and spicy sauce.

Lower Egypt: Northern region, from Dashur, Delta region to the coast.

Mastaba: often small a tomb built alongside a pyramid.

Mysteries: secret wisdom revealed to adepts in initiation ceremonies.

Negative Confessions: 42 spells uttered to prove your purity of heart.

Nemes: ornate striped headdress, often with uraeus in front.

New Kingdom: 16th to 11th century BC, the height of the Egyptian empire.

Nubia: Southern part of Egyptian empire, rich in gold and granite.

Obelisk: monolithic stone with pyramid on peak, to reflect divine rays.

Old Kingdom: 3rd millennium BC, pyramid-building and cultural peak.

Opening of the Mouth: ceremony to re-animate a mummy or statue.

Osirion: subterranean structure in Abydos, symbol of mound of creation. Also thought to be the burial place of Osiris.

Osiris Complex: sacred chambers in Temple of Sety I, used for initiation ceremonies, the Mysteries of Isis and Osiris.

Ostraca: pottery sherds or stone tablets used to write on.

Peret: growing season, when the land emerges from the flood, around November-February.

Punt: Eastern Africa, exotic land rich in flora, fauna, gold and incense.

Pyramid Texts: oldest religious texts, shamanistic verses to reach eternity.

Sarcophagus: ornate stone coffin to house deceased pharaoh in tomb.

Sekhem: the eternal life force of a person, god or statue.

Shadouf: ancient frame with lever, to draw water from the river.

Shemu: harvest and low-water season, final season in old calendar, around March-June.

Shisha: Egyptian water pipe or hookah, designed to cool tobacco.

Sistrum: sacred rattle used by priestesses in rituals and dances.

Star of Isis/Sirius: star's rising signalled summer solstice and the flood.

Stela: a funerary stone honouring the deceased's life and good deeds.

Upper Egypt: southern region, stretching from Aswan to Dashur.

Uraeus: rearing cobra, symbol of sovereignty, invincibility, protection.

Wisdom Texts: first written in the Old Kingdom, providing moral and ethical instructions for pupils.

Bibliography

Israel Gershoni & James P. Jankowski, *Redefining the Egyptian Nation: 1930-1945*

Laura Bier, *Revolutionary Womanhood: Feminisms, Modernity and the State in Nasser's Egypt*

Robert Bauval, Thomas Brophy, *Black Genesis: The Prehistoric Origins of Ancient Egypt*

E.A. Wallis Budge, *The Book of the Dead*

--------*Egyptian Magic*

Steven Cook, *The Struggle for Egypt: From Nasser to Tahrir Square*

Jonathan Cott, (collab. **Hanny el Zeini**) *The Search for Omm Sety*

Hanny el Zeini, Catherine Dees, *Omm Sety's Egypt: A Story of Ancient Mysteries, Secret Lives, and the Lost History of the Pharaohs*

Christopher Dunn, *Lost Technologies of Ancient Egypt*

Pamela Eakins, *The Priestess: Woman as Sacred Celebrant*

Normandi Ellis, *Awakening Osiris*

Raymond Faulkner, *Concise Dictionary of Middle Egyptian*

Timothy Freke, Peter Gandy, *The Hermetica: The Lost Wisdom of the Pharaohs*

Selim Hassan, *Excavations at Giza*

--------*Excavations at Saqqara, 1937-1938*

Danielle Rama Hoffman, *Temples of Light: An Initiatory Journey into the Heart-Teachings of the Egyptian Mystery Schools*

Miriam Lichtheim, *Ancient Egyptian Literature, vols 1 & 2*

Edward F Malkowske, *The Spiritual Technology of Ancient Egypt: Sacred Science and the Mystery of Consciousness*

Margaret Murray, *The Osireion at Abydos*

Jeremy Naydler, *Shamanic Wisdom in the Pyramid Texts*

Michael Newton, *Journey of Souls: Case Studies of Life Between Lives*

David O'Connor, *Abydos: Egypt's First Pharaohs and the Cult of Osiris.*

W.M. Flinders Petrie, *Abydos, parts I & II*

Ellen Cannon Reed, *Circle of Isis: Ancient Egyptian Magic for Modern Witches*

DeTraci Regula, *The Mysteries of Isis: Her Worship and Magic*

Alison Roberts, *Hathor Rising: The Power of the Goddess in Ancient Egypt*

Gay Robins, *Women in Ancient Egypt*
Sharron Rose, *The Path of the Priestess*
Omm Sety (Dorothy Eady), *Omm Sety's Abydos*
 --------**Hanny el Zeini,** *Abydos: Holy City of Ancient Egypt.*
 --------(ed. by Nicole B Hansen, Kent Weeks), *Omm Sety's Living Egypt: Surviving Folkways from Pharaonic Times*
Stephan Schwartz, *The Secret Vaults of Time: Psychic Archaeology and the Quest for Man's Beginnings*
Laird Scranton, *Cosmological Origins of Myth and Symbol*
Nicki Scully, Linda Star, *Shamanic Mysteries of Egypt*
Joyce A. Tyldesley, *Daughters of Isis: Women of Ancient Egypt*
Richard Jacquemond, David Tresilian, *Conscience of the Nation: Writers, State, and Society in Modern Egypt*
Leslie Zehr, *The Alchemy of Dance: Sacred Dance as a Path to the Universal Dancer*

Impression of Harp of Joy, by Anne Killeen

Lightning Source UK Ltd.
Milton Keynes UK
UKOW04f0604190917
309457UK00001B/29/P